The Travelling Man

Ring A-Roses
Maggie Craig
A Leaf in the Wind
Emma Sparrow
Gemini Girls
The Listening Silence
Lisa Logan
The Clogger's Child
Polly Pilgrim
A Better World Than This
A World Apart

The Travelling Man

Marie Joseph

GUILD PUBLISHING
LONDON · NEW YORK · SYDNEY · TORONTO

This edition published 1990 by
Guild Publishing
by arrangement with Century Hutchinson Ltd

For Ali . . .

CN 8486

Printed and bound in Great Britain by
Mackays of Chatham PLC, Chatham, Kent

1

Down in London, Queen Victoria's coffin, borne on a gun carriage and covered by the royal standard, was taken to the mausoleum at Frogmore. Londoners wept openly in the streets, and up in the industrial heart of Lancashire the Old Trouper, as the working man called her, was talked about with pride. For wasn't she one of them in the way she had carried on fighting, signing her papers right up to the week before she died? They doubted if they'd ever see the likes of her again.

It was the end of an era.

It was 1901.

At the back end of that year Jack Clancy told his daughter Annie about the lodger.

'A lodger? *Here?*' Her eyes almost popped out of their sockets. 'Where is he going to sleep then? You're never going to let him sleep in your room, are you, our Dad?'

She could tell her father was in one of his blustering moods. He always blustered when he was in the wrong, especially when there wasn't the drink in him. Annie watched him warily from one side of the square table in the front living-room of the terraced house. It was always as well to have the width of the table between them when her father was in one of his rages. Often the best thing to do was to scarper out the back way and hide up for a bit till he calmed down.

But first she'd have a go at reasoning with him.

'You know full well there's only the two rooms upstairs – you in one, the five lads in the other – and me down here in the back scullery.' She folded her arms across a sacking apron. 'There's no room in this house for a lodger, unless he's going to sleep on the clothes-line!'

For once Jack Clancy was being on his dignity. If he could have stood up straight fixing his daughter with a look, he would have done so. But after working underground for more than thirty years, crawling on his knees for a lot of the time, he would never straighten up properly again. His face was a map of criss-crossed blue scars, and the mark of an old injury stood out on his forehead like a bulging vein.

The truth he would never admit to was that he *regretted* offering a stranger a place to doss down in the two-up, two-down house, though he would rather die than say so. He knew it had been the ale talking, but he wasn't going to admit that either.

'He can sleep on that.' He jerked his head at the rag rug by the fire. 'Laurie Yates has been a sailor, so he won't be expecting to sleep in a four-poster with sheets and blankets. Anyroad, like I said, he's coming, and when he gets taken on at the pit and starts bringing money in . . .'

'You mean he hasn't even got a *job*, our Dad! No job an' no money? You mean I've got to feed him as well as all the others? Do you know what there is to last us till Friday? A measly rabbit, half a bag of oatmeal, some spuds sprouting their eyes out, and a piece of scrag end as thin as a sheet of tissue paper.'

She was so mad she could feel tears warming the back of her eyes, but she wasn't going to let them fall. Annie Clancy was no crier. 'Crying never got the baby a new bonnet,' she always told herself when things got too bad and *somehow*, since her mother's death four years ago, she had managed, even on the money her father grudgingly tipped over to her. And now her eldest brother Georgie was twelve and working, things were beginning to look up.

Annie was a good manager and she knew it. She could make a stew that stuck to your ribs out of a few bones, a handful of vegetables and a good scattering of barley. She knew how to simmer an ox-tail in the fire oven till the

2

meat dropped from the bone as tender as butter, and she could roll oatcakes so thin you could see the graining on the table through them.

Oh yes, she'd managed all right, even though there were times when she'd gone to bed so hungry she could have gnawed the table leg. She had seen to it that the boys never went to school barefoot; she had coped with the dirt her father and Georgie brought back from the pit.

She wore a dark patterned cotton blouse that day, a long brown skirt, and two aprons, one of shiny black fent and the top one of sacking. Her hair was tucked up into a man's flat cap, and her hands and wrists were the reddy-brown of potted meat. She was as thin as a picked chicken and her eyes, an unusually dark blue, were the eyes of someone who, while hoping for the best, more often got the worst.

'There's six of you!' she was shouting now. 'All lads. And now you tell me you're fetching another one to live here!'

Frustration and fury welled up in her throat, making her feel sick. She could hear herself yelling, she knew she was sounding as common as dirt and that her mother would have been ashamed of her; accepted she was making as much noise as Mrs Greenhalgh at the bottom of the street did when she was having a go at her daughter-in-law. Yet Annie was *glad* the door was open. She hoped everybody in the street was listening. Let them all crowd round the door and hear what she had to say, because she hadn't finished yet, not by a long chalk she hadn't.

'No wonder me mother never got over the last one of us being a boy. She was sick and tired of listening to rough talk; sick of cooking stews that got gulped down in a minute, and tired out of having to do everything herself, without anybody stretching out a finger to help her. You even let her fetch the coal in from the back when she was expecting . . .'

3

Annie knew she was going too far, but nothing could stop her now. In a strange way she was glorying in the sound of her raised voice, exulting in the fact that she was daring to speak her mind.

'One more mucky face, one more pair of clogs under the table! You must think I'm doo-lally!'

Totally beside herself, no longer in control of the words spilling from her mouth, Annie stared at the thick-set man across the table, infuriating her by remaining uncharacteristically silent. She lowered her voice to a fierce whisper:

'An' while we're getting a few things straight, it wasn't the consumption that took me mother off neither. It was malnutrition, our Dad. *Starvation!*'

Jack Clancy took a menacing step forward, leaning on the table edge, gripping it with his hands. He could feel his throat swelling and hear blood pounding in his head. He'd vowed after the last time when they'd had to bring the doctor to her, that he would never hit Annie again, no matter how much she provoked him. But what she'd just said ... . Good God Almighty, he'd be less than a man to let her get away with that. Some of the things she came out with would make even the Angel Gabriel spit.

When he hit her she rocked back, clutching at the chair to save herself from falling. The stinging pain in her left ear made her eyes water, so that all she wanted to do was to rock backwards and forwards, moaning the pain away. But the white hot anger inside sustained her.

As her father reached the door she was there, shouting after him as he walked away from her, hunch-shouldered down the cobbled street. Just like Mrs Greenhalgh at the bottom house, Annie stuck her chin out, put her hands on her hips and screamed at the top of her voice: 'If that bloomin' lodger comes in at our front door, then it's me out the back, our Dad!' She stepped out on to the uneven flagstones and shook both fists in the air. 'I'm telling you! So think on. Think on!'

Jack didn't bother to turn round. He was used to his

daughter's ways. He could afford to bide his time, knowing she would calm down as quickly as she'd flared up. She was one on her own all right – had been from the day she was born. He turned the corner, hob-nailed boots ringing on the flags. Annie was as different from the boys as chalk from cheese. Where they sulked or merely shrugged their shoulders, Annie yelled. Old Doctor Bradley had called her the strongest lad in the family, and by the left, he was right. It was as if a fire burned inside her, giving her the strength of a man. She could hump the coal in from the yard, or turn a flock mattress without catching her breath. Yet she wasn't the size of two pennorth of copper. But he'd best her. He'd show her who was boss. He turned up his jacket collar against the wind which felt as if it was coming straight from Siberia.

Jack Clancy's father had brought his son over from Ireland to work on the farms around Ormskirk, but the minute he could get away Jack was down the mines, working alongside men who talked his language, doing a bit of wrestling in his spare time, playing pitch and toss on Sunday mornings instead of going to nine o'clock Mass. He had ordered the priest from his house on more than one occasion, and had managed to convince himself that all church-goers were hypocrites. His wife had been a Methodist. In Jack's opinion the worst hypocrites of all.

Instead of going back inside, Annie went two doors down to the house where Grandma Morris lay in bed in the front room; she had been a bedridden invalid for as long as anyone in the street could remember. All Annie knew was that the old woman had bad legs, but she was always working at something with her strong arms and hands – knitting, sewing, peeling potatoes, earning her keep as she often said. When Annie lifted the sneck on the front door and walked in, Grandma Morris put down the sheet she was hemming and took off the steel-rimmed glasses she wore on the very tip of her nose.

5

Annie came straight to the point – there was no other way. Grandma Morris missed nothing that went on in the street, though she kept what she saw and heard to herself, never skitted about it or passed on a confidence. Nobody knew how she'd come to be called Grandma by everybody. There were certainly no grandchildren of her own, as her only daughter Edith was a spinster teacher of fifty summers who played the harmonium at Sunday School and said she had need of no other friend in her life but Jesus.

Since growing older, Annie had begun to believe that Edith was a bit of a trial to her mother, though she understood how difficult it would be for the old lady to be even faintly nasty to the daughter who kept her so clean. Spotless, in fact.

'I expect you heard me shouting after me dad?' Annie stood at the foot of the bed. 'You can't have missed it with both our doors being open. I gave him a right tickin' off.'

Grandma Morris nodded towards the fire. 'Put another of them big cobs on, love. It's not time for Nextdoor to come in for a bit yet and there's a real nip in the air today. No, don't shut the door, love. The winter'll be here soon enough, God knows.' Her eyes twinkled. 'Well of course I heard you bawling your head off. I'm not *that* deaf. I reckon if they'd been handing out the medals for who could shout the loudest in this street, you'd win hands down. Mrs Greenhalgh down the bottom end would have to split her tonsils before she could yell as loud as that.'

She knew that young Annie would rather die than tell about the clout she'd had, but the left side of her face was as crimson as a port wine stain, and tears still glistened on her eyelashes. If Grandma Morris had spoken aloud what she was thinking about Jack Clancy, the very air around her would have turned blue. The man was a boor and a bully but, to be fair to him, he was doing his best to fetch up six kids on his own since his wife died, so maybe

6

there was some good in him. Though you'd need a search warrant to find it – you would 'n' all.

'Me dad wants us to have a lodger.' Indignation flared Annie's nostrils. 'A bloomin' *lodger* who hasn't even got a job. A sailor!' She clasped work-roughened hands round the brass knob at the foot of the bed. 'I know me mother would have been put to shame to hear me behaving like that, but she's dead and gone, and there's only me. If I don't stand up for meself I'm a gonner. Me dad would treat me like a doormat if I let him. An' I know I shouldn't be talking about him, *calling* him like this, but you don't know how selfish he is, Grandma Morris.'

The tears, held tight inside her, suddenly overflowed. 'He still has the front bedroom all to himself, not caring a toss that three of the boys have to squash in a bed in the back, with the other two lying on a mattress on the floor. It's a wonder me mother doesn't come back and haunt him. You know how kind to everybody *she* was.' A great sob burst from Annie's throat. 'I cry for her more now than when she'd just died. *You* liked her, I know.'

'I'd have laid her out when she passed on if I could have got to your house, love. That's how much I thought about her. They don't grow them like your mother all that often.'

Annie twisted away from the bed. 'I know it's a wicked thing to say, but *why* did she marry him, Grandma Morris? They'd nothing in common. Nothing!'

'He married *her*,' the old lady said, nodding her head mysteriously. 'Don't go making a big drama out of something you know nothing about. An' don't go working yourself up into a lather about your father, or giving him cheek at the top of your voice. Things'll only go from bad to worse if you carry on like that.'

It was no use. Annie had come to have her say, so there was no stopping her now. Who else *could* she talk to? Who else would listen? The shame of being hit made her cringe inside; each time it happened it left her feeling more diminished – yes, that was the word – *diminished*.

7

'My father doesn't like me! I stopped trying to make him *love* me a long time ago, but it's come to me lately that he doesn't even *like* me. He looks at me sometimes with such a terrible expression on his face. I'm not imagining it. There's murder in his eyes some days.' She gave a sob. 'An' it's me birthday today, Grandma Morris. I'm seventeen today. It's me birthday, and nobody knows!'

Not for nothing was Grandma Morris known as 'the peacemaker'. So many confidences had been poured out to her from the foot of her bed she could have set every single family in the street at each other's throats if she'd been inclined to gossip. So, at the risk of sometimes verging on the side of hypocrisy, she would listen, swallow what she was really thinking, and soothe, smooth over wounded feelings, dispense wisdom from the bed set under the window in the front room of the small terraced house.

She looked long and hard at Annie and told herself, not for the first time, that but for the clothes she was wearing Mary Clancy's young lass could be taken for a lad. Not a vestige of hair showed beneath the floppy flat cap; the sleeves of the cotton blouse were pushed up to reveal Annie's thin arms, ending in hands as red as if they'd been boiled in a bag. The small circular shawl she was wearing round her shoulders was crossed at the front and knotted at the back. Grandma Morris sighed. Annie didn't take after her mother for looks, nowt was more certain. Mary Clancy had had hair as black as the soot from the chimney-back, and skin like the cream skimmed from the top of the milk. Annie's mother, before she wasted away to nothing, had been a raving beauty, a woman to make men lust after her. No wonder her husband had seen to it that every year since he married her she was either expecting, nursing or burying a child.

'When I was your age,' she said carefully, 'I remember thinking that anyone who tried to tell me what to do hated me. I was growing up, love, just like you're growing up. I thought I knew best, better than anybody. How dare they try to tell me how I should think, or how to behave myself!'

There was a question in Annie's eyes, but it would never be asked. 'Did your father hit you?' it said. 'If you dared to speak your mind, did he lay about you?'

Nextdoor coming in at that very moment was a bit of a blessing, Grandma Morris thought. Annie almost knocked her over in her dash for the door.

'That lass's father was bog-Irish, and it's coming out in her,' Nextdoor said, rolling the blankets down to give the bed a bit of an airing while her neighbour was on the commode. 'Mary Clancy thought herself a cut above, just because she served her time to millinery and dressmaking.'

Grandma Morris said a diplomatic nothing. It never mattered whether you answered Nextdoor or not. She was always far too busy listening to herself, in any case.

'Did you know they've got bugs across the street? I've seen two men going in this morning with elastic bands round their trouser bottoms to stop the flecks crawling up their legs.' Nextdoor was giving the flock mattress a good pawing to even out the lumps. 'One thing about young Annie. She does her best to keep their place clean. Did you hear her creating merry 'ell a bit since? Her mother'll be turning in her grave if she was listening.'

'I've finished, thank you,' Grandma Morris said. In a voice as quietly dignified as circumstances would allow.

When Annie got back home she was joined almost immediately by a small boy with the build of a stunted gnome.

'Where's me tea, our Annie?' Snatching off his cap he skimmed it on to the table. 'Me back's sticking to me front I'm that clemmed.'

Annie rounded on him, her anger far from spent. 'How many times have I to tell you, our Georgie, not to

9

put your mucky cap on my clean table?' She jerked her head. 'Out in the back with it, then get your head underneath the tap before the boys come in from school. You're all sitting down together for once, and if our dad misses his tea then it's his own look-out!'

Not all that long ago Annie had been able to talk to her younger brother. She'd been able to confide in him, unburden herself to him. A month ago he would often get the coal in for her, side the table, chivvy the other boys to bed, crack a joke with her, but now he was a miner he was above behaving like a sissie. Already Annie could see him turning into a replica of all the other pitmen she knew who treated their women with a superior contempt. Annie had seen the same happen to a lot of lads once they followed their fathers down the mine. She had noticed that the relationship between them changed from that very first time they stood together in the pit cage, to drop far, far below the ground. From that day on they were brothers, not father and son.

'Where's me dad gone to?'

Georgie had no intention of doing what he was told, and Annie knew it. He was staring at her with eyes set in a face as black as pitch, narrowed eyes showing her who was boss.

'I don't know where he's gone. Your dad never tells anybody where he's goin', an' you know it.' She moved to the fire to stir a brown stew glistening with globules of fat, then took the poker and moved the trivet away from the glowing coals. 'I suppose if I ask you about this lodger he's wanting to bring here, you'll say you know nothing about it?'

Straightening up, she saw her brother slowly backing away. 'Oh, our Georgie, why don't you stick up for me like you used to? Just this once?'

Opening a drawer set in the side of the big square table she scattered spoons in a heap before setting them out: 'Billy, Timmy, Eddie, John, Georgie, our Dad, and me, if there's time to sit down.'

She dropped onto a stool as a stab of pain shot through her ear. Closed her eyes and pressed her lips tightly together.

When she opened her eyes again Georgie had gone out, and standing in his place was a man she had never seen before.

2

The September sun was as weak as blue milk, but even so, coming out of it into the gloom of the small front room, Laurie Yates thought the bowed figure was a boy. But when Annie straightened up he saw her blouse straining across her chest and guessed it was Jack Clancy's daughter. He held out his hand.

'Miss Clancy?'

Her hair was bundled up into a man's cap; she had the pointed features of a half-starved child, but her eyes wore the bleak expression of a disillusioned woman. A piece of sacking round her waist formed an apron of sorts, and her feet were stuck into miner's boots. She would be, he reckoned, about fourteen years old. If that.

'Miss Clancy?' Was she deaf, dim-witted? Or both?

Annie felt her mouth drop open and forget to shut itself. Nobody had ever called her Miss Clancy before. Not even the priest, and he knew his manners if anybody did. The shock of it brought her to her feet. The pleasure of it made her blush. Wiping her hand first on her long skirt, she shook hands with the stranger, too flabbergasted to think of the right thing to say.

'Your father said I would find you here.'

Annie couldn't hide her astonishment. So this was the lodger who was looking for a place to stay and a job down the mine? This man had an ease and grace about him, with a voice that held the lilt of music. To her way of thinking all sailors had rough red faces half hidden behind bushy beards, but this man was clean-shaven with a head of close black curls. His skin was different too, swarthy, not grey like her father's when the pit dirt was washed from it. He was out of place; he didn't belong. As out of place as a flower on a muck midden.

'I'm Laurie Yates,' he was saying. 'I told your father I would look around for a bed, but he insisted I come here.'

Annie was getting her breath back now. For a minute or two she'd been in danger of letting herself be taken in by a soft voice and a wheedling smile. But this Laurie Yates was only another man, with an appetite to satisfy and dirty clothes to wash. She wasn't going to let him soft-soap *her*, even if he had got round her father over a tankard of ale.

Deliberately she turned her back on him to get seven plates down from the range.

'You can't stop here, Mr Yates, there's not the room.' She set the plates round the table. 'One, two, three, four, five, six, seven. Not even room for a little 'un.' She turned round suddenly, long skirt swinging out. 'You can see how it is without me having to spell it out for you.'

Laurie Yates could see how it was all right. When the fresh colour had drained from this young girl's face, he had seen the clear imprints of fingers on her left cheek. Oh, no indeed, there was no room for an extra one in this small room dominated by the big table and the black fireplace with its lofty mantelpiece. He smiled on her.

'I'll be on my way then, Miss Clancy. I'm sorry to have bothered you. A man only needs half an eye to see that one extra would be an intolerable burden on your hospitality.'

'Sit down!'

Annie pointed to her father's rocking-chair. 'I'd be a disgrace to me mother if I didn't offer you a sup of something or a bite to eat.' She studied him, hands on hips. 'She never sent a stranger away from the door without giving him a crust, even if it was the last in the house. So for me mother's sake, Laurie Yates, sit yourself down.'

She added a good handful of oatmeal to the stew simmering in the big black pan, bending over showing the rounded shape of her buttocks, totally without self-consciousness, like a child, not caring how she looked or what she revealed.

Laurie was intrigued. She wasn't a child, and yet she was entirely without feminine guile, if that was the word he was thinking of.

She straightened up and pointed the wooden spoon at him. 'Have you ever been down a mine, Mr Yates?'

The smell coming from the pan was bringing the saliva to Laurie's mouth. He had walked from Blackburn, and apart from a hunk of bread and a drink of water, his stomach had remained empty all day. He was so hungry he could have snatched the spoon from her and helped himself to the thick bubbling stew, stiff with potatoes, laced with onions and nutty with oatmeal.

Yesterday a woman tending her herb garden had invited him into her cottage and heaped a plate with potato cakes fresh from the griddle, spreading them with butter that ran down his chin as he ate. She had told him he reminded her of her dead son, but Laurie had known she was lying. Her dead lover, more like it, he'd guessed, trying not to look too relieved when her husband had come in from the quarry covered with white dust, none too pleased that this black-haired stranger was sitting there calmly eating what should have been *his* tea.

'Aye, there's a job going at the quarry,' he told Laurie. 'There's a man needed to wheel the rubbish away on a bogie to the tip. A *muck-chucker*,' he added spitefully, licking his lips as Laurie chased the last dregs of runny butter with his finger. 'Hard work, but then I suppose you're used to that?'

'Not in my line, I'm afraid.' Laurie sat back patting his satisfied stomach. 'But thanks all the same.' He had walked away, leaving husband and wife at each other's throats, squaring up to each other like a couple of fighting cocks.

He smiled at the memory. 'No, I've never been down a mine, Miss Clancy.' If this ragamuffin had resembled, however remotely, a woman, he would have had her on

14

his knee whistle-quick. As it was, she was best humoured if he was going to get a taste of that stew.

'But you've been across the sea?'

He grinned. 'You could say I've been across the sea.'

'Where to?'

Laurie turned his head away from the tantalising smell. Any minute now and he'd be down on his knees pleading with her to give him a bowlful of the magnificently bodied broth, or whatever she chose to call it.

'Oh, to lots of places,' he forced himself to say. 'Too many to tell.'

'To India?'

'Yes. To India.'

She was at the table now, sawing away at a cob of crusty bread. He clenched both hands hard to stop himself from leaping out of the chair and grabbing a piece. He set the chair rocking. 'A mucky, dirty place, India.'

Immediately the ragamuffin stopped what she was doing and pointed the knife at him.

'*Mucky?*' Her voice shook. 'I learnt about India when I went to school, and my teacher didn't say nothing about it being mucky! I've seen pictures of India in a book. The sky was blue, and all the people were dressed in white. *White*, Mr Yates. Out in the streets in white.' She put the knife down on the table. 'You wear a white blouse or a white shirt here and it's mucky before you've had time to fasten the buttons. The dirt's in the air here, an' if it's damp, which it usually is, you fetch the washing in covered in sooty flecks. I wash for three families round here as well as my own, so I know what I'm talking about.' She attacked the bread again. 'You go down that mine, Mr Yates, an' you'll soon wish you were back in India looking spotless.'

'You mean to tell me you take in washing? As well as looking after your family? You don't look old enough to have left school.'

Annie ignored him. 'An' what about when you're out

15

at sea? Is the *sea* mucky? Is the *air* mucky? Best thing you can do is go right back to where you've come from before you end up like me dad, and like our Georgie.' Her voice rose. 'An' like our Billy, our Timmy, our Eddie and our John. Because they'll all go the same way once they've left school and gone down the mine.'

She tossed the pieces of bread one by one on to a plate, her tongue protruding slightly as she counted them.

'Want me to tell you something for nothing, Mr Yates?'

The pain was back in her ear; it was a frightening pain, as if a red-hot needle was being poked into it. That was the ear her father always boxed, him being right-handed, and lately there had been tell-tale yellow marks on her pillow in the mornings. As though something was festering away inside. She felt the shameful prick of tears behind her eyes.

'One of these fine days I'm going to walk away from this place an' never come back. Just as soon as our little John is big enough to look after himself.' A sob rose in her throat. 'I don't know where I'll go but I'll find a place somewhere.' She held out her hands. 'I can work with these till I drop. I'm strong as an ox. Me mother used to say I was the strongest lad in the family.' Her voice was ragged with tears. 'When she was on her last I could lift her in and out of bed.' She cupped her hands. 'Before she died, her neck was no bigger than this, an' her wrists . . .' she made a circle with a finger and thumb '. . . as tiny as that. She was wore out with having babies, one after another. She had nine altogether, but lost three after I was born. There was only eleven months between our Eddie and our John. When she died she only had half a shroud because me dad went out and drank his wages away. *Half* a shroud, Mr Yates! To save money!'

The needle in her ear was twisting itself round and round. She couldn't help putting a hand over it. It was driving her mad. It was making her speak so freely to this

16

stranger, she could hardly believe the words coming from her mouth. It was as though she was saying things that had been dammed up inside her for a long, long time.

'An' I'll tell you another thing. Some day I'm going to have a house with a piece of carpet on the floor, an' I'm going to have a tablecloth on a table. A white lace tablecloth, Mr Yates, that'll come up lovely each time it's washed and starched, an' keep its whiteness too with a bit of dolly-blue in the rinsing water.' She banged her hand down hard on the big square table. 'An' it won't be this shape. It'll be round, so that the cloth can fall down in folds.' She clasped her hands together. 'I saw one once, an' I've never forgotten it.'

Laurie Yates didn't know what to make of this young lass standing there, trying not to cry, pouring out her heart to him, a stranger she'd met only a few minutes ago. He was hungry and tired. He needed food and a bed. In that order, so with an effort he summoned up the charm that never failed him.

'I'll buy you a lace tablecloth, love. When I get my first pay packet I'll be away to the nearest market to pick out the whitest and laciest cloth I can find.'

When she rushed out to the back he stretched both arms above his head and grinned, fully aware of the effect his words had had on Annie. He closed his eyes to shut out the sight of the bread so tantalisingly near. She'd counted them too carefully not to miss a piece, and if he was to get his feet underneath the table he had to tread warily.

Something told him he might just be in luck here. Missing his ship in Liverpool hadn't dismayed him for long. It had been his own fault anyway, dallying with a night woman with a tongue on her like a whiplash. Her temper had made him laugh, and the more he'd laughed the madder she'd got. He could still hear her strident voice as she'd yelled abuse after him, shaking her fist through the open window of her room in the tall, overcrowded house near the docks.

'I don't need to work for bloody nowt, sailor!' she'd shouted, and the thought of her slack body had bothered him for a few miles, until he shrugged her memory away.

Now, after being on the road for almost two weeks, he was ready to get his head down for a while. Sleeping rough had made him thankful that the fine weather had held. The long walk had soothed the restlessness inside him, brought him to some kind of peace with himself. Now he had run out of money, he accepted it was either find work or starve.

What was she doing, the strange young girl, out there at the back? Letting the tears come, he guessed. Splashing her face with cold water from the tap her father had boasted about.

'Most summers,' Jack Clancy had explained, 'the houses at the top of our street are without water for three months or more. There's just not enough for the source to supply all the houses. It's all got to be fetched. Every bloody drop.'

Had young Annie been carrying the water up the steep cobbled street all summer long? Bucket by back-breaking bucket? Laurie assumed a hang-dog expression as she came through the door. He picked up his bundle.

'I'll be on my way. God go with you, Miss Clancy.'

That did it. Annie had grown up with a lot of respect for the Almighty, even though her mother had become a non-believer and her father was a lapsed Catholic.

'Do you believe in God, Mr Yates?'

Laurie, sensing his luck could be on the turn, immediately crossed himself. 'I walk with Him. Every step of the way,' he said.

Annie knew when she was beat. Folding her arms, she nodded sternly at the rag rug in front of the stone hearth.

'You'll have to sleep on that. There's no bed. An' just for the night – that's all.'

'You're an angel of mercy, Miss Clancy.' Laurie doffed an imaginary cap.

18

'You'll soon find different,' Annie said.

A clatter of clogs on the cobbles heralded the four young Clancy boys coming home from school. Annie moved towards the great soot-blackened pan on the trivet, nodded at the bench drawn up to the table.

'Get yourself a seat, Mr Yates. It'll be a bit of a squash, but that's your lookout. If I can make this stew go round seven, I don't suppose one more will make much difference. You'll have to fill up with bread.'

Laurie was at the table in a flash. Annie could read his face easily. He was as hungry as a hunter. Sick from the want of food, she guessed. Her own expression softened for a moment, then hardened again. What was he but another man, another mouth to feed? As black-haired and wily as the boys coming through the door.

'Billy, Timmy, Eddie, John.' Laurie chanted their names as they formed a semi-circle to stare at him. 'Bless the bed that I lay on.'

'Who's yon fella, our Annie?' Billy, coming up to eleven, obviously reckoned nothing of the stranger sitting in what was normally his place at the table. 'Has he come to his tea?'

Annie half smiled an apology at Laurie. 'We're not used to company,' she said in way of explanation.

'Except when Father O'Leary comes.' Timmy at ten, the serious clever one, took everything that was said to him literally. 'Once when our Annie had made an oven-bottom cake he scoffed the lot.'

'An' licked the butter from his plate.' Eddie, at eight already the black sheep of the family, narrowed dark eyes into wicked slits.

'The cheeky monkey,' little John added, wanting to get in on the act. Then he sat on the end of the bench and wriggled his way along till he came close to Laurie. 'I got whacked at school today,' he confided. 'For spittin'.'

'How far?' Laurie wanted to know, and they all burst out laughing.

19

That was the moment Annie decided that as long as he didn't overstay his welcome, Mr Yates could stop on for a while.

She was very quiet as she ladled out the full-bodied stew. Her father and Georgie sidled in and took their places at the table as promptly as if she'd stood at the door and banged a gong. It was a long time since she'd heard laughter like that round the table. The boys were looking at Mr Yates as if he'd dropped in from heaven, listening to him spellbound. And her father obviously thought he was a fine fellow.

Annie supposed he *was* quite a cut above the young men roundabouts. It was his brown skin, she supposed, and the different way he had of speaking. There was an open-air look about him that set him apart. She passed him the last piece of bread.

'Do you mean that your grandma was a real proper gypsy, Mr Yates?'

Annie didn't need to raise her head to know who had asked that question. Timmy wanted to know about everything. He had what his teacher called an 'enquiring mind', even at ten years old. Now his small face was puckered into a grave fascination.

'I learned about gypsies at school. They was in a book, with a picture of them cooking rabbits in a pot over a fire in a field. They come from Egypt millions of years ago.'

Billy gave his brother a sharp dig, furious at not being the centre of attraction. 'Gypsies are dirty,' he said loudly.

Laurie wouldn't have believed it if he hadn't witnessed what happened next. In one bound Annie was behind her brother, yanking him from his seat on the bench and shoving him towards the door.

'Out!' she shouted. 'An' if you come back before bedtime you'll get the leatherin' of your life.' She sat down and smiled at Laurie, changing her expression and her way of speaking. 'I apologise for my brother's shocking manners, Mr Yates. He's old enough to know better. Would you care for a drop more stew?'

Subduing a shout of laughter, Laurie passed his plate over. 'Your daughter's a very good cook,' he told Jack, sitting morose and silent at the other end of the table.

'When she bethinks herself.' Jack stood up, wiping his mouth with the back of his hand. 'Which isn't often. I'll see you later on.'

Laurie looked at Annie to judge her reaction to her father's behaviour, but the polite smile was still curving her mouth.

'My father suffers with his chest,' she explained. 'Like most of the men round here.' She passed the steaming plate over. 'It makes him nowt as a wasp at times. No, you *can't* leave the table!' she shouted at the boys, altering her tone and her accent with bewildering speed. Then changing back, she addressed Laurie again. 'They can be little buggers at times,' she told him in cultured tones.

'Don't have them stay on my account.' Laurie fell into the rhythm of her speaking. 'I find this stew delicious, Miss Clancy.'

'Miss Clancy!' Georgie made to follow his father out of the house. 'Cheese and flippin' rice. Pity our dad's not heard that. He'd wet himself laughing.'

'It's only our Annie,' John explained kindly. 'She's not Miss Clancy, mister. She's *Annie*.'

'Would you like me to tell your fortune? Like a *proper* gypsy?' Laurie took John's hand and turned it over. 'Let me see now.' He narrowed his eyes. 'That's your life-line.' He traced his finger across the grubby palm. 'Ah, yes. You're going to live to at least a hundred. And judging by what I see here you're going to be rich and live in a castle.'

'You're having him on, mister.' Timmy held out his hand. 'Does it say I'll be a teacher?'

Laurie stroked his chin. 'Well, let me see now. Ah yes, I see a glittering career ahead of you. I'd have to look into a crystal ball to see more detail, but if you want to be a teacher, then it looks promising. Very promising.'

Annie began gathering the plates together. Her mother would have said the lodger talked through his hat. 'Like an 'apenny book,' she'd have said, putting this unusual man in his proper place. Her mother had been able to weigh folk up after a first glance. It was a funny thing, but even though she had been dead for four years now, Annie found herself seeing most things through her mother's eyes. Sometimes she even heard her voice, and once she'd whipped round, half expecting to see the ghost of the quiet little woman standing behind her.

'I'll tell *your* fortune if you like, Miss Clancy.'

There he was again, trying to get round her with his Romany ways, just as he was getting round the boys. Apart from Billy who had no intention of being charmed by anybody. Eddie had just been told that he would be going on a long journey to a far-off land.

'To Manchester?' Eddie had wanted to know, his eyes round with awe.

'To London,' Laurie smiled. 'To see Buckingham Palace.' He gave Annie an impudent wink.

She held out her hand, wiping it first on her skirt. 'Go on then. Make something nice up for me.'

'I only say what I *see*.' Laurie bent his dark curly head over her palm. 'Ah, yes . . . I see . . . what do I see?'

'Go on, mister.' John's small sharp nose quivered with excitement. 'Tell us about our Annie.'

'I see a room . . .' Laurie Yates's voice deepened. He ran his finger round and round Annie's palm, making her want to snatch her hand back. 'I see a room, a big room, with polished furniture in it, a great fire in the range with flames leaping up the chimney-back.' Laurie dropped his voice to a whisper. 'There's a beautiful girl sitting on a low chair sewing. There's a lamp on the round table beside her, and the cloth, a *white lace* cloth, is hanging down in folds . . .'

'Shut up!' Annie forgot to use her polite company

22

voice. 'Stop skitting me!' She hated him so much she could have landed out at him and knocked him flat on his back. She had told him her dream and now he was spoiling it for her. He was making fun of her, laughing at her with his head thrown back, showing his white even teeth. She loathed him so much even his teeth revolted her. Surely there were too many of them?

'Get out, the lot of you!' Her small face beneath the kneb of the greasy cap was pinched and plain with hurt. She whirled round on John. 'Go through in the back and wash that mucky face. You could grow potatoes on the tidemark round your neck.' The pain in her ear was thumping again, and when Eddie said something underneath his breath she reached out and gripped his arm. 'What was that you said, our Eddie?'

With a jerk he was away, but by the door he turned and yelled at the top of his voice: 'You're a naggin' owd witch, our Annie! That's what I said, an' it's true an' all.'

With a ringing of clog irons on the cobblestones they were gone, leaving Annie standing hands on hips, waiting for Laurie to follow them.

Instead, he walked over to the corner and picked up his bundle. 'Is that what you always do when you're in a paddy? Chuck people out?' He nodded towards the door. 'And what do you do when they refuse?' He opened the bundle and sorted through the jumble of clothes inside, bringing out a length of blue ribbon. 'I wasn't laughing at you, lass. They weren't to know it was our secret.' He dangled the ribbon in front of her. 'And I *could* see you in a room, just like I said. Why don't you clean yourself up a bit and tie this ribbon in your hair? I know you've got a bit because I can see some coming down at the back. Take that terrible cap off and let's have a proper look at you.'

The humiliation and shame were so great Annie wanted to crawl away from him and hide her face. Instead she stepped back a pace. 'You can put that ribbon away, Mr Laurie Yates. And I'm not dirty. I

23

wash meself all over on a Friday, and bits of me every day. An' I wear this cap because it sets me apart, an' that's the way I want it.' The tears were running down the side of her nose, dripping from her chin. She tried to wipe them away with the back of her hand. 'The girls round here think I'm a bit barmy because I never go down to the Mission Hall or to Chapel. But I can't go with them when I've no proper clothes to wear, can I? This skirt is the one me mother was wearing right up to the day she died.' Annie took hold of a fold of her blouse. 'An' this doesn't fit me proper neither, now that me front's got too big.'

Laurie blinked twice. The straightforward utter simplicity of this young lass had him beat. She looked so small, so vulnerable standing there, glaring at him with the tears rolling down her cheeks, he felt the faint stirrings of a compassion that hadn't troubled him for a long, long time.

She hadn't finished with him yet. Annie's cry was a childish wail of anguish. 'It's me birthday today and nobody knows, an' don't you go telling anybody because if they've forgot they've forgot.' She glanced at the table. 'So if you'll just go I can get on with things. It's time I was lighting the lamp and getting the coal in. You'll find me dad in the Ram's Head bending his elbow; it'll be going up and down like a pump handle.'

Laurie scratched his head, struggling to say something to help, anything to comfort and bring a smile back to the small hard face buttoned up with misery because he'd implied she wasn't clean.

'You got me wrong, love,' he said at last. He backed towards the open door, anxious to be away. 'It's such a pity that a lovely girl like you hides herself beneath her dad's old cap. There's a raving beauty hiding away inside those clothes. I'm sure of it.'

Nodding twice, feeling he'd done his best, he walked out into the cool of the September evening, leaving behind him the bright blue ribbon looped over the back of a chair, the one splash of colour in the dingy room.

*

24

When all the boys were in bed, including Georgie who had to be up at four the next morning, Annie went into the back scullery and filled an enamel bowl with cold water. First she washed her top half with the same hard yellow soap used for scrubbing floors and clothes. Then, making sure the door was bolted, she climbed out of her long skirts and washed the lower part of her thin body. Her hair she saved till the last, rinsing it with a jug of water from the rain butt outside.

She put her mother's old cloak over her long flannel nightdress, just in case her father and Mr Yates came in before she'd had a chance to get to bed, but for Jack Clancy to stop drinking before chucking-out time was unheard of. It was said he could sup a canal and still walk a straight line home.

All the same, she hurried with her preparations for the morning. First the fire had to be built up with slack packed tight, but not too tight to allow a tiny spurt of blue flame here and there. Then the big brown earthenware crock-pot had to be filled with the oatmeal, water and salt so that it would give a decent lining to the stomach for the breakfast porridge. Annie laid a blanket and her father's heavy winter coat over a chair, and as she did so her fingers touched the blue ribbon. Picking it up, she let it slide through her fingers, feeling the silken slipperiness of it, holding it up to the lamp-light to admire its bright periwinkle blue.

She woke to the rhythmic thump-thump of the pit's winding engine, rolled out of bed and dressed herself in the dark, fumbling with dead-ended fingers at tapes and buttons. She perked up slightly after splashing her face with cold water, and before she went through into the living-room bundled her clean-smelling hair up into the cap.

Laurie was up too, tending the fire, laying the coals on with care and holding the blower in front of it to get a good draught up the chimney. The blanket and coat were folded neatly, and there was nothing to show whether he had slept on the floor or in the rocking-chair.

Hardening herself against him, Annie decided she didn't care one way or another. There was too much to do anyway. There were three snap tins and three bottles of water to be put up instead of two. No cold fatty bacon to lay between the thick slices of bread this morning because the money had run out, but lashings of dripping instead, seasoned with salt and spread thick.

Nobody ever spoke at that time in the morning. Jack liked his porridge as thick as a poultice, and Georgie sat huddled in his pit clothes, a small weary scarecrow, his hands cupped round a pint mug of scalding tea.

'I hope you get taken on, Mr Yates.' At that moment Annie was her mother again, gentle and polite, wishing her lodger well.

Laurie nodded, used by now to her rapid changes of mood and speech. A kid, play-acting, he thought, stepping out of the front door into the street to join the throng of men and boys clattering their way down to the pit.

Annie went straight back to bed, shivering in spite of her heavy serge skirt and long black woollen stockings. If they didn't want him he'd be back within the hour, by which time she'd be up for good as today was the day she did the washing for Mr Thwaites and his three motherless children. Annie closed her eyes and tried to drift off to sleep, but it was no good. Mr Thwaites was a real tartar, examining his shirts and snapping his collars round his hand to see if they were starched stiff enough. As the pit manager he wore a suit and a bowler hat to work, and drank at nights in a different pub. He was clumsily built, often made uncouth gestures with his hands, and had a nose on him like a ripe tomato. Annie couldn't take to him at all. She was always glad to be shut of the folded washing and be on her way back down the hill. For a boss he was – she tried to think of the right

26

word – too *unpolished*. His head was too round, his light brown hair too coarse, and there were dents in his forehead as though someone had once taken a chisel to him.

The wicker basket with the Thwaites's dirty washing was over in the corner. There was nothing to it really, she supposed, not when you compared it to pit clothes stiff with sweat and dirt. She pulled the rough blanket over her head, but it was no use, she wasn't going to get to sleep again.

She broke off from her washing to get the four boys off to school, standing over John to see he got some porridge down him. The Thwaites's whites were already in the copper, the dirt loosened from them after a good soak in the wooden dolly-tub. Annie had scrubbed them well first, paying special attention to Mr Thwaites's combs and to his shirts where he sweated underneath his armpits. The things that would shrink in the boil she set to with the dolly, lifting it up and down in the soapy water so that its four legs churned the clothes round and round.

When she heard the 'Tubs to mend' man coming down the street she wondered for a second if he would replace the broken steel hoop on one of the washtubs, giving her till the next time he came round to pay what she owed.

'Not him!' she muttered fiercely, giving Mr Thwaites's flannel nightshirt a vicious poss, swilling it so hard the water slapped over the rim of the tub on to the flagged floor.

Although the day was fine, Annie could feel dampness in the air, so she decided to dry the white things inside rather than bring them in covered in black specks. She felt she couldn't face having to do them again. To turn the handle of the big mangle she stood with her feet well braced and far apart, as she fed the sheets in the wooden rollers straight into a tub of rinsing water.

27

When the boys came in for their dinner they sat uncomplaining in a room so full of steam the dampness ran in rivulets down the walls. Annie had no time to sit down herself. She'd put too much dolly-blue in the pillowcases and tablecloths, which meant they'd have to go through another water, at least once.

The boys were at it again. Fighting like savages, locked in hand-to-hand combat. Annie finished pouring boiling water on to the starch, stirring it to the consistency of frog spawn before separating Billie and Eddie who looked set to kill each other.

'The strap's behind the door if you want a proper larruping,' she shouted, slapping the nearest pair of legs. 'Get out of me sight, the lot of you!'

She stood at the door watching them dawdle their way up the hill, one of them holding a rag to a bleeding nose, another stuffing a torn shirt into ragged trousers. Openly defying her by sparking their clog-irons on doorsteps, knowing full well there was no money to pay old Barney the clogger to fix them back on again when they came home with them hanging loose. Billie snatched Timmy's cap from his head and threw it into a pile of horse dirt in the middle of the street. Annie stepped quickly back into the house and closed the door.

By half-past two the actual washing was finished, so Annie upended both tubs and swept the water out of the back. Her ear still ached, and she'd got a splinter in a finger from the worn poss stick, but there was the mangle to wipe down and the copper to empty, saving a bucket of good soapy water to give the oilcloth up in the front bedroom a good going over.

Annie could still remember her mother and Georgie bringing the roll home from the market, carrying it between them like a stepladder. It wasn't quite big enough, and the green and orange colours shouted at you as soon as you opened the door, but it had gone for a song because it was an off-cut, and as Annie's mother had said, the colours would fade. You could get used to anything. 'You could stand on your head for three days if you were forced to,' she was fond of saying.

The fire was half-way up the chimney-back and steam rose from the washing draped over a massive clothes maiden, drying them nicely. There was the ironing still to do, but by eight o'clock that evening everything would be folded away in the big wicker basket, ready to be taken to Mr Thwaites's red brick house overlooking the spare land at the top of the next street.

Annie hoped it would be the eldest girl who paid her. Last week the pit manager had given her a funny look and held on to her hand as he passed over one shilling and threepence, counting each coin separately, and pressing them into her palm before closing her fingers over them. He had stared at her with a blank expression on his face. As if he was going to be sick, Annie thought. As if he'd lost a tanner and found a threepenny bit.

3

Annie was well on with the ironing when Laurie Yates came in from the mine.

'It rains as hard down there as it does up here. Did you know that?' He slumped down in the rocking-chair. 'I could sleep on a clothes-line.' He closed his eyes. 'Your father's down in the bottom house seeing his woman, but he'll be back for his tea, and your Georgie's playing football in the pit yard with some of his mates.'

'Our dad hasn't got a woman!' Annie's voice was deceptively calm. The transformation from the good-looking, impudent young man to the exhausted figure sprawled in the chair shocked and disappointed her. In his pit dirt Laurie Yates looked like all the others; worse than most, with his white teeth flashing in his black face. She had thought he was different, with his alien way of speaking and his gentlemanly manners, but she'd been wrong. He was bending down to his boots, so tired he was fumbling with the laces. Doing it less than a foot away from the clothes maiden with Mr Thwaites's combinations steaming in the heat from the fire.

'You're having me on about the woman,' she said, still in that same quiet tone. 'There's a Mrs Greenhalgh in the bottom house, a widow who lives with a married son and his wife.'

'That's her. Mrs Greenhalgh.'

Annie could feel the heat from the iron coming up at her, flushing her face. Her dad wouldn't go with Mrs Greenhalgh. Not that fat sloppy woman with scragged-back hair and a voice on her like a corncrake. Not Florrie Greenhalgh, who'd been seen more than once fighting in the street with her daughter-in-law, pulling her hair and thumping her between the shoulders.

30

'Our dad wouldn't *look* at Mrs Greenhalgh, not if she was the last woman on earth.' In her agitation Annie pulled off the atrocious flat cap, releasing the long fall of her hair. 'If you'd known me mother you couldn't even *think* a thing like that.'

Laurie was staring at her in total disbelief. Annie's hair was *beautiful*. He couldn't take his eyes off it. He supposed it was red, but red was far too ordinary a name for it. More gold than red. He half stretched out a hand, then drew it back quickly, anticipating the way she would swipe it away. Titian . . . the glinting warmth of a shining copper pan. That hair accounted for the paleness, the creamy tinge to her skin and the way a spattering of freckles marched across the bridge of her nose.

She was still going on about the woman down the street. 'She's *known* for it . . .'

'For what, Annie?'

'For going with men.'

'Your father's not exactly an old man, love. It's only natural. He's got to find his bit of fun from somewhere.' Laurie reached out for his sack. 'I've got to wash this muck off me when I've found a dry pair of socks.' He groped around in the bottom of the sack. 'Forget about your dad and the ravishing Mrs Greenhalgh, love. Where do I go to get clean? Through there?'

To his amusement, Annie changed at once into the woman of the house, a polite and solicitous hostess, with an accent to match.

'There's a hip-bath through there at the back, and if you want to have a proper all-over wash you can put some cold in it and warm it up from the kettle. Georgie and me dad make do with a lick and a promise till Friday, just head and shoulders, but if you want a decent soak you're very welcome.'

'Will you come through and wash my back?'

His low chuckle turned to a shout of laughter as Annie upended the iron, snatched a grey shawl from the peg

31

behind the door, and in one swift graceful movement swept her hair up on top of her head beneath the flat cap. She spoke to him over a disappearing shoulder.

'I'm going down to the shops. I'll not be long.'

She was off out of the house as quick as a lick. He saw her head bobbing past the window, heard her call out to someone in her normal voice.

She was a funny kid all right . . .

Laurie went through into the back room, out into the yard where the zinc bath hung from a nail hammered into the wall. A lick and a promise might do for the likes of Jack Clancy, but it wasn't good enough for Laurie Yates.

Annie averted her eyes as she walked past Mrs Greenhalgh's house. The front door was closed, which made a change. Usually, when the weather was fine, the big blousy woman propped the door open with a chair and sat there, missing nothing that went on in the street. Or stood on the doorstep with arms folded across her bolster-bosom. Or came out on the flags to sit on the window bottom. All signs of bad bringing up, as Annie's mother had often reminded her.

Mrs Greenhalgh's son Jim was on the late shift at the mine, and Dora his wife would still be down there working on the screens, raking over the coals with her bare hands, festering her finger tips into open cracks. Annie turned the corner with head bent, muttering to herself.

It wasn't right. There was so much that wasn't right. Annie's mother had often said that when real poverty came in at the door, dignity flew out of the window. 'Dignity,' she would say, 'when God made woman He meant her to have *dignity*, Annie. Always remember that.'

Past the forge, across the street, past the house with sixteen children, two sets of twins and one of triplets among them. Annie often wished she could see inside, but they never used the front door, always the back. She supposed they came to the table in relays and slept top to toe, but how on earth did their poor mother manage to feed them? A man carrying a wicker basket of oatcakes on his head turned round from knocking on a door, but Annie was too quick for him. He'd have to whistle for the sixpence she owed him till Friday.

In the next few weeks the extra coming in from the lodger made quite a bit of difference. Annie not only paid the oatcake man, but bought a fresh batch from him to hang over the end of the clothes rack to dry out. Most days she had two pennorth of greens to boil up as an extra vegetable, and one day when she couldn't get the washing dry for love nor money she ran out and bought shop meat-and-potato pies instead of making them herself.

'Though you'll need a search warrant to find the meat,' she warned Laurie. 'That woman probably did no more than run past the oven with a spoonful of Bisto.'

Jack noticed the change in his daughter, but said nothing. She seemed to have shot up in the last few weeks. She had stopped wearing her cap, and started tying her hair back with a blue ribbon. She was sitting where her mother used to sit, on a stand-chair drawn up to the table, with the work-basket to hand beside her, sewing a patch on one of the lads' trousers. A bobbin of black cotton fell on to the floor and when she bent forward to pick it up he saw the hollow between her breasts.

Jack averted his eyes. It would be boys next. Boys from the mills or the pit, or even soldiers from the barracks, coming round with eager eyes, wanting to take her for walks. Wanting to fondle her. He felt the heat rise in him.

'Dad?' It took him a second to realise she was speaking. Her eyes seemed unnaturally bright.

'Do you think you could put me money up this week,

so I can buy some material to make a dress?' Putting the patching aside she clasped her hands together. 'I know you sold the sewing machine, but I could make it by hand. I'd do it plain, no fancy bits or anything. There's a social on down at the Mission Hall, with dancing and a bit of supper. The tickets are only sixpence.' Her voice shook a little. 'I can't go in an old skirt, an' I'm growing too big for me blouses. I can't move the buttons any more.'

Jack's face set hard. He could hardly bear to look at her gazing at him with tears in her eyes and that red wavy hair slipping its ribbon, falling down over one shoulder, reminding him . . . reminding him . . . With a fierce thrust of a foot he set the chair rocking.

'I've never had a dress, not since me mother died.' She was whingeing now, like a child who must have its way. 'I have to go. Can't you see?'

'*Have* to?'

Annie's quick temper rose to meet her father's angry stare. 'You can't shut me away inside for ever! I'm seventeen years old! The lads are my *brothers*, not my sons. I'm not their mother, though God knows I'm trying to be.' She went to stand beside him. 'There'll be time enough for me to settle down when I get married, but first I want a bit of fun. I want to dance and laugh, I want to go to the social. Laurie said you'd let me if I asked you properly.'

Jack's hands were clenched tight on the arms of the rocker. He stared up at her and saw the way the emotion inside her was heaving her breasts up and down. In a minute she'd be going off into one of her old tantrums.

His hand shot out and gripped her arm. 'You know well there's no money for fancy clothes.' His hard fingers dug into the flesh of her upper arm. 'But even if there was, you're not going to any dance. Not at seventeen, eighteen, or even nineteen. Not while I'm here to see you don't!'

Annie only took in what he said about the money.

When he stood up, still holding on to her, she saw that his eyes were on a level with her own. And it came to her in that very moment that if she kept on growing, the day would soon come when she was taller than her father. Taller than any of her brothers – she knew that too and somehow the knowing of it gave her courage.

'If you spent less on drink you'd have more money to give to *me*.'

Had *she* said that? Annie clapped a hand to her mouth, but the expression in his eyes goaded her on to say even worse. He hated her. It was there in his eyes, filling them, narrowing them to menacing slits.

'I bet if Mrs Greenhalgh from the bottom house asked you for money for a dress you'd cough up,' she said in frantic desperation.

When he hit her, rocking her head back, Annie accepted that she had certainly asked for it this time. When he unfastened the buckle of his belt she twisted away.

'No! Not that, our Dad. Please, no!'

The shame and humiliation were already there in her cry, but she'd gone too far. She had spoken to her father as an equal, and there was no way he was going to stand for that.

Laurie Yates had missed two cages through taking his time back from the coal face. The work appalled him, and every back-breaking day the conviction grew in him that it was time he took to the road again. His job as a newcomer to the mine was to push the tubs, each containing four hundredweight of coal, down water-logged steps, then up again. The cork-filled thrutcher he was forced to wear on his head to help him push the heavy tubs was an affront to his pride, even all those miles underground. That day two tubs had come off a faulty rail, and the miners helping him to get them back had made Laurie feel it had been his fault. He had sweated like a stuck pig in spite of wearing nothing but an old pair of football shorts, and in a fit of towering rage had cleared the last of the coal out to give whoever took his place a clean start in the morning.

But it wouldn't be him. No, by God, it wouldn't be him.

Only that day he'd learned that because the seam was running out they would be sinking a new shaft another two miles away. He didn't need telling that he would be working on it, and he didn't need telling either that it was one of the most dangerous jobs in the mine. He wasn't ready yet to die choking for breath in an airless dank dark tunnel. He wasn't going to end up with a cob of coal in place of his lungs, not if he could help it.

He wouldn't be missed. The miners would never see him as anything else but an interloper, though young Annie might miss him for a while. He smiled at the thought of her as he collected his tackle and started off up the hill. Let them as wanted crawl about on hands and knees far below the ground, but he would be off the next morning, and back in Liverpool he'd sign on the first ship available. Then it would be the wind on his face, salt spray cooling him, and in time he'd forget the searing heat of the mine and the time he pushed a heavy tub along in the black dark, wearing a cork-filled bag on his head.

Lifting the sneck on the door he walked in to see Annie sitting at the big square table, her head down and her arms spread wide. What was left of her blouse hung in shreds to her waist, and the red-gold hair only partly concealed the weals net-worked across her bare back.

'Oh, you poor little love . . .'

Something stirred in Laurie's black heart as he stared down at the result of Jack's heavy hand. There was no blood, no skin broken, just the raised purple weals, an ugly sight on the smooth fair skin. How young she was – how achingly slender. He touched a bare shoulder.

'Annie? Look at me, love. What in God's name did he do that for? What could you *possibly* have done to anger him like this?'

The kindness in his voice, the compassion, made her raise her face, so that she saw the lodger through a mist of tears, saw the handsome face covered in coal dust. And saw the deep pity in the dark eyes.

'Oh, Laurie . . .'

There was a desperate ache in her for comfort. Her mother had been dead for four years now, but it was her mother she had been crying for when Laurie walked in. Her father would never have dared to use his belt on her if his wife had been alive.

'I said some terrible things to him, Laurie. I wanted a dress to wear to the social, an' when he said no I went for him with my tongue.' Her eyes swam with tears. 'I have an awful tongue on me when I can't get what I want.'

Tenderly Laurie pulled her to her feet and into his arms, holding her carefully, drawing the tattered blouse, up, trying to cover the soft curves of her young breasts. Swearing to himself that if her father had come through the door at that moment he would have killed him and not thought twice.

'Hush-up, love.' He was a good caring father comforting a child, rocking her in rhythmic soothing movements, feeling her body curve into his.

Did she turn her mouth to his or was it a deliberate movement on his part? Afterwards he wondered, trying to assuage his guilt. All he knew was that even as he kissed her the rocking went on, sending an ache through him, seeping away every vestige of self-control. Had he carried her through into the back room, or had she gone readily, allowing herself to be led? It had been a long time since the woman in Liverpool, and Annie was all soft willingness, clinging to him as he laid her down on the small truckle bed.

Her cry of pain as he took her should have brought him to his senses, but by then his senses were aflame with the searing triumph of possessing her. Of knowing he was the first man ever to have touched her.

'It's all right. All right, love.' He couldn't stop his

hands from shaking as he buttoned her into a clean blouse from the stack of freshly ironed clothes on the small chest of drawers. Even then he was cursing himself for being a fool, for using young Annie when tomorrow he would be away from this place, away from this house where the walls ran damp. But most of all away from the mine where the sky was so far away a man could forget it was even there.

When he went through into the living-room she came and knelt down by his chair, her face upturned to his.

'Will we be married?'

Laurie had to close his eyes to hide his expression. He drew her close, tangling his fingers in the soft weight of her hair. Of all the bloody stupid things he'd done in his life, and he'd done many, making love to this young innocent lass beat the lot. If he hadn't decided a long time ago that remorse was a wasted emotion, he'd be having a good wallow in it now. Why did he always act first and think second? Starting from the day he'd insisted on leaving school, when his father would willingly have seen him through college. Why had he turned his back on the academic career that could have been his?

'Laurie?' She was waiting, gazing at him, her eyes limpid with the trust she had in him. 'Will we be married soon?'

If she didn't get up from where she was kneeling the boys would be in from school. Or her father would walk in.

Laurie spoke quickly: 'Of course we'll be married, love. But first I have to go away.'

'You can't! Not now. Not after . . .' She looked away, too shy, he guessed, to meet his eyes.

'Listen, love.' Keeping one eye on the door Laurie gently raised her up, guiding her towards one of the stand-chairs round the table. Pushing the work-basket towards her before going back to his place by the fire. 'I'm never going down that mine shaft again. It's how I imagine hell will be, but worse, because down there is hell on earth.' He sat forward, feeling better now that he'd got her sitting away from him, even though her face was as white as bleached cotton.

'But what we . . . what we just did?' Her voice faltered. 'That means we belong. Only night women an' . . .'

'Mrs Greenhalgh?' he prompted, hoping to get a smile out of her.

'You can't leave me now,' she said, hysteria thick in her throat. 'What if . . . ?' Terror stared from her eyes, choked her voice.

'What if you have a baby?' Laurie said it straight out. It was the first thing they all said, the girls like Annie, the inexperienced, the first-timers. From where he sat he willed her to take a hold of herself. 'You won't have a baby,' he told her firmly. 'I made sure of that.'

She had no idea what he meant but it was what she wanted to hear so she believed him. The terror faded from her eyes.

'If you got me into trouble, our dad would kill me first then you next.' She came over to him, lifted his hand and gently kissed it.

'Your dad will come in and catch you if you don't look sharp.' His mind was working overtime. The quivering girl must be calmed down. Fast. 'I'll come back. I promise.'

'When?' She was clinging to him like a bloody limpet.

'A year from now. Less than a year. On your birthday. Exactly to the day I came here. I'll save every penny, then I'll come back for you.'

'And we'll be married?'

'We'll be married, sweetheart.'

He tried to put her from him, but she wasn't ready.

'Let's say it together, Laurie. Like we were standing together in church.'

'I promise to marry you,' he said through clenched teeth.

'I promise to make you a good wife,' Annie whispered,

39

feeling her heart contract with love. 'For ever and ever, Amen. An' you'll come back for me?'

'I'll come back for you. I promise.' The school must have loosed. Laurie could hear the clatter of clogs in the street outside. 'Amen,' he said with fervour. 'In the sight of God,' he added. For good measure.

'An' you won't forget me?'

'I'll *never* forget one single word we've said.'

Firmly he put her from him.

As soon as her father and George had gone off to work the next morning Annie packed a hunk of bread and a nice thick slice of potted meat for Laurie to take with him.

'To put you on,' she told him, 'till you get well on your way.' She added an apple, first wiping it carefully down the front of her blouse. 'Your clean socks are in your sack, and a starched white collar. In case you have to go in front of an interviewing body to get taken on.'

She was behaving like a wife already. So trusting, so naïve, so young, Laurie couldn't get out and away quick enough. He was inordinately relieved when Timmy came downstairs complaining of the toothache, crouching down between them on the rug, holding a rag to the fire then pressing it against his cheek. Eyeing them up, taking all in.

'Will you write to me often?' Annie stood on the step with the door closed behind her, dry-eyed and outwardly composed.

'Better not, love. Your dad would be bound to find out, then there'd be hell to pay.' He risked touching her cheek, only to find his hand caught as she turned her lips to kiss his fingers. 'I won't be responsible for him hitting you.'

'He will never hit me again, Laurie.' Her eyes were very bright. 'Now that I have you loving me, there's no need for me to keep on trying to make *him* love me. I'm not afraid of him now, so write to me when you can. There's nothing he can do to hurt me now.'

Laurie touched a finger to his forehead, turned and walked away, leaving her standing there sending up a silent prayer that God would keep him safe and bring him back to her. He remembered to stop at the bottom of the sloping street to turn and wave.

Annie went inside, heart bursting with love, to minister to Timmy's tooth by pressing a piece of cotton soaked in oil of cloves against it.

Grandma Morris from two doors down had had a bad night, but at first light when Laurie Yates went past her window she was sitting up in bed with a pillow underneath her knees to ease the grinding pain.

'Yon lodger's just got on his way,' she told her daughter. Edith was running about like a scalded cat getting her mother settled and spotless before she went off to work. 'He's a fine looking man.'

Edith didn't hold with men and never had. Her mother had stopped wishing she would find someone to marry a long time ago. Always wanting to best men, take them down a peg, that was Edith. Look at her now, getting a dish of cowheels into the side oven and shoving the nigget into place so it would cook slow, when all the time her mother would have made do with a bowl of the leek and potato soup Edith had made last night.

'The Clancys' lodger?' Edith sniffed. 'I wouldn't trust him as far as I could throw him. I wouldn't touch him with a barge pole.'

'Chance would be a fine thing,' her mother thought, with uncharacteristic bile.

'There's an understanding between us,' Annie confided when she came round to collect the Morris's washing, already folded and graded into whites and coloureds by Edith. 'It's a secret, a deadly secret, but by this time next year I could be married. Laurie is going to sea to save as much money as he can then he's coming back for me.'

'Very nice too,' the old lady said, not believing a word

41

of it. 'He's a fine looking man, love.' Well, that was true enough, she thought, though his complexion was so swarthy you could be forgiven for thinking he had a touch of the tar brush in him.

Not that she would use such a phrase to her daughter. Edith had once wanted to be a missionary going out to Africa to bring the word of Jesus to the black children. Edith never noticed the colour of a person's skin. It was their souls that mattered.

'I've never seen a black man,' Grandma Morris had told her daughter once. 'And neither have you.'

But Edith had ignored her. The opportunity of being a missionary had long since come and gone. Now, with her mother totally bedfast Edith didn't even have the chance to work full-time at weaving. The days were too long for her mother to be left alone, even though the neighbours were goodness itself. So for the past five years Edith had been a 'sick' worker, standing in for absentee weavers, waiting outside the mills some mornings for over an hour on the off-chance somebody failed to turn up. The old lady sighed. Being a burden was bad enough, but knowing you were one was worse.

'It looks like our Edith has got taken on this morning, else she'd be back by now.'

It was Annie's turn to ignore her now. She was standing there at the foot of the bed staring at the wall as if she'd seen a vision.

'Laurie has Romany blood in him. He could tell fortunes. *You* liked him, didn't you?'

'He was a right bobby-dazzler, love, and educated too. I asked him why he hadn't settled down to a proper job, but he only laughed at me.'

'He has to feel *free!*' Annie's face was transformed by her love. Laurie had been gone for two hours now and the need to talk about him was overwhelming. 'He hated the mine. The dark and the heat hurt him here.' She thumped her chest. 'His father wanted him to go to college but it would have finished him off. He has to be

42

able to open a door and walk away when the feeling of being stifled comes on. Nobody can tie him down. Nobody!'

'And he's coming back to marry you, love?'

With a little rush Annie moved round to the side of the bed, sitting down on the counterpane and lowering her voice to a dramatic whisper.

'We are already married, Grandma Morris. In our hearts. We love each other so much we made our vows, just as if we were in church. Promising to love each other for ever and ever, Amen. Oh yes, Laurie will be back for me.'

She went through and got the heavy basket of washing from the back, walking as if there was air beneath her feet and not the oilcloth scrubbed by Edith every Friday night. Poor Edith, she was thinking, to be fifty and never known what it was to have been loved by a man. No wonder she was as sour as unsweetened rhubarb.

Annie often left the front door wide open to the street while she did the ironing. Her mother had always stood on a cushion to save her feet from aching, so she stood on one too. She pressed a traycloth carefully on the right side then turned it over and ironed the wrong to bring up the lumpy splendour of Edith Morris's French knots. Tears came to her eyes as she thought about Laurie going further away from her with every hour that passed. He was making for Bury first, he'd told her, because he had a friend there who would give him a bed for the night. Annie rolled up her sleeves to well above the elbow and fastened her hair back with Laurie's blue ribbon. Then reached for a pillowcase fringed with Edith's exquisite crochet-work.

On his way home Bertram Thwaites stopped to catch his breath and saw Annie at the table ironing.

'There's a bit of a nip in the air today, Annie.' He took a step inside. 'Nights'll be drawing in soon.' He took off his billycock and wiped his bulging forehead with the back of his jacket sleeve. Drawing attention to the dents.

'I reckon he fell on a pitchfork once,' Annie had told her friend Janie Whittaker at school, and they'd giggled so much the teacher had sent them both from the classroom.

'Yes, Mr Thwaites. Winter'll be here before we can turn round.' Annie wished he would go away. He made her feel uncomfortable somehow. He had pale eyes that stood out like chapel hat-pegs, and a neck that rested on the rim of his high collar. Since his wife had died of double pneumonia it was said he was looking for a new wife to bring up his children, but Annie couldn't imagine anyone applying for the job. Not unless they were really hard up and none too fussy.

'You're making a good job of the ironing, lass.'

He was staring at her bare arms, making her wish she had kept her sleeves buttoned at the wrists. She folded the pillowcase neatly into the shape Edith Morris liked for putting away in a drawer, and looked up to see the thick-set man still staring at her.

'You'll be up tonight to pick the washing up?' he asked, never taking his eyes off her.

Then, much to Annie's relief, he smoothed back his light brown hair and replaced his hat. Perhaps he'd go now, and good riddance, she told herself, remembering how Janie had decided that his hair must have come off a coconut, it was that coarse and sparse.

'About eight o'clock, Mr Thwaites. If that's all right with you.'

'I'll have the brass ready, lass.'

She nodded and started on a table-runner worked in cross-stitched daisies at the ends. Tomorrow she'd be washing Mr Thwaites's yellow combs and ironing his shirts, dipping his collars into the bowl of starch and doing his socks by hand, being careful not to shrink them.

The iron was cooling so she changed its solder for the

44

one heating up in the fire, taking it out with the tongs, dropping it into the iron and closing the shutter with a loud thud. Whoever was hard up enough to marry Mr Thwaites would have to take on his washing, yellowed combs and all. Annie spat on the base of the iron and tried it out first on one of Edith Morris's dusters.

When that too grew cool she pulled the blue ribbon from her hair and pressed it carefully. Bringing it up like new.

4

It was late November before Annie forced herself to admit that she was in a trouble so terrible the mere thinking of it almost stopped her heart.

Lying in her narrow bed in the back room cluttered with washing tackle – dolly-tubs, mangle, copper, posser, rubbing-board, wicker clothes-baskets – she let the living nightmare take over. It squeezed the breath out of her; it brought her out in a cold sweat.

Laurie had taken her face between his hands and reassured her that nothing could go wrong. He said he had made sure of that. Annie brought an arm up across her eyes. How had he made sure? She groaned – a piteous little sound. Her old school friend, Janie Whittaker, had got married a year ago and told Annie that there wouldn't be any babies for a long time yet, not with her and Jake wanting to get a few bits of furniture together first. Jake was 'being careful', she said.

How careful? In what way careful?

Annie called in at Janie's mother's house on her way back from delivering a load of washing. Mrs Whittaker wouldn't let her daughter or her new son-in-law lift a finger between them when they came in from standing in the mill all day. She was there at the table, having a good knead-up with her strong hands. Flour on her nose, happiness shining out of her now her future was secure with a married daughter living at home, just as if she'd never left. Things were going to go on just the same, she was sure of it.

Mrs Whittaker thought Annie looked a bit off. It was a pity her hair was so red, it drained what colour there was from her cheeks, and made her freckles stand out like

46

brown measles. She had quite a nice bust on her, though her blouse needed the buttons letting out. Her mother would have made her a new one in no time, having served her time to millinery and dressmaking. Little Mrs Clancy had been a lovely woman, with time for everybody. Thought she was a cut above in some ways, but then Mrs Whittaker had heard she'd come from a quite well-to-do family in Manchester. Big Methodists, from what she'd been told. How she'd ever come to marry Jack Clancy was a mystery. She'd never turned Catholic for him, though. Mrs Whittaker couldn't stand the sight of him, always giving women the glad eye, even when his wife was expecting. *Especially* when she was expecting, poor soul.

Annie went after about twenty minutes. She was never going to get a word on her own with Janie, not with Janie's mother standing there with both ears wagging.

She was passing the house with sixteen children just as the father came out.

'Nasty neet, Annie.'

'It is that, Mr O'Mara.'

Annie watched him cross the street swinging his arms like a soldier on parade. She turned the corner, averting her eyes from Mrs Greenhalgh's house. It was all very strange. What was Janie's husband doing right that Mr O'Mara was doing wrong? Was it because the O'Maras were Catholics, while Janie's husband was Chapel? Had Laurie been a Catholic?

Annie slowed her steps. There was so much about Laurie she didn't know. Not a word had come from him since the bright morning he'd walked away from her with his sack across his shoulder. But he'd write to her. The minute he'd found a ship. She was sure of it.

The blind was down in Grandma Morris's house. Annie guessed that the old lady would be dozing with Edith sitting by the fire busy with her embroidery. Annie knew she would be welcome if she popped in for a minute, but how could she sit there chatting when her mind was so filled with worry it felt as if maggots had taken over her brain. Besides, they were such good people, Edith and her mother. Annie didn't suppose Edith had put a foot wrong in the whole of her life. Lately the entire world seemed to be full of good people who never thought of sinning – people who would be shocked to the very depths of their souls when they found out that Annie Clancy had let the lodger have his way with her.

She stood for a moment on the flags outside the window. A warm yellow light shone out through the blind. The desire to knock on the door and go inside was an ache inside her. Edith mopped the window bottom every day, and as Annie drew a finger along the neat yellow-stone edging, an idea suddenly occurred to her.

Edith bought *Home Companion* every week and sometimes passed it on to Annie to read. Towards the end of the magazine there were letters from girls at the end of their tethers, asking the editor for advice on how to solve their problems. Annie moved on, trailing the empty wicker clothes-basket behind her. That's what she would do. She'd write a letter, signing herself 'Worried Blue Eyes' and wait to see what the answer would be. Whatever was printed she would act upon. She would . . . she would do whatever the editor thought best.

She stopped with one hand on the sneck of her own door. About three weeks back a young lady had been strongly advised to resist her fiancé's caresses, remaining pure till their wedding in two years' time. Making love out of wedlock, the editor had said sternly, was considered by all right-thinking people to be both vulgar and unfortunate.

That editor would likely tear Annie's letter up and drop it straight into the waste-paper basket. A girl making love with the lodger, still in his pit dirt. The editor would be sick at the mere idea of it.

The maggots were nibbling away at her brain again. She could feel her breasts tingling; she could feel them growing bigger. 'Oh, dear God, help me now,' she whimpered. 'I am asking You from my heart. Please, *please*, help me now. I ask You from my very soul to make things come all right.'

She opened the door and saw Eddie sitting on John's head, while the two other boys fought to the death over a large glass marble.

And knew in that moment that nothing and nobody could help her now.

One morning, just after Christmas, in the hour before the boys were up, Annie made up her mind to kill herself.

There was no choice.

She crouched over the fire coaxing it to a good blaze so that she could carry a shovelful of coal through to heat the water already in the copper. But when she got it there the iron door was sticking so that, in struggling to open it, she almost dropped her fiery burden on to her feet.

She knew she was going to be sick again, heaving and retching over the slopstone with nothing to get rid of by now but a thin white froth. Silently she rocked herself backwards and forwards, her face pinched with anguish. It wouldn't be long before her father cottoned on to what was wrong with her and when he did . . . when he did she was *dead*. It wouldn't be any use trying to tell him that Laurie had promised to marry her, that they were already married in the sight of God.

Annie straightened up from the slopstone, turned on the tap and as she did so it was as though the maggots in her head swelled so much they threatened to burst her head open, like a ripe pomegranate.

She ran outside into the yard and when she banged her head against the blackened wall she felt no pain at first. It was only when she went back inside that she felt a trickle of blood down her face.

'There's something sadly wrong with young Annie.'

Edith Morris was checking over the week's washing before storing it away in lavender-scented drawers.

'She's not herself,' she told her mother. 'She just took the money tonight and went.'

'I'd just nodded off,' the old lady said. 'She wouldn't want to wake me, and you were busy making the cocoa.' She stretched out her hand for a cup. 'Young Annie's not been right since that lodger of theirs went away. She talked daft to me about him coming back to marry her.'

'You never said.'

'It was private.'

'Well, why are you telling me now?'

They stared at each other over the rims of their cocoa cups. Both of them doing rapid sums in their heads.

'She's put a bit of weight on,' Edith said.

'She's no fatter in the face.'

'No, not in the *face*.'

'Oh, my God!' Grandma Morris said in her head. Not aloud because Edith would have accused her of blaspheming.

Annie had taken to wearing the flat cap again, bundling her hair up into it, not caring a toss how she looked.

Early January brought a frost so hard that she brought the sheets and towels in off the line as stiff as planks. Even a handful of salt in the rinsing water, supposed to stop them freezing, had no effect.

By now the waist-band on her skirt was a long way off meeting, so she used a big nappy pin she found in a drawer, and wore her small shawl tied loosely. She had stopped praying to God to make things right, and she no longer thought up ways of killing herself. The frantic never-ending worry had taken her strength, sapped her spirit, and the only way she could get through the days was to divide them into hours, living each one from one dragging minute to the next.

She stood at the mangle, feet well apart, purposefully feeding treble thickness sheets through the wooden

50

rollers, straining at the big iron wheel till every muscle in her body ached. But nothing happened. She forced herself to jump from halfway up the stairs, landing heavily, and she worked at her wash-tubs with the posser till the sweat stood out on her forehead.

It was strange how the mind worked, she told herself, remembering how her mother had done all these things. 'My poor, poor little mother . . .' Annie conjured her up, small and gentle, and remembered that in that gentleness lay a lot of strength. She would have known what to do. Somehow they would have faced up to this terrible, unbelievable thing together.

'Help me, Mam . . .' Annie closed her eyes and put her hands together. 'Tell me what to do. Send me a sign showing me what to do.'

When the knock came at the door she jumped. When she opened the door and saw the priest standing there she knew her prayer had been answered so promptly she could only gape in wonder, holding out both hands as if to warm them at a glowing fire.

'Father!' She drew the priest inside, pulled the rocking-chair closer to the fender, pushed the kettle over the coals.

'You'll have a pot of tea, Father? It's blowing outside fit to whip your tonsils out. The wind's been whacking at the windows all night.' She moved an outsized clothes maiden festooned with steaming undergarments away from the fire. 'I bet it snows when the wind drops. I bet it does.'

Father O'Leary unfastened his long black cloak and draped it over the back of a stand-chair. Annie's mother had had her roots deep in Methodism but she had always made him welcome, listened to him gravely, then sent him on his way feeling that somehow she had been too clever for him. Her husband now . . . well, Jack Clancy was another matter.

'No good coming here for a hand-out, Father,' he'd say. 'And no good trying to persuade me to come to

Confession. I'd keep you too long. There's not much short of murder that I haven't done!'

Putting his fingers together like the steeple of a church, the old man smiled on Annie.

'A warm drink wouldn't come amiss, and by the look of you, my child, you'll be glad of one yourself.'

He was taken aback when Annie suddenly dropped to her knees by his chair. 'You've come in answer to a prayer, Father.'

'Indeed, my child?'

What a pathetic sight she was in that man's cap, bundled up in clothes not fit for the rag bag.

'Take your time, Annie,' he said, removing his glasses which had steamed up and no wonder with the room like a Turkish bath.

'I don't know how to say it, Father.' She had her head down, speaking so quietly he couldn't hear a word she said.

'Speak up, child. There's nothing so bad that a good confession can't put right.'

'I didn't know what I was doing, Father . . .'

'I'm listening. Take a deep breath, and take your time.'

'There was a man, Father.'

The priest drew in a deep breath. Surely . . . ? Oh, no! He had often grieved for the life this young girl led since her mother's untimely end. It was all wrong that young Annie Clancy should be bringing up a family of boys, taking in washing to keep them fed. Never leaving the house as far as he knew except to lug a heavy clothes-basket round the streets. And look at her . . . just look at her . . . He shook his head. For a minute he'd thought the worst.

'This man. Did he say something to frighten you, my child?'

Annie's head drooped even lower. 'He came as a lodger, Father, back last September. Our dad told him he could stop here. He was a sailor.'

Light was beginning to dawn. 'And now he's sailed away on a troop ship?'

'No! He doesn't . . . he didn't work that kind of ship.' Her voice was ragged with shame. 'I'm going to have a baby! An' nothing will shift it. Nothing!'

Father O'Leary closed his eyes, but not in prayer. What he was thinking at that moment wasn't fit for anybody's ears, let alone God's. The blind panic in Annie's eyes shocked him into an anger so great he could feel himself beginning to tremble with the force of it.

'To even *think* of trying to get rid of a baby is a mortal sin, child,' he said automatically, in the instant before his natural compassion took over. 'Are you *sure*?' His mind groped for an explanation. 'You can't have a baby with just kissing a man, Annie.' He put the glasses on again and coughed. 'Did your mother not talk to you before she . . . before she died?'

'I did more than kissing, Father.'

Annie stood up, and as she did so the shawl dropped away. The kettle came to a spluttering boil and she leaned over to lift it from the trivet.

It was true . . . Father O'Leary glimpsed the thickening of her normally slender waist, saw the big safety-pin bridging the placket of the brown skirt. He covered his eyes with a hand at the terrible pity of it.

'Have you seen the doctor, child?'

'Oh, no! Don't tell me to see the doctor, Father. The last time we had him was when our Eddie had rheumatic fever bad, an' it took more than a year to pay him off.' Tears spilled from her eyes. 'I don't need no doctor. I just need to be told what to do. I don't *know* what to do. I ask meself every minute what to do . . .'

'Kneel down, child.'

Over the bowed head and shaking shoulders, over the sounds of her sobbing, the priest said a prayer. It was a prayer vague in content, asking for forgiveness for Annie's sins, unproductive even to the old man's own ears.

'You must hand over your worry to God. He alone can show you the way,' he finished, then reached for his cloak. 'In the meantime there must be some woman, some *good* woman you can talk to . . .' His voice tailed away. He should have been prepared for what this child had been trying to tell him – it was a confession he'd listened to often enough, but she had knocked him for six. He turned at the door. For a man to take advantage of young Annie Clancy, little scarecrow that she was in her bunchy ragged clothes, was an obscenity. It was a spitting on the face of God.

'No, don't go doing anything foolish. Will you promise me that?'

Annie bowed her head. A dreadful certainty was dawning on her. Father O'Leary hadn't known what to do, either. She'd embarrassed him by what she'd told him. He hadn't been able to get out of the house quick enough. His face was as red as if he'd had it boiled up in a pudding cloth.

Automatically, with a quiet desperation, she reversed a vest and a pair of bloomers on the clothes maiden. Giving their other sides a chance to dry.

It was an almost primeval rage that had flushed Father O'Leary's face to scarlet. He was known in that part of Lancashire as a man of God, with a wealth of charity and forgiveness in him, a priest first but a man a close second. In his young days, before he left Ireland, he had worked on and off as a fairground boxer, taking on anyone for the price of a meal and a pint of good milk stout. He'd had it in him to turn professional, they'd said, and that might have been if he hadn't killed a man one day, felling him with a single blow to the head.

It was not his fault. The man could have died at any given minute from a clot of blood just waiting to be dislodged. It was all part of the game, they said. And let him bear in mind that when he turned professional things would be more ordered, with doctors examining a man before he stepped into the ring. He was a potential champion, they swore. Altogether in the world light-heavyweight class.

Father O'Leary walked slowly down the sloping street, clenching and unclenching his hands, feeling that same strength in them from so long ago. From that time to this he had never once lifted a hand in anger, but this day . . . He stopped and stared down at his hands, balling them into fists.

If Laurie Yates, sailing a far distant sea at that very moment, had been able to see the expression on the old priest's face, he would have wished himself ten fathoms deep.

It was later that afternoon when Father O'Leary came up with an idea and acted upon it. Poor little Annie Clancy had been wrong about it being too windy for snow. It was coming down like a great white curtain, soundlessly, from a leaden sky. Snow meant chilblains on the priest's knobbly toes and fingers, swelling them up into a purple agony. His boots leaked, and the woollen mittens on his hands seemed to soak up the wet before he'd gone ten yards.

To get where he was going he had to pass the Clancy house, and to his shame he was glad to see the door closed and no sign of Annie. He walked on down the street, being careful where he put his feet, knowing it wouldn't be long before her young brothers slurred and slithered down this stretch of flags, turning them into a lethal slide as smooth as glass.

He was passing the house with the old lady in bed by the window now. He couldn't see her, but he knew that behind the cream lace curtain she was more than likely watching him. So he raised his black hat. To be polite.

At the bottom of this street, he had remembered or been nudged by God to remember, lived a homely widow with her son and his wife, a nondescript young woman who was disappointingly childless after three years wed. Week after week the daughter-in-law came to Mass, praying for a miracle that never happened. Kneeling there in church with her poor sore hands clasped in supplication, putting a strain on the relationship between her and her mother-in-law, so the priest had heard. So maybe Annie's baby would altogether be a blessing in disguise.

Father O'Leary stepped as gingerly as if he walked on hot coals and not a snowy pavement to the bottom house, lifted the iron knocker and knocked three times on the door.

'Yon Catholic priest's been down the street twice. Once this morning and once this afternoon. When Nextdoor came in to see to the fire she told me she'd seen him going in young Annie's house.' Grandma Morris submitted to being helped out of bed to sit on the commode, while Edith gave her mattress a good pawing over before she got the tea. 'I nearly knocked on the window the second time, and asked him to come in for a bit. He looked frozen to the marrow.'

Edith was bone weary. She had stood outside three mills that morning before the fourth one had let her take the place of an absentee. Working as a 'sick' weaver was a thankless job. You just got used to one lot of looms then the regular weaver came back and you were out. But what else could she do when there were days when her mother couldn't be left, when her breathing was so bad Edith kept the steam kettle on the go all day.

She gritted her teeth, waiting for her mother to finish, then helped her back into bed, feeling herself almost shaking with self-pity and a rarely acknowledged bitterness.

'Would you like lentil sausages for your tea, Mother?'

In her mind Edith was already mixing the ready boiled lentils with mashed potatoes and onion, binding them together with an egg before forming into sausages and frying in hot fat. She was like that, one step ahead all

56

the time, never wasting a minute. Meeting herself coming backwards, as she often said.

'I don't mind what I have. I could understand the Father coming once, but why twice?'

Edith's halo slipped a bit. 'I don't *care* why he went twice. I don't care if he came down the street *seven* times. I just hope he can do something for that poor young lass.'

Edith was filled with an emotion she couldn't put a name to. She wanted to say: 'I'm going through the change, Mother, and you've never even noticed. I'll never have a baby now.' She wanted to blame her mother for keeping her tied to her apron strings, for stopping her marrying, even though nobody had ever asked her.

'I'm going round to see Annie when we've had our tea,' she said. 'I'll tell her I'll make her baby everything it needs – its whole layette. I'll make it a christening robe and a bonnet. I'll line a clothes-basket with flowered stuff and I'll knit it a blanket.' She blinked hard to stop the tears falling. 'I'll be its godmother if she likes and I won't listen when the tongues start wagging. There'll be no condemnation coming from *me*!'

She jumped up to go through to the back, shaking her small head from side to side as if to emphasise her determination to stand by Annie. After no more than a minute she reappeared.

'How do I know how I would have behaved? I can't set myself up as judge and jury, can I, when nobody ever tempted *me*! When no man has ever tried to lay a finger on *me*! How do I know what I'd have done?'

Grandma Morris sank back exhausted on her pillows. Wondering what she'd said to bring all that on. But seeing the awful sadness in it, just the same.

Father O'Leary was so relieved to get inside out of the cold he made straight for Mrs Greenhalgh's fire, failing to see Jack Clancy, still in his pit dirt, scarpering up the stairs.

'I've come on an errand of mercy,' he said. 'Knowing you've never been known to pass by on the other side.'

'If it's in my power, Father.' Jack's jacket and waistcoat were there, in full view of the priest, with his boots set side by side under the table, but the saintly old codger would think they were her son's. 'We only pass this way but once.' Florrie Greenhalgh put on the pious expression she saved for going to Mass.

Father O'Leary leaned forward. Best to come straight to the point. 'Young Annie Clancy's got herself into trouble.' He bowed his head. 'With a man. I'm feared she's going to have a baby.' His head jerked up. 'What was that?'

'Nothing, Father.' Florrie had to think quick. 'Sometimes the next door's cat gets in and knocks things over.' She hoped she didn't look as alarmed as she felt. 'Are you sure you're right? Begging your pardon, Father, but young Annie's always been a bit fanciful. Is it not some fairy-tale she's made up, thinking to shock?'

'I pray you're right, Mrs Greenhalgh. I pray you're right altogether.' Father O'Leary gathered his cloak round him. He'd forgotten how enormously fat this good woman was, how her eyes kept disappearing into little cushions of flesh. Homely. Motherly. Just what was needed. 'If you could go and have a straight little talk with her.' He reached for his hat. 'It's a mother she needs at the moment . . . but alas . . .'

'I'll go up right this minute, Father. I'll just get me shawl.'

'God bless you,' Father O'Leary muttered, stepping out into a raging snowstorm, his hands and feet already numb. 'May His blessing shine upon you.'

He had hardly turned the corner at the top of the street when Jack Clancy hurtled out of the bottom house, followed by Mrs Greenhalgh, puffing to keep up with him, but leaving enough breath to yell at the top of her voice: 'You lay a finger on that lass, and I'll have the law on you, Jack Clancy!'

Annie heard them coming, and the shame of it made her feel sick. The front door slammed back with such force that flakes of plaster fell from the wall. She wanted to turn and run out the back way, but forced herself to stand her ground, holding the ironing blanket she'd been folding in front of her like a shield.

A part of her, a small unacknowledged part, bowed to the relief of having been found out. When her father started to unbuckle his belt she accepted that to have the shame beaten out of her might even be a good thing. Once it was done it would be done.

'Is it true? Is what Father O'Leary's just come out with the truth?' He ran the thick belt through his fingers.

Mrs Greenhalgh snatched it, then gave Jack an almighty shove that took him off his feet and sent him sprawling into his chair. Annie's mouth dropped open with the shock of it.

'Shame on you, Jack!' Mrs Greenhalgh stood over him, wobbling with indignation. 'It's that sailor you should be fighting, not this child. I warned you there was gyppo blood in him, but you wouldn't listen. Not you!' She spoke without turning round. 'Is it true, lass?'

'Laurie said he wanted to marry me. He said he would be coming back for me. An' he will. He *will*.'

Mrs Greenhalgh's broad back expressed disbelief. 'He was all talk and nowt else. I could have told you that, chuck.' A fat finger was poked in Jack's chest.

Annie could hardly believe what was happening. Laurie had been right. There *was* something going on between her father and Mrs Greenhalgh from the bottom house. He was cowering back in his chair with the blowsy woman bending over him, supporting herself on the arm-rests.

'Aye. All talk and nowt else,' she shouted. 'Like someone else I could mention.' She stabbed him in the chest. 'No wonder you and that gyppo got on so well together. You're two of a kind. No you don't, miladdo!'

When Jack tried to get up she put a hand on his chest and pushed. 'Me own son gave me my marching orders this morning. Said I could go to the workhouse for all he cared. How's that for honouring your poor old ma? But what chance does he have against that sod he's married to?'

Jack made a valiant effort to have a bit of a say. 'Your Jim wouldn't do that. I know him better.'

'Do you?' Mrs Greenhalgh's broad behind quivered. 'But you don't know that daughter-in-law of mine, do you? There isn't the room for her and me in the same house, not one day longer. So do I move into here, and do we get married, or do I go to the workhouse? You've promised to marry me often enough. I reckon we've been courting for at least twelve months.'

Courting? Unnoticed, Annie crept through into the back to sit on her bed and stare unblinking at the round-bellied copper. Her father and Mrs Greenhalgh married? The loud-mouthed common woman living *here*? Taking the place of her mother? Sharing her father's bed? She shuddered. What would the boys think to it all?

As if reading her thoughts the raucous voice from the other room bellowed: 'I only had the one lad, but he's caused me more bother than all your five put together. I'll look to them, Jack. You know that.'

'And Annie?'

Was that her father asking the question, as meek and mild as if butter wouldn't melt in his mouth? Annie held her breath. She leaned forward, a hand to her mouth.

'The day I come here, out she goes.' Mrs Greenhalgh was making no attempt to speak quietly. 'Two women can't share the same house. I know that better than most. It doesn't work.'

There was a silence, then the noise of the rocker moving along the flagged floor. Annie clutched her throat at the inference. That loud-mouthed woman was sitting on her father's knee. She hadn't wanted Jack to

60

belt his daughter, because that would have taken his mind from the real issue. And the real issue was that she was determined to move in here.

'Annie could get a job at the mine. She's young and strong; she could work on the screens for a long time yet.'

Annie couldn't believe it. Her father was pleading for her . . . he was . . . and surely that meant that he must care? Not much, but a little? She moved to the door to hear better.

Mrs Greenhalgh's next words chilled her through.

'An' how long would that last once they found out she was expecting? Have a bit of sense, Jack. She can go to the workhouse to have the baby, they've a special section for girls in her condition. Come on, Jack. Think of the talk once it gets out. Starting with that mealy-mouthed Edith Morris . . .'

Annie leaned against the whitewashed wall. Oh, dear, dear God, how could she have let it happen? Here on this bed, over so quickly, paining her so much. She closed her eyes, in her mind a picture of Laurie Yates sliding the torn blouse off her shoulders, kissing her and whispering words of love. She remembered the way his body had trembled, and the heat coming from him. All she had wanted was to be held and given the comfort she craved. 'Oh, Laurie,' she whispered. 'Come back to me. *Please*. Don't wait a year. Come back *now*.'

'I'm going down the street.'

Jack stood in the doorway and stared at his daughter. He couldn't see any difference in her; she looked just the same to him, with the flat cap on her head and her clothes bunched round her as if she'd put them on all at once. Then she uncrossed her arms and he saw the unmistakable enlargement of her breasts, the slight swell of her stomach as she stood up to face him. Anger rose in him, a fierce and burning anger as if a naked flame had been run up and down his spine. He clenched his hands to hold himself back from striking out at her.

Florrie Greenhalgh was right. And she didn't know

the half of it. If he felt like this now, what would he feel like when Annie's condition became obvious? He turned from her, almost spitting his contempt. Taking no notice of her outstretched hand.

'You dirty little whore,' he muttered. 'You filthy little bitch.'

Her world might be coming to an end, but there was still the boys' tea to get. Annie moved from fire to table, table to fire, with glazed eyes and dragging movements.

'The snow's sticking, our Annie.' Billy spoke through a mouthful of stew made with tripe bits and onions. 'We'll be able to make cloggie-boggies.'

'I bet we can get stilts that thick.' John showed her how thick with his thumb and forefinger. 'We'll knock 'em off before we come in. Honest.'

'Where's our dad gone to?' Georgie looked sly. 'He came up the cage before me.'

Annie waited until the younger boys had rushed straight from the table into the darkened street, whooping with delight at the way the snow was piling up, then she sat down and said, 'Our dad is down the street at Mrs Greenhalgh's house. He'll be having his tea there because they're going to get married.'

She waited for the outburst that never came.

'He's been hanging his cap up there for a long time.'

'You mean you knew?'

Georgie's eyes were those of a man of forty, a man well used to the ways of the world. His father had decided to take a woman, and since his wife had been dead for a long time, what was wrong with that?

''Course I knew.' The old eyes in the black face were weary. 'Anyroad, what difference will it make? I like Mrs Greenhalgh. She gives me sugar butties.'

Annie stared at the unwashed face, black with coal dust, at the pink lips, parting over small white teeth. She had been going to tell Georgie about the baby, making a sort of story out of it, but faced with the hard stare, so much at variance with the childish features, she knew she could never bring herself to say the words, however much she wanted to. Conditioned by her mother's puritanical upbringing, remembering how her brothers had arrived mysteriously in the room upstairs, Annie bit her lips, chewing on them till they hurt. For all his pitman's talk, Georgie was still a little boy; for all his pretence of not caring, his acceptance of Mrs Greenhalgh had more than a bit of bravado in it, she realised with a pang of pity.

'I'm going away,' she said.

The shrug of the thin shoulders could have meant anything.

'*Georgie*? I may be gone a long time.' She struggled to explain. 'But Mrs Greenhalgh will look to you all. Our dad'll see to that.'

She half stretched her hand out to the black paw emerging from her brother's tattered jacket, but drew it back as she sensed his stiffened withdrawal. It came to her in that moment that the small boy in his filthy pitman's working clothes was as frightened as she knew herself to be. Why hadn't she realised before this that he was scared stiff every single day of his life? But if he hated the mine so much, why hadn't he said so? Why didn't he *talk* and express his feelings?

She softened her voice. 'There are jobs going at Howard and Bulloughs if you don't like the mine. There's no law saying you have to work down the mine all your life. You could perhaps go to the Technical College in a few years. You were always top of the class at school, and the Co-op might pay your fees. They're paying for Tom Carmichael across the street.' She was trying her best. She was saying things that should have been said a long time ago. Her mother would have seen to it that Georgie's brains weren't wasted. She'd have sat him down and talked to him. Annie knew what store her mother had set on education. 'Listen to me, Georgie.'

'What's it got to do with you what I do? You're going

away.' For a moment brown eyes looked into blue. 'Where are you going, our Annie? Is it because Mrs Greenhalgh is coming to live here that you're going away?'

The door flew open, catapulting John into the room.

'Our Eddie's fallen down and bumped his head on the lamp-post. He slurred right into it. Miss Morris came out to tell us off for making a noise and she went full length on the slide we'd made. On her bum. And our Billie's thrown a snowball at Mr Thwaites and knocked his billycock off . . .'

Annie snatched her shawl from the nail behind the door. When she turned round Georgie had gone.

The next week Jack Clancy and Florrie Greenhalgh were married by special certificate. In Father O'Leary's eyes they wouldn't be married at all, but his cough had turned into a pneumonia of the double variety and he'd been rushed by ambulance to the hospital.

When he was told the news he thanked God that poor little Annie now had a mother to see her through her trouble.

'God moves in a mysterious way,' was quoted as being the last thing he whispered, before crossing his chilblained hands over his chest and closing his eyes for ever.

Jack Clancy had steadfastly refused to speak to his daughter since the day he had found out about her shameful condition. There was an expression in his eyes that terrified Annie. It was as though he couldn't bear to look at her; as though to be in the same room with her taxed his self-control to the limit.

The snow had gone, leaving a grey wet slush on the pavements, though it still sparkled white on the hump of Pendle Hill and lay in uneven patches on the moors.

Now that the wedding had taken place Annie knew that her days in her own home were numbered. Her father had put it about that she was to go into service in a big house on the Yorkshire border, and knowing how bad the situation had been between Florrie Greenhalgh and her daughter-in-law, the story was accepted in the street as being the best solution in the circumstances.

Edith Morris knew her mother was on her last. Since Christmas she had been sleeping the hours away, eating like a bird and taking no notice of the life in the street. When Nextdoor told the old lady about Annie going away, Grandma Morris tried to bring to mind what Edith had said. Some kind of trouble . . . Her eyes blurred over with the effort of trying to remember, but it was no good. The worries of this world had nothing to do with Grandma Morris now. She could recall events from her far away childhood, but not what happened yesterday. Quite peacefully she slipped in and out of her dreams, going happily back to the time when she lived with her mother and father on their farm high up on Whalley Nab. She whimpered in her sleep as she relived the day when the Press Gangs came, rounding up men for the Battle of Waterloo. She could still hear their loud voices as they thrust their bayonets into the hay where her father was hiding, narrowly missing impaling him to the barn floor. She remembered the day when the cholera epidemic spread from Blackburn, claiming three of her sisters and two brothers in one dreadful month.

'They're sending Annie away,' her daughter told her one day.

'Annie would have lived if the fever had broke,' her mother said, and Edith knew she was talking about her youngest sister, the one she suspected her mother had loved the most.

'They're sending young Annie Clancy away. She's not wanted since her father got a new wife.'

Bertram Thwaites heard the women gossiping down at the mine.

'Is what I've heard true?' he asked Annie when she brought the washing back that night.

'Is what true, Mr Thwaites?'

Disturbed by the unkempt look of her and the lingering sadness in her eyes, he curbed his normal abrupt way of speaking. 'That you're going away into service?'

'It's true.' She was holding out her hand for the money, wanting to go, rushing away with that desperate look on her face, bundled up into old clothes like a woman of the roads. Suddenly he couldn't accept that.

'Do you *want* to go?'

To his surprise she gave a hard dry laugh. 'No. I don't want to go, Mr Thwaites, but needs must.'

'What do you mean, needs must?'

He snatched her hand and held on to it. He was flushed in the face, as out of breath as if he'd run all the way up from the mine without stopping.

'There are reasons I have to go away.' Annie tried to free her hand, to pull away from him, but his grip was iron, his big red face contorted out of shape with the force of his feelings.

'It's because of that Greenhalgh woman, isn't it? That son of hers finally got the courage up to give her her marching orders, and not before time. She's vicious, that old fat slob. She'd make mincemeat out of you if you were forced to live in the same house. Oh, aye, I can see that for meself. It's diabolical!' he shouted, thrusting his face even closer.

Annie was horrified. The dents in his forehead were surely more pronounced than ever, and she could swear his thick neck was swelling and pulsating like a toad's.

'I have to go now, Mr Thwaites.' He was sweating cobs. She felt sick. 'Please. I've got a lot to do before morning. Before I leave . . .'

'There's no need for you to leave, lass.'

With a jerk he pulled her tight up against him, pressing her head hard against the rough serge of his jacket. He smelt of tobacco and of the pit.

'I'll *marry* you, Annie.' His gruff voice spoke into the top of her head. 'I've always had a soft spot for you. I've watched you grow up into a fine looking lass. I'll marry you then there won't be the need for you to go away, and that Mrs Greenhalgh can go and take a running jump at herself.'

Any minute now and he was going to kiss her. Annie clamped her mouth tight shut, clenching her teeth together. When his tongue wormed its way into her mouth she brought her knee up, fast and hard, so that he let go of her, backing away, clutching himself.

'You young devil!'

In one bound he was on her, forcing her up against the table, bending her over, but Annie was ready for him. Her arms, grown strong with all the daily mangling, possing, the carrying of the heavy clothes-baskets, were slender ropes of steel. She was off out of the house before Bertram Thwaites had time to pull himself together. The money he owed her was there on the table, one shilling and a sixpence.

'She can whistle for this,' he muttered, putting it back in his pocket, before tying his muffler round his neck in a fierce knot, slamming his billycock on his head and going out the back way. To soothe his pride in four pints of ale at the Pig and Whistle.

Outside in the street, Annie leaned against the wall to get her breath back. When Mr Thwaites had come at her like that she had wanted to kill him. Remembering the sickening kiss, she took a crumpled hankie from up her sleeve and rubbed her mouth hard with it.

'All right, Annie?'

The man from next door came slithering past her on the icy pavement on his way to the night shift at the mine.

'You want to mind you don't fall. They've been queuing up at the hospital all day with broken arms and legs. It's the freezing on top of a thaw what does it.'

He had known her since she was a child. Once he had won a coconut at the fair and brought it round for her. He was a kind man with a John the Baptist face.

Annie watched him slide his way down the street. He still considered her to be a child, yet in the morning she was leaving home for good to have a baby in some unknown place by a man whose face she was beginning to forget. It was unbelievable, but true.

The doctor was going into Grandma Morris's house. She saw Edith let him in, her long face stiff with suffering in the light of the street lamp.

Annie opened the door of her own house and saw Mrs Greenhalgh putting coal on the fire with her hands, then wiping them down an already filthy pinny.

'Put the wood in the 'ole, chuck,' she called out cheerfully. 'You'd best keep the money from Mr Thwaites's washing to pay the carrier with tomorrow. It's like getting blood out of a stone getting money from your dad, the tight-fisted old beggar.'

She was laughing as though it was funny. The boys were sitting round the table stuffing their faces with doorsteps of bread spread with margarine and lavish sprinklings of sugar. They liked their new mother because she let them run wild, eat what they fancied, and never asked them about what had gone on at school, what Miss had said, or whether they'd washed their necks in the past week.

Not like their Annie who inspected their ears and pinned a clean rag on their jerseys when they had a cold to save them blowing their noses on their sleeves. The brown-paper chest protectors smeared with goose grease she'd insisted on them wearing were soon ripped off and flung to the back of the fire with Mrs Greenhalgh looking on and laughing. She laughed at everything; she laughed at nothing, and funniest of all, she wobbled when she laughed.

'Are you the fattest lady in the world?' John had asked her one day, fascinated by the sight of her getting her enormous behind stuck in his dad's rocking-chair. 'I expect you could be in a show with it costing a penny to go in.'

'A penny!' The laugh had nearly ripped the plaster off the walls. 'More like twelve pennies to see someone my size!'

Annie need have no qualms about leaving her brothers to the slap-dash ministrations of her father's new wife. Neglected they would certainly be, but she had a feeling they would thrive on it.

Florrie wasn't laughing the next morning when she and Annie had the house to themselves.

She was explaining about the workhouse. 'You have to be properly destitute to get in, so you can't take much with you. An' if you could faint on the doorstep you might have a better chance of being taken in.' She reached up with her fat arms to put one of her own ornaments on the high mantelpiece. 'It's a pity you don't show more, but they'll have you examined so that's all right. They'll likely put you to work in the laundry, but you won't need any training for that.' She stood back to admire the blue glass jug flanking the clock that Annie's mother had brought with her when she was first married. 'The time will soon pass, then you can leave and get work outside. They can always find places for the babies born in there, especially if they're handsome and healthy. You'll be all right, chuck.'

Annie picked up the small bundle she'd placed on the floor behind the door. It was better this way, going without having said goodbye to the boys. They'd come home from school for their dinner caring nothing that it was bread and jam again, eating standing up if they'd a mind to, putting four spoonfuls of sugar into their cocoa if they felt like it, playing truant if they thought they could get away with it, all her good bringing up forgotten.

She looked round the room, a bare room but for the

essentials, but cosy with the firelight washing the walls to a soft shade of apricot.

'I'll be off then,' she said.

Florrie had a sudden urge to go to Annie, take her hand and bring her back into the warm. In her mother's old cloak, with a scarf tied round the flat cap, the child looked like a tramp – like an old, old woman of the roads.

'It's for the best, chuck,' she said, trying to convince herself. 'Things allus turn out for the best.' She crossed herself quickly. 'Some things are meant to be . . .'

Annie opened the door and walked out.

5

It didn't register with Annie that the blind had been pulled down over Grandma Morris's window until she was in the carrier's cart on the road away from the town.

Did it mean the old woman had died? Was that why Edith's face had looked even more mournful than usual as she let the doctor into the house the night before? Annie swayed from side to side with the movement of the cart, huddled into her mother's old cloak, the flat cap pulled low over her forehead, too cold and miserable to make herself care much one way or the other. No, that wasn't true. Grandma Morris was a saint – even if you couldn't blow your nose without her knowing about it. Annie wished she'd called in to say goodbye; wished she hadn't been too ashamed to tell them why she was going away. Grandma Morris would have felt nothing but pity, whereas Edith . . . Annie shook her head. Edith would be disgusted.

'Too cold for more snow, I reckon.'

There were pieces of stiff sacking covering the carrier's back and legs. A top hat, green with age, was pulled low over his weathered forehead. He glanced sideways at his passenger, at the small set face, blue with cold, and the hands clutching her bundle as if it had the Crown Jewels wrapped up inside.

'Cat got your tongue, lass?'

He flicked his whip, urging his horse on faster. Suited him all right her not wanting to talk. He'd only been trying to be kind. It wasn't as if he was much of a talker himself. His own mother had sworn he was tongue-tied till he was five – even had a go at it herself with the scissors. He began to hum . . .

Once he'd got this job done he'd go back to working on

funerals. This road was a killer in the winter. He sucked his teeth. There were always plenty of funerals at this time of the year. Seemed as if folks decided to last out till Christmas, then just gave up. He hummed a slow march. He was a sight cheaper than the professionals with their fancy carts and their horses plumed like fairies. There was dignity in the way *he* did it. Just a plain box laid with proper reverence on the cart, and the relatives walking behind, decently overcome. There were funerals and funerals, of course. Babies fetched the best price. The outlay for a baby wasn't all that much for him. Just a hat box for the corpse and his young niece walking in front of the cart with a purple sash on her dress and a wreath of artificial daisies on her head. Yes, the coming months were the best for mortalities. The old and the young – snuffed out like candles the minute the frost began to bite. The outlook was quite cheery really.

'It might never 'appen, lass,' he said, neither expecting nor getting any reply.

Annie's eyes darted from one side of the road to the other. She had no idea how long they'd been travelling, but the ridge of distant hills loomed ever closer. The stony road wound uphill now and the horse made a ferocious snorting noise, the breath from its wide nostrils steaming in the freezing air. She had often wondered what it would be like to travel away from the town. There'd been little enough time for walks since her mother died, but she remembered as a child, one clear summer's day, standing with her mother on a hilltop, looking away from the smoke of the mill chimneys to Pendle Hill in the north, the bump of Boulsworth and the fells leading to the Pennines in the east. 'Look at the world!' she'd shouted excitedly, throwing her arms wide. 'Mam! Look at the world!'

When the carrier stopped the cart to disappear for a minute or so into the bushes, Annie climbed down to stand by the side of the road, waiting for him.

'You can leave me here,' she told him. 'Thank you for the ride.'

The carrier looked at her with suspicion. 'Nay, lass. I can't leave you here on the fell road. There's nowt round here for miles but the odd farmhouse, and mebbe a cottage or two.' He took off the top hat and scratched a shiny bald head. 'Look 'ere, lass. I know it's none of my business, but my guess is you're running away from home.'

'I'm going into service.' Annie pointed to a building in the far distance. 'See that cottage with a lot of black smoke coming out of the chimney? Over there, to the right of that row of trees. Well, that's where I'm going. The wife's got bronchitis bad and can't do the outside work, so they're taking me on.' The lie came easily. Annie could actually 'see' the farmer's wife coughing herself sick by the fire, 'saw' her husband lead her gently away to her bed, telling her that the girl would be coming that day to take over and ease her pain. 'It's very sad. It's more than likely that she's consumptive,' Annie embroidered. 'I was told her mother went the same way.'

'Aye, well . . . as long as I know you've a place to go to.' The carrier swung himself back onto the cart. 'You've a fair walk across them fields.'

Annie nodded, raised a hand in salute and stood perfectly still by the side of the road, clutching her bundle, waiting until the clip-clop of the horse's hooves faded away.

Now she was really alone. Now she could turn her back on the road to the workhouse and walk until she found a farm with plenty of jobs for a strong and willing girl to do. It would be a while yet before her shape gave her secret away and by that time . . . by that time . . .

She threw her bundle over a drystone wall, climbed after it and set off across a field with horses standing beneath the bare branches of a spreading tree, their heads lowered against the biting wind. She wouldn't

73

think about what might happen when the baby showed. That was the future. What mattered was now, and finding shelter before it got dark.

Round about four o'clock when it was time to light the lamps and get the coal in for the night, Edith Morris went round to the Clancys' house to break the news that her mother had died.

She was finding it hard to understand why Annie hadn't been round to pay her respects. Nextdoor had made a lovely job of laying her mother out, sliding her on to a board to keep her straight, putting pennies on her eyes and crossing her hands over a nightdress with a pin-tucked bodice. Young Annie had thought such a lot about her Grandma Morris – it really was a mystery why she hadn't been. Edith knocked at the Clancys' front door.

It was immediately obvious that Jack Clancy's new wife had no intention of asking Edith in.

'Annie? You're asking after Annie?' She lifted a pendulous breast and had a good scratch. 'She's gone away and she won't be coming back, not if she knows what's good for her.'

'Hold on a minute!'

Edith took a step forward, just too late to prevent the door being slammed hard against her. For a long moment she stood irresolute on the pavement, chewing on her thin lips till they almost disappeared, holding her head up as if she scented the sounds of battle in the air.

Edith Morris had just spent the worst forty-eight hours of her life. Not one tear had she shed in front of the neighbours crowding into the little front room to pay their last respects to the old woman who could be trusted to keep her mouth shut, no matter what tempting secrets they confided in her. Edith's eyes might be dry, but inside her she was weeping tears of blood. What would she do with her life now her mother was dead? Who would *need* her now? She was too distraught to look even a day ahead.

74

'Where's young Annie gone? That's all I want to know. Where, in the name of God, has she gone?' She burst into the Clancy house like a tornado, eyes flashing.

Florrie was flabbergasted. You could have knocked her down with a feather, as she told Jack later on when he came up from the mine.

'I don't remember asking you in, Miss Morris!' She could only stand there gaping at the scrawny-necked woman, with eyes bulging from their sockets like shiny marbles. Gone clean off her chump, by the look of her.

'Annie was pregnant. Mother and me guessed,' Edith said straight out. This wasn't the time nor the place for fancy words. 'Pregnant!' she said again. Overcome by too much emotion she put a hand out to the table for support. 'Just tell me where she's gone and I'll find her – go after her and bring her back.' The shiny eyes rolled wildly. 'I'll look after her. She can live with me. I'll help her bring her baby up. The Lord giveth even as He taketh away. Don't you see? My mother is dead, but Annie will bring new life into my house. It is the will of God. He has made His purpose clear.'

'Best thing you can do, chuck, is go home and have a bit of a lie down.' Florrie mentally crossed herself. It was funny how religion turned some folks' heads. Couldn't this potty woman see that bringing Annie back to the street was out of the question? She could just imagine Jack's reaction to the news that his daughter was moving back with her shame. 'Don't take on, chuck,' she soothed, coming round the table and taking Edith by the elbow. 'I'll come back with you to your house and have a look at your mother, and as soon as we hear from Annie I'll let you know.'

'You promise?' Edith's anguish had gone straight to her neck as usual, flushing it up like a scald.

'On my honour, chuck. On *God*'s honour,' Florrie soothed, feeling that would carry more weight.

'She's a sight for sore eyes,' she said, crossing herself as she stared at the corpse. 'Have you touched her up yourself, or did you have the Co-op in to do it?'

'Where's our Annie gone?'

The boys were getting their teas down as fast as they could so they could join their mates round the lamp on the corner of the spare land. Two of the miners on the early shift were due there to play a game of marbles for higher stakes than had been known for many a day. Threepence a hit was rumoured, and some said it was as high as sixpence. Eddie could hardly wait for the excitement to begin; he could almost hear the iron bobbers pinging against each other. One thing about the teas his new mother made: you could eat them standing up if you wanted. They never varied much. Thick slices of bread with jam in between them; sometimes potted meat. And shop meatpies followed by pineapple chunks on a Saturday, when she was flush.

'Annie's gone working away.' Florrie was passing round half-pint pots of strong sweet tea. 'Maid to a Duchess, I shouldn't wonder.'

'When will she be coming back?' John's mouth drooped. 'Why didn't she tell us she was going?'

Florrie ruffled his hair. 'Because she was called to go sudden, chuck, that's why.'

'Can you show me on the map where she's gone?' Timmy went to the shelf for his beloved atlas. 'Is it as far away as Scotland?'

'Ask your dad. He'll be in any minute now.'

But there was no time for that. Not with the game due to start any minute, not with stakes as high as was rumoured. When Jack Clancy came through the door, a black bent figure wearing old clothes and heavy clogs, his wife was frying four lamb chops, two for him and two for her, her fat rear swaying from side to side as she turned the meat over and over in the hot fat.

Annie was long past feeling hungry. She just kept on going, placing one foot in front of the other, with no real idea of her whereabouts. She had accepted of course that

76

there *was* a world outside the town where she'd lived all her life, but had never once asserted her right to explore it. Now, after two miles of steady walking, her boots were rubbing blisters up on her heels, making every step a burning agony. The wind blew flurries of frozen rain into her face, pricking as sharp as needle jabs.

The sky looked dark and swollen, a much bigger sky, Annie was sure, than the sky she'd left behind. She seemed to be walking into nowhere, up a muddy lane flanked by drystone walls, with no sign that anyone had lived there, ever. A mile further on the walls petered out at a derelict cottage, open to the sky, and she knew she was lost, knew that when it was properly dark she would have no idea in which direction she was walking.

She remembered how during the spell of bad weather before Christmas, a woman in the next street had wandered out from the town, crazed in her mind after her baby was born dead. How she'd been found, frozen stiff, her features set in a horrific mask, her mouth wide-open as if she'd cried out for help right to the last. Quite dispassionately Annie wondered how long it would take for her own body to set hard as a rock. Two hours? Four? And would it hurt, or would she merely drop off to sleep, then wake up dead?

Sitting herself down on the ruins of a low wall she gingerly eased a foot out of a boot. What she saw made the tears spring to her eyes. The blister had burst, and the black wool of her stocking was sticking to it in a patch of wet blood. The sensible thing to do, the right thing to do would be to walk back to the top road. At least she'd get somewhere that way. Here was the middle of nowhere, the 'back of beyond', as Grandma Morris used to say about her nephew who had gone to live in the village of Whalley. 'Burying himself and his new bride alive,' she'd said.

It was funny how the old lady kept popping into her mind. It was because she hadn't gone in to say goodbye, Annie decided.

Closing her eyes against the agony, she eased her foot back into her boot. By now, if she'd done as she was told, she could be inside the workhouse, sitting at a long table with rows of tramp women in white caps, eating pobs out of wooden bowls, being silently grateful for every single mouthful they took.

Grandma Morris would have understood that the workhouse was an unthinkable solution. She was forever saying that she had never been beholden to nobody – even though Edith waited on her hand and foot. Edith would think Annie had got what was coming to her for being so wicked as to lie with a man before she was married.

Annie stood up, pulled her cloak closer round her throat and took a painful step forward.

By now it was almost dark and the skyline was so bleak and hopeless Annie felt like lifting up her face and howling her misery at it. Soft yellow lamplight shone from the windows of a row of cottages, but she limped on by. It was the big houses she must make for, the mill and pit owners' mansions, where they would be glad of an extra pair of hands. The long twilight seemed to be never ending, as she stumbled, head down, staggering from side to side of a deeply rutted cart-track.

When the horse appeared suddenly round the bend of the road she was too late to dive for the ditch on her left. In her dark cloak, with her head down, she was practically invisible, but as the horse reared up its rider had a split-second view of her face, eyes wide with terror, mouth open in a soundless scream.

As she fell, he jerked hard on the reins, his reaction as swift as was humanly possible, but just too late to prevent his startled horse kicking out as it struggled frantically to regain its footing.

Seth Armstrong slid from his saddle to bend over what he took to be an old woman of the roads. With fingers grown skilled at tending animals, he examined the crumpled figure as well as he could beneath the cloak and the layers of clothing, relieved when his hands came away unbloodied. The tramp woman was alive, thank God, though deeply insensible. As he lifted her easily into his arms, her head lolled back, her face an indefinable blur in the darkness.

Turning the horse he set off for home, holding Annie and her pathetic little bundle in front of him. He urged the horse on, upwards towards the hills, then across a narrow path hung over with the bare branches of trees, his horse treading the familiar path by instinct.

'Mrs Martindale? *Mrs Martindale?*'

Seth was calling out before it was even faintly possible that she could hear him, but his housekeeper was there in the front room of the old stone-built house; he could see her moving about lighting the lamps, coming over to the window to draw the long velvet curtains.

'Mrs Martindale!' The woman was more deaf than she would admit to, and it was Biddy's afternoon off though time she was back. Seth led the horse right up to the glassed-in porch and dismounted.

From round the back of the house Biddy Baker disentangled herself from her current sweetheart's arms. Quickly she adjusted her clothing, ramming her felt hat down over ruffled hair.

'What's he yammering on about? It's no use him shouting his head off. Old Ma Martindale wouldn't hear him if he fired a starting-pistol up her nose. I'd best go before he splits his tonsils.'

By the time she got there Seth was lifting what looked like a dead woman down from his horse.

'The door, Biddy!' he shouted. 'The door . . .'

Biddy thought the animal doctor looked terrible, and by the expression on Mrs Martindale's face as she came out of the parlour, she thought so too.

'The lamp, Biddy!' she cried, all of a twitter. 'Hold it high so the master can see where he's going.'

79

'Nay, sir,' she protested, when he kicked the door of his own room open, 'you can't put her in there.' She bustled up to the bed. 'She's a tramp woman, sir. The spare room's where she belongs. Just look at the dirt from her boots on my nice clean spread.' She glared at Biddy as if it was all her fault. 'You should have called *me*, sir. I was drawing the parlour curtains or I'd have seen you.'

Seth didn't bother to turn round. 'Put the lamp down there, Biddy, and I think we'll have the candles lit as well. I'm going to need all the light I can get.'

'*I'll* see to them, sir.' Mrs Martindale almost snatched the box of matches out of Biddy's hand.

'I couldn't avoid her . . .' Seth pulled the scarf and the flat cap from Annie's head, releasing the long fall of her hair. 'Good God, she's only a child! I was sure she was a vagrant making for the nearest barn.' He started to unfasten the clasp at the top of the black cloak, his hand cold against Annie's throat. 'Let's see what damage is done.'

At once Annie opened her eyes, saw the face of a strange man bending over her and moaning, tried to twist away from him.

'Best leave her to me, sir.'

Nellie Martindale didn't know what to do for the best. She was so overcome with embarrassment she could hardly speak. Surely the master could see it was a young woman he was undressing and not a child? And that silly Biddy was having a bit of a cough to disguise the fact that she was laughing her head off. It was all right the master running his hands over an injured animal, keeping his fingers clear of bared teeth, reaching for his phial of chloroform, whispering in that special voice of his that even animals seemed to understand. But this was a different kettle of fish altogether. She moved to the bed as Seth slid the girl's cloak away, before making a determined start on her blouse buttons.

'Nay, sir.' Forgetting her place for once, Nellie

80

actually tried to push him aside. 'Let me do that. See, she's gone over again, the poor soul. You just leave this to me.'

'Hot water, Mrs Martindale. Towels. And my box from downstairs!'

Nellie moved away. She knew that tone of voice. One word from the master when he was in that mood and you jumped to it. Quick!

'Come with me, Biddy.' She marched straight-backed towards the door.

Seth's voice was a whisper, but it seemed to come at them like a pistol shot. 'Stay where you are, Biddy!' He continued undressing Annie. 'I might need you to hold up the lamp when I've got all her clothes off.'

Nellie Martindale could hardly stop her legs from dithering, she was that upset. Dismissing her as if she was nothing but a maid of all work! Speaking to her like that in front of Biddy! Calmly stripping that ragamuffin. Slipping her blouse down, whipping her skirts away. It was disgusting!

Downstairs in the stone-flagged kitchen, tut-tutting to herself, Nellie took a cross-stitched holder down from its nail and lifted the kettle from the hob. She poured a stream of hot water into a bowl, added cold from the tap at the wide slopstone, then still chunnering snatched three towels down from the airing-string above the fireplace.

Nellie Martindale looked far older than a woman in her early sixties had any right to look. Her hair, screwed up on top of her head in a sparse bun, was the dirty grey of well-trodden snow. Long, long ago she had married a dashing soldier who had failed to tell her that he was a deserter trying to avoid being shipped to India. The union had hardly been consummated when two detectives had burst into the room to snatch Nellie's bridegroom from her arms. Three weeks later he had been shot at point-blank range when the military, hounding him through a wood, mistook the branch in his hand for a gun.

81

From that day Nellie had never glanced at any man in what she would have described to herself as 'that way'. She was saving herself, she told Biddy, for when they met again in heaven, where they would carry on where they had left off.

Exactly where they'd left off? Biddy found the notion fascinating.

Nellie started for the stairs. It should have been her and not Biddy up there in the master's room. Mr Armstrong might be the best animal doctor for miles around, but that didn't make him into a proper doctor used to dealing with people. Only last week Nellie had seen him splinting a wild cat's leg, holding the spitting and snarling creature still, talking to it in that special way he had. But this wasn't the same, not at all the same.

The doctor should have been sent for, though Nellie didn't have much time for doctors, either. One had wanted to examine her once when she had told him about a pain in her side, but she'd given him short shrift. 'Make me a rubbing bottle up. I'll get it right myself,' she'd told him, and though the house reeked of wintergreen for three weeks the pain disappeared, never to return.

She stood still on the bend in the wide stairs. When the master had untied the young lass's skirt, hadn't there been a soft swell of her belly? And what about the blue veins on the full breasts? Nellie gripped the bowl so hard the water sloshed up the side.

'Nay . . . never . . .' she said aloud.

The girl before Biddy had kept her shame a secret for months till the day Nellie had gone into her room without knocking and caught her stark naked, staring at her reflection in the wardrobe mirror.

Nellie's small head moved from side to side as the certainty grew on her. There was no wedding ring, but then there wouldn't be, would there? Nellie forced herself to continue her way upstairs. The workhouse was the right and the only place for fallen girls, and that was where this one would go as soon as she was fit to stand. She, Nellie Martindale, would see to that personally.

Annie lay perfectly flat in the high bed watching the firelight flickering on the flowered wallpaper. She was dreaming. No, she was awake. She closed her eyes and remembered walking, head bent, along a narrow lane. There was a gale tearing the breath from her body, sending hard shafts of frozen rain at her, blinding her, so that when the horse came straight at her she was conscious only of a huge black shape towering over her, blotting out the sky.

She sat up, held out her arms and saw she was wearing a nightdress so shrunk in the wash that the sleeves ended six inches from her wrists. There was a pain down her side and a nauseating throbbing in her head.

'So you've come to, then?'

The girl sitting in a shadowed corner of the room came towards the bed smiling. The first thing Annie noticed about her was the roundness of her face. Pert and pretty, she had an upturned nose and a cloud of fly-away brown hair, topped by a shrivel of a lace cap.

'You mustn't get bothered,' she was saying. 'Mr Armstrong says there's nothing broken, though you're going to be black and blue tomorrow. It was his horse what kicked you.'

Annie closed her eyes as the ceiling dipped and swayed towards her, but then the feeling of sinking down through the bed was worse. There was a scorching pain in her side and a dragging ache in the small of her back. When she opened her eyes again the brown-haired girl was leaning over her, speaking in a hoarse whisper.

'Were you running away?'

Annie bit her lip. 'Running away from the workhouse, really. I was looking for a place to work.'

'This isn't a big house,' Biddy said, as quickly as if she'd read Annie's mind. 'There's only me and the housekeeper.' The round eyes narrowed. 'She nearly fainted dead away when Mr Armstrong whipped all your clothes off.'

Annie tried to sit up. 'My clothes? My bundle?' She swung her legs over the side of the bed, stood up – and gave a soft little cry as the floor came up and hit her smack between the eyes.

There was a man standing by the side of her bed when she surfaced once again – a powerfully-built giant of a man, with an abundance of silver-fair hair and a wind-brown face. His eyes were filled with genuine concern.

'How are you feeling now?'

Annie turned her head towards the window. Surely the last time she'd looked out the curtains had been drawn against the night, and a girl with brown curly hair had talked to her. Now it was light, and huge flakes of snow fell silently, straight down, like a beaded curtain.

'I'd best get up.' She raised herself on an elbow, only to feel a firm hand on her shoulder.

'You'll stay where you are.' The big man walked to the door. 'That snow's not pretending.'

'But I've got to get on my way!' Annie could hear herself becoming agitated. The dizziness had almost gone, the throbbing in her head was less acute, but the soreness down her side and the ache in her back were worse. 'I've got to find a place before the snow starts to stick.'

Seth turned, a hand on the brass door handle. Already the snow was a spread blanket, merging the fields and the paths into one. His calls would have to be made on foot and he would have to go now to get back before dark. The girl seemed comfortable enough and the swelling on her forehead was going down a little. He'd ask Biddy to make sure to keep the fire going, and he'd ask Mrs Martindale to make one of her milk jellies. He felt impatient to be away, and yet responsible for the girl being here at all.

'The least I can do is keep you here till you're fit to leave.' He opened the door wide. 'Is there any family

84

fretting about where you've got to? Anybody expecting you?'

'Nobody fretting and nobody expecting,' Annie told him.

'I see . . .' He nodded, his mind seemingly on other more important things. 'I see.'

Then he was gone, his heavy boots clattering down the stairs. Annie heard him calling out as he left the house, giving orders in a deep voice, slamming a door behind him.

Biddy wondered what Mrs Martindale would do if she found out that the girl upstairs was expecting. She doubted if the old bat would be making her a milk jelly, measuring out the gelatine, the tip of her tongue poking out between her thin lips. But Biddy had realised a long time ago that what Mr Armstrong said was gospel where his housekeeper was concerned. If he'd asked her to sit on the fire she'd have done so. When he spoke Biddy noticed she gave a little bob, not quite a curtsey, but as near as damn it. Mrs Martindale had been trained donkey's years ago in a big house teeming with servants, a little cog in a big wheel, Biddy suspected. Now she was a big cog in a little wheel, with just one underling to boss about.

'Annie Clancy,' she was saying now. 'That's what she says her name is.' The milk was poured grudgingly into the gelatine. 'Wouldn't you say Clancy was Irish, Biddy?'

'Not Welsh, Mrs Martindale.'

'And if Irish, it's ten to one the girl's an R.C.'

'Beholden to the Pope,' said Biddy, in the mood for stirring things up.

'Having children for His Holiness. Dozens and dozens of them so that one day they take us all over.'

'An English Pope on our throne.'

'She'll have to go,' said Mrs Martindale, stirring so vigorously that the milk slopped up and spattered the scrubbed table.

·By nightfall there was no sign of Seth. A blizzard had blown up, shifting the thick powdered snow into dunes, rippling it away as far as the eye could see. Biddy's sweetheart had failed to appear at their arranged time and Biddy, growing tired of him and of all the panting and struggling for the virtue she had no intention of relinquishing, told herself she didn't give a tuppenny damn.

Mrs Martindale had done what she'd been told to do for Annie, and not a thing more. So it was left to Biddy to carry the slops, make the fire up in the spare room's tiny grate, help Annie along the landing to it, and wrap a hot brick in a blanket for the bed, shoving it in at the bottom and telling Annie to get her feet on it and be blowed to chilblains.

'I've never been as warm in my life,' Annie whispered. The pain in her back was spreading round to her front. It was like the grinding ache she was used to experiencing every month. Annie drew her knees up to ease it.

'I think you've got yourself into trouble, Annie,' Biddy said all of a sudden.

'I've not!' Annie's reaction was swift. 'Why do you say a thing like that?'

'Because I know the signs.' Biddy sat down on the side of the bed. 'Two of my sisters got themselves into trouble, with men who promptly disappeared – that's why Mam sent me here to keep me safe. She thinks that only pigs and cows do that kind of thing in the country.'

Annie didn't know what to say. In her mind, a memory of Laurie Yates bending his dark curly head to kiss her bare shoulders, the way his body had swayed against hers, the way she had allowed him to lead her through into the back room . . .

'He's coming back to marry me!' she cried. 'In September. On my birthday. He's away at sea. We're as good as married now; every bit as good.' She drew in a breath as a pain tightened in her back, spreading itself round to her stomach in a warm wave of agony. 'I've just got to keep going until September. Find a place. Work.' She held out her hands. 'I can do the work of three men, Biddy! I'm as strong as any lad. Stronger!'

'Biddy? What are you doing up there?' Mrs Martindale's tinny voice spiralled up the stairs. 'Fetch two candlesticks down. Quick! Mr Armstrong's come back. He looks fit to drop.'

'So it's all hands to the pumps,' Biddy said cheerfully, picking up a candlestick from the top of a mahogany tallboy. She turned at the door. 'She'd lick the snow off his boots if he asked her to.'

Mrs Martindale couldn't do enough for Seth. She took away his heavy coat sodden with snow, and sent Biddy to fetch his slippers. She gave him a towel to rub his hair, though Biddy could see her fingers were itching to do it herself.

She loves him, Biddy realised all at once. Not in the way a woman loves a man. Not with her being old enough to be his mother, but like a mother. Fussing, cosseting, and getting nowhere fast, because if ever there was a man who could fend for himself it was the animal doctor.

Biddy knew that he'd been married to a wife who went completely mad when their first baby had been born perfect in every way, but dead. She had tried to get the details from Mrs Martindale, but all she could find out was that the poor demented girl had refused to eat, ending up with no more flesh on her than a plucked sparrow.

'It was a blessing when she passed on. She had shoulder blades on her like coat-hangers,' the housekeeper had said. 'You could have dropped her through a grid and it wouldn't even have taken the skin off her big toe.'

'There's some nice hot broth ready for you, sir.' Mrs Martindale bent over the black pan on the fire. 'You go through to your den where it's warm.'

Seth snapped his fingers and a black and white dog woke at once from a twitching sleep and moved to his side. 'How's the girl?'

Mrs Martindale was already spooning the broth into a dish. 'Coming on nicely, sir. She'll be able to leave in a few days.'

Seth glanced up the stairway as he walked across the wide flagged passage-way. 'If the snow clears . . .' All the signs of a long hard frost were there. Already a fox had come down from the high slopes and massacred five hens. Not a domestically-inclined man, Seth nevertheless reminded himself that the spirit lamp in the outside privy must be kept alight to stave off the frost. He turned back to the kitchen.

'You can leave it all to me, sir,' Mrs Martindale assured him. 'Go to the outside and see to that lamp,' she told Biddy the minute he had closed the door behind him.

'The old flarcher,' Biddy muttered, putting a shawl round her head and stepping out into a freezing snow-filled wind that tore her breath away.

At three o'clock the next morning as the house slept Biddy woke up with a shuddering jerk.

The temperature in her room was below freezing, and when she padded over to the window to draw back the curtain, the pane was opaque with whorls of ice. She had definitely heard something, but what? Some noise had prodded her awake when normally she was so tired she slept the sleep of the dead. She listened, her head on one side. She padded to the door, opened it and listened again . . .

And heard the girl in the spare room moaning and whimpering like an animal caught in a trap.

Not many hours before she had watched her employer dose Annie Clancy with a sedative. With her own eyes she had seen him measure it out carefully, promising Annie that she would sleep like a baby and wake feeling much, much better.

Holding her candlestick high, Biddy moved along the landing.

Annie's face was wrenched out of shape with pain. Her knees were drawn up, her long red hair almost black with sweat.

Biddy pulled back the piled blankets and saw the blood-stained sheet. She set the candle down on the high bedside table. 'Your baby's coming away. You're losing it.'

'Thank God for that! Oh, thank God for that!'

The words said themselves. Annie's eyes were wide, her voice too high.

'I tried to get shut of it by mangling the washing folded thick. I prayed on me knees. I jumped down the stairs – but nothing would budge it.' She lay back as a pain gripped her. She turned her head into the pillow, tears rolling down her flushed cheeks. 'The Lord be praised.'

'You wicked, wicked girl!'

Mrs Martindale stood framed in the doorway, two grey plaits as thin as ropes hanging over her shoulders. 'Do you know what you're saying?' She walked flat-footed over to the bed, wincing as she saw the sheets.

'I'll get them clean.' Annie was wiping the tears away with the back of her hand. 'A good soak in salt water then a boil with a drop of ammonia in the water will bring them up as good as new.' She clutched her back, talking too quickly, hardly knowing what she was saying, just wanting to be left alone to bear the pain, and get whatever had to happen over with quick.

'I think we ought to wake Mr Armstrong up.' Biddy covered Annie up again, smoothed the damp hair back from the hot forehead. 'She doesn't know what she's saying or doing. It's my guess she's been going quietly off her chump these past few months.'

'It's you what's going off your chump, Biddy Baker.' The housekeeper turned round to see Seth standing quietly in the doorway. He was fully dressed.

'You've been falling asleep in your chair again, sir.'

89

She chided him as if he was a naughty boy. 'Get you off to bed, sir. It's no place for a man in here. Me and Biddy can see to things.'

In her agitation she moved round the bed as if to block any glimpse of what might be happening from him, but he was too quick for her. Before she could stretch out a hand to prevent it he pulled back the bedclothes, held his candlestick high.

'It's all right, Annie. You know that you're losing the baby you were expecting, don't you?' His voice was gentle.

'She doesn't care!' Mrs Martindale chewed the end of one of her plaits in her agitation. 'She's been trying to get rid of it, she said so.'

Annie's eyes flew wide with fright as a pain gripped and burned and twisted low down in the small of her back.

'You can't stop in here, sir.' The thought of it was making Mrs Martindale go hot and cold. 'It's one thing with animals, but yon's a young woman, not a cow or a horse. It's not seemly for you to . . .'

'Off to your bed, woman!'

There was no gentleness in Seth's voice now, no compassion in the rain-grey eyes. Biddy was thrilled with the drama of it all, sure in her mind that if the old bat hadn't scuttled from the room Mr Armstrong would have lifted her bodily and chucked her out onto the landing.

6

They were well into February, with no sign of a thaw, though some mornings the temperature rose briefly above freezing, causing trees and the overhanging eaves of the old house to drip continuously. The wind was still in the east, screaming at times in fury across the vast wastes of pure white snow banked high in places like miniature mountain peaks. It was beautiful and it was terrible, and Annie thrived on it.

In some ways she was a child again, able to push the night when she had lost the baby right to the back of her mind. Mr Armstrong had done things for her that flooded her with shame, though Biddy had explained that delivering calves and horses was all in a day's work to the animal doctor, so the sight of a bit of blood and a half-finished baby wouldn't exactly put him off his breakfast.

She told Annie that sometimes when she was stuck for what to read she borrowed a book from the big glass-fronted bookcase in his den to look at the riveting pictures of animals' insides. In great detail, she explained what had to be done when a calf was coming out backwards. 'First an arm and a hand has to be soaped, then . . .'

Annie's eyes grew rounder as she listened. Fancy her never knowing that a cow had four stomachs, or that if they made too much gas the cow swelled up just like a balloon. Not sparing the details, Biddy told Annie what happened when a sharp instrument was jabbed in, so that compared to all what he had done for Annie it wouldn't amount to more than pulling a tooth.

'Mrs Martindale thought it was awful, him seeing to you, but then Mrs Martindale thinks having your bowels moved is rude,' Biddy went on to explain, narrowing her eyes into concentrated slits as she tried to remember the illustration showing the procedure for gelding a horse.

'For *what*?' Annie wanted to know.

Biddy told her – in great detail.

On a day when a blizzard kept the sky dark all day, Mrs Martindale went outside to the privy and slipped on a patch of black ice, badly spraining her right wrist and twisting an ankle.

Seth examined the wrist carefully, bent her fingers back one by one, assured her there were no bones broken, made her a sling out of a three-cornered kerchief and told her to rest up for a while. 'Annie's here to help Biddy,' he said, an amused glint in his eyes at the furious expression on his housekeeper's face. 'You don't give her enough to do, though it strikes me she's very capable. I suppose she told you she was bringing five younger brothers up after her mother died?'

'Before she got herself into trouble,' Mrs Martindale felt obligated to remind him.

In the days that followed Annie was wound up with what she recognised must be happiness. The house, with its carpets and gleaming furniture, was like the houses she had read about in the magazines she used to borrow from Edith Morris. The coal sat by the fires in scuttles, not buckets, and there were long curtains at the windows instead of torn and yellowed paper blinds. Mr Armstrong ate his meals with a white damask napkin spread on his knee, and there was even a small screen to stop the fire from being too hot on his face when he sat in his winged armchair reading, often well into the night.

Everything was soft instead of hard, glowing with colour instead of being drab and grey. Footsteps were silent all round the house except in the kitchen and scullery, and the small outhouse the vet used as his surgery. There was even, in a corner of the barely used lounge, a round table, covered with a white tablecloth hanging down in lacy folds. It drew Annie like a magnet, and when she was dusting in that room she would spend a lot of time stroking the aspidistra leaves with a cloth dipped in milk to bring up their shine. She would touch the cloth to savour the cobwebby feel of it, remembering the day she told the travelling man about her dream.

Now, since Mrs Martindale had hurt her wrist, it was Annie who did the cooking, Annie who took over Biddy's job of doing the washing in an outhouse, bringing it in for ironing shades whiter than it had been before.

Biddy, too, was in her element. With the housekeeper more or less tied to a chair, she could skive off for hours, to lie on her bed reading paper-back novels about servant girls marrying lords and exchanging their print frocks for silken gowns and feathered hats. Biddy was in the wrong job and she knew it. When she married, she admitted, she would cheerfully sweep the dust under the dresser, and swear to her husband that the heat of his body would bring the creases out of his shirts, to save her the job of ironing them properly.

She watched through the window as Annie thawed out the pump when the tap in the kitchen froze solid, and she held the basket while Annie dug up as many root vegetables as she could before they were hardened into the earth. She knew she was lazy, she said, and laughed when Annie said that crafty would have been a better word.

Mrs Martindale sat in her chair in the kitchen, taking everything in. She saw the way Annie blossomed by the day, saw that no task seemed to be too arduous or too dirty for the bright-eyed girl with the red hair tucked up into one of Biddy's caps. And she noticed how Mr Armstrong's eyes followed her when he came into the kitchen. Noticed and dwelled on the fact.

Late one cold grey afternoon Seth caught Annie tending the fire in his den, kneeling down on the rug and working the bellows, encouraging the flames to leap up the chimney-back.

He was cold and bone weary. The previous night's

gales had brought even more snow, tearing down the delicate branches of a willow tree by the frozen stream. He had walked five miles, pushing his way through snow-drifts to find four cows so diseased they were fit for nothing but slaughter. There was no treatment for Johne's disease, and already three of them were lying in great distress in their own liquid excreta. Telling the farmer, a man well into his sixties, hadn't been easy, and Seth felt he could have handled it better if the old man had ranted and raved, or even cursed Seth for not getting there sooner. Instead, he had pushed his cap to the back of his grey head and said that what must be, must be, he reckoned, even though the cows had been like his own family. They even came when he called their names, he'd explained. Stoical people were the very devil; Seth had often thought that. The way they looked at you defied you to help them.

He sat down by the fire and immediately Annie stood up and backed away from him, remembering that Mrs Martindale had told her she must never remain in a room alone with her employer because it wasn't right and proper.

'Are you feeling quite well now, Annie?' Seth reached for his pipe and began to fill it, pressing the tobacco well down in the bowl with a practised forefinger.

'I'm feeling more than well, Mr Armstrong.' Annie couldn't help the smile spreading across her face. 'I've never felt better in me whole life.' She turned and walked towards the door. 'I've never been as *warm* in the whole of me life.'

'You certainly know how to build a fire.' Seth took a taper from a box in the hearth and held it aloft, as Annie began to close the door behind her. 'Annie?' He raised his voice. 'You didn't know I was speaking to you, did you?'

She explained at once. 'Only because I had my back to you, Mr Armstrong. I can hear you fine when I can see you.'

'How long have you been like that?' Seth busied himself lighting his pipe, watching the way she narrowed her eyes in concentration when she couldn't see his lips move.

'It's only at one side, Mr Armstrong. A lot of people are a bit deaf in one ear.'

'At seventeen?'

Automatically Annie put a hand over the ear her father had boxed more often than she cared to think about. 'I've no trouble when folks don't mumble,' she said, escaping round the door. Closing it firmly behind her.

Like a flash Seth was across the room, wrenching the door open and calling out in a loud voice, taking no chances that she couldn't hear him: 'Annie! Come through into the surgery. I want to have a look at that ear!'

'He's got no right examining her,' Mrs Martindale chuntered. 'She hears what she wants to hear, that madam does.'

'Likely he remembers the marks on her back and guessed her father had done her ear as well. I think Mr Armstrong's got a soft spot for Annie,' Biddy said, just to make the housekeeper mad. 'You know what he's like when he finds an animal that's been ill-treated. He can't do enough for it.'

'Annie Clancy isn't an animal. She's a girl with bad blood in her who thinks she's landed on her feet.'

'That was a lovely stew she made today,' Biddy said, rubbing salt in. 'Mr Armstrong had two helpings.'

Mrs Martindale felt sure her blood was actually boiling. There was no justice, no justice at all. There was she laying with nobody else but her husband, and that only the once, while Annie Clancy had miscarried her illegitimate baby in the spare room upstairs, gloating that she was glad to be rid.

Nellie withdrew her right hand from the sling and

pulled at the tight bandaging. By the end of the week she would be on her feet. A thaw was coming, she knew the signs. Yesterday she had watched through the window as starlings landed on a large frozen puddle down by the field path, but tomorrow there could easily be the first faint signs that spring was on its way. Annie had come in with a clutch of snowdrops in her hand, sighing over them as if they were the first she'd set eyes on.

'They *are* the first she's seen,' Biddy said. 'There was no green anywhere in the street where Annie lived.'

'Pull the other leg,' said Nellie Martindale, wiggling the fingers of her right hand up and down. To get them going.

The way young Annie looked at him after he'd carefully examined her ear reminded Seth of the old farmer bravely accepting the loss of four of his small herd of cows. It was a look Seth equated with the passive indifference of someone who, while used to hoping for the best, had come to expect the worst.

'Who did this to you, Annie? And *this?*' He touched her back, laying the flat of his hand against her shoulder blades.

'I don't know what you're talking about.' Annie twisted away from him. 'I'm in fine fettle, Mr Armstrong. I always have been. I'm as strong as an ox.' She smiled. 'An' why shouldn't I be? It's like being on me holidays working here.' She gave him a mischievous smile. 'Three strapping women running a house like this? I could do it meself with one hand tied behind me back.'

Seth's surgery was furnished with the bare essentials. Most of his work was done out in the fields, in the outlying hill farms. He had crawled on his hands and knees the last mile back to the house that afternoon, a mile that had stretched into fifty as he had fought his way through snow-drifts frozen to iron hardness, on and on through a landscape held in a pitiless white grip. The cold was still steeped inside his bones. Out there in the freezing wilderness he had been seized with such a sensation of loneliness that the hurt of it had taken him totally unawares.

Frantically he had tried to beat it away, groping his way back along the well-known path, merged now into one vast freezing field. Who would care if he never got back to the house? Mrs Martindale? Yes, she would care; she would grieve for him as a mother grieves for her child. He had winced as his gloved hand, brushed against his face, scraped hard ice down his cheek. Someone else, surely? Since his wife died, his isolation had been self-induced. Friends, turned away and rebuffed too often, stayed away.

He turned his back on Annie and walked quickly out into the passage.

'Sir?' She followed him into his den. No wonder Mr Armstrong's face had set as hard as a block of concrete after she'd told him she could do the work of the whole house with one hand tied behind her back. She had no means of knowing just how wealthy he was, but he couldn't be making a fortune when some days it took him all his time to visit just one poor hard-working farmer. Perhaps even now he was wondering how he was going to pay his bills, and whether he could afford to keep on both Mrs Martindale and Biddy, never mind her.

'I was only swanking what I just said.' She stared straight ahead. 'Both Mrs Martindale and Biddy work like galley slaves.'

'What did you say?' From his chair Seth stared at Annie's troubled face, crimson with the effort of covering up what she saw as an enormous blunder. 'Shut the door and sit down.'

'One person really couldn't do all the . . .' Annie did as she was told, perching on the very edge of a stand-chair, determined to set things right.

'It was your father who beat you, wasn't it?'

The shame of it brought Annie to her feet.

97

'Did you know that by constantly hitting you hard across the side of your face, he's managed to perforate your eardrum? Do you realise that you may always be hard of hearing in that ear? You must never go back home, Annie. Never!'

Before he could lean forward to light a taper at the fire, she was there, holding the light to the bowl of his pipe. 'I will have to go back come September, but only to be there when my . . . when Laurie comes to claim me.' She went back to her chair. 'I've thought it all out, Mr Armstrong. My stepmother will let me stop a while. She's all shout, really.'

'Laurie? The sailor? The man you told me about that night?'

Annie blushed and nodded. 'The man I'm going to marry.'

'Who went away when he found you were going to have his child?'

'He didn't know!' The words burst from her in a great wail. 'He told me he'd seen to it that I wouldn't have a baby. That's how wrong you are!'

When the door banged behind her Seth sat for a long time smoking his pipe and staring into the fire. The burning anger he'd felt at being taken unawares by his own vulnerability out there in the snow that afternoon was now replaced by a towering rage against a man he had never met, or was ever likely to.

Nor was young Annie likely ever to see the travelling man again. Why in God's name hadn't she cottoned on to that fact months ago? She was far from stupid. Far, far from that. An untutored intelligence shone from her eyes, and if she'd told him once that she'd been top of the class at school she'd told him a dozen times. Seth smiled to himself. She could change her accent in a flash. Look at the day when the rather superior gardener from up at the Lodge had appeared at the back door with a sick and sorry-for-itself black and white puppy pushed down deep inside his jacket.

'Mr Armstrong won't keep you waiting long. He's busy with another patient,' he'd heard her say. In an accent so cut-glass it almost shimmered.

For the first time in a long and weary day he laughed out loud. She had such a unique turn of phrase. When she came into a room it was as though a light came on. Seth shook his head at his fanciful thinking, puffed away at his pipe and relaxed properly for the first time that day.

Mrs Martindale stared at Annie Clancy in trembling disgust. The girl was worse than a hair-shirt to her, always irritating. Not a scrap of respect for her betters.

'It was you slamming the master's door just now, wasn't it?'

'It was.' Annie leaned over the sink and angrily swished a tablespoon through the tepid water. 'He'd no right to say what he did.'

Nellie Martindale actually felt the skin tighten on her scalp. A wisp of red hair was straggling down from beneath Annie's cap, and she had an almost uncontrollable urge to hobble across the flagged floor and yank Annie's head back with it in order to spit in her face. Not once in all the years she'd worked in this house, no matter what the circumstances, had she expressed feelings. She'd been trained to accept that the lower orders weren't expected to show emotion in front of their betters, that your heart could be bleeding inside but you never let on. Never!

Her voice shook. 'What did Mr Armstrong say?'

'Not much. He didn't need to. He just hinted that he didn't believe I would be getting married come September.' Annie plunged her hands deep into the grey washing-up water. 'He was laughing at me! I'm not daft. I know when I'm being laughed at.'

'He has every right to laugh at you.' Nellie's voice quivered with the intensity of her feelings. '*I'm* laughing at you. *Biddy's* laughing her head off, though she does it behind your back. Anybody with an 'apenth of sense is laughing at you .'

Annie swung round, the dish-mop brandished like a truncheon. 'You know nowt!' she shouted, all attempt at refinement forgotten. 'You'll all be laughing at t'other side of your stupid faces when Laurie comes back to claim me. An' when I'm married to him I'll drive past here in my own waggonette, and I won't give you the time of day! You'll still be working every hour God sends when I'm sitting on a velvet chair giving me orders to the likes of you!'

'How *dare* you!' Nellie sprang up too quickly, winced and sat back again. 'The minute yon snow's melted you're out of this house quicker than a stick of greased lightning, then we'll see . . . My God, we'll see . . . A velvet chair,' she chuntered, setting her chair rocking furiously, staring through narrowed eyes at Annie's irritating back, which of its own volition seemed to be trying to best her. 'Just wait till a thaw sets in, madam.' Nellie felt she could afford to let the matter drop for the time being. 'Just wait . . .'

At the end of the next week the weather suddenly turned warmer. The snows melted, overflowing the stream at the bottom of the garden, so that for the whole of one day it roared like a torrent. At the end of the following week a watery sun set the lingering snow glistening like sugar in a crystal dish.

'So when will you be going, Annie Clancy?'

Mrs Martindale asked the question straight out, her small eyes as hard and grey as moorland stones.

Annie was peeling potatoes into an enamel bowl in the stone slopstone. They were green in parts where the frost had got at them, but there was still enough for a good boiling in what was left when she'd cut the bad away. She jabbed her knife into a gnarled and knobbly specimen.

'I'll mention it to Mr Armstrong,' she said, hoping the

fear wasn't showing in her voice. Since she'd cheeked Mrs Martindale the other week the housekeeper hadn't referred to the matter at all. Now Annie knew she had been merely biding her time, waiting for the weather to change.

That morning Seth had ridden out at first light to visit the outlying farms rendered inaccessible by the long weeks of snow and frost. Biddy was supposed to be giving the upstairs rooms a good going over, but Annie had seen her take a heavy tome from the bookcase and stagger upstairs with it. To gloat over the pictures, Annie knew that. She flinched as the housekeeper repeated her question.

'When will you be going, then? You weren't banking on stopping here for good, were you?'

Nellie lifted a batch of dough from a wide stone crock and began to knead it with her left hand, holding the right one awkwardly to steady the bowl. She had given a lot of careful thought to what she was going to say next, and with Biddy out of the way, this was her opportunity.

'I'm going to speak out of turn,' she said. 'Best face me so you can hear me properly. I don't want to shout.'

'I can hear you, Mrs Martindale.' Annie stared hard at the small working mouth. 'I can hear you even if you whisper.'

Nellie jerked her head up at the ceiling. 'Biddy doesn't pull her weight. I know that and so do you. But she'd have to pull her socks up if you weren't here. You've taken her job on, Annie Clancy, and the lazy tyke's let you.'

'I haven't meant . . .'

'Well of course you haven't *meant*. You've just wheedled yourself into the running of this house, trying to make yourself indispensable.'

'That's not true!'

Annie could feel her temper rising. The housekeeper was misjudging her cruelly. What she had done, the work she had undertaken willingly, had been a service

101

given in good faith, in gratitude for the kindness shown to her. Couldn't this thin stick of a woman see that in return for kindness Annie Clancy would do *anything*? That here in this quiet house, where voices were hardly ever raised in anger, she had found a peace never known to her before.

'What I did was out of gratitude,' she said. 'But if Mr Armstrong says I must go, then so be it.' Her head drooped. 'I'll speak to him myself when he comes back this evening.'

Annie could feel that her hands, clenched by her sides, were trembling. What a fool she'd been to go on happily from day to day, thinking, believing that she was . . . that she belonged. She began to feel sick.

Nellie Martindale dusted the flour off her hands and sat down. The lost look on Annie Clancy's face was upsetting her, and she didn't like being upset. Nobody could say she was a hard woman, but what she was doing was right. What had happened that morning had convinced her. She twisted a tea-cloth round and round till it resembled a rope.

There'd been no call for Annie to get up to see the master off on his rounds, but she had looked through her window that morning and seen Annie laughing up at him as he sat on his horse. She had seen her handing a small bundle up to him, her red hair hanging loose down her back. Food to sustain him, she'd explained when challenged, and hot cocoa and a dried haddock creamed in the pan for him to eat before he left the house.

'He took some persuading to sit down at the table,' she'd laughed, 'but I told him I was used to feeding men in the middle of the night before they went to work, so in the end he gave in.'

The laugh had done it. That and the little touching scene with Annie outside in the cold morning air with no more than a neck shawl over her dress, and that long red hair waving down her back, not decently hidden beneath a cap. She had looked like a young wife seeing her

102

husband off to work. Nellie's heart contracted as she remembered the way Mr Armstrong had leaned down from the saddle to touch Annie lightly on her cheek. Couldn't he see that she was bamboozling him? Making herself indispensable? Was he like all men after all, a soft touch when it came to a pretty face, especially a pretty laughing face?

She decided to play her trump card.

'It will be Biddy who has to go if you stay. Mr Armstrong can't keep three of us in a house this size. He's not made of money.'

'Biddy?' Annie's expression was one of horror. 'Oh, no. Biddy can't go away from here. She's happy. They don't want her back at home. Her mother would make her go back to work in the mill. She did it for a month and she hated it. For me to stay and Biddy to go would be wrong. Mr Armstrong wouldn't . . .'

'You think you know him, don't you?' Nellie stood up. 'You'd not set foot over this doorstep at Christmas, and you think you know him better than me who's looked after him for years? How do you know what Mr Armstrong would or would not do? Did you know him when he carried his dead baby down the stairs in his arms, his face like a mask? Were you there when he tried to force his wife to eat, spooning the food into her mouth then wiping it away when she let it dribble down her chin?'

There were limp grey strands straggling down the housekeeper's neck from the bun that hadn't been properly fastened up that morning. On a young girl they would have looked endearing, but they gave Mrs Martindale the look of an old woman well into senility.

Suddenly Annie felt sorry for her.

'Biddy need have no fear for her job,' she said quietly. 'If one of us has to go it won't be her.'

That night Seth motioned to the high-winged chair by the fire for Annie to sit down when she went in to collect his tray.

103

'I feel like talking tonight, Annie,' he told her. 'You got me off to such a good start this morning I rode out farther than I'd intended.'

'Forgetting you'd got to come all the way back.'

Seth grinned. 'Take that silly cap off. Whose is it, anyway?'

'It belonged to Mrs Martindale when she was a kitchen maid to a real lord.'

'And did *he* like it? I very much doubt it.'

As Annie took off the offending cap, Mrs Martindale put her head round the door.

'Annie's needed in the kitchen, sir.' Her lined face was stiff with distaste at the sight of Annie Clancy sitting there round the fire with her master, just as if she was his equal.

'*Good night*, Mrs Martindale.'

'Dismissing me as if *I* was a nothing,' the housekeeper told Biddy. 'Who was it said that virtue had its own reward?'

'Not me, Mrs Martindale.'

Biddy went back to her novelette. She had just reached an exciting part where the eldest son of a Duke had fallen from his horse in a riding accident, thus putting his inheritance in jeopardy. Now if *he* died, the younger brother, who hadn't a decent bone in his body, could become the next Duke and what would happen then? Would he become a reformed character, or would he gamble away the family fortune? And what about Lady Ursula, the beautiful bride-to-be? Would she die of a broken heart? Slowly Biddy ran her finger along another line.

Nellie crouched over the kitchen fire, brooding on the fact that in all the years of working in this house, she had never once been invited to sit down in the same room as her employer. Or had that madam sat herself down without being asked? She wouldn't put it past her. Leaning forward, she poked the fire so fiercely that a piece of coal dislodged itself to fall into the hearth sending up a shower of sparks.

104

*

'Do you ever think about your father, Annie?'

Seth stretched out his legs across the hearthrug, avoiding the dog sprawled there, leaned his head back and closed his eyes. The fire was so bright with flames he could see them dancing through his closed eyelids. It was good to sit with a woman again, to close his eyes if he wanted to, to talk or not to talk.

'Do you mind if I go and get my sewing, sir?' She sounded worried.

'What on earth for?' Seth folded his arms comfortably across his chest. 'Can't you just sit for once?'

'Not without a terrible feeling of guilt I can't.'

'Guilt?'

She tried to explain. 'It's not right to sit without something in your fingers. Mending, or patching. And then only when you've done all that is to be done.'

'Good God! What a dreadful outlook on life. You mean you never stand and stare, Annie?'

'What at?'

He shook his head. 'Never mind. Let me ask you a question again. Do you ever think about your father, Annie?'

'Not if I can help it.'

'Because he beat you?'

'No. Because he didn't like me.' She sighed. 'You can't keep on and on trying to make someone like you. There comes a day when you just stop trying.' Annie looked down at her folded hands. 'Would you like me to mend that tear in your jacket while I'm here?'

Seth ignored her. 'I was a great disappointment to *my* father, Annie. I wasn't prepared to grow into the mould he'd planned for me. In the end I killed him.'

'Shot him?' Annie's eyes flew wide.

'Indirectly I killed him.' Seth's right hand was on the dog's head. He needed to talk. Oh, dear God, how badly he needed to talk. 'My father owned a cotton mill this side of Bolton. It was built by my grandfather at the

105

beginning of the last century, then about forty years ago my father extended it to twice its size, using one of the new buildings for manufacturing velvet. Twenty years on, the cardroom was extended and business boomed.'

Annie blinked as a piece of coal suddenly dislodged itself to fall into the hearth. Instinctively she got up to reach for the fire tongs.

'Leave it be.' Seth waved her back to her chair. 'I'll see to it.' He took his pipe from the rack and cradled it unlit in his hand. 'As the only son, it was considered inevitable that I would go straight into the mill from school, and this I did.' He stared at the pipe in his hand. 'To tell you I hated it wouldn't convey how much I loathed it. The non-ending clatter of the looms pounded in my head till I thought I'd go mad. I felt I would choke on the cotton fluff. Our house was so close to the mill you could hear the growl of the caged machinery, and the black smoke from the chimneys coated everything within miles. I'd been away to school down in Sussex, a school set in the midst of rolling fields with the sea so close you could taste the smell of it on your tongue.'

'Tell me about the sea,' Annie wanted to say, but she knew that now wasn't the time. Mr Armstrong was busting to get something off his chest, and the kindest thing she could do for him was to listen and keep her own mouth shut.

'My mother died about this time and left me some money, and when I told my father I wanted to leave the mill and enrol at the Glasgow Veterinary College to work towards passing the Royal College examinations, he was so angry he swore he would never speak to me again.'

Seth raised his eyes to stare directly at her and when she saw the pain in them, Annie found she had to look away.

'My father kept his word. All my letters to him were returned, and when I tried to see him at the house he ordered his manservant to throw me out. Then one day I

106

went to the mill. It was shut down for the night but I knew my father would be there working in his office. The mill was his life, you see, especially after my mother died.'

Annie held her breath.

'We had a terrible row. I reminded my father that his brother's three boys were all working willingly in the mill and that any one of them would be able to take his place when he retired. I also reminded him that it would mean there would still be an Armstrong at the helm. I tried to make him see that my life from now on would be working with animals, not in some town practice, but in the country away from the smoke and the grime.'

Seth's voice was now no more than a whisper so that Annie had to watch his mouth carefully to read what he was saying.

'We said terrible things to each other. He accused me of betraying my heritage; he said that if I was half a man I would buckle to and take my rightful place by his side in the mill. He raised his hand to strike me, but I held his arm quite easily. We glared at each other without speaking for what seemed to be a long time – then I turned on my heel and walked out, leaving him reaching for the whisky bottle.'

'You look like you could do with a drop yourself, sir,' Annie whispered. 'Shall I . . . ?' She motioned towards the round table with the whisky decanter on it, but Seth shook his head at her and made a slicing movement with his hand, so that she sat still, as silent as he obviously wanted her to be. There was a ragged despair in his voice when he began to speak again.

'My father liked his drink, Annie, but he could hold it, yet that night he must have got blind drunk . . .'

'Don't go on if you don't want to, sir.' Annie felt a small knot of fear tighten low down in her stomach. Why was he talking to her like this? Telling her things she could swear he'd never opened his mouth about before. Delaying her, so that Mrs Martindale would have yet

107

another reason for sending her away. She half rose from her seat.

'Cotton fluff is oily, Annie. My father used candles as well as gas lighting. He'd been promising to replace the wooden beams by cast-iron, but he'd never got round to it. He'd been talking for years about an idea of replacing the pitch roof with a flat one to be connected to the water in the mill lodge by a pipe. He'd talked about sprinklers . . . Talked . . . and done nothing. The worst happened that night. The mill caught fire and the whole building was burnt out within the hour. It went up like a torch.' His head slumped forward. 'The charred remains of what had once been my father were found slumped at his desk. The only faint consolation I have is that they said he must have been overcome by the smoke before the flames got to him.'

'But you didn't kill him, sir!'

Annie was at his side like a flash, kneeling by his chair, reaching for his hands to pull them away from his face. There were tears on his cheeks, and when she saw them she was at a loss to know what to do. She had never seen a man cry before and the sight shocked and upset her. She twined her fingers in his.

'The mills were always catching fire round where I used to live, Mr Armstrong! I remember me mother taking me to see one once. She lifted me up to see better and the whole sky was as red as if it was bleeding. Them mills used to catch fire on their own. Like an explosion. There wasn't nothing you could do, sir.'

When he raised his head and looked at her, as if he wondered who she could be, Annie knew it was time to leave him be. She felt that for her to remain would be a terrible embarrassment to him when he pulled himself together. No man wanted a woman to see him cry.

'It's done you a power of good to talk to me, sir,' she said softly, 'but I'll be off to bed now. Good night, sir.'

Seth drew her to him, lifted her and held her close against him.

'Annie . . . little Annie . . .'

Her eyes, wide and startled, were the dark blue of a bruised bluebell; she smelled as clean and sweet as new mown hay. It had been months since he held a woman in his arms. Afterwards he blamed it on the dancing firelight, the sweetness of her, the kindness in her eyes. But most of all it was the urgent need in him.

As he kissed her his arms tightened round her, holding her close and fierce against him. For a brief wild moment he was so sure she responded, the kiss deepened as he trembled, all control gone. When she stiffened against him, twisting away, beating at him with her fists, pushing him away with all her strength, he opened his eyes and saw naked fear in her face. At once he set her from him.

'Annie . . . Annie, love . . . I've no wish to frighten you.' He still held her by the arms. 'I thought . . .'

Annie closed her eyes against the very sight of him. In those last few moments he had been Laurie Yates all over again. He had been the black-haired Laurie with his mouth on hers, giving her feelings that had led to her letting him do what he wanted with her . . . giving her a baby . . . The terror tightened in her throat, crept up to her eyes, filling them with tears.

'Let me go, sir,' she whimpered. 'Oh, please, *please* let me go.'

When he released her she almost fell, but before she could reach the door he was behind her, jerking her round to face him.

'Is that what he did, the travelling man? Forced you against your will?' His face darkened. 'You're safe enough with me, little Annie. I've never taken a woman against her will yet, and I never will.' The sheer terror on her face maddened him so much he lashed out in fury. 'You really think the gypsy is coming back to marry you? After what he did?' Tilting her chin he forced her to meet his eyes. 'He's not coming back, and you know it. Why don't you grow up, Annie, and face a truth you must know?'

109

When she pummelled her fists against his chest, he let her go, standing in the panelled hallway as she pounded up the stairs. When he heard her shoot the bolt on her bedroom door he went back to the fire and kicked at the coals with a slippered foot, sending a shower of sparks up the chimney.

Seth was away and gone before Annie came down to the kitchen the next morning.

'Where will I go?' she asked Mrs Martindale, when the housekeeper told her that the carrier would be calling with his cart within the hour, and that today was as good as any for her to leave.

Nellie hadn't been born yesterday. She had heard the way Annie had rushed up the stairs to shut herself away in her room, and she'd half expected to hear Mr Armstrong follow her. But then she'd realised that a forward girl like Annie Clancy wouldn't stand a chance with a gentleman like Mr Armstrong. He could pick and choose; soiled goods wouldn't do for him. Deliberately she closed her mind to the woman he visited in Manchester every month or so, stopping for two nights at a time.

'I can give you her name,' her informant had told her. 'She's been set up in a house by at least five men from the Exchange. They have their set times for visiting. She's a high-class prostitute.'

The very word had upset Nellie no end. There was no proof, so she chose not to believe it. When the master went to Manchester he went on business, that was all.

Bending down to the fire-oven, she took out the first of a batch of crusty one-pound loaves. 'I'll fill this one with brawn and that should see you right till you get home.' She straightened up. 'You know that's the best thing for you, don't you?'

'You *know* I won't go home, Mrs Martindale. I'm not going home till September when Laurie will be coming for me. I'd rather die than go back there now.'

'Well, we can't have that, can we?'

Now that the matter was settled Nellie was inclined to be generous. Something akin to pity stirred in her flat bosom. Leaving the bread to cool on a wire-mesh tray, she rubbed the side of her long nose.

'I've been thinking, Annie. Let's have our cocoa. You mix it ready and I'll get the kettle back on the boil. There's a farmer I know by the name of Barney Eccles. His wife is a cousin of mine in a roundabout way.' She sniffed. 'Not that we've spoken in many a long year.'

She closed her eyes briefly at the memory of the pretty girl who had got herself into trouble, been overjoyed that the man had stuck by her, married him and gone on to have a baby every other year, or so she'd heard.

'There's a big family, Annie. So help won't come amiss and I'm sure if you mention my name they'll take you in. Lily always had a kind heart. That was probably her downfall,' she added. 'You must tell her that you looked after your brothers on your own after your mother died.' She passed a cup of frothy steaming cocoa over to Annie. 'I'll have a word with the carter. I'm pretty sure he goes out that way of a Tuesday. One thing I'm sure of. You won't be turned away. The farm is miles from nowhere and the Eccles's seem to have trouble keeping their servants. Young girls don't like being so far from the town.' She gave a thin sarcastic smile. 'But with you being betrothed and more or less passing time on until your fiancé comes to claim you, that won't bother you, will it?'

'Why so sudden?' Biddy wanted to know.

'Well, I can't stay *here*, can I?' The concern on Biddy's round face made tears smart suddenly in Annie's eyes. 'Mr Armstrong only took me in till I was better, then the snow came. I've outstayed my welcome as it is.'

'Does he know you're going?' Suspicion sharpened Biddy's nose. 'It seems funny to me you going all at once like this.'

111

'Of course he knows.' Annie told the lie easily. 'The carrier won't be passing this way for another week, maybe not that if the cold snap comes back.' She forced a smile. 'Anyway, I've got a place to go to.'

'A decent place?'

Annie nodded, walked quickly to the door and climbed the stairs to her room. Before she shamed herself by sobbing on Biddy's shoulder.

She never actually said goodbye to Biddy. Instead she stayed in her room, looking her last on the polished mahogany chest-of-drawers, the matching dressing-table with its oval stand-mirror.

She stripped her bed, folding the sheets ready for the wash, and she stood by the window staring out at the pearl-grey sky banked with heavy grey clouds. She looked her fill at the river-like stream with the willow tree trailing broken branches into swirling brown water.

Then she sat down on the edge of her bed and in her small even handwriting, using the stub of a pencil rather than go downstairs for the bottle of ink, wrote a short letter.

Dear Mr Armstrong,

This is to tell you that I am sorry to be leaving this house, and I would not be going if there was any way I could stay.

She swallowed the lump in her throat, and widened her eyes as if challenging the tears to fall.

Thank you for everything. I have been very happy under your roof. Mrs Martindale knows the place I am going to. It is a relative of hers who is always needing help.

Yours truly, Annie Clancy

A pathetic letter, saying nothing and meaning less.

112

Annie hesitated for a moment before folding it up into a neat square. Did she owe him a letter at all?

Her hand smoothed the mattress. This was the room where her baby had come away from her in a long night of pain. With him caring for her, holding her hands, wiping the sweat from her face. Each time she had opened her eyes he had been there, watchful by the fire, his grey eyes steady when he looked at her. Promising her that all would be well.

Annie heard the rumble of wheels on the drive outside, got up from the bed and gathered her things together.

Oh, yes. For that alone she owed the animal doctor a letter.

'Well, Annie?'

The carter was waiting, impatient to be gone. Annie could see him outside hunched over his knees on the high seat of the cart. What did the housekeeper expect her to say? By going she was making it possible for Biddy to keep her job, and after last night to stay was out of the question. So what was there left to say?

'Well, Mrs Martindale?' Annie opened her mouth to say more, then closed it again.

There were no tears, no last look round the by now familiar kitchen. 'Say goodbye to Biddy for me.' Annie was leaving in dignity – she was determined of that.

But as the carrier's horse clip-clopped its way down the drive, Annie twisted round in her seat for a last glimpse of the old stone house. Hoping, in spite of her resolution, to see Biddy shaking a duster out of one of the bedroom windows.

But Biddy was lying on her bed at the back of the house, eagerly devouring an article in a magazine telling her how to enlarge her bust by six inches in less than thirty days, without resorting to pills, massage, or wooden cups. She gloated over four pictures of a woman in the throes of transformation. In the first one as flat as if she'd been spoke-shaved; two slight bud-like swellings in the second; on the third the swellings had taken on balloon-like proportions, but the last defied description. Biddy felt sure the model would never be able to stand up close to anyone again!

Annie was trying hard not to cry, and seeing this the carter left her alone. It was obvious the girl was trying to sort something out in her mind; he could see her lips moving.

What Annie was trying hard to sort out was how quickly and unexpectedly kindness could turn into something else. She shuddered. Laurie had been kind. At first he had held her gently . . . The animal doctor had shown her such a wealth of kindness, talking to her, telling her his secrets, so that she had felt safe with him too. She had trusted him – just as she had trusted Laurie.

Annie shook her head. Mr Armstrong must have thought her so naive, sitting with him in his room, taking off her cap the minute he asked her to, shaking her hair free. Thinking that the expression in his eyes was nothing more than pleasure at the sight of her hair. He had told her more than once it was the colour of russet leaves.

Mrs Martindale had tried to warn her. 'Never be in the same room as the master on your own,' she'd said. *Warning*, when all the time Annie had thought she was just being her bitter pernickety self.

And yet, last night when he had told her about his father, she had seen the pain in his eyes, she had responded by going to him and twining his fingers in her own – with *kindness*. Annie frowned. Because he had accepted that a girl who was going to have a baby by a man she confessed she hardly knew could hardly be an innocent, he had . . . he had . . .

A groan escaped her as she remembered the way he had pulled her up towards him, holding her so close she could feel the hardness of him, kissing her so that her lips still felt bruised . . .

'All right, lass?'

The carrier, a man of forty-nine, with two daughters of his own, raised his eyebrows as this young lass shot him a look of such apprehension he almost fell off his seat. And all for trying to be kind, he muttered, relapsing into silence once again.

When Seth rode back that evening, a bedraggled puppy with a broken foreleg curled up in his saddlebag, he was exhausted and as hungry as the proverbial hunter. Striding into the house, he made straight for the kitchen.

'Where's Annie?' He put the puppy down by the fire. 'Give him some warm gravy when you've finished what you're doing, Biddy. They weren't prepared to nurse him where I found him, and I'd be damned if I was going to put the little fella down.'

His own dog lumbered in from the hall, circled the puppy for a while then began to lick it.

'Where's Annie?' Seth said again.

The network of wrinkles on his housekeeper's forehead deepened before she answered him. 'She's gone, sir. She went with the carrier this morning. I packed her some food and she went.'

'Went where?' Seth towered over her. 'She had nowhere *to* go, for God's sake! What the devil are you talking about, woman?'

'I tried to stop her, sir, but she'd made her mind up.'

'Biddy?' Seth's face was working in disbelief.

'She told me you knew, sir.' Biddy refused to look at the woman standing by the table, twisting her hands together. 'She said she had a place to go to, and that if she didn't take the carrier's cart today she could be here indefinitely.'

'I knew nothing!'

Seth was aware of his housekeeper and his servant girl staring at him as if he'd gone mad. He made for the door. Whenever Annie Clancy went or wherever she went wasn't his province. He had brought her here limp and

115

unconscious, thinking she was a tramp woman, and he had tended her, just as he would have tended a distressed animal, when she had lost her baby that night. Her bright presence had gladdened his heart. She had been happy here, he could have sworn it. When she was better and the colour had come back to her cheeks, her trusting eyes had given away her happiness.

But last night he had betrayed that trust. In one unthinking moment he had put the fear of God in her. She had bolted her door against him, believing that he would break it down. The freezing wind had stung his cheeks to scarlet, but now the colour drained away, leaving him grey and ill-looking.

Nellie stood up and gripped the back of her chair hard to still the trembling of her hands. The lie came easily to her lips.

'I tried to stop her, sir, but she'd made up her mind.' The small head went to one side. 'She seemed upset about something.'

For a moment she thought her employer would strike her. He was staring at her with such a blazing anger in his eyes, his whole face distorted. He was remembering how last night, as he had stood in the hall watching young Annie rushing up the stairs, he had caught a glimpse of a door opening slightly, the door of his housekeeper's room. And now she was putting two and two together and coming up with God alone knew what.

'You let her go?' he thundered. 'You allowed a young girl like Annie to go with the carrier in this weather? She could die out there! Do you realise that? Didn't you even *try* to stop her? Didn't you even ask her where she was going?'

'It wasn't me what upset her, sir.'

The words were said quietly, but they struck home. Seth crumpled as if he'd been punched from behind. 'How long has she been gone?'

'All day. She'll be miles away by now. Back home by this time, I feel sure of that.'

116

'Did you know the carter?'

'It was one I've never seen before.'

Clicking his finger and thumb for the dog to follow him, Seth crossed the stone passageway and went into his den, calling out first for his meal, telling them to look sharp about it. Slamming the door so hard that the very foundations of the old house seemed to tremble.

Nellie Martindale knew then that throwing Annie Clancy's letter on the fire had been justified. The master was badly shaken; she knew him too well for him to be able to hide a thing like that. She wouldn't put it past him riding out to fetch Annie back if he knew where she'd gone. But he didn't know, did he? She stared into the fire as if she could still see the flames licking the note, shrivelling it away.

7

Edith Morris was a single-minded woman. If she had been able to persuade herself years ago that her duty lay with the black heathens in Africa rather than with her mother she would, she often told herself, be running a Mission School by now, teaching rows of woolly-haired children about reading, writing, arithmetic and Jesus.

She was too old at fifty to realise her ambition. She accepted that, but since her mother's death her life had taken on an emptiness that terrified her. She was working full-time at the mill, going out in the dark and coming home in the dark, but it was closing the front door behind her, knowing that she wouldn't even hear the sound of her own voice till the next day, that defeated her.

The bed by the window had been taken back upstairs. It left a gap that Edith filled with a tall pedestal table bearing an aspidistra plant. She would sit by the fire after the evening chores were done remembering the days when she had gone to work sharing her mother's shawl, because there wasn't the money for a coat for the painfully thin twelve year old girl. Her father she couldn't remember at all, but her mother had told her how he was killed on a factory outing, trampled by the horse drawing the waggonette. 'The man who got him from under the wheels was drunk for a month afterwards,' she would say.

Edith wondered what it would have been like if she'd married. If her mother hadn't taken to her bed all those years ago, tying her daughter to her as surely as if she'd had her at the end of a rope. She wondered if the rest of her life was going to be as empty as this. Coming home to this hurting silence, staring at the aspidistra plant, almost willing it to talk to her.

She couldn't envisage a future so barren. She started a purl row, felt a sharp pain stab at her heart, and knew there was something she *could* do about her loneliness if she was persistent enough.

The inside of the Clancys' house appalled her. The table didn't look as if it was cleared between one meal and another. The ashpan was so filled with dead ashes it was pushed out into the hearth, and she was sure a bird could have nested in Florrie Clancy's hair without anybody being any the wiser.

'I've called to see if you can give me Annie's address,' she said straight out, looking at Jack Clancy who was sitting on a low stool by the fire with a last gripped between his knees, nailing a clog-iron back on to its wooden sole.

He shot Edith a look, a look of disgust and contempt, then went back to his hammering, banging away, ignoring her.

'I'd like to write to her,' Edith said, standing her ground, determined not to be intimidated by a mere man. 'I'd like to know how she is, and I'd like to go and see her.' She finished on a rush. 'An' if she's not happy, bring her back.'

The staccato hammering stopped immediately. Jack lurched to his feet, clattering last, clog and hammer to the floor. To her horror Edith found him standing next to her, his face pushed into hers, his eyes on a level with her own. He smelt of drink and sweat. His closeness was an affront to her fastidiousness. She could feel the heat and the violence emanating from him. She was sure he was going to strike her.

'We don't talk about Annie in this house. Not now, and not ever! There's no address and there will never be no address, an' if we ever got one it would go straight to the back of the fire!'

The spirit in Edith that would have taken her into the African jungle to confront far worse than this filthy slavering man squaring up to her, glaring at her with his bloodshot eyes, rose up in her.

'Mark my words,' she said, in a whisper that seemed to echo round the room. 'I will find Annie. I will find her wherever she is, and if she's not happy I'll fetch her back to live with me.' She spun round on her heel to fire a parting salvo. 'She's not had much luck with the men in her life, that innocent child.' She flung the door open to step out into the night. 'My mother used to say it was a man's world, and by all that's holy she was right! The only good man that's ever lived was put to death. On a *cross*!'

'She's barmy, chuck. Not right in the head.'

Florrie's hand on her husband's arm was firm. She could feel his anger subsiding even as she led him to his chair. In the months she had been married to Jack Clancy she had come to know him very well. All shout and bluster, a man who asked for little else but his beer and his food, and a bit of the other two or three times a week. A father who never laid a finger on his sons, leaving their upbringing entirely to her. Not a man for inconvenient hobbies like most of his mates with their pigeons and their ferrets. Not the sort of man who went off at weekends walking the fells, fishing the streams, or climbing the hills, coming home whacked out and good for nothing.

'She should be locked away,' she soothed. 'Put away for the rest of her natural.'

'She doesn't know.' Jack's head was down, his hands hanging loosely between his knees. 'How can she know . . . the potty old maid.'

'The ugly sod,' said Florrie, to make him feel better. 'If she'd ever had a man she wouldn't talk such rubbish. She'll not find Annie. Your Annie will have let on her feet, you mark my words.'

Annie had never been so cold in her life. Huddled deep into the long black cloak she saw birds wheeling over sodden fields; she saw flowing ditches and the flooded gardens of stone-built cottages. When they came to a river the driver pointed out the height of the fast-flowing water.

'Another foot and yon bridge wouldn't take it. Yon's more like a highland stream this year.' He spat a trickle of brown saliva from the side of his mouth. 'Some folks say they've seen the signs of an early spring but there's nowt I've seen yet to back them up. I wouldn't be surprised if it snows again. It's cold enough for it.'

Annie was too miserable to care one way or the other. When she had told the driver where she was going, a strange expression had crossed his weather-beaten face.

'Tha knows Barney Eccles then?'

'No. Do you?' Annie had asked him.

'I knows *of* him,' the carter had told her. 'Aye, I knows of him all reet. Tha're sure tha wants tekking there?'

Annie merely nodded. She was too unhappy to think straight. It had all happened too quickly. It was hard to believe she wouldn't be going to bed that night in the room with the shining furniture. Hard to accept that she'd been wrong about the animal doctor all along. But all that was behind her now. She had left her room as clean and tidy as time had allowed. She'd rolled her mattress up and tied it into a sausage with string – as if she had died of the typhoid and the mattress was ready for burning.

She shuddered, and when the driver said he would have to set her down as his horse couldn't climb the high road to the Eccles's farm, she thanked him for his company.

'Tha's not said two words, lass,' he muttered. He jerked his head at the hill still patched with snow. 'Tha're sure . . . ?'

Annie nodded, stumbling away from the narrow road, on up the rocky uneven path, clutching her small bundle, keeping her head down against the freezing wind. When the man appeared suddenly from the fringe of gaunt bare trees she was too terrified even to cry out.

Barney Eccles almost dragged Annie the rest of the way up the hill. Then at the house he gave her a push that almost sent her sprawling.

'Lily? Where the 'eck are you, woman? You'll never believe it when I tell you what I've found!' A hand as large and red as a knuckle-end of ham gripped Annie's shoulder. 'She says Mrs Martindale sent her. Your cousin Nellie. That sourpuss who came to our wedding and give us a pair of bloody sugar tongs for a present.' He snorted like an outraged bull. 'Nay, surely if I can remember her, you can! Once seen never forgotten, I'd say, with a phizog like that!'

'Oh, *her*.'

Lily Eccles, a bare-bottomed child clinging to her skirts, a baby balanced on her hip, slapped yet another child away. Leaning perilously close to the open fire, she stirred something in a large black pan.

'What's she want?' She turned to stare at Annie. 'Our Nellie's husband did himself a favour when he got shot through the head.' She kicked a scrawny cat out of the way. 'Never did owt for nothing our Nellie didn't.'

Annie, still staggering from the blast of heat, wrinkling her nose from the stench, stared round the large living-kitchen in dismay.

Seven children, the eldest no more than ten years old, sat, crawled or lolled, white-faced against the walls. Seven heads of thick white-blond hair turned uninterested stares in her direction. Every single surface of the big room was covered with piles of clothes, unwashed pans, odd boots, clogs, stacks of old newspapers, the handlebars of a bicycle and an assortment of unwashed crockery, whilst underneath the table a cat lay in a dirty cardboard box, nuzzled by four tiny kittens, each one anchored firmly to an overflowing nipple.

'She wants to know if there's a chance you might be needing some help?' Barney's ruddy complexion

122

deepened to purple. He slapped a leg with the flat of his hand. 'She says your Nellie thought we might take her on.' His laugh was so loud that three of the children began to cry.

'How much does she want?'

For the first time the woman straightened up from the fire, put the bare-bottomed baby down on the filthy flagged floor, and looked directly at Annie.

'The last girl wanted two shillings a week and all found, but we can't afford nothing like that. We're not moneyed people.'

Annie tried to hide the note of desperation in her voice. It was already going dark outside, and it would take her at least an hour to slide and slither her way back down the hill-slope. Lily Eccles was a woman near to breakdown; you didn't have to be a doctor to see that. She was so dirty, so slovenly, that compared to her, Annie decided, the woman her father had married looked like she'd just been pressed with a flat iron. The hardness of Lily's thin body was reflected in her expression. She was daring Annie to say she would stay, but so deep into hopelessness that to ask her would be impossible.

'I'll stay for one shilling and sixpence a week. And all found,' Annie said clearly. 'With nothing binding on either side.'

Lily looked at her husband. 'Does she know how to look after children?' She hoisted the baby back on to her hip, and Annie noticed that one of his feet was not only clubbed but turned completely inwards, at right-angles to a stick-thin leg.

'I'll leave all that to you, Lil.' Barney clattered his way to the door. 'You set her on if you want. I've got the milking to do. The yard might have been mud yesterday, but now it's frozen like a skating rink.'

Annie nodded. 'I can look after children. I was bringing five brothers up before I left home.'

'She's not well.' Lily Eccles pointed her stirring spoon

123

at a small girl with a hand up her dress, scratching herself feverishly. 'Her skin's flaking off. Are you good at getting up?'

'My father's a miner, on the early shift, so I'm used to being up at five.'

'Well, that's an hour *later* than what you'll be getting up here.' Lily seemed determined to scare Annie off. 'You'll have to weigh the milk, then lift the cans on to the cart to have them down on the bottom road in time for the pick-up. Then there's the scouring-out to be got through long before the second milking.' She jiggled the baby up and down as it began a thin plaintive wail. 'Then there's the breakfast to be got and the three big ones to get set on the walk to school. They're off at the moment with their chests.' She stuck a finger in an open tin of condensed milk on the table and gave it to the baby to suck. 'And there's the washing, though where to get it dry's the big problem this weather . . .'

'You've just the one fire?'

'Not even that when the coal runs out.' She jerked her head at the door. 'He tells me he'll see to things, then he forgets. Slap-'appy, that's 'is problem.' She raised her eyes to the ceiling. 'Things have got a bit cluttered and messy in the bedrooms, but a bit of tidying will soon put that right. Down here I can keep more of an eye on everything.'

Annie was too cold to see the irony in this. She held out her arms to the baby. 'I'll give you a hand with getting the children to bed. Starting with this one.'

'You don't look much more than a child yourself.' Lily was staring directly at Annie, her head to one side. 'What did you say your name was?'

'Annie. Annie Clancy.'

'Catholic?'

'Nothing,' Annie said firmly.

'You're not in any trouble?'

'No trouble.'

'No baby on the way?'

124

'Definitely no baby. No baby coming, no trouble of any kind.'

'No mother?'

'No. An' no father either. Leastways the one I have doesn't like me. Hates me is nearer the truth.'

'Mr Eccles doesn't like our children.' Lily nodded in understanding. 'He ignores them as much as he can. They don't like him neither.'

There wasn't a hint of black humour in the statement. No suspicion of a dry twinkle in Lily's hard eyes. Annie guessed that any sweetness lingering in her soul must have been driven out of it a long, long time ago. She felt sure that the exhausted grim-faced woman wouldn't have recognised a joke if it had been told to her by a clown wearing a big red nose.

Annie followed her new employer out of the kitchen, down an unmopped flag floor, up a flight of stairs with tattered remnants of an old carpet, as though someone in a frenzy had ripped the carpet from the treads and thrown it away.

'Barney threw the stairs carpet through the landing window five years or so ago,' Lily said. 'His mother fell down from top to bottom and split her skull open. Caught her foot in a frayed piece of carpet. Not a speck of blood to be seen, but she was dead all right. Barney buried her at the bottom end of the garden, near where the children have their swing. We never said nowt to anybody. There's three babies out there as well.' Lily opened a door on the right. 'Barney doesn't bother with undertakers. Or doctors. He delivers all the babies himself. And buries them, if needs be.'

The smell in the bedroom was overpowering. The bed was covered by a heap of dark-grey blankets. A rickety chest-of-drawers, its surface dotted with candle-grease, stood underneath a window so thick with dirt that it would be hard to tell night from day. The contrast to the room Annie had just left behind her was so great she almost turned and ran. Then asked herself, where to?

125

'I'll leave you to settle in.' Lily held out her arms for the baby. 'Unless you'd like him in here with you?' She nodded in a satisfied manner when the baby wound his arms round Annie's neck and nuzzled his head into her, making little whimpering sounds. 'I'll fetch his cot in, then. He's taken to you. He keeps the two he's in with awake half the night with his crying. He's never stopped whingeing and moaning since the day he was born.'

When the cot came Annie tucked the frayed blankets round the baby's neck. The cradle-cap darkening the rounded forehead made her want to take an oiled flannel to it, gently easing it away, the way she'd seen her mother do when John had been born with the same thing.

'What's he called?'

'Benjamin. That means last son. An' that's what he's going to be.' Lily's voice was as hard as flint. 'There'll be no more babies.' She stood with one hand on the door handle. 'Eleven in twelve years, and him not taking to a single one of them. He even sent our Toby away when he saw the lad was turning out to be tuppence short. Only tuppence, mind you – there was a lot of good in that lad.' She made a spitting motion from the side of her mouth. 'Men! The only good 'uns are the dead 'uns. I wouldn't give you a tuppenny bun for the lot of 'em!'

'Me neither,' Annie said, bringing what could have been taken for a smile to Lily's thin lips.

Annie stared at the closed door. Was Mrs Eccles making all that up? She walked over to the window, rubbing a small section of the pane clean. Down at the bottom of the garden, she'd said, by the swing. Three babies and one grandma – *buried* there? Peering intently, she made out the outline of a swing. Oh, dear God, how Biddy would have relished a tale like that. A split skull and no blood? Had Mr Eccles given his mother a push? Biddy would have convinced herself he had. She winced as the sounds of his loud laugh spiralled up to her from the yard. Was he talking to himself? Laughing at himself? Did he really dislike every one of his children?

Unfastening her cloak, Annie looked down on the baby's red twitching face. Weak blue eyes met her own and the plaintive wail changed to a hiccoughing sob. Pinkly swollen eyelids fluttered vainly, then were still. With the suddenness of a stone dropping down a well, the baby had fallen fast asleep.

'The first chance I get I'm going to wash you all over,' Annie whispered, 'because you smell terrible.'

Day after day it rained till the last of the snow and ice were gone. The farm ditches overflowed, and the farmyard was a lake of mud.

When Barney Eccles knocked on Annie's bedroom door each morning, she struggled up through dense layers of sleep, sure she had been in bed for no longer than a few minutes. She soon stopped caring what she looked like, piling layers of clothes on top of each other, wrapping her woollen scarf round her head before crossing it at the front and pinning it at the back.

Spring might well be in the air, but Annie took no notice of it. A long time ago, when her mother was alive, she had gone regularly to Sunday School, to be told by Edith Morris that the Lord Jesus was everywhere. That if you closed your eyes and sat quite still you would feel His presence holding you still.

One dark streaming morning as she swilled out the cowshed, Annie thought about that. Her hands were stuck with cold on the handle of the almost bald long brush. For one thing there wasn't any time for sitting still and closing your eyes, but even if there had been, Annie felt sure Jesus had never visited this terrible desolate place set in the side of a hill. Up here there was nothing but hard faces and cold hard words, and that terrible loud laugh when Mr Eccles decided something was funny. Hatred exploded between him and his wife whenever they came within shouting distance of one another, but he never lifted a hand to her. Just turned on his heel and let out a great bellowing roar, as if he was

127

relishing a sick and personal joke. As if he knew something nobody else did.

The children, too, were strangely unlovable. Sticky, sly and devious, they would grab food from the table, wolf it down without chewing, swallowing it whole as far as Annie could judge. Like dogs. They stared at her with flat pale eyes, scratching their barley-pale heads, picking at sores on their chins.

The smaller ones shivered with fear rather than cold when she stripped off their clothes to stand them in a dolly-tub when she couldn't find a bath anywhere. She sat the older ones on the wooden draining board and told them to wash themselves all over, but they left black tidemarks round their necks and green ropes of slime descending from their nostrils. They dribbled down their chins. They were in a state of constant wetness.

'I don't know why you bother,' their mother said, staring into the fire, her eyes blank. 'They get enough colds as it is. Every one of them had the convulsions when they were teething. The boys worse than the girls. That one under the table was blue and stiff for an hour. Too much water on the body saps the strength. Anyroad, you've no sooner got them clean than they're mucky again.'

'I can't get them to respond to me at all,' Annie worried.

'I don't think they like you,' Lily said, taking a hair-pin from her slipping bun and rotating it round and round in her right ear. 'They never take a liking to anybody. I know they don't like *me*.' She picked a small scab on the side of her nose. 'Our Toby liked me, but he's best off where he is with nobody taking to anybody round here.'

Benjamin appeared to like Annie. He clung to her like a leech, so that she became adept at carrying him around on her hip. She propped him up in a wooden box as she worked, talking to him, and sometimes a semblance of a chuckle would startle her so much she would have to stop what she was doing to rush over to him and cover his pale little face with kisses.

Yes, spring might well have been in the air, but there wasn't time for Annie to be bothered with it. Yet one bright day a bedraggled goose laid an egg, and on her way out to the far field she saw rabbits huddled in the hedges, flushed out of their burrows by the never-ending rain.

Every day she told herself that she would have to get away. To where, she didn't know, but to stay here was becoming impossible.

One morning, after finishing her work in the cowshed, she came out into the yard and sensed rather than saw the deep blackness of the night changing imperceptibly into the soft grey light of early dawn. She wished she could walk away down the hill without even turning round, so that never again would she have to hear Barney Eccles's raucous inhuman laughter, or listen to his wife moaning her lot or screaming in demented frustration.

They needed her, and yet she knew that if she went away they would forget her in less than a week. Within a few days the big farm kitchen would be as cluttered as on the day she came, the children as filthy, their clothes and bodies unwashed from one week to the next. They would walk about bare-bottomed and bare-footed, mauve with cold. And they would somehow survive. But what would happen to Benjie if she left?

It was for Benjie's sake that she stayed through a blustery March and an April when daffodils and cowslips covered the long slope down to the stream as the land slowly dried out. Barney Eccles set two men on to help him with the planting, one a fourteen year old boy with vacant eyes, and the other a burly Irishman with tangled eyebrows meeting over the bridge of a plum-red nose.

'Yon's young Annie Clancy,' he told Barney one day. 'I'd know that red hair anywhere. Her father's married to a far distant cousin of mine.' He wrinkled his high forehead so that the eyebrows mingled. 'The lass got into trouble with a sailor and they chucked her out.' His rheumy eyes watered. 'But if she's expecting then it's a mystery where she's hiding it.'

Annie had shed the thick cloak and the long woollen scarf. That day she was wearing her hair tied back from her face, but already the fresh wind had teased curling tendrils on to cheeks as rosy as flowering poppies.

Barney stared hard at her. 'T'were a false alarm,' he said, then as if that was unbearably comical, threw back his head laughing uproariously. 'A sailor!' he managed to gasp between great gulfs of laughter. 'Young Annie and a bloody sailor – if that doesn't take the biscuit! She acts that pure she'd make even the Virgin Mary seem like a wrong 'un.'

From that day on Barney's attitude to Annie changed completely. He observed her slyly. He came into the kitchen at times, ignoring the children but staring at her. One day he watched her boil peas before draining them into a basin and covering them with a crust. Another day he brought her a rabbit and showed her how to skin it, running his finger along the pink exposed flesh, looking at her with his mouth slightly open and the tip of his tongue showing. He pointed out a weasel running across the field with a robin in its mouth. When she cried out, he slapped his thigh and roared with glee.

The warmer weather came in May and for a few days Annie worked outside without her shawl. Barney told her that if she washed herself all over with the morning dew it would improve her looks. He muttered something else she didn't catch and then he laughed – the everlasting mindless laughter.

Annie knew he was only biding his time, so she shot the bolt of her bedroom door at nights and tried not to be alone with him more than she could help.

But for Benjie she would have left the farm. He was far from well. Annie had seen her brothers with summer colds and coughs which never seemed to clear up, but Benjie was different. When a coughing spell was on him he flayed his little arms about, as if he would pluck his breath from the air. She lay awake at night listening to him snuffling, knowing he was going to sick up a thin frothy liquid that was sometimes streaked with blood.

'He needs a doctor,' she told Lily Eccles.

'An' I need some money. An' I need to lie down. An' I need another drink of tea.'

Annie thrust Benjie at her. 'I've got to get the cans on the cart yet.' Gently she touched the baby's lilac-tinged lips. 'Keep him warm till I get back.'

'Benjie's ill,' she told Barney. 'You should have the doctor to him. He's not hardy like the others. He's different. He needs more care.'

Slowly Barney finished tying the cans into position, taking his time. When he turned round he was grinning all over his big flat face. 'There's always a runt in every pack,' he said. 'Didn't you know that? It's nature's way.'

As soon as she could Annie ran back into the kitchen. Lily was sitting there, staring over the baby's head into the fire, rocking herself backwards and forwards, patting Benjie's back.

'He's gone off to sleep,' she said. 'Best take him upstairs.' She held him out to Annie.

'What's happened to him?' With a despairing cry Annie looked down at the pinched face, the blue-veined eyelids. 'He wasn't like this early on. What's wrong?' She knelt down by the fire. She loosened the ties of Benjie's nightshirt, patted the still face. Refusing to acknowledge what she knew to be true. 'He should have been seen by a doctor! I told you he had a bad cold.' Fear caught at her throat. 'He should have been kept down here by the fire. Wake up, Benjie! Wake up, little love!'

'He's gone,' Lily said in a matter-of-fact voice. 'He's never been strong. He'd never have walked, so we must think on it as a blessing.'

Annie couldn't take her eyes from the baby's face. It

was a pot face, reminding her of a doll she'd seen on an Easter fairground long ago. His hands were pot hands, strangely heavy when she lifted them up. Hysteria was a lump in her throat; terror pricked at her armpits.

'Fetch his box,' Lily said, in that same flat tone. 'Barney will see to him. No good delaying it. Best get it over and done with.' She took the dead baby from Annie's arms. 'The box. Go and fetch the box.'

Annie couldn't believe it. What in God's name had happened to this woman to make her as she was? There was more feeling in a hard grey moorland stone.

'He was your *baby*! You gave him birth! Don't you *care* that he's dead?' Annie was beside herself. 'He wanted loving, that was all. That's all your children want. Nobody's ever loved them, so they don't know how to love back. But Benjie was different . . . He would have grown up different from the others. He was special, and you didn't want to know!' She got to her feet. '*I* loved him even if nobody else did.'

''Spect you put him in the place of the one you lost.'

The words were said quietly, but Lily's expression was sniggering and sly.

'You know what they say about sailors. Here one day and gone the next, not caring a toss where they hang their caps.'

Annie backed away, a hand to her mouth. How did she know such things? How could she say them in that soft voice with her lips half smiling, while holding her own dead baby in her arms?

'Go and fetch him,' Lily was saying now. 'He'll have to bury Benjie right away, before the others come down.' She raised her voice. 'An' there'll be no blabbing about this to nobody. See? We don't need no doctor, nor any busybodies coming up the hill asking their questions. Funerals cost money an' we haven't got none.'

Stumbling across the yard and into the cowshed, tears running down her face, Annie was already making plans to get away. To where it didn't matter, just as long as it

132

was far enough away from this God-forsaken, desolate place, where no one laughed except to mock, and where a baby could die without its mother shedding a tear.

Ten minutes later, standing at the window of her room, she saw Barney Eccles walking out across the field with the box held carelessly underneath an arm. He carried a spade over his shoulder, and by the swagger in his walk she felt sure he was whistling. Annie knuckled her fists against her mouth to prevent herself from screaming.

She worked inside the house all that morning, but early in the afternoon when she went outside to empty a bucket she saw Barney Eccles standing by the pump watching a man on a horse riding down the long hill-slope. There was something familiar about the rider in the slouch hat crouched low in the saddle. Annie dropped her bucket with a clatter and ran across the cobbled yard.

'Mr Eccles?'

'Aye?'

'Who was that?' She pointed down the hill. 'The man on the horse. Who was it?'

The familar mirthless smile widened the slack mouth. 'But you know who it was, Annie. You know full well exactly who it was.' To her horror he caught her by the wrists. 'The high and mighty Armstrong, that's who it was. Trying to tell me I ought to be sending for the knacker man instead of doing his job properly and getting my best cow back on its feet.' The shifty eyes narrowed. 'I'm having no knacker man nor no inspector up here asking questions, poking their noses in where they're not wanted.'

He turned his head to spit over his shoulder, and as he did so Annie tried to break away, but he held firm. She forced herself to meet his eyes.

'Did Mr Armstrong ask after me?'

Barney's bellow of laughter was a nauseating view of

133

brown uneven teeth, and the rancid smell of foul breath. 'Ask after *you*? Now, why should he ask after the likes of Annie Clancy?'

'Because I was living in his house not all that long ago!' Annie was almost dancing with frustration. 'Because he knows I'm here, that's why, an' even if he didn't want to see me I know he wouldn't ride away without enquiring after me.'

Barney shouted aloud with glee. 'So you thought he would be enquiring after you, then? Well, he never said a word about you. He couldn't wait to get away after the mouthful I gave him.'

'But he *must* have mentioned me!' Annie twisted round to stare frantically down the long hill. 'Just to ask how I was? Just to say he hoped I was all right?'

Her distress had flushed her cheeks, brightened her eyes. Barney felt the ache of wanting her tightening his loins.

'No need to moither yourself about him, nor over that sailor fella.' With a sudden jerk he pinned Annie's arms behind her back and lifted her into the shadow of the house, well away from the windows. 'I know you think I'm a hard man with what I had to do for our Benjie, but what man wouldn't grow a skin as thick as a bleedin' rhinoceros having to live with that apology for a woman back yon?' He ground himself against her. 'Do you think I enjoyed what I had to do?'

'I don't think it bothered you at all.'

Annie could smell the sweat on him. It stood in beads on his red face; it ran down his grizzled sideburns. Breathing heavily he forced a knee between her legs, pinning her to the wall.

'I need a bit of what you let that Armstrong fella have, an' what you give that sailor fella. I wouldn't treat you like they did.' His voice slurred into a whine. 'Lil's not got an 'apporth of affection in the whole of that mangy stringy body of hers. I'll come to you tonight, Annie, and we'll forget about that little babbie sleeping under the ground.'

134

There was a frenzied cruel urgency about him. His strength was that of a roused bull, and Annie knew she could never break free. She took hold of the hand groping for the fastening of her skirt.

'Not here, Barney.' She used his Christian name for the first time. 'Save it till tonight.' She forced herself to touch his hair, to run her fingers through the coarse stubbled feel of it. 'I'll be waiting for you. The need's in me as well.'

'He been beggin' you to let him have his way with you?'

When Annie went into the house she was still breathless from the struggle, still shaking from the horror of what had so nearly happened. Lily Eccles bent down and removed a gritty crust from the hand of a small boy, then passed it on to a blade-thin dog Annie didn't recall seeing before.

'He come in from God knows where,' Lily explained. 'Thinks he's let on his feet here, the silly beggar.' She shrugged thin shoulders. 'You don't need to look at me like that. I knew as soon as you come in what he'd been up to. It won't be the first time he's spit on his own doorstep. Not by a long chalk.'

'You don't for one moment think . . . ?' Annie took a step backwards. 'You couldn't think that I would let . . .'

Lily was leaning against the edge of the table, shaking her head from side to side.

'Oh, stop staring at me, Annie Clancy, with those great blue eyes of yours! Do you know how old I am? Go on! Have a guess? Forty? Fifty?' She hunched lower, supporting herself by blue-veined hands. 'I'm twenty-eight, that's all. I used to be as bonny as you. Bonnier! With long gold curls, and a waist that Barney could span with his two hands. I was married in a white dress with bands of blue braid round the hem, and umpteen tiny buttons all fastened with tiny little loops.' She straightened up. 'Nobody wanted me to marry him, but you

135

should have seen Barney in those days. The girls couldn't leave him alone. He had yellow hair that glistened in the sun, and a smile that made you want to do anything he asked of you.' Suddenly she sagged into a chair. 'And now . . . For the sake of that girl I used to be, get yourself away from here. He'll not give up once he's set on having you. It's not too late, is it?'

'Oh, no!' Annie was wiping the hand that had stroked his hair down the side of her skirt. Wiping, wiping, as if to destroy the feel of it. 'I'll never . . . never . . .'

Lily nodded. 'Then go now. This minute, while he's in the top field. Now! Before he comes in.' She lowered her head so that a clutch of white hairs were clearly visible springing from a wavy parting. 'An' don't risk going to say goodbye to Benjie. Let him rest in peace where he is. Go, *now* before it's too late.'

'But what about you?' Annie knew how it would be for the grey little woman struggling on without help. 'Now I know you're on my side, perhaps we could . . .'

Her voice tapered away as Lily's head came up with a jerk. 'I'm on nobody's side, Annie Clancy! Nobody's. D'you hear me? I hate the whole rotten world, you included. An' him out there most of all.'

Annie took her black cloak down from a nail behind the door. 'What about . . . ?' She glanced upwards. 'My things . . . ?'

Lily whipped round on her, eyes blazing. 'For God's sake, go! An' run like the wind, because he'll kill you if he catches up with you.' She hoisted a whining child up from the floor, slapped its bare bottom, and turned her back.

Annie felt the fear start to grow in her; it was the squeeze of a hand round her heart, a trembling of her legs. She stepped out into the yard, and without even a glance behind her ran down the steep hill, dreading the sound of heavy footsteps following on, or a rough voice calling her name. She ran when there was no need to run any more, until the sudden cry of a blackbird startled her to a stop.

136

There was nothing to see for miles but green undulating hills and patchwork fields dotted with buttercups. She sat down by a low stone wall and unfastened her cloak, holding a hand over her wildly beating heart, trying to catch her breath. The air was heavy with the scent of May blossom, the leaves glistened with an early summer sheen. Annie closed her eyes and forced herself to breathe deeply until she grew calmer.

In her desperate tearing hurry she had left everything she owned behind. Already her throat felt dry and rough; soon darkness would come and the sky to the west told of rain.

'I am never,' she told herself, 'going to feel as alone and unhappy as I do at this moment.' She said it aloud, speaking slowly and deliberately.

Her mother had told her that once the barometer had dropped as low as it could, there was only one way for it to go, and that was up. Annie's smile was grim. She admitted that at that moment she ached with loneliness. She could cope with the fear, but loneliness was another thing altogether.

Taking her unawares, a sudden anguish shouted aloud in her head. 'You have run away again, Annie Clancy, and this time there is nowhere to run to! This time you could die out in the fields and nobody would care. Not one single person in the whole of the world! You could lie beneath a hedge until you rot, and nobody would even know.' She didn't want to believe it but it was true. There was no place for her because she wasn't needed. Anywhere.

Why *should* Seth Armstrong have asked after her? She had bolted her door against him that night because he had shown her he was no different from other men. He and Barney Eccles were two of a kind. In fact, Barney Eccles was to be preferred. At least he had never *pretended* to be kind. Not like the animal doctor who had talked to her as if he really liked her. There was nothing to choose between them, nothing at all.

Annie said it aloud, then covered her mouth with her hand in a gesture of comfort, knowing that it wasn't true.

Seth suspected that the abscess on the fetlock of Barney Eccles's cow had been caused by a heavy blow. He had bathed the infected area to induce a pointing, then rubbed Elliman's embrocation well in until he'd found a spot soft enough to lance. The strip of tow pushed deep into the wound would be all that was necessary now for the healing, unless the weather turned unseasonably hot and the flies got into it.

He rode on down the hill and away from the farm, deep in thought. He had done what he could, but the poor beast's condition cried out for nourishing food and a well-drained pasture. There was no distension of the belly, but to be on the safe side Seth had given a one ounce dose of chlorodyne. And before he called back he would mix up a tonic of iron, gentian and cordial seeds, ground and mixed with linseed and bran mash. The hill farmer was over-fond of using the stick when gentle handling would have got far better results.

A neglected beast never failed to fill Seth with loathing for its owner. He had told Eccles exactly what he thought about him and ridden away with relief. And yet had felt a strange compulsion to turn back . . .

A great unease had come on him as he stood in the damp and draughty cowshed. All at once a weight had tightened his chest, and the notion that had he been in the least fanciful his eyes would have filled with tears.

Even now, within sight of home, the inexplicable melancholy shadowed his thinking and saddened his heart.

8

When Annie heard the sound of voices she jumped to her feet and ran on blindly, sure it was Barney Eccles coming after her. Keeping to the shelter of a ridge of trees she stumbled on, paying no heed when she tore her long skirts on a thorn bush. She was certain she could hear the farmer's loud coarse voice calling her name. She imagined his hands on her, heard his bellow of a laugh, smelled his rancid sweat.

At last, on a road winding on towards the vast stretch of moorland, she stopped. Her breath rasped in her throat, a burning pain raged down her right side. She had lost her mob-cap, so that her hair tumbled down over her shoulders, the hair of a madwoman, unbrushed, unkempt. All she possessed was back at the hill farm, her one change of clothes, her hairbrush and her Bible. She could never go back for them, never. Yet how was she to go on without them? And how could anyone stretch out a hand to help her when the very sight of her would send them running in the opposite direction?

She slept that night in a derelict cowshed, huddled uncomfortably on the dirt floor, jerking awake then dozing for what she was sure could be no more than minutes. At first light she crawled on hands and knees to the opening in the shed's rotting timbers and saw a family of rabbits nibbling grass. They were eating furiously, sitting straight up every few seconds, their ears working like antennae as they listened for the faintest suspicion of danger. The moment Annie moved they were off.

She stood up and looked around her. At the hills showing purple against the bright morning sky, at the far-off sweep of moorland, the dark patches of woods, the fells sloping down to the flowering fields spread like counterpanes along the valley.

The sun was already up. She was hungry, she craved a drink. She had wiped the night's tears from her cheeks with dirty hands, her arms were peppered with bite marks, from what form of life she had no wish to know, and when a tiny hedge-sparrow flew up in sudden alarm from a small hawthorn bush she screamed.

For the whole of her life Annie had lived in a street. If a blade of grass had dared to poke its way up between the cobbles, the soot-filled air had quickly choked the life out of it. The coming of spring meant merely that the washing had an even chance of drying outside, and the boys could manage without their brown paper chest protectors.

The springs that Annie had known were no more than a gradual blending of one season into another, an imperceptible lightening and lengthening of the days, but here in the country spring burst out with a vengeance. A myriad flowers bloomed, buds popped and bees hovered. In the town spring was a glance through a window at the unexpected blueness of the sky. Here, the sky was all around, wide and suddenly terrifying.

Annie felt she wanted no part of it. More used to warmth that came from a coal fire than from the sun, she dropped to her knees in the dew-wet grass. Inside her there was a burning anger, an emotion far different from the despair she had felt when she left home. Then she was lumbered with a pregnancy, at the mercy of anyone kind enough to stretch out a hand to help her. Now, at least, she was free of all that. Fate had chucked just about enough at her for the time being. She was going to *make* things happen from now on, not just let them happen to her.

'So what are you going to do, Annie Clancy?' she said aloud. 'Where are you thinking you might go now?'

She bunched the torn skirt up in her hand and tried to tuck it back into the wide waistband. She slithered her way down a bank of cow-parsley to a running beck fringed with tiny yellow flowers. The water was cool on her face. She drank deeply of it from her cupped hands, and when she'd tied her hair back with a strip of lace torn from her petticoat, she felt ready to go on.

Where to?

Trailing her long cloak behind her, she started walking, taking to the winding road but hiding her face when she heard the rumble of a cart coming towards her. Hunger pains gnawed at her stomach; her throat was soon parched again, but the water in a boggy ditch was muddy and brown and she let it trickle away through her fingers.

By the late afternoon she was light-headed and exhausted. Laurie had said he had gypsy blood in him so he would have known how to keep alive. He would have picked leaves, scrabbled in the long grass for mushrooms, filled his mouth with the juice from the scarlet berries on an overhanging bush.

Sobbing and swaying from side to side, Annie caught her foot in a deep wheel-rut and fell forward, flat on her face.

At a row of cottages she stopped at the gate of the first one and asked a woman in a sun bonnet picking herbs from her garden if she could have a drink of water.

'I'm not short of pegs. Not today, thank you,' the woman said, bustling inside and closing her front door.

A little way further down the lane Annie came face to face with a small girl in a pink cotton dress carefully carrying a pitcher of milk. Annie wished her good afternoon – or ought it to have been good evening, she no longer knew – and stood blocking her path.

The little girl was probably six or seven years old. The pink cotton dress was topped by a white pinafore. She was clean, her brown hair shone as if her mother brushed it for her every night before she went to bed. She had been brought up to be kind and good, polite to strangers, but this lady with glittering eyes frightened her. She gave Annie an uneasy smile, trying to step round her.

141

'Please can I have a drink of your milk?' Annie was babbling and swaying, desperate for the smooth feel of the creamy milk on her tongue. She held out her hand for the jug. 'I don't mean to frighten you, love. I'm thirsty.' She forced a smile. 'I'm spittin' cotton for a drink.'

'Me mam says that.'

'My mam used to say that, too.' It was taking every bit of Annie's self-control to keep her voice low. 'Give me the jug. *Please.*'

Annie saw fear cloud the wide eyes; cringed as the little girl opened her mouth wide in a surprisingly loud wail. She grabbed the jug from her.

'I'll tell me mam on you! Me dad'll get you with a big stick!'

Annie drank the sweet frothy milk. She drank it the way she had often seen her father sup his ale, in a long swallow with her head thrown back. It was stealing, she supposed, wiping her mouth with the back of her hand. It had been an ungodly thing to do, snatching the milk from a child's hands, scaring the living daylights out of her. But needs must. Oh, dear God, how needs must.

She set the jug down carefully on a moss-covered stone and ran as fast as she could, on down the lane, past a farm with a barking dog straining at a chain, across a ploughed field and into the cool shade of a wood.

Leaving her cloak behind her where she'd dropped it as she'd snatched the jug.

The milk had given her fresh hope and an upsurge of energy. If only she could knock on a door, *any* door, and ask for work. If only she looked more presentable, less like a living scarecrow. The loss of her cloak didn't seem to matter. To go back for it would be impossible. She moved further into the wood.

As she came out of it, she heard a dog bark, then stepped back in alarm as a collie with a muddied tangled coat ran towards her, tail wagging, panting with excitement.

'Down boy! Down!'

142

Turning round quickly, Annie saw a man carrying an axe, a square, heavily-built man with a face almost covered in hair. She held her breath, poised to run. As he came closer she could see the sharp cutting edge of the axe and imagined he was weighing it in his hands before he struck. The euphoric mood brought on by the pint of milk had long since gone. She knew that she looked like a crazy woman out of Bedlam, with her trailing and torn skirts, her dirty hands and face, and no dignity to her at all.

The shadows were lengthening. Soon it would be dark, and as far as she could see she was mile upon mile from anywhere. The hills seemed to be closing in on her; it was very quiet, the only sounds being the song of a bird and the far distant sound of children's voices as they played out in what was left of the light.

She stared at the man standing in front of her saying nothing. Biding his time before he pounced – that was obvious. Why didn't he move? Why didn't he say something?

'Get away from me!' she shouted, picking up her skirt and turning to run, stumbling over tree roots, making for the sound of the voices. When she tripped and fell she lay there, her arms over her face, awaiting the inevitable.

'Haven't I seen you somewhere afore, lass?'

The voice was concerned, the question so unexpected that Annie could only twist round to stare up at him, her mouth wide. The whiskery man had large creamy teeth, a broad forehead, high cheekbones and penetrating brown eyes.

'You wasn't running away from *me*, was you, lass?' Shifting the axe to his other arm, he held out a hand to help Annie to her feet. 'I know I'm not exactly God's gift to women, but I'm not that bad, am I?' His eyes sobered for a moment as he took in Annie's appearance. 'You wouldn't exactly pass for the May Queen either, lass.' He took off his cap and scratched his head. 'I know now where I've seen you afore. It was early on in the New

143

Year when Rex here had half his nose bit off by an alsatian the size of a Blackpool tram.' He laid a hand for a moment on the dog's domed head. 'I took him over to Seth Armstrong's place and you was there. I saw you in the kitchen with that housekeeper of his – the one who looks as if she's lost half-a-crown and found a threepenny-bit. Mr Armstrong asked me to go through into the house for a warming drop of whisky.'

As he mentioned the vet's name, he jerked his head in the direction of a wooded slope. Annie spoke quickly. 'Is Mr Armstrong's house close to here? I was sure I was miles away. Miles and miles.' Her eyes were bleak with despair. 'I've lost my way good and proper.'

'Well, it's more than a good spit away, lass. It were a long walk, cold enough to freeze your cockles, but folks walk further than that to see Seth Armstrong. There's nowt much goes wrong with an animal that he can't put right. You running away from there, lass? I wouldn't have thought . . .'

'The housekeeper,' Annie said quickly. 'We didn't get on.' She fell into step beside him. 'But I've not come from there.' She hesitated. 'I don't suppose you know the Eccles's farm? I've been working there.'

'Barney Eccles!' The man turned and looked at her sharply. 'How on earth did you come to be working for him? He's a real bad lot is Barney Eccles. He'd make owd Nick himself look like he was wearing an 'alo.'

'Mrs Martindale sent me to him. She said Mrs Eccles was a distant cousin.'

'Everybody round here's a distant cousin to somebody. That filthy old devil hasn't been . . . ?'

'No!' Annie said at once. 'I wasn't going to give him a chance.' Her chin came up. 'I'd've kneed him if he hadn't been as strong as a bull. So I ran away. Without stopping to get me things.'

'When?'

'Day before yesterday.'

'An' you slept rough last night?'

144

'Yes.'

'Food? Water?'

'Milk,' Annie said. 'A whole pint. I whipped the jug out of a little girl's hands and drank it down.' She lowered her head. 'And now you know.'

'Cheese and flippin' rice!' Adam Page was at a loss what to say or do. He blamed Seth Armstrong's housekeeper for this lot. She knew right enough what went on at the Eccles's farm. He glanced sideways at the slightly built girl trudging along by his side. She was sticking to him like a stray dog would if you chanced to give it a kind word or a pat on the head. Nellie Martindale should be shot at dawn for sending this young lass to work for Barney Eccles. If ever a man deserved a long spell in prison he did. Hanging was too good for him. Hung, drawn and quartered would be more like it.

Annie looked up at the sky. 'It's spittin'.'

'Aye, I think you're right, lass. It's been threatening to rain all day.'

Adam's mind was working overtime. If he asked the lass into his cottage he could be letting himself in for more than he'd bargained for. Besides, Clara would have something to say about him turning up with this bedraggled creature. Sick in her body Clara might be, but her mind was as keen as a newly-stropped razor.

They trudged along in silence for the best part of half a mile. It was raining in earnest now. Annie lowered her head and let the weather do what it willed. She had stopped trying to hold up her torn skirt or prevent it trailing along behind her. She stubbed her toe on a loose stone, and wished she was dead.

'My wife's delicate,' the man beside her said suddenly.

Annie knew what he meant right away. She'd heard that word often and it always signified the same thing. Delicate meant consumptive. It meant a member of a family lying downstairs in a bed in the same room with

145

the cooking being done on the fire, meals eaten round the table, family life carrying on as usual. It meant coughing and spitting blood at the end, then the inevitable funeral with the box on a cart and relatives with black armbands on their coats walking behind it through the streets to the cemetery. Being delicate meant you were on your last.

'I'm the gardener at that big house you can just see over yon through those trees.' They were out of the field and down on to the lane now. Adam pointed. 'You can just about see the chimneys. I live a bit further on, round that corner. In a cottage that goes with the job.'

'I see.'

Annie accepted that he was preparing her for the moment when he left her at the door of his cottage. She was embarrassing him, putting him under some sort of obligation walking with him all this way, sticking to him like a limpet. But soon it would be dusk, then dark. Last night it had been fine – tonight it looked as though it was going to rain like the clappers.

'T'master up at the big house promised me the cottage for the rest of my life. I've worked for him since I were ten years old.'

'That's a long time,' Annie said automatically, concentrating hard on putting one foot in front of the other.

'Thirty year, man and boy.'

In spite of her despair Annie couldn't help but turn in surprise. This man with the straight back, the leathery face – what she could see of it – was the same age as her father, give or take a year or so. A sudden picture came into her mind of her father coming up the street stoop-shouldered in his pit clothes, carrying his big tea-can, his snap-can fastened to his belt. She remembered how he had often been too tired to wash, and how he'd just sat there in his chair by the fire, the whites of his eyes gleaming from his black face. When he'd washed his face it still never looked clean. Beneath the coal dust his face was grey, criss-crossed by blue scars, dented with old injuries.

For a moment something akin to pity made the tears prick behind Annie's eyes. Something that could have been mistaken for love.

Jack Clancy had just about had enough of that old maid Edith Morris pestering him about Annie. With her sunken cheeks and tight lips pressed so closely together they were almost hidden away, she was a menace, a proper pest.

'Annie is not at the workhouse. I've made enquiries and she's not at *any* workhouse for miles around.' Edith was determined to stand her ground. To best this uncouth man sitting gaunt-faced and subdued, waiting to go off on the night shift down the mine.

The week before Jack had twisted his back escaping a sudden fall of coal. It was paining him badly but he accepted the injury, as he had all the others, as part and parcel of his working life. He had the house to himself for once, and was relishing the fact. He'd been savouring the quiet, drawing it into himself for a precious few minutes, until now.

'So she's not at the bloody workhouse?' Jack's eyes flicked sideways. 'Does it matter where she is? The divil melt her. What's it got to do with you where she is?'

'She's your daughter, Mr Clancy! Your flesh and blood.' Edith looked away from the greasy black frying pan in the middle of the unscrubbed table. Bacon and cabbage by the smell of it. The immigrant Irish seemed to live on the stuff. 'If she didn't land up at the workhouse, then where is she?' Edith stabbed a finger in the air.

What Jack Clancy said after that was best forgotten, Edith told herself, hurrying back down the street to her silent tidy house. You had to remind yourself that we were all God's creatures, the uncouth, the blasphemous, and the filthy-tongued. Inside every man or woman was the God within. Edith had always believed that. The most hardened sinner had that grain of goodness deep in

147

his soul. But what if a man was without a soul? What if his wicked tongue had shrivelled it away? She was sure that where Jack Clancy's heart should be was a big slab of coal.

The brass pot holding the aspidistra needed a bit of a rub up. Edith went to the drawer for a nicely folded clean duster. She muttered to herself as she polished, drawing her lips further in, giving the impression of being toothless.

'I'll find young Annie if it's the last thing I do. I'll find her if it costs me my last farthing . . .'

She refused even to think that Annie might be dead. Lying out there on the far moors, turning up as a skeleton in years to come. She also refused to entertain the notion that Annie might have let on her feet and be far happier than ever she was living at home. The yawning gap in Edith's life had to be filled. She had to be needed, and since her mother had died no one had asked anything of her, never even knocked at her door and asked for a drink of water. Her prayers to the Lord Jesus had as yet been unanswered.

'I am an empty vessel,' she cried aloud in the middle of the sleepless night. 'Fill me with the goodness of Thy love. Do not send me empty away.'

Adam Page stopped at the gate of his cottage with one hand on the latch. The lass stopped too, just as he had known she would, staring at him with her big eyes. The rain dripped from her hair, her nose, her chin. She shivered and shook; she was a drowned rat. He had the feeling that if she stood there for long enough she would run down herself, ending up as a puddle.

'Do you think they might take me on up at the big house?' she was saying. 'I'm a good worker. I had five brothers at home, and at the Eccles's farm there were seven children, and one of them a baby.' At the thought of Benjie she gave a loud sob.

Adam was a slow thinker, but when he spoke he said

what he meant, and meant what he said. Working on the land since the age of ten, marrying a woman who never used two words if one would do, he was totally out of his depth when it came to making decisions. Now he was faced with a big one. To make time he clicked the gate open then closed it again. Getting involved was something of which he had always fought shy. He could take the lass in to the fire; he could feed her up, then what? She was on the road, when all was said and done. Homeless. A tramp. She said she'd run away from Barney Eccles, and he could understand that. But why from home? And why from Seth Armstrong's place? There was something fishy about a young lass who was always running away.

'I'll be on my way, then,' Annie said, watching his face. There was a lamp set in the window of the cottage. She bet the kettle would be on the hob, and a crusty loaf on the table. In the place where her stomach should be there was a great empty hole. She felt ill.

Suddenly, without any warning, what Mrs Greenhalgh had said on that last morning at home popped into her head: 'If they won't let you into the workhouse, faint on the doorstep,' she had advised. 'A decent faint never comes amiss.'

'Needs must,' Annie told herself, buckling her knees, closing her eyes and sinking to the ground.

'You were sent in answer to a prayer, Annie Clancy. I hope you realise that.'

Annie had been at the gardener's cottage for two days. Two nights of sleeping in a comfortable bed, on a feather mattress so billowy it folded itself round her, like flower petals closing. There was a bedding chest and a bamboo table holding a flowered water jug and basin, and in a small locker by the side of the bed, a matching chamber-pot.

There was a well in the back garden, not too close to the privy; there was wood for the gathering, a big black kettle hanging over the fire for constant hot water, and a copper in the alcove behind the fireplace if more was needed for washing clothes. There was a deep red frill round the cornice and a red bobbled chenille cloth on the table, flowers in pots on the wide window sills, a grandfather clock in a corner, pewter tankards in a row on the mantelpiece, a bare brick floor and a box of Sunlight soap set to harden on a high shelf.

Adam's wife, Clara, had the feverish eyes and highly flushed cheeks of the consumptive. She had 'enjoyed' bad health for years, never coughed once when twice sounded better, and foretold her death in the tone of one who had never looked on the bright side for the simple reason that she would have found it much too mundane. As a permanent invalid she got the attention she craved, and now with this red-haired girl waiting on her hand and foot, even to the extent of anticipating her needs, she had actually found herself smiling once or twice.

'I've not got long to go, Annie,' she said one sunny morning.

'You mustn't say that, Mrs Page.' Annie was standing

on a four-legged stool, taking the pewter tankards down from the high mantelpiece to give them a much needed dust. 'I've known hundreds of folks with your complaint,' she exaggerated, 'and they all lived for years and years. Have you tried scooping a turnip out and filling the hole with honey, then letting it ferment? A neighbour across the street from us swore by it for her son.' Deliberately she pushed from her memory the sad day when the child had been boxed and carried out to the cart, with every window-blind in the long street pulled down to show respect. 'It did him a power of good,' she lied.

'Tell me about your street, Annie.' Clara lowered herself down on to the horse-hair sofa drawn up at right angles to the fire. 'Adam told me about you working for Mr Armstrong then going on up to Barney Eccles's farm, but what about before?'

Annie got down from the stool. She had taken a liking to the gardener's wife, with her doom-laden voice and her way of relishing and enjoying bad news. It had taken her no more than these two days to discover that the way to Clara's heart was to tell her details of terrible accidents, preferably fatal. She had worked out that hearing of tragedy somehow helped Clara Page to cope with her own misfortune.

'I'll be getting on with the rabbit for the dinner while I tell you about what happened before,' she said. 'You lie back and get your feet up. I learnt how to do this at the Eccles's place.'

The rabbit lay on the bare table, its eyes wide open, its mouth drawn back from its teeth in a last desperate grimace. Annie took up a long knife and steeling herself, brought it down with a whacking thump on the rabbit's lolling neck.

'My father threw me out because I was expecting,' she said. 'He couldn't bear the shame of what people in the street would say.'

Clara's whole face was transformed. Incest was common enough in the teeming streets of Liverpool where she'd been brought up, but she'd never come across it at first hand before.

'Oh, you poor child,' she said, coughing into her hand. 'Men like your father should be hanged. By their johnwillies.'

'It wasn't my father, Mrs Page!' Annie stared down at the spilling tendons of the dead rabbit, feeling her stomach rise up in protest. 'The only time my father touched me was to wallop me one.'

'Some men get their satisfaction in that way.' Clara nodded wisely.

Annie looked her employer straight in the eyes. If she was going to stop on here in this lovely cottage she had to tell the truth. Word got round; rumours spread. Anyway the truth of what had happened would cheer Mrs Page up no end.

'A sailor came to lodge with us. He was kind to me and I thought he was the most . . . the nicest man I'd ever seen in my whole life. He had black hair that curled over his forehead; he had a brown face and he said things that made me laugh. He told me stories of where he'd been. He'd been to India, and China, but when he went to work down the mine he changed.' She sighed. 'He even looked different, and it wasn't just the pit dirt, it was the way he walked and talked. The mine would have killed a man like him.'

'And you were sweet on him?'

Annie raised the knife again. There had been plenty of time to think as she walked the roads, hungry and thirsty, not knowing where she was going to end up. A lot of the time she had been thinking about Laurie. She wished she could remember his face clearly, but there were times when she saw it merely as a blur, like a photograph not quite in focus. That's what he was, a blur. He was never going to come back, not on her birthday in September, or ever. He had pretended to go along with her talk of marriage and plans for their future together. She brought the knife down hard again.

There was no future for them. There never had been . . .

'Annie? *Were* you sweet on the sailor?' Clara had forgotten to cough.

'I loved him till my heart ached,' Annie said. 'He came in the door one day just after my father had given me a good beating.' She closed her eyes at the memory of it. 'So Laurie comforted me in the best way he knew.' She slit the rabbit's skin from the neck down. 'I let him do it. He didn't force me. I'd only myself to blame, you see. I didn't struggle.'

'What did he say when you told him you'd fallen for a baby?'

'He never knew.'

'You never told him?'

'I never had the chance. He went away the very next day.'

'What a shocking thing to do.' Clara's eyes softened with genuine sympathy. 'There's some terrible men in the world.'

Annie raised her eyes. 'Oh, he promised to come back and marry me on my next birthday. An' I believed him! Can you credit that? We stood together in the sight of God and made our vows, an' all the time he was planning on going away the very next morning.' She wrapped the rabbit's head in a sheet of newspaper, and as she did so the picture came into her mind of Biddy following the animal doctor's instructions and wrapping something up in newspaper at the bottom end of the bed. 'I lost the baby,' she said, feeling again the dragging pain in her back. She tore at the rabbit's legs with her hands. 'I ought to be saying I'm sorry, but I'm not. If I've to get by on my own from now on a baby would be a big handicap.'

'That's a hard thing to say, love.'

Annie shook her head. 'Do you know where I'd be if I'd gone on and had that baby? For a start it would have been born in the workhouse, to be taken from me if it was healthy for adoption by a couple who couldn't have babies.'

153

'Like me,' Clara said, in her suffering voice. 'Though I've never been strong enough to rear a child. What sort of a life would a child of mine have had? I couldn't have looked after it, that's definite. I would probably have died in childbirth anyroad. In agony.' That prospect seemed to cheer her. 'Then what would Adam have done? He needs me. Them up at the big house work him till he's fit to drop.' She swung twig-thin legs to the floor. 'There were drifts of snow high enough to bury a standing man in February. Adam used to come in with icicles on his eyebrows, and the dog plastered in snow with just two holes to show where his eyes were. But did them up there care? I doubt if t'master would have lifted a finger to dig Adam out if he'd got himself buried in a snow-drift.'

'Mr Page seems to speak well of them.'

'Mr Page would shake hands with the devil. Then ask him to his tea,' said Clara, staring mournfully into the fire.

In June the long sweep of lawn in front of the big house became scorched in patches by the heat of the sun. Over in the fields the hay was baled, but before it could be got inside the rain came. At the end of June, Adam took Annie to one side and asked her if she would forget her intention of getting work up at the big house and stay at the cottage to look after his wife.

'I reckon she'll be bedfast by the winter. Will you promise me you'll do that, lass?'

That night when she went to bed Annie sat without moving for a long time on the edge of her narrow bed.

'Promise?' She said the word aloud, kicking out at a cut rug, sending it skidding across the floorboards. She wanted nothing to do with promises. Laurie had promised her on his life that he would love her for ever, and now she was hard put to it to remember the way he looked or the way he talked. The blue ribbon was gone. The last time she'd seen it, it had been draped over a

154

spotted mirror in her room at the Eccles's farm. Even the memory of Laurie's footsteps as he'd walked away from her down the street, the sack over his shoulder, was dimming fast.

She knew what the gardener had meant when he'd asked her to promise to stay to look after his wife. Stay till the end, he'd meant. Stay till she went to skin and bone, and her eyes stared from her head like chapel hat pegs. Stay till she took to the couch by the fire, coughing her heart up, bringing up buckets of blood.

Annie walked over to the window and looked out into the garden. There was the rumbled menace of thunder to the east, the air was hot and sticky. That afternoon Clara had sat outside the door for a while, reminding Annie so much of her own mother that her heart had turned over. She couldn't go through that again, not the agonised watching and waiting as someone died. Mr Page would have to understand that she couldn't promise him anything. Annie clenched her hands. What was a promise, anyway? Just words to be broken, that was all.

'I promise,' Laurie had said in his lilting voice.

'He'd be one of the travelling men,' Seth Armstrong had explained. 'They have the urge always to be moving on, they can't be tied down. Are you listening to me, Annie?' he'd asked her.

Oh, yes, she'd been listening, but she wasn't going to give him the satisfaction of knowing that.

The rain was falling now, sweeping down from black curling clouds. Annie moved away from the window and snatched off her white cap, one of Clara Page's hand-me-downs. Sometimes the things people said, especially the hurtful things, lingered on in the mind and wouldn't go away. As he talked to her that day the animal doctor had been trying to revive a dying bird, a thrush caught up in the wire fence at the bottom of the long garden. Annie had watched, holding her breath as the ends of the wing feathers were tied before being glued to the flank of the terrified bird.

'Will it live?' she remembered asking, even as the fluttering suddenly stopped.

'Nothing lasts for ever,' he had said. 'Even promises are often broken.'

Annie knew exactly what he was trying to tell her. She had ignored it though, so why was she remembering it exactly after all this time?

She unbuttoned her blouse, her frayed camisole, and began to wash her top half, working the soap into a good lather with the soft water. Patting herself dry, she slipped one of Clara's old nightgowns over her head before soaping her lower half. For decency's sake, the way her mother had taught her.

Soon the family up at the big house would be coming back from France. Mrs Page had explained that Mrs Gray was half French, with two step-daughters well into their twenties and shamefully unmarried. Annie climbed into bed. If she was to get work at the big house she would have to apply the minute they got back. Closing her eyes, she tried to bring to mind a story in one of Biddy's magazines.

It was about a girl with raven-black hair who worked for a noble family living in a remote Scottish castle. This girl wore a black sateen dress, a white muslin apron, and a frilled cap on her high-piled hair. She had never known who her father was, but you could tell he'd been gentry by the way she'd inherited small feet and dainty ankles. She was waiting at table one evening, the Glen outside the castle filled with the scent of heather, when all at once she saw the Duke staring at her with blue fire in his eyes. She was so overcome that she dropped a dish of roast potatoes on to the silken lap of an honoured guest, and burst into silent tears which slid pitifully down her creamy cheeks.

It was love at first sight, and after many vicissitudes the Duke married her. His mother not only overlooked the girl's humble beginnings, but personally turned her into a lady, correcting her speech and showing her which knife and fork to use.

The story had made Annie laugh out loud, but the black sateen dress and white frilled cap had stayed in her mind.

Throwing back the blankets she went to the mirror scooping her long hair up on top of her head, imagining herself with a froth of white pinned on to it.

Up at the big house she would be working with and touching beautiful things. She had never been inside, but she knew in her head exactly how it would be.

And she knew more than most how it would be if she promised to nurse Clara Page till she died. It was her mother over again; it was the smell of sickness, and the sponging down of a body racked with pain, wet with sweat. She wanted . . . oh, dear God, she wanted a bit of *life*. She wanted a lot of life, the chance to be young and to wear a dress specially made for her. All at once she was back pleading with her father for just that. Instinctively her hand went to and covered her left ear, holding the pain in as she remembered it.

The next day she told Adam that she would stay, and the following week the family from the big house came back from the south of France.

Margot Gray was driving herself in her own pony-cart down the long avenue lined with trees when she first saw the gardener's little protegée chasing a wandering hen back across the road. Immediately she pulled on the reins.

So this was the tramp woman Adam was supposed to have fetched in from the rain! Her eyes twinkled at the sight of the small girl with red curly hair wisping from the confines of a blue headscarf. This was no orphan waif with pallid looks and downcast eyes. There was what she would guess to be a wealth of intelligence in the bright eyes, a hint of spirit in the way the girl bobbed only half a curtsey.

'So you are to housekeep for Adam, and nurse his wife?'

157

'Yes, ma'am. For the time being, anyway.'

'And then?'

'What will be, will be, ma'am.'

'Do you mean that?'

'Not really. I'll probably have to prod things along a bit.'

Margot was intrigued. The girl was talking to her as an equal. It was obvious she had never gone into service, never been taught the rudiments of deferential behaviour.

'Your name is . . . ?'

'Annie, ma'am. Annie Clancy.'

Margot nodded. 'You must take good care of Adam, child. He's been around this place even longer than I. He could grow a flower from a stone. You know that?'

'Yes, ma'am.'

'Then look after him well, Annie Clancy. You hear me?' With a flick of her whip Margot urged the pony on, leaving Annie looking after her spellbound.

Plain Mrs Gray she might be. Not Lady Gray as she deserved to be, but Annie could recognise gentry when she saw it. In her dress made up of two different plaids, with a small velvet hat pinned to her upswept dark hair, she had looked every inch a Duchess. The encounter was the closest Annie had ever been to the aristocracy, and she felt suitably overawed. Manners, breeding, all were there, along with the dignity on which her mother had set such store.

'We never saw anybody like her down our street,' she told Clara when she went inside. 'She spoke to me just like she was an ordinary person.'

'I'm not going to last long,' Clara said.

'What's puzzling me is how she got her hair to stick up at the back of her hat like that. It looked as if it had been brushed over a pin cushion. Nobody could have hair that thick. Biddy told me that she'd once worked for a titled lady who sat for an hour every morning having her hair brushed and pinned up. Fancy having a maid to brush your hair! Biddy said she . . .'

'I keep getting this numb feeling in my hands and feet,' said Clara. 'Feel at my fingers, Annie. It's the same with my toes. I'm dying inch by inch.'

Annie obliged, rubbing the cold hands between her own, taking off Clara's slippers and doing the same to her thin, blue-veined feet.

She couldn't get the sight of Mrs Gray out of her mind. All that splendour, all that colour! Even the pony looked as if it had been polished up with a silk scarf. And the blues and greens of the plaid dress, a misty blue and a muted green. Clara had said all Mrs Gray's dresses came from Paris, and that she had a maid to help her on with her clothes.

'And nothing wrong with her neither?' Annie had cried.

'It's not true that we're all equal in the sight of God,' she told Clara now, as she dealt with one icy-cold foot then the other. 'Mrs Gray is more equal than any of us. I can't get over her. I really can't.'

'It's a sign that you're on your way out when your extremes go numb,' said Clara. 'I won't see Christmas.'

Margot Gray nurtured a guilty disappointment in her step-daughters. Her husband's first wife had possessed an hour-glass figure and a cameo-like prettiness, but by some unfortunate distribution of genes, both Dorothea and Abigail resembled their father, even to the florid face, hawk-like nose and thick-set body. Puddings, Margot considered them to be, with high fashion wasted on them. Their slow minds were attuned to horses, horses, horses and even, God help them, Harry's fine herd of pigs.

Her observant eye had taken in the slimness of Annie's waist and the voluptuous swell of her breasts in the too-tight dress. Given the right clothes and the right accent, of course, Adam's waif and stray could have every eligible bachelor for miles hovering on the doorstep.

The hair could be a problem, though. Margot clearly

159

remembered red-haired children being left to live out their days hidden away in workhouses because of the colour of their hair. She touched her own hair. God alone knew what colour hers would be without its weekly rinse of cold strong tea. She leaned closer to the tripled mirror on her dressing-table, pushing at the front of her hair, searching for any sign of greyness at the roots. The gardener's girl would almost certainly go a pure white if she lived to be old. Red-haired women were lucky in that way. Now she, if she let hers go the way nature intended, would be a dirty battleship grey. She shuddered.

Annie Clancy had intrigued her. Margot never listened to servants' gossip, naturally, but according to Dorothea they were saying down in the kitchen that the gardener's girl had been found wandering the roads without a possession to her name. Thrown out by a hill farmer who had got her pregnant and abandoned her.

Margot plucked out a suspect hair. But if that were true where was the baby? How had Adam got his puritanical wife to accept a fallen girl living in the cottage? It was all a great mystery.

Margot sighed. Middle-age was a bore. Old age she refused to contemplate. She lifted her chin and slapped it hard with the backs of her hands, wincing at the incipient double chin.

It would be interesting to know where young Annie Clancy had come from. Her accent had Margot puzzled. There was a refinement about it that conflicted with another story she'd heard that Annie was a product of the workhouse.

Thinking about the workhouse reminded her. What Margot saw as 'the servant problem' was a constant worry. She had been advised to write to the vicar's wife to ask if she knew of any village girl who would be willing to live in. A much more acceptable way of solving 'the servant problem' than applying direct to the nearest workhouse.

Margot couldn't bear the thought that she was getting

wrinkles round her mouth, but the mirror never lied. Maybe if she did her lip stretching exercises more often she could keep them at bay.

'Ee aw, ee aw, ee aw,' she said, doing them now.

She suddenly stopped in mid-stretch. If the gardener's girl hadn't come from the workhouse, why had she been running away? With nothing but the clothes she stood up in, according to one tale.

It was better than a story in one of the weekly magazines her parlour maid liked to read.

Biddy Baker missed Annie a lot.

She couldn't get over Annie leaving like that without saying a proper goodbye. Nothing in the house was quite the same somehow with no one to have a bit of a laugh with. Mr Armstrong was out all the hours that God sent, coming back cold and wet most days, slamming the door of his den behind him and forgetting to go to bed some nights, according to Mrs Martindale.

The old woman was a flamin' pain in the neck, always kow-towing to the animal doctor, fawning on him till his temper flared. Once or twice Biddy had wondered aloud how Annie Clancy was faring, only to have her head bitten off as if she'd said something too rude to repeat.

Biddy had made a lovely story up in her head. It went like this:

Annie Clancy turned up at the house one day dressed to kill, wearing a fur hat, a fur muff and kid gloves with a ribbon-trimmed green velvet dress. It turned out that down in London, in an antique shop, a locket had been found containing a silken strand of bright red hair. On the back of the locket was an inscription giving the name of a man related to royalty. The antique dealer had traced him and it had all come out that Annie was the daughter of the man's mistress. On his deathbed the old man had whispered a Lancashire address, and through this Annie had eventually been traced. No further proof was needed when the hair in the locket was matched to

161

Annie's hair, and from then on she was able to lead a life of luxury with her own carriage and servants to tend her every whim.

Biddy had always felt that Annie was a cut above herself and Mrs Martindale. She felt no rancour about this. Breeding would out any old day. Look how Mr Armstrong had taken to her, always teasing and talking with her, just as if he knew that deep down the pair of them came out of the same drawer. He'd never once asked Biddy to sit with him in his room, driving old Nellie mad. Biddy could quite see why. She hadn't a ladylike bone in her body – her own mother was always telling her that. 'You'd think you'd been dragged up instead of fetched up,' she was always saying.

Maybe if the story came true and Annie did turn up at the door swathed in velvet and fur, Mr Armstrong would take one look and fall madly in love with her. Seeing her for the first time as the aristocratic personage she really was. Personage . . . Biddy liked the sound of that word a lot. Mrs Martindale was a person. Biddy was a person. But Annie was a personage. Definitely.

One warm day when skylarks were singing high above the fields, a fox got into the outhouse and bit the heads off a newborn litter of kittens. The animal doctor sat up for two nights running, trying to nurse the grieving mother cat back to a semblance of normality.

Biddy thought he looked shocking and said so. 'He's not been the same since Annie Clancy went,' she said unwisely. 'I think he misses her. They were just getting really thick when she went.'

'Getting thick?' Nellie's neck flushed up like a scald. 'What an expression! You're beginning to talk like those magazines you read.'

'I might go and see Annie when I have my weekend off.' Biddy spread a layer of jam on a slice of bread. 'I'd like to know how she's getting on.'

'She's not at home,' Nellie said too quickly.

'Where, then?'

'I don't know. And I don't *want* to know.'

All at once Nellie made a snap decision. She knew Biddy Baker. The stupid girl would make a mystery out of nothing. Once she got her teeth into anything she never let go. Wiser to shut her up once and for all.

'I wasn't going to tell you this . . .' Biddy sat up straight, both ears flapping. '. . . but the truth is that Annie blotted her copy book good and proper the night before she left. That was why she went in such a hurry without saying a decent goodbye.'

'What did she do?' Biddy held her breath, hoping for the worst. 'She was in Mr Armstrong's room till late, wasn't she?'

'Exactly.' Nellie nodded her small head up and down three times. 'Exactly.'

Biddy put a hand to her mouth. 'You mean she . . . they . . . ?'

Nellie put up a hand. 'We don't talk about things like that. Especially at the table. Suffice to say that after that night Annie had no choice left to her but to leave in disgrace.'

'You mean *she* seduced *him*?' Biddy could hardly bear the excitement. 'An' he spurned her so that to save her face she had to go?' Her eyes were as round as pin-wheels. 'An' all the time he thinks it was his fault and he's no better than one of the animals he tends. An' why he's so bad-tempered and why he doesn't go to Manchester any more to see his fancy piece?'

'That will do! I've got my palpitations coming on again, and is it any wonder?' Nellie got up and held a hand to her flat bosom. 'I think I'll go for a lie down.'

Biddy went straight into the room at the end of the long hall. She couldn't get over it. Annie and Mr Armstrong, slaking their passion on the horse-hair sofa . . . She sat down and stroked its shiny prickly surface. The thought was so beautiful she could hardly bear it. She rocked herself to and fro, imagining . . .

Seth, from force of habit, made straight for the fire when he came in and the face Biddy turned to him was so vacant, so filled with longing, he asked her if she felt ill. If she did, then of course she must go up to her room until she felt better.

Biddy found it hard to close her mouth. How handsome he was. How romantic his profile. What a beautiful couple he and Annie would make. She slid from the sofa and backed towards the door.

'Mrs Martindale and me were talking about Annie Clancy earlier on,' she said, watching his face for the slightest hint of emotion. 'Mrs Martindale says Annie never went home.'

He turned away so fast Biddy could only guess his expression.

'And does Mrs Martindale know where she is now?'

Surely his voice shook? Biddy felt a prickle up her spine. 'She says not, sir.' She slipped round the door. 'I'm very sorry, sir.'

Seth stared hard at the door after Biddy had closed it behind her, then wrenched it open, calling down the hall in a voice that had Biddy all of a tremble.

'Mrs Martindale! Will you come here, please?'

In the kitchen Biddy clasped her hands together across her disappointingly flat chest. He was fired with thwarted passion – it was there, in his whole manner. Mrs Martindale *did* know where Annie was. Biddy hadn't been born yesterday. Nor the day before that, neither. The old bag knew something she was keeping to herself.

'Annie Clancy!' Seth went straight into the attack. 'Why didn't you tell me where she is?'

Nellie turned her head towards the door as if she sensed someone listening outside. 'Who said . . .' Her eyes were wary. 'I never . . .'

'I've found out exactly where she is!' Seth lied, his voice entirely devoid of emotion. 'All I want to know is if she's happy there?'

164

'She's all right, sir.'

'You've heard from her?' Seth sat down at his desk, picked up a paper-weight and held it lightly in one hand. 'Is she well?'

Nellie swallowed. 'Quite well, sir.'

'Kind to her, are they?'

'Oh, yes, sir.' The soft rhythm of the conversation had Nellie bemused. 'Lily Eccles is a second cousin of mine. She . . .'

The desk chair was sent spinning as Seth sprang to his feet. 'Lily Eccles? Barney Eccles's wife?'

Too late Nellie realised she'd been taken in. Mr Armstrong hadn't known where Annie was, and now he looked ready to throw the glass paper-weight at her. She clenched her hands, turned and walked with controlled dignity out into the hall.

Seth started after her, then stopped. He had to get a hold of himself first before he shook her or slapped her thin sallow face. Barney Eccles! A sharp pain stabbed at the side of his head. There wasn't a woman this side of fifty safe from the hill farmer's groping, filthy hands. Sitting down again at his desk he buried his head in his hands.

And he'd *been* there! Back in April. He had stood with Barney in that filthy yard, itching to get away once he'd seen to the cow. And all the time Annie was there, somewhere in the house, or out in the fields. Living with that awful woman and her sticky brood.

He remembered too the inexplicable ache of sadness as he'd ridden away. As though he was being called back.

Suddenly he hurled the paper-weight at the stone fireplace, striding from the room as it splintered into tiny pieces.

'What have you been saying to Mr Armstrong?' Nellie Martindale was breathing as fast as if she'd run a mile.

Biddy feigned total amazement. 'Me? Mr

Armstrong?' She opened her eyes wide at the house-keeper, who looked as white as a sheet. 'I don't know what you mean.'

Whatever Mrs Martindale had been going to say was left unsaid as the kitchen door slammed back so hard that little flakes of plaster dropped from the ceiling.

'At first light,' the vet shouted, looking like the wrath of God, 'I am going to ride over to the Eccles's farm and bring Annie back with me. When I arrive I expect to find you gone, Mrs Martindale. Out of my sight, out of this house. Do you understand?' With that he turned on his heel and made for the door.

Biddy gasped at the sight of the prim and proper Mrs Martindale rushing after her employer, yelling like a common fishwife.

'It was *you* what upset Annie Clancy. *You* what made her run upstairs and bolt her door against you! You think you can put the blame on me, but you can't! I was listening.' She followed him right out into the hall. 'It was to protect her from you that I sent her away!'

With every shouted word her voice rose higher and higher. Biddy felt she would die with the thrill of the drama enfolding before her eyes. A *real* drama this time.

'You mustn't upset yourself, Mrs Martindale,' she said insincerely, as the housekeeper staggered back into the kitchen, clutching her heart.

She wasn't even heard.

'You've been nothing but trouble since you first came to this house! You're a lazy, stupid, wicked girl. I hope you're satisfied with what you've done.'

The first slap rocked Biddy's head back on her shoulders, the second knocked her off her feet. The carving knife was on the table. Biddy scrambled to her feet. She wouldn't put anything past the crazed woman with the staring eyes and the bun of hair coming undone. But the housekeeper was wailing, her mouth wide open, all control gone.

'He doesn't mean it, Mrs Martindale,' Biddy said,

166

accepting that this time her imagination had perhaps exceeded even its own brief. 'When he comes back with Annie things will settle down and be just the same.'

But things would never be the same, and Biddy knew it. She got behind the table, putting its width between her and the housekeeper. The anger was draining from the thin pointed face, leaving in its place a terrible, unacceptable despair.

Lily Eccles would never to her dying day forget the sight of the vet striding into the house and demanding to see Barney. Lily had always known that Seth Armstrong was a big man, but at that moment he looked at least seven feet tall.

'Where's Annie?' He strode to the foot of the stairs and shouted: 'Annie Clancy?'

The three kids playing with a half-chewed mouse on the dirty floor were open-mouthed, round-eyed with astonishment. Not frightened, never that. How could they be when loud yelling voices had filled their days since they were born.

'Annie's gone,' Lily told him. 'She run off a while back.' Her eyes turned sly. 'Barney tried his old tricks on her and she was off like a skelped rabbit.'

'Where to?' The unwashed pots on the table jumped in the air as he brought the flat of his hand down hard. 'Tell me where she's gone.'

'How should *I* know?' Lily had found a place underneath her right armpit in urgent need of a scratch. 'That's Barney just passed the window. Ask *him* where she's gone.'

Lily thought about it afterwards. She didn't exactly want Mr Armstrong to kill her husband, but when Barney was lifted clean off his feet and held dangling there for a minute before being on the receiving end of a blow that sent him flying across the room, to land up sliding down the wall with blood streaming from his nose, she supposed she had quite enjoyed it. It got better, too, as the vet yanked her husband to his feet, frog-marched him out of the door, across the yard to the pump where he worked the handle so violently that within seconds Barney was soaking wet, gasping for breath.

Then he leapt astride that great black horse of his and galloped off, going faster, Lily was sure, than the wind itself.

When Barney crept into the house, dripping water, slinking upstairs like a whipped dog, Lily was hard put to it not to laugh.

But thought better of it.

Biddy wasn't in the least surprised when Mr Armstrong came back without Annie and shut himself in his den, not going to bed at all that night.

She *was* surprised when he told Mrs Martindale the next day that she could stay until she found another place, just as long as she kept out of his way. The animal doctor might have a temper on him as bad as old Nick's, but he would never throw an old woman out on her heels. Biddy told herself she should have known that.

But Nellie Martindale couldn't accept those conditions. For her master to treat her with coldness would have destroyed her slowly, piece by piece. So when her sister in Padiham had a stroke and sent word that she was having a job to manage, Nellie took it as a sign from above, packed her things and was gone within the week.

Leaving Biddy to muddle through as best she could.

10

On a warm muggy day Mick Malone was called in to repair the lean-to coal shed at the back of the Clancys' house. After the job was done he stood on the pavement talking to his distant cousin, the second Mrs Clancy, Florrie Greenhalgh that was.

'There's a long-nosed woman two doors down sweeping her flags. Haven't I seen her carrying the banner on last week's Bank of Hope march?'

'More than likely,' Florrie said. Her plump arms were folded across the front of a none too clean apron. Now and again as they talked, she moved aside to let a boy with ragged trousers and uncombed hair slip past her into the street. 'That's Edith Morris.' She tapped the side of her head. 'Daft as that brush she's sweeping up with. She was going to be a missionary looking for heathens to pray over. Now she's set on finding young Annie, the silly beggar.'

'Young Annie? Annie Clancy?' Mick's tangled eyebrows merged together as he frowned with the intensity of his struggle to think coherently. 'She got herself into trouble and ran off, didn't she?'

Florrie waited until Edith had gone inside and closed her front door. 'Young Annie was given her marching orders by her father. He couldn't stand the sight of her – used to break out in a sweat when she came in the room, especially after he found out she was expecting.' She lifted a pendulous breast to ease herself. 'He won't have her name mentioned now.'

'A hard man, Florrie. How did you come to marry a man like that?'

'I could've done a lot worse for meself, Mick. Though there's not many men who would send their only

169

daughter to the workhouse. Poor little lass.'

'Well, I'll be off,' Mick said, doing a little sideways shuffle before moving off down the street. 'Tara, Florrie.'

Thinking always bothered Mick. He avoided doing it as much as possible, but mention of the workhouse never failed to upset him. He could bring tears to his eyes just with thinking about it.

It wasn't until he was sitting with a second pint of ale in front of him, the first pint nicely settled in his stomach, that he allowed his memories to come creeping back.

'Aw right, Mick?' An old crone sitting in a corner wearing a man's cap skewered to her head with hat-pins, shouted across to him.

'Fair to middlin',' Mick said back.

'Coming o'er here?' She patted the seat beside her.

Mick shook his head.

'Suit yoursen',' she said.

Mick gloomed at the stippled wall in front of him. It was no wonder that even a mention of the workhouse depressed him. His father had brought Mick and his brother over from County Cork, only to break both his legs during his first week's work as a carter for a brewery firm. The firm said it was his own fault, that he hadn't handled his horses properly, so he got no compensation, and within a month he was dead.

Mick took a reflective sip of his ale. His mother had worked and slaved to keep them out of the workhouse, going out cleaning, taking in washing – anything. They moved from the two-up two-down house they were renting to a single room infested with cockroaches. Mick could remember his mother shaking their clothes to get rid of them. She had even tried to work as a street trader, selling kippers at a penny a pair, until so many customers wanted them on tick she couldn't carry on.

They had walked to the workhouse. Mick and his brother holding on to his mother's hands. It was a walk Mick would never forget, not ever, no matter how long he lived.

The pauper's uniform of drabette coat, check neck-cloth and fustian trousers had filled him with horror. At eight years old he was given the job of carrying tools for one of the stone-breakers, an old man crippled with rheumatism, hardly capable of holding his hammers as he struggled to break down block stone to road-metal size.

When the old man died out on the fells with the rain beating down on his face, Mick had turned his back on the road leading to the workhouse and walked away, to live rough for the next three years, stealing, scrounging and begging where he could, until at twelve he had let on his luck and got a job living in on a farm.

He clenched his big hands on the table in front of him. But young Annie Clancy *hadn't* ended up in the work-house, had she? So he was moithering himself and getting upset about nothing at all.

He'd seen her. He was sure of it. When had he seen her? Where had he seen her? The eyebrows mingled again as he forced himself to concentrate. When the answer came to him, he banged his fist hard on the table. Barney Eccles! The run-down farm on the high hill, with kids being dragged up in conditions not fit for animals. Barney's wife, Lily, with a face like a witch, and a soul even blacker. Married to that terrible man who was so mean it was said he would pinch the pennies off his dead grandma's eyes.

Mick punched his forehead with his fist as if to beat out the explanation he was groping for. Knowing that young Annie's father wouldn't thank him for news of her, but trying to bring to mind someone who would.

Edith Morris was in two minds whether to let him in when he knocked on her door. She recognised him, of course. Most folks knew Mick Malone, the odd-job man who would turn his hand to anything you asked him to do in return for a meal or a few coppers. Besides, she'd seen him talking to Annie's step-mother not above an hour ago, so most likely he was looking for work.

'I've nothing needs doing, thank you, Mick,' she said. making a move to close the door.

Mick snatched off his cap at the sight of this handsome woman with cotton-flecked hair who looked every inch the lady. All the way up the street he'd been planning what to say, and how to say it, fearful lest he was poking his nose in where it wasn't wanted.

'I'd like a word, Miss,' he managed at last. 'About young Annie Clancy.'

When he'd gone, Edith climbed the narrow stairs to her bedroom and knelt at the altar she'd made from a small table covered by a purple cloth. She spoke directly to the wooden cross.

'Thank You for sending Thy messenger with the news I've been waiting for. Forgive me for despairing and forgetting to trust.' She got up from her knees. 'Let it be fine on Sunday when I go to fetch her back.'

Mick Malone spent a lot of time that week trying hard to think what to do for the best. The neatness of Miss Morris's front room and the spotless cleanliness of herself stayed in his mind. You couldn't live the whole of your life moving from one hostel, one lodging to another, without appreciating the sight and feel of a proper home. From the gleaming fire brasses to the magnificent aspidistra in its blue bowl, he doubted if he'd ever seen a more inviting or better furnished room.

'You mean you've never had a home of your own?' Miss Morris had looked flabbergasted.

'I'm of no fixed abode, Miss,' Mick had told her proudly, quoting the description of himself in the paper the time he was up in front of the magistrates for being drunk in charge of a three-wheeled truck. 'No fixed abode,' he'd said again.

'I'm coming with you to the Eccles's farm,' Mick said straight out when Edith opened the door to him. 'I've been thinking, an' it's no place . . .' He shuffled his feet, stared down at them. 'For a lady,' he finished.

'You'd better come in.' Edith opened the door wide, trying not to show her pleasure. She accepted that she was indeed a lady. Her mother before her had been one, and her mother before her, but this was the first time she'd been told it straight out.

Mick Malone was a rough diamond of a man, but he had been so kind when she'd broken down and cried tears of joy on being told that he knew where to find young Annie Clancy. There was a gentleness about him and a way he had of coming out with something so unexpected it caught at the throat.

'I've been sick to my heart at the thought of you going up yon on your own,' he was saying now, accepting the chair by the fire and stretching out his long legs to the blaze. 'There's a wind that cuts through to the bones, and besides, Barney Eccles has a tongue on him as filthy as the Thursday night shit-cart.'

Edith didn't even flinch. 'Do you read your Bible every day, Mick?'

'Never been learned how to read, Miss. Never stopped in one place for long enough to have anywhere to keep a book.'

'So you've grown up without knowing Jesus, without having Him as your friend?' Edith leaned forward eagerly, flushing like a girl at the thought of bringing the Word to this plum-nosed, cheerful, hairy man who needed her as much, if not more, than the black heathens in far away Africa.

It looked as if her loneliness was coming to an end, for she would teach him to read, and when they brought Annie and the baby back with them on Sunday her joy would be complete.

The carrier hadn't minded giving Miss Morris a lift. He thought she gave his cart a bit of tone, sitting up beside him on the seat, but Mick Malone was another thing altogether.

173

Didn't Miss Morris know that Mick had been scraped up from the floor of all the ale houses from here to Rishton? Couldn't she see that he'd swipe the smile off your face if that was all you had left? Look at the conk on him for a start. If he was bled it would be beer coming out of him, not blood.

Surely, if what he had heard was right, Miss Morris had carried a banner in the Band of Hope. Wasn't she a temperance reciter down at the Mission Hall every Tuesday night, warning people of the evils of drink? In verse? She was right set up today about something, no mistaking that.

'We'll be there waiting to be picked up at the time you suggest,' she was saying. 'The four of us.' She was bobbing about on the seat like a young girl. 'I don't suppose you remember young Annie Clancy? Used to live in the same street as me.'

The carrier raised his eyebrows. 'Seeing as 'ow I dropped her off along this very stretch of road, I should remember her. Poor little beggar. I couldn't get a word out of her that day, though she told me she was going to work for a couple with a new bairn in one of those cottages over there.' He pointed with his whip. 'You can see the smoke rising up by that line of trees. Shall I stop for you to have a proper look?'

'No need. We know she didn't end up there.'

'Poor little beggar,' said Mick Malone, sitting up straight with his cap clutched tight in his ham-shank hands. 'It must have taken her the best part of a day to walk to where she did end up.' .

'She'll be safe now,' Miss Morris said, and actually patted one of Mick's corduroyed knees. 'The Lord is guiding us to her, Mick.'

'Amen,' said Mick, his beer-stained moustache quivering with an emotion that the carrier mistrusted with every fibre of his being.

'She's there, Mick! She's there!'

Edith had thought the climb up the rough winding road to the farm at the top would finish her off. The searching wind had already whipped her hat half off and whirled her skirts up round her ankles. She stopped to catch her breath and pointed to where a small girl was scattering feed to a dozen or so scrawny hens.

'See, there she is! Annie!' Her normal reserve tossed on the wind, Edith ran off the road and across the field, holding out her arms. 'Annie! It's me, Miss Morris. Come to take you home . . .'

But the slightly built young girl turning round to face them wasn't Annie. Was nothing like Annie.

This girl had a tiny wizened face of a heartbroken monkey. But she was wearing a blouse Edith had seen before, made out of a remnant of black cloth patterned with blue circles. She even remembered Annie's mother coming home in triumph from the market with the yard and a half of material marked down to sixpence.

'You're wearing Annie Clancy's clothes!' Edith's voice rang out like a clarion call. 'Where is she?' She grabbed a wrist as thin as a twig. 'Why are you wearing clothes that don't belong to you? Who are you?'

With a surprising strength the girl upped with her boot and gave Edith a kick that sent her sprawling, gathered up her skirts and ran, head bent, towards the farmhouse.

Mick helped Edith to her feet, brushing her muddied skirts down with his hand, looking with dismay into her white face and her eyes wide and black with shock.

'Holy Mary, Mother of God!' he soothed. 'Come away with me now, Miss. This is a terrible place to be. It's not for the likes of you. Just you get yourself down to the bottom road, and leave me to deal with them evil sods up at the farm.' He balled huge hands into fists. 'If Barney Eccles has laid as much as a finger on your young Annie I'll smash his ugly mug to a bloody pulp. I'll separate his breath from his body, Jaysus that I will.'

Edith flinched, but there was time enough to correct

his unfortunate use of blasphemy. All she knew was that she wasn't for letting the big fella go up to the farm on his own.

'Follow me, Mick,' she ordered, leading the way. 'Remember the Lord is with us, so we have nothing to fear.'

'No, Miss Morris.'

Mick looked up at the lowering sky and crossed himself. As an extra precaution.

No matter that she went back down the hill a lot faster than she'd gone up it. No matter that Lily Eccles was waving her arms about and shouting obscenities at them, yelling that it was the second time her husband had been felled with a single blow. First by Seth Armstrong and now by Mick, leaving his eyes rolling in his head as he lay stunned and bloodied on the floor.

'What's he supposed to have done?' she screamed. 'He never laid a finger on Annie Clancy. I can vouch for that. What the 'ell is he supposed to have done?'

'The wicked shall fall by his own wickedness!' Edith turned to shout back at her. 'They shall perish . . . they shall be as the fat of lambs; they shall consume; into smoke shall they consume away!'

But after that Mick could see that the wind and fire seemed to have gone from her.

'What a silly woman I am.'

'That you're not, Miss.'

'I am, Mick. How could I be foolish enough to think that Annie would be there with her baby, ready to run upstairs to get her things the minute I stepped over the doorstep.' She shook her head slowly from side to side. 'She was always such a bright, loving girl. Now God alone knows where she is. You must think I'm a proper gobbin.'

They were sitting side by side on a low stone wall waiting for the carrier's cart. Mick thought that Miss Morris suited her hair all wispy like that, with little curly bits escaping from the neat little bun. Couldn't she see that he felt it a privilege just to be out with her? As for her being a gobbin, nay, the only gobbin sat on that wall was himself.

'You'll find Annie one of these days, Miss. She can't have run far without her bloody belongings.'

'Don't swear in front of me, please, Mick. There's always better words to use than swear ones.' Edith turned and spoke directly to the glowing nose. 'Though I can't thank you enough for sticking up for me in front of that terrible man, and that dirty woman.'

Mick spat on his swollen knuckles and gave them a good rub on a trouser leg. 'I've allus wanted the chance of giving Barney Eccles a good pasting. He's known for miles around for being a bad lot. There's more little butter-nobs running round the countryside than you've had hot dinners.'

'Mick!'

'Sorry, Miss.' Somehow he couldn't wipe the smile off his face.

Miss had asked him to stop to his tea last night after she'd given him his reading lesson, and a wonderful meal it had been. His mouth watered at the memory of it. First Miss had piled his plate with tater pie, with a crust on it that melted in the mouth, then she'd given him a dish of creamy rice pudding thick with sultanas and a nice topping of nutmeg to give the brown skin a bit of flavour. To go with his pot of tea, she'd buttered him a decent sized wedge of oven-bottom cake.

Was he wicked for being glad they weren't taking Annie Clancy back with them? Miss Morris would have no time for him with young Annie and a baby there. He plucked a blade of grass and began to chew on it, wrinkling his forehead in an agony of concentration. Barney Eccles had laughed his socks off when Miss had mentioned a baby. Told her there'd never been one. Roaring and yelling, slapping his thighs, he had laughed till tears came in his blood-shot eyes. It was then that

Mick had come to the conclusion that force might have to be used. He spat on the bruised knuckles on his right hand. He had no idea how things would turn out. For Miss's satisfaction he had searched every corner of the farmhouse, but Annie Clancy wasn't there. He believed Barney's wife when she insisted that Annie had run away. Nobody should linger in a place like that. He glanced sideways at Miss.

'It pained me to see you in yon house,' he said. 'You were like a rose in a muck-midden.'

She smiled at him, patted his arm, making Mick want to leap from the wall and go running down the lane, waving his arms about like the true gobbin he was. Not much had ever gone right for Mick Malone, but there was one thing he knew – that never, in the whole of his bloody life had he been as happy as he was at that moment. Pardon his French, of course.

The long summer months lay ahead of him, filled with Miss giving him lessons, talking to him across plates of steaming tater pie about the love of Jesus. He'd landed butter side up this time, right enough.

In September the leaves on Adam's rose bushes curled in on themselves and were tipped with brown. In the far meadow crane-flies with wings of gauze and trailing legs hung suspended in the still air.

On a warm day Annie saw a bat in swooping flight as she walked back from taking Adam's dinner to the big barn where he was helping to stack the bales of straw for winter feeding. Clara said that seeing the bat was a bad sign, and later in the afternoon she remarked that the sun was going pale to bed. 'So 'twill rain tomorrow, it is said.' She gave an extra deep sigh.

In the past weeks the flesh seemed to have dropped from her. She wore her neck shawl all day, coughed her hard dry cough, and when Annie tried to feed her, turned her head away so that the sweetened gruel ran in rivulets down her chin.

178

'I've not long to go,' she said, over and over again. 'I won't be here at Christmas,' she warned. 'You promise me you'll stay with Adam till then?'

Promises, promises.

One misty morning Clara asked to be helped upstairs to her bed, lay down on it with a quiet resignation and quietly died. Adam was distraught, totally bewildered. He stood at the foot of the bed and stared at his wife lying there with the colour drained from her cheeks, her hands crossed over the front of her best nightgown.

'She told me that often she was on her last,' he said, 'but somehow I never thought it would happen.' He banged his fist on the bed-rail. 'You know why she died? You know why we never had no children? Because she was dragged up, not brought up, that's why!' The collie dog crept into the room to nuzzle his nose into Adam's hand. 'The wife was half-starved when I first saw her.' His voice was choked with tears. 'Her father came home drunk one Friday night after supping most of his wages away, lay down in a stupor on the rug and pegged out. Her mother went off with a man who couldn't stomach children, and Clara and her young sister lived with a so-called decent woman who took them in because she could work them to death filling match-boxes. She kept them in a room no bigger than the outside privy and when the young one died she . . .'

'Come away, Mr Page. Come down to the fire.' Annie took him by the arm. 'She's out of it all now. She's finished with her pain. Look how peaceful she is.'

He stumbled behind Annie down the steep narrow stairway. 'That's why she couldn't see the bright side of things. Because there'd never been a bright bloody side for her to see!'

It was the first time Annie had heard the gardener swear. She hoped it did him good. Anger was better any old day than the numbing misery that had clouded Clara's thinking, day in and day out.

'I'll make you a cup of tea, Mr Page,' she said.

'The house that woman lived in was no bigger than a dog kennel! And the place Clara and her sister worked in . . .' He spread his hands wide. 'Room for a table for them to work at, but no room for chairs. They stood up all day long and well into the night, working with candles. Lily was half-blind, Annie, you guessed that?'

'Here's your tea. Drink it while it's hot.'

'She went as a doffer in a weaving shed when she got away from that woman. She was that small, that under-nourished, she once told me she sweated cobs of fear when she walked between the looms, the space was that narrow . . .'

'Have a little sip, Mr Page.'

'Is it any wonder she never laughed? The laughter had been all kicked out of her a long time ago. An' what good was I to her, going out of the cottage before she got up, coming back most nights when she was ready for bed? Too tired to be much company to her, eating the food she set before me on the table, but never thinking to tell her how much I enjoyed it. Taking her for granted all the time, letting her wait on me hand and foot even when she wasn't fit . . .'

His hand trembled so much that Annie took the cup away from him. When he began to weep with harsh dry sobs, she left him alone with his grief.

On the day of Clara's funeral the rain held off until the late afternoon. Dressed in Clara's grey serge dress and jacket, hastily trimmed with bands of black crêpe, Annie walked by Adam's side behind the cart carrying the wooden box to the churchyard. She kept her fingers lightly on his arm in case he stumbled in the deeply rutted lane, but he gave no sign that he even knew she was there.

As they stood together by the open grave, a carriage drew up, its horse brasses jingling and sparkling in a sudden spell of sunlight. Annie watched from beneath lowered eyelashes as Mrs Gray and her two step-

180

daughters walked across the grass, closely followed by a pot-bellied man wearing a greatcoat patterned in grey and black checks.

When Annie looked up and caught his eye the wink he gave her almost sent her toppling into the open grave, so from then on she kept her glance firmly fixed on Clara's old boots padded at the toes to make them a more or less reasonable fit.

What a peculiar family they were! One quick glance had convinced Annie that Clara had been right about the girls. They looked like men dressed up as women, the frills and flounces and ruched ribbons on their hats only adding to the impression. It looked as if the Mediterranean sun had got at their noses too.

Annie felt shame wash over her at thinking such thoughts at a time like this, and especially at the way her mind wouldn't settle on more serious things. Why was that? It wasn't because she hadn't liked Clara Page, because she had. She'd even managed to make her laugh once or twice and that was no mean feat.

Maybe it was because today was the day when, all things being equal, she would have been standing at the door of her father's house looking down the street for the sight of Laurie turning the corner, keeping his promise to come for her on her birthday. To honour the vows they'd made in the sight of God. Her lip curled. How young she'd been then. How trusting and ready to believe in people. She even believed in God at that time.

'Dust to dust, ashes to ashes.'

Annie risked a quick glance upwards and thought that the minister looked as if he was on the wrong side of his breakfast.

'Seems like Adam's let on his feet. That's a bonny lass he's got for himself.'

Margot Gray sat bolt upright in the carriage for the short ride back home, trying not to look at the girls slumped across from her, frilled as brothel-keepers, and

181

talking, she guessed, about pig-swill or horse manure.

'You're wrong, Harry.' She turned to look through the window. 'That bonny lass isn't for anybody but herself.'

'She was wearing one of your old hats, Mama.'

'With her hair pinned up underneath it like a beehive, Mama.'

'I gave it to Clara years ago. Because you said you hated me wearing black.'

'I *hate* black,' Harry Gray said. 'Especially on women. Makes them look like a lot of old crows. Which reminds me, the rooks have returned to the rookery. Seemingly overnight.'

Annie knew that folks were saying that she was living over the brush with the gardener. How they could even think such a thing was beyond her, when they must know for a fact that he was old enough to be her father. Anyway, since his wife's death he had gone about as if he carried a heavy parcel of misery on his back. It had taken her all her time to persuade him to sit down at the table and eat. It took even more nagging to get him to change his clothes, and as for his hands . . .

'Muck is muck,' she told him firmly. 'It can come from down the pit or from the soil, but it's still the same. *Muck.* It was hard work forcing the lads at home to wash their hands before they came to the table.' Her eyes clouded. 'My dad never bothered. He used to say we'd all to eat a ton of dirt before we died, anyroad.' Using the tips of her fingers she rubbed lard into the bowl of flour. 'I swore I'd never go back, but mebbe one day . . . just to see how they are.'

Adam was at the open door of the cottage, brushing his dog's moulting coat. 'You can't go back,' he said quickly. 'It would only upset you, and besides, that woman your dad married won't want you now any more than she did then.' He looked anxious. 'You're all right here, aren't you?'

'I'm more than all right here, Mr Page. Looking after

you and this cottage is nowt-a-penny to what it was when I lived at home. D'you know what me mother would have said?'

'No.' Adam went on brushing the dog's tail. 'What would she have said, Annie?'

'You've let on your feet there, Annie Clancy!'

When she laughed he put the brush down and stared hard at her. For a whole week now there had been a thick dank mist filling the valley like smoke in the mornings, and he was pretty sure the swallows had left. The harvest was safely gathered in and soon, unless the ploughed land dried out, the land work would begin. He had always been a man who liked his home comforts, and with Annie around the place he accepted that he had never been looked after as well in the whole of his marriage. In the whole of his life, in fact. Clara had done her best, but even before she took really ill she was always a bit slap-dash about housework and baking. Now this young lass, she'd have him in the dolly-tub on washday if he wasn't careful.

'There!' she was saying now. 'You've smiled and your face hasn't cracked – wonders never cease!'

Her arms were flour-spattered, there was a blob of it on her nose. Months of good food, mostly from the garden, had brought a healthy glow to her cheeks and made her eyes sparkle. Adam looked away from her and frowned at the handfuls of hair coming away from the dog's lifeless coat.

Annie poured just enough warmed water into the larded flour. 'To tell the truth, I've never had such an easy life. I can clean through in a day, and even sit down and read a book when I've a liking to. If I'd ever been on my holidays, I'm sure this is what it would be like.' She tipped the bowl so that the flour came from the sides and began pummelling it into a dough. 'If I'd been a boy, I know I'd never have gone down the mine to work.' She gave him a shrewd glance. 'It would have finished you straight off, Mr Page, you being a man of the soil.' She thumped the dough down onto the table. 'Oh, I knew

183

there were fields and hills not far off, but I always played out in the street like everybody else when I was little. After my mother died there wasn't the time for going walks in the country.' She blew a strand of hair away from her hot face. 'Five brothers take some seeing to, Mr Page. I was for ever mending their britches and darning their jumpers, and what I baked went down their throats as quick as it came out of the oven. On top of all that, my father had to bring a lodger home one day.'

Adam sat back on his haunches, the niggling worry in his mind that there was something sadly wrong with the dog forgotten. Clara had never been a one for chattering, and it was pleasant to sit back on his heels and listen to Annie's light young voice going on and on.

'You know about the travelling man, Mr Page?'

'Aye. Clara told me.' He wished Annie hadn't brought it up. He hadn't wanted to hear about it when Clara had explained why Annie had run away from home, and he wanted to hear about it even less now. The thought of Annie and some gyppo from God knows where – the very thought turned his stomach. She was so young; she had such an untouched look about her. God forgive him for comparing her to Clara, but beside his wife she was all freshness and joy. Clara never saw the bright side of owt. If the sun shone she said it overheated her blood, and if the wind blew it gave her a headache. He lowered his head. Annie would go away soon, there was nothing more certain. Leaving him alone.

'Some men aren't made to manage on their own.' He was talking as if to himself. 'They need a woman about the place.' He stood up slowly. 'I'm one of those men, Annie.'

'You're right about that.' She laughed out loud again. 'I reckon you'd burn a pot of tea if you tried to brew one for yourself. You're as much use around the house as a rubber hammer.' She was enjoying the feel of the dough in her hands, he could tell, kneading it with her fists, turning it over and kneading it again.

184

'Would you ever think of marrying me, lass?' he whispered.

At once Annie swung round, staring at him with wide startled eyes, the laughter silenced. 'You, Mr Page?' She backed away, bits of dough dripping from her fingers on to the floor. 'But you're . . .' her voice faltered, but he knew what she had been going to say.

His hands tightened on the dog's brush. 'It's all right, lass. I'm not going to touch you. An' I know what you're thinking.' He walked to his chair by the fire and sat down. 'You think I'm soft in the head because of Clara dying. You think I don't know what I'm saying. You think I'm too old, but forty-five isn't old. You wait till you're that age and you'll know.' His ruddy complexion deepened. 'I wouldn't expect you to sleep in my bed, Annie. Not till you'd got used to me, used to being married. I'd leave you be, lass. God knows I've had enough practice at that in the last few years.'

Annie reached for a towel and wiped her hands. Clara's death had turned his brain. It must have. He was taking a plug of tobacco from the jar on the mantelpiece now, cutting it into pieces with his pocket-knife before rubbing it into flakes between his hands, a simple homely gesture she'd seen him make over and over again. Did he realise what he'd just said?

'I'll have to go away if you talk like this, Mr Page.' Annie looked round the room with its shining brasses and polished dresser. 'I love this cottage, and I get on well with you, Mr Page, but it's not like . . . Look, I don't want to have to go away, not just yet, but if you talk like this I'll have to go. You're spoiling things, Mr Page. I wish you'd never . . .'

'Come with me, Annie.' He got up from the chair so abruptly it startled her into backing away. At the foot of the stairs he held out a hand and smiled. 'Come on! I've not gone mad in spite of what you think. Aw, come on, lass. I'm not going to touch you.'

Reluctantly, Annie followed him up the narrow

185

stairway, hesitating at the door of his bedroom, but he was over by the window, down on his knees, prising up a floorboard with the knife he'd been using for cutting tobacco not five minutes before.

'Over here, Annie . . . over here.'

He pulled hard at a loose board and, moving into the room, Annie saw how it had been sawn into a short length, so that when it was lifted it revealed a gaping hole. Adam sat back on his heels holding a bag tied together at the top with garden twine.

'Kneel down here beside me, Annie.'

The knot in the twine needed picking at before he could open the bag. Slowly he upended it, to let a shower of sovereigns cascade down into Annie's lap. They fell in a shining heap, more money than Annie had ever dreamed could exist. She put her hand to her mouth.

'Oh, my God! Shove it back, Mr Page!' She began to scoop up the coins. 'Put that bag back!' She was so shocked she hardly knew what she was saying or doing. 'Hide it away again. Oh, dear God! I wish you'd never showed me that. There's a king's ransom there!'

'Annie!' Adam couldn't have wished for a better reaction. 'Every penny is come by honest. There's a lifetime's savings there – my father's as well as mine.' He bit hard on a coin and beamed. 'Every penny saved for the bag, Annie. When you can live off the land, with rabbits for the snaring, eggs from the hens, and vegetables from the garden, you're never short of a bob or two to put by. I've been a saver since I was old enough to tell a tanner from a florin.' He bared large creamy teeth and Annie recoiled.

How had she come to think that he was a generous man? Not a penny in wages had she been given since she came to the cottage. Come to think of it, she never remembered him spending a penny on anything at all. If it didn't come from the garden, if it couldn't be dug up free from the soil, it didn't come into the cottage.

'I wish you'd never showed it to me.' Annie scooped

186

up the last remaining coins and handed them back to him. 'When you wouldn't bring the doctor to Mrs Page I thought it was because you couldn't afford him; when you never offered me any wages I was just grateful to work for you for bed and my keep.' She stood up and backed towards the door. 'I know the condition of your wife's clothes because I'm wearing them. Rags! Patched that often it's a job to see what they were like when new. But the worst thing of all was you seeing your wife shivering by a fire no bigger than a match flame, an' I thought it was because you couldn't afford the coal to bank it up with.'

She ran down the stairs, leaned against the table catching her breath for a moment, then picked up the dough and took out her feelings on it. Trying to pound away the sight of the crouching man upstairs gloating over his savings, letting them run through his fingers, smiling at them with his big teeth. She slapped the dough down so hard that two one-pound loaf tins rose in the air in protest. She could hear a hammering upstairs and pictured the floorboard being banged into place and the rug placed over it again.

When Adam came downstairs he placed five gold sovereigns on the flour-dusted table.

'I didn't mean to upset you, lass.'

He was the man she thought she'd known again. Soft-spoken, quick and quiet in his movements, edging towards the door as if he couldn't wait to get out into his beloved fresh air. Annie saw with amazement that his face was filled with satisfied pleasure at his giving.

'Next week, when the carrier calls up at the house, I want you to ride with him as far as Blackburn, and I want you to take this money with you and buy yourself a new dress and hat. *Two* dresses and *two* new hats, if you've a mind.'

He was at the door in two strides, obviously well pleased with himself. As he walked down the path Annie heard him whistling, an obviously reluctant dog at his heels.

187

She had to sit down to get a grip on herself. The sovereigns were there on the table. One, two, three, four, five of them. Hers if she wanted them. Leaning forward, she picked them up and wiped them on her apron. With money like this her mother could have had meat and eggs and milk to build her up after John was born. With money like this to spend on doctors and medicines Clara Page might never have died. A sudden picture of her hunched on the edge of the horse-hair sofa, clutching the threadbare neck shawl round her throat, coughing her life away, misted Annie's eyes.

She thought of her husband's shining eyes as he handed her the money and anger rose up, heating her whole body, flushing her face. There were places where consumptives could be nursed, special hospitals where the patients could lie in bed all day to rest their lungs. What rest had poor Mrs Page had till she came along? And what about Annie Clancy – so grateful to be taken in that she worked for nothing, worn cast-off clothes no self-respecting pawnbroker would look at.

With a sudden movement Annie threw the sovereigns to the far end of the room. Then asked herself why she hadn't hurled them to the back of the fire? The Annie she used to be would have done just that. The Annie she used to be had a temper the colour of her hair and would have felt a certain dignity in refusing to spend such money.

Annie stood up and stretched out her arms, stretched them wide in the shape of a cross. 'Oh, Mother! My poor misguided little mother, who set such store on dignity. What does that matter compared to sticking up for yourself and fighting for what you believe to be right? You wouldn't have touched money saved at the expense of a dying woman, not you.' She lowered her arms. 'But I am not you, Mother. I am me, Annie Clancy, and it's time I stopped trying to be like you and trying to please you. An' my commonsense tells me that chucking good money away is no way to best that flamin' old miser!'

188

In a totally undignified manner she got down on her hands and knees to recover the money. Flat on her stomach to reach a coin that had rolled underneath the dresser. One, two, three, four, five. She counted them again before taking them upstairs to her room.

'Men!' she said aloud, when they were safely put away. 'Edith Morris always said it was a man's world and she was right.' Standing there at the window staring down into the garden she decided there wasn't a man alive worth a tinker's cuss. Her anger was so enormous, so bursting out of her, it was like a great clearing of the brain, a facing of a truth she'd been too slow to acknowledge, even to herself.

Starting with her father. When had he ever said a kind word to her? When? Drinking his money away so that she had to take in washing to make ends meet. Scrubbing the sweat stains and worse from Mr Thwaite's revolting combs. Annie's fury knew no bounds.

An' the animal doctor. What about him? Talking to her as though he liked her, putting his hand to the side of her head the day he discovered her father had made her hard of hearing, then making a grab for her the first chance he got. She leaned her hot forehead against the glass. She had thought he was special, but she was wrong. How could he be special when he was a man?

Slowly she went back downstairs, her face set in lines of determination. Why should she walk out like she'd walked out of her father's house, out of Mr Armstrong's house, away from Barney Eccles's farm, to wander the roads like a tramp woman? Mr Page wouldn't touch her, not now she'd got his measure, not since she'd seen the expression on his wind-burned face as he'd tipped the bag of sovereigns into her lap. Money was his god, always had been and always would be. She greased the tins before dusting them with flour. But her mind wasn't on what she was doing.

Her mind was on the hat she was going to buy from the hat market in Blackburn. It was also on the dress, the

189

first dress she would ever have chosen for herself. White, she thought, remembering reading in one of Biddy's magazines that white was the only colour for an unmarried girl to wear. Annie nodded her head up and down furiously. That was exactly what she was – in spite of Laurie Yates and his promise. She was eighteen years old, only just eighteen. An' she was going to have a dress that fitted her properly. Tight over the bodice and hips, with a little jacket pleated into a basque and a flat bow at the back, only a bow, because the bustle was old-fashioned now.

It had said in one of Biddy's magazines that a fish-tail skirt was popular down in London. There had been a picture of one, tight-fitting right down to the ankle. The mannequins showing them off had to wear an ankle chain to stop them from taking too big a stride and splitting! And underneath they wore a chamois leather narrow petticoat so their knees could only move an inch at a time.

Biddy had nearly bust herself laughing when Annie had demonstrated how she imagined the mannequins would be forced to walk, wiggling her way down the hall taking tiny mincing steps. Annie's mouth set hard as she remembered Mr Armstrong coming in the front door and grinning at the sight of her.

She dismissed that memory with a narrowing of her eyes. Seth Armstrong was no better than the rest, and maybe worse, because he had pretended to care.

When Adam came in from work his meal was ready and waiting for him as usual. Annie told him that she accepted the five sovereigns, thank you very much, and suggested he paid her four shillings a week, to be back-dated to two weeks after the day she arrived.

'Do you think I'm bow-legged wi' brass?' he wanted to know, as she slid a nice helping of plum pie in front of him, but she knew he would give in.

'An' we won't mention the other matter, Mr Page?'

'You're a hard woman, Annie Clancy.'

'I know.'

'An' you'll stop on?'

'If you agree to what I've just said.'

He took a slice of buttered new bread from the plate and folded it in two with an angry movement. 'By heck, Annie, you drive a hard bargain.' But the light was back in his brown eyes.

She knew she had won.

During the night the dog was sick and when he tried to follow Adam to the door, his legs buckled beneath him. For four days he refused his food, lying on a sack by the fire with glazed eyes, his coat as dull as the ashes in the pan Annie carried out each morning to the midden.

Adam cornered Harry Gray down by the stables and asked if he could take half a day off work to wheel the dog in a barrow across the field to Seth Armstrong's place. 'It's serious this time, Mester. Yon dog's never been off his food for as long as this.'

Harry Gray had a habit of addressing his outdoor workers over a shoulder as he walked away from them. 'I'll do better than that, Adam. I've a horse needs looking at and my wife was only saying last night that it's time we had Armstrong over to dinner. I'll get a message to him today.'

When Adam told Annie that he'd managed to get her a ride into town with the carrier for the next morning she was delighted, but when he told her that Seth Armstrong was coming to look at the dog, her smile vanished as rapidly as if an Indian rubber had been taken to it.

'You don't think much of him, then?'

Annie nodded towards the basket in front of the fire where the dog slept, a twitching, pain-filled sleep. 'If anyone can make him better Mr Armstrong can. Biddy said he had the healing touch in his hands.'

'Biddy?'

'The girl who worked for him.'

191

'I never saw no Biddy the last time I was over there. I saw that weasel-faced housekeeper of his, and I saw you.'

Annie neatly side-stepped his outstretched hand and walked out into the garden. The late afternoon sun warmed the leaves to russet-gold, and there was the scent of wood-smoke in the air. Annie turned as usual to look back at the cottage.

She must have been more than a bit doolally to think that the gardener would be willing to carry on treating her like a daughter. He'd started trimming his moustache and combing his thick brown hair, and today he'd brought a great bunch of michaelmas daisies inside and watched her arrange them in a copper jug, never taking his eyes off her. Twice last week he'd come up behind her when she was at the slopstone, so close that she'd felt his breath on her neck. Once she'd imagined that he had touched her hair, and known that one small step backwards would have brought her close up against him. She shook her head from side to side. Why hadn't she realised, long before he spoke out, that he was getting ideas? Why had she believed he was old enough to know better?

'Men!' she said aloud, sounding so much like Edith Morris that if she'd recognised the resemblance for herself she would have burst out laughing.

She was glad she wouldn't be there when Mr Armstrong came the next day. Meeting her again would be a terrible embarrassment to both of them. 'Annie Clancy!' he'd say, pretending he was so happy to see her again. 'So this is where you got to!'

Just as if he'd never talked to her till midnight, set her tongue wagging with a glass of wine at times, told her his life story, a real sob story, thinking he was softening her up for what he had in mind. Just as if he had never gone to Eccles's farm, knowing she was there but never asking after her. Riding away down the hill on his black horse in that silly black hat.

Annie walked slowly back down the path. Oh, yes. She was glad all right that she wouldn't be there when the animal doctor called the next day.

192

11

Seth always hated telling a man that his dog would have to be put down. Some men openly wept, while others pretended they had expected it anyway, agreeing that it was for the best.

The gardener's expression was hard to read. 'I knew he was bad, Mr Armstrong. His age goes against him, doesn't it?'

Seth nodded, explaining that the form of dropsy Rex was suffering from was abdominal, an obstruction of the liver.

'But you can treat him, Mr Armstrong?'

'If he was a young dog, yes. I'd suggest two to five grains of calomel a week, and show you how to rub his right side here, from the last rib to the hip with embrocation, but . . .' Seth stroked the dog's face. 'I only wish there was some way, but it would be cruel to put him through so much suffering for nothing. He's very jaundiced, Adam.'

Adam Page was looking so different from the last time Seth called as to be almost unrecognisable. Then his shirt had food stains down its button-trim, with the muffler knotted loosely round his neck as stringy as a frayed piece of rope. The cottage was different, too. Now the brasses gleamed, the hearth was swept, and from the appetising smell Seth guessed that a piece of meat was slowly cooking in its own juices.

'You've trimmed your beard,' he said, trying to give the silent man time to think.

'Aye.'

'You've got everything looking very nice in here.'

'Aye.'

'You've obviously got help in since your wife died?'

193

'Aye.'

As Seth bent over the dog again, stroking its face and ears, the dry nose nuzzled itself into the palm of his hand.

'It's the kindest way, Adam.'

'I know that, Mr Armstrong.'

'Well then . . . ?'

Margot Gray listened gravely as Seth told her about the gardener's dog. She was sorry, of course, but an animal was just an animal when all was said and done. Not a human being, for God's sake. Harry would see that a replacement was delivered to the cottage as soon as possible.

What she was more interested in was watching Seth's face as he talked. His eyes were the kindest she had ever seen in a man, almost as if they had a light shining from behind them. His hair was as sun-bleached as if the sun shone down on it every day. Seth Armstrong was a beautiful man. Yes, that was the right word. But to use it to describe him didn't mean that he was in the least effeminate. Mon Dieu, no! There was a strength in him that almost shouted at you. Quick-tempered, too. She had once seen him snatch the whip off a hired man out in the yard to put a stop to him beating a wretched dog into submission. He had snapped the whip in two as if it had been a mere twig.

She shifted her position on the couch, spreading her skirts more attractively about her. There was nothing more exciting than a handsome man who seemed to be totally unaware of the effect he had on women. A vain man was an abomination, but this man's open, friendly attitude was almost an insult. Margot pouted. She might as well be another man, for heaven's sake!

Seth was well aware that Margot Gray was flirting with him. She was waiting for a compliment on her appearance, and she'd get one in due course. They always played this game together when they met. If he hadn't thought that her marriage was as solid as Pendle rock . . .

194

'I can never quite decide on the colour of your eyes, Margot,' he said. 'Hazel? Amber? What colour would *you* say they were?'

Margot fluttered her eyelashes. 'They are whatever colour you would like them to be,' she whispered, tilting her head to avoid him noticing her double chin. 'Seth, dear Seth. Why have you never married again?'

At once his expression darkened, so that she knew her light-hearted teasing had gone too far. She shrugged her shoulders. 'I'm sorry. It's just that you're so wasted, so terribly wasted . . .'

'Is my wife proposing to you again?' Harry rubbed his hands together as he came into the room, then held them out to the fire. 'There was no need for you to bury Adam's dog yourself, Seth old chap. If it was too upsetting for him you should have got one of the stable lads to do it.' He turned his back to the fire, spread his legs wide. 'Was he very cut up about it?'

Seth shook his head. 'It was hard to say what he was feeling. He just wasn't the same man. It must have something to do with the woman he's got in to look after him. He looked spruce enough to attend a wedding.'

'Perhaps he will be going to one before long.' Margot held out a foot to admire the soft bronze sheen of the pointed-toed shoe. She paused for full dramatic effect. 'His own.'

'You mean that young lass?' Harry laughed out loud. 'But his wife's only been dead for . . . Well, I'll be danged!' He moved to the bell-pull at the side of the fireplace. 'He's old enough to be a grandfather.' He gave two tugs at the rope. 'Not too early for a drink, is it, Armstrong?'

Margot sat forward, not wishing to let the subject go. 'How old do you think the gardener is, Seth?'

'Fifty-five? Sixty? It's hard to tell with most of his face covered in hair.'

'Early forties,' Margot said triumphantly. 'Try and picture him without the undergrowth, and you'll have a different man altogether. Men with beards always look as if they've something to hide.'

Harry had lost interest, but Seth was grinning, enjoying Margot's pleasure in her little bit of gossip. 'The girl? What's she like?'

'A splendid little . . .' Harry stopped in mid-sentence as a swarthy man carrying a silver tray with glasses on it came into the room. 'Over there,' he said, indicating a small table by the side of the fireplace. 'And ask Johnson to come up and see to the fire. It needs more coal.'

Margot could see by the expression on Seth's face that he couldn't see why Harry didn't take the tongs and lift the coal from the scuttle himself, instead of waiting for a maid to do it. That was one of the many things she liked about him. In spite of his obvious good breeding there wasn't an ounce of snobbishness in him. When Johnson came in to tend the fire Margot saw the way his mouth tightened briefly and his eyes slid away from her struggle with a cob of coal too large for the tongs to take. Yet he wouldn't intervene, not when he was a guest of the house. How petty and small-minded he must think they were.

'I think I'll pay a call on the gardener's girl one of these days,' she said, when Johnson had left the room. 'She probably has no mother to advise her – I'll talk to her . . .'

She looked at Seth to see how he was taking this, but he was engrossed in telling Harry something about a cow that had aborted itself twice. She got up and swept from the room, her skirts swishing out behind her.

True to her word, a week later she called at the gardener's cottage. She was followed up the path by Kit Dailey, the handyman hired by her husband a year ago. A small dark man, he staggered a little beneath the weight of a huge cardboard box filled with jars of preserves.

Margot suspected that she had overdone the Lady

Bountiful bit. She was no lady of the manor calling regularly at the cottages in the village wearing a floppy hat, knowing all the children by their names. It smacked of patronage to Margot; it seemed to her to be an intrusion into privacy, and she had told herself many times she would have no part in it. But the gardener's girl intrigued her, had done so right from the beginning, and the box of preserves was a good excuse to meet and talk with her again.

'Anyone at home?' She pushed the door open and stepped inside.

The cottage was charming. Like a cottage in a fairy-tale illustration. The firelight set the brasses twinkling; the blue and white plates on the dresser gleamed as if newly glazed. A small hand sewing-machine stood at one end of the scrubbed table, with scraps of material scattered around. There was a paper of pins, a reel of cotton and a bigger one of white tacking thread. Over the back of a stand-chair a length of scarlet ribbon trailed to the floor.

'Anyone at home?' Margot walked to the foot of the stairs. 'Are you there, Annie? It's Margot Gray.'

Annie put a hand to her throat. Margot Gray? Mrs Gray from the big house, downstairs in the living-room, with the place looking like a pig-sty. No cloth on the table and the best chair covered in paper patterns! Dropping in uninvited! Oh, dear God! And here she was, half dressed, the front of the bodice pinned and the hem only partly tacked up. Bits of cotton on the floor. No cake in the tin . . . So flustered she could hardly speak, Annie called out that she was coming and ran downstairs.

At the sight of her Kit Dailey put up a hand and sleeked back his already smooth hair. So this was Adam's housekeeper. No wonder the old codger was keeping her to himself. No wonder he kept his mouth shut when they asked about her. Compared to the ailing wife this girl was all colour, glowing vivid colour. Compared to Clara Page, this one was the ruddy Fairy Queen!

'You may go now, Dailey.' Margot nodded a dismissal. She smiled at Annie. 'May I sit down, dear?'

Kit Dailey left them to it, remembering first to touch his forehead in a way that made the gesture look like an insult. 'You may go now, Dailey. Wait outside.' Something inside him cringed every time he was spoken to in that way. Why did the possession of money give anyone the right to speak to another human being like that?

He climbed back into the trap and folded his arms. He couldn't get over the sight of the gardener's girl and the colour of her. That blue dress and that glorious red hair. He bet the shiny material had cost a bonny penny. How had a young lass persuaded a miser like Adam Page to fork out money like that? Happy as a pig in muck when he got his wages, but nobody had ever seen him spend a brass farthing of it. Kit's lip curled. Talk about a dark horse. The sly old devil had definitely spruced himself up lately. No tobacco stains down the front of his waistcoat now, whereas not all that long ago you could have stood Adam Page side by side with the scarecrow in the bottom field and not told the difference.

Kit laughed out loud.

To cover her confusion, Annie was now talking nineteen to the dozen.

'Mr Page gave me the money to buy a new dress, but I went on the market for a good look round and got two dress lengths and this second-hand machine for the same money.'

Margot made a small circle with her finger for Annie to turn round.

'The bow at the back was a bit tricky.' Annie tried to peer over her shoulder at it. 'But it had to go on to hide the gathers. It's the first time I've ever made a dress right from scratch, with new stuff and everything.' She smoothed down the pin-tucked bodice with obvious pride. 'I had a terrible job with the button loops, they kept twisting all over the shop, the fiddly things.'

'It's simply lovely, Annie.' Margot guessed that Annie was chattering away not from over-familiarity, but because she'd had no formal training, obviously not knowing any better. Annie had never been taught to be servile, therefore she could be herself. In her present mood, Margot found the situation much to her liking. She smiled. 'You have a precious gift there in your fingers, Annie. I could almost believe you've served your time to dressmaking.'

'Thank you, Mrs Gray.' Annie remembered to give a little bob. 'I must have got it from my mother. She could make a blouse from a duster, and her feather stitching was that fine you'd need a magnifying glass to see it.'

Margot smoothed down her skirt. She hadn't enjoyed herself so much in a long time. Her mother had once told her she came from peasant stock, so that could account for the fact that she felt completely at home in the tiny room with the rag rugs on the floor, and the furniture so crowded together there was hardly room to squeeze a body between the table and the overloaded dresser.

For another thing she was warm for the first time in weeks. The fireplace in the drawing-room up at the house was large enough to take an ox for roasting, but the room itself was as cold as a dank tomb. Her feet were perpetually numb, and although she knew she should wear heavier shoes, she wasn't ready to give in to her age for a long time yet. It was bad enough having two enormous step-daughters clomping about in unspeakable footwear. She looked down at her pale green, high-buttoned shoes, turning an ankle this way and that to admire them. The day was a long way off when she would be inclined to put comfort before fashion.

'May I?' She unbuttoned her long duster coat.

Annie looked embarrassed enough to cry. 'Take it off if you want to, Mrs Gray. I never thought you'd be stopping or I'd have asked you to do so before.'

Margot shook her head. 'I won't take it off, thank you, Annie. I really came to say how sad it is to see Adam

199

going about his work without a dog at his heels. We gave him the dog as a puppy when one of our border-collies had an unfortunate meeting with a stray.' She sighed. 'Mr Armstrong said he'd hated putting the dog to sleep.'

Moving a piece of paper pattern from a chair, Annie sat down. 'Mr Armstrong thinks more of animals than he does of human beings.'

Margot sat up straight. 'You know Seth Armstrong?'

'I should do. I lived at his house right through the cold snap.'

'Do you mean you were working there?'

Annie knew her face had gone red. She wished she'd kept her mouth shut, but there was no going back on it now. Not with Mrs Gray's eyes standing out from her head on stalks. 'In a way I was, an' yet in another way I wasn't. It was all because he knocked me down – at least his horse knocked me down – on the top road on the edge of the moors. He took me back to his house till I got better.'

'When was that, did you say?'

'Early on in the year. When we had all that snow.'

'So you saw him yesterday?' Margot frowned. In that case why hadn't Seth admitted that he knew the gardener's girl? She sensed an intriguing mystery.

Annie's chin was up. 'No, I never saw him yesterday. I made sure I was away to town before he got here.'

'You don't like Mr Armstrong?'

'It's not for me to like or dislike him, Mrs Gray.'

'You mean for the likes of me, don't you, Annie? A remark like that doesn't become you. Tell me why you've taken such a dislike to him. I wouldn't have thought a man like that had an enemy in the world.'

Annie could hardly bear to look at the elegant woman sitting in Adam's chair. Mrs Gray was playing a game. She was pretending they were two neighbours having a good old gossip by the fire. But they weren't, were they? This woman with prune-coloured hair puffed up like a barmcake, circles of rouge on her cheeks and button-bright eyes was bored to death sitting around all day doing nothing. She was here to pass the time on, thinking she might learn something to have a good laugh about with her family that evening. Right then. Why not give her something interesting enough to pass on? Then they could all enjoy themselves.

'To tell you why I don't like Mr Armstrong, I would have to start at the beginning,' she said, too loudly.

'I'm listening, Annie.'

Annie stood up, feeling that what she had to say would come better from a standing position. In that moment she was once again Annie Clancy standing at the poss-tub day after day, wearing a man's flat cap, her mother's old blouse and over-large pit boots. She took a deep breath.

'My father is a collier. When I lived at home he would come in reeking of pit muck and sweat. There'd be cockroaches in his clothes, and I used to shake them out and bang his trousers against the backyard wall to get the worst of the dirt out. He drank most of his wages away, so that there was never enough for food, and what there was my mother gave to me and my five brothers.' She took a shuddering breath. 'My father used to take his leather belt off and hit me with it. Just me. Never my brothers.'

Margot put out a hand. 'Don't go on if you don't want to, Annie. I have no wish to pry,' she said insincerely.

She was ignored. It was as though all the bad things in Annie's life, all the remembered hurts, the suffering, rose up in her, not in sorrow but in anger. Not all that long ago it would have been in sorrow, but not now. Never again.

'My mother died when I was twelve. Of malnutrition, the doctor said. Of years and years of reckoning on she had eaten, when all the time she was so hungry she could have gnawed the table leg. So when she took ill there was nothing there to give her strength. No resistance.' Annie fought for control. 'My father brought a lodger to the

201

house, a sailor, a travelling man he called himself, an' one day he saw me crying after a beating, an' because I was upset I let him lay with me. The next day he went away, after promising to marry me. Soon after that I found I was having a baby.'

'Go on, Annie.'

'I wanted to kill myself, but I hadn't the nerve, so I hid myself with a loose shawl and I went on working, doing other folks's washing and looking after the boys.' Her voice fell almost to a whisper. 'Then one day Father O'Leary knocked on the door. I saw him standing there in his big black hat, carrying the walking stick that looked more like a shillelagh. So I asked him to pray to God on my behalf, and what did he do but tell Mrs Greenhalgh from the bottom house that I had got myself into trouble. He didn't know that my father was there in the house listening, and what did *he* do but come tearing up the street with that woman, telling me they were getting married and that I'd have to go to the workhouse.' Like a child she knuckled a tear away from her eye. 'But I wasn't going to no workhouse, so I walked over the top road to find work, an' it was then that Mr Armstrong's horse knocked me down.'

'And the baby?'

'I lost it.' Annie was calming down now that the relief in speaking out was flooding through her. 'An' I was glad. I was happy to get rid.'

'Under circumstances like that I would have felt exactly the same.'

Annie was so surprised she sat down again.

'I mean it, Annie. Babies should never come where they're not wanted. How could you have looked after it at your age, without money or a roof over your head?'

'I was glad,' Annie repeated. 'I could have sung aloud I was that glad. I can't tell you how glad I was.'

Margot shot her a shrewd glance. 'Now tell me why you hate Mr Armstrong.'

'Because he . . .'

202

She had been going to say she hated him because he had tried to take advantage of her that last night. That he was like all the rest, not to be trusted. Pretending to be kind to her, even treating her like a lady, talking to her, telling her she had the character and the looks to make herself into anything she wanted to be. The anger was still in her, and in that telling moment she was back in the old stone house, in the fire-lit room, held closely in the animal doctor's arms. She could feel the hardness of his mouth on her own, feel the heat coming from him, see the way his eyes had darkened as he held her so close the breath went out of her.

But the words coming from her weren't the words she wanted to say. There was something calming about the over-painted, plump little woman sitting so still, listening, waiting.

'Well, Annie?'

'I hate him because he made me see the truth,' she said quietly.

'Which was?'

The admission came out on a long drawn-out wail. 'That Laurie never meant it when he said he would come back and marry me. That I will never see him again. That he never meant one word of his promise.'

'And you still care for him?'

Slowly Annie raised her head. 'I never did care for him. I know that now.' Her voice rose. 'Because of what we did I felt I had to love him, that to have done that without love would have made me like a night woman, a trollop.'

'So the vet was right?'

Annie's head drooped low. 'That is why I hate him,' she said. 'For being right. For telling me something I should have admitted to myself a long time ago.'

Adam was flabbergasted at the way he'd come in from the fields to find Mrs Gray sitting there by the fire with Annie, gabbing away as if they were equals. And what was Annie doing wearing a dress only half-way sewed, all gaping at the bodice and showing her chemise? Why did Mrs Gray have to jump up at the sight of him as if she'd just remembered Kit Dailey sitting outside in the trap? Adam sniffed. Hardly likely. He doubted if Madam Gray cared a tinker's cuss about anyone but herself.

'She never came once to see Clara,' he grumbled, when she'd gone. 'Clara had a decent and proper respect for her betters.' He pointed at the big box of preserves. 'Anyroad, what did she come for? We don't need her charity.' He sat down and began to unlace his boots, not bothering to carry them out to the back porch. He was still smarting at the taunts shouted at him from the trap outside in the lane.

'You're a wily old varmint, Adam Page. Keeping her all to yourself.' Kit Dailey had thrown back his dark head, laughing out loud. 'Though I can't say I blame you. They don't grow them like your little Annie all that often.' He had pursed his lips and whistled, rolling his eyes.

Adam could feel the blood pounding in his head. 'Those jars and bottles are only an excuse to get inside and have a proper look at you. An' you give her an eyeful, didn't you? Who carried that lot in? Kit Dailey? Did he get an eyeful as well? You want to watch him. He's bad, through and through, really bad.'

Annie tried to change the subject. 'Mrs Gray asked me if I'd like to work afternoons up at the house.'

'*What* did you say?'

Annie said it again. It wasn't news that would keep, anyway. 'Mrs Gray has asked me if I'd like to work afternoons up at the house.'

Adam's eyes bulged. 'And you told her no! I'm waiting to hear you told her no!'

'I told her yes.' Annie began to gather her bits and pieces together. 'I'm to sew for her. She couldn't believe it when I told her I'd made this dress in less than two days. She said if I could make dresses like this for her step-daughters she'd be delighted, but of course I'm being set on mainly for mending the linen, and darning and patching.' She twirled round, almost beside herself with excitement. 'I thought rich people just threw things away when they got torn, but that's not the way with Mrs Gray. She wants them mended. You can be wrong about rich people, you know, Mr Page. Sometimes they can act quite ordinary.' Annie was so pleased with herself, so chuffed about the prospect of working up at the big house, she almost danced round the table. 'Mrs Gray said the housekeeper would see to the money side of it.'

'I'll see to the money side!' Adam thumped the table with his fist. 'I've told you – there's all the money you'll ever need upstairs.'

'You look like a pitman,' Annie said, trying to tease him out of his bad mood. 'I'll have your tea ready in a minute.' She lifted the sewing machine.

'Leave that be!' Adam thundered. 'So I look like a pitman, do I? An' so would you, so would you if you'd been working with the horse-roller since first light.' He spread his big hands wide. 'That's soot from the burnt stubble.' He pointed to his chin. 'An' it's on my face too, is it?'

A nervous giggle escaped from Annie's throat. 'You've got a nose as black as the fire-back.'

Because she was half-way to being scared, she could hear herself being childish, and the angrier Adam became the more difficult she found it to wipe the smile off her face. But if only Mr Page would turn round and look in the mirror behind him, he would see for himself how funny he looked. He was baring his teeth now, the large creamy teeth like newly-scrubbed tombstones. The nostrils of his sooty nose were flaring. The angrier he got the more the laughter bubbled up in her.

'I'm sorry.' When he gripped her wrist she stopped laughing. He was close up to her, so close she could see the way his eyes were bloodshot, red-rimmed with exhaustion. 'I'm sorry, Mr Page,' she said again, sobered up now. 'I wasn't laughing at you, not really.' She pulled away from his grasp. 'I was just so happy I didn't know what to do with myself. Don't you see? I haven't felt this happy in a long, long time.' She rubbed at her wrist. 'It must be this dress.' Her eyes were pleading with him to understand. 'It's the first dress I've ever had that fits me. Because it's been made for me. Just me.' She came to stand in front of him. 'Don't be cross, Mr Page. Don't spoil it all for me.'

He could see the way the blue dress would cling to her shape when the buttons and loops were finished. His heart began to beat with such force he felt she must surely see it. How lovely she was! Into his mind flashed a picture of how she had looked on the day he had found her, skirts caked with mud, her hair clinging black wet to her head, so that he saw the glorious colour of it only when it dried by the fire. She looked so much older now. The touching vulnerability of her had quite gone. He wasn't surprised that the master's wife had been so taken with her. Annie Clancy was no ordinary lass. She was dead set on making something of herself, and one day she would go away. She would stay with him out of gratitude for a while, but one day she would just open the door and walk out. He bowed his head, the very thought of it nigh on killing him.

'You've been very good to me,' she was saying. 'I'm not likely to forget it.'

Adam muttered from the hurt deep inside him. 'Oh, aye? Bread eaten's soon forgotten.'

She shook her head at him. 'You're wrong. You took me in when I might have died of cold out there. I can't ever repay that sort of kindness.'

'An' you'll forget about working at the house?'

'No!' Annie hoped he wouldn't realise how scared she was, but she knew she had to stand her ground. 'I'm not ungrateful to you. I'm not. You must know that. But I

206

paid you back in kind, Mr Page. I looked after Mrs Page and I kept house for you. Since she died there isn't enough for me to do. I can't sit doing nothing. I wasn't brought up to it.'

'You're not going up there to work, and that's that.'

'You don't own me, Mr Page.' The angry spots of colour on her cheeks were as scarlet as the trailing length of velvet ribbon. 'I don't belong to anyone. I accepted the position Mrs Gray offered me and I start the day after tomorrow.'

Suddenly the temper Adam never believed he possessed took over. Terror at losing her brought him up out of his chair, sending it skidding across the floor.

'I tell you you're not going!'

As he raised his fist, Annie stepped back, blue eyes daring him to touch her. 'You hit me, an' I'll walk right out of the door. Now! Just as I am. There's nobody ever going to hit me again. Now move away! Get back!'

She hesitated when he crumpled into his chair, his face so contorted it was almost unrecognisable. For a terrified moment she thought he was going to die on her, to drop down on the floor from a seizure brought on by his blazing fury.

'You ought not to have raised your hand to me.' She was shocked at the sudden way he seemed to have shrunk into himself. 'Mr Page! Are you all right?'

'Can't you call me Adam? Even yet? I wouldn't have struck you, lass. I'd rather cut off this arm than strike you. You must know that.'

His head was down, his soil-ingrained hands loose between his knees. The thick brown hair was thinning on top, showing a round and balding spot. Her father had one, just the same, she remembered. You couldn't see that one either till he'd bowed his head. She said the gardener's name with difficulty.

'Adam. Listen to me. I'll stay here and housekeep for you. I'll look after you till you feel able to stand on your own two feet. You've not got over Mrs Page dying yet;

you're all mixed up in your mind.' She stretched out a hand to touch him, thought better of it and drew it back. 'I'm going to work up at the house in the afternoons. You'll not change my mind. You getting so angry about it showed me how right I am.' She risked coming round his chair to stand before him. 'I don't belong to nobody, Adam. I don't think I ever will. What I have to do, I have to do by myself. Can't you even begin to see that?'

But he couldn't, and upstairs in her room Annie took off the blue dress. If she worked on it till late and again tomorrow she could finish it in time to wear on her first day at the big house. She would rather die, she told herself, than go in one of Clara's hand-me-downs in a drab colour that didn't suit, fitting only where it touched.

She stroked the fine material, being careful not to snag a thread on her work-roughened fingers. Perhaps if she soaked her hands in a solution of soft green soap they would look better, more presentable, fit to be seen up at the big house.

She laid the dress carefully on the bed. It was so beautiful she couldn't stop smiling even just looking at it. Dress like a tramp and folks treated you like one; wear another woman's ancient cast-offs and get regarded like a nobody. The smile spread right across her face. But dress like a lady and what a difference that made. Mrs Gray had been really impressed by the dress. It was probably the dress that had brought on the offer of a job, Annie felt sure of it.

She took the candle from the chest-of-drawers, held it high to admire it once more, before she went downstairs to make the tea. It wasn't just luck that Mrs Gray had called and seen her looking refined and ladylike. It had been meant to be. Her mother had always said that when things happened unexpectedly – good or bad – they were meant to be. It looked as if her luck was in at last. An' the look on her face when she'd seen the dress! Annie would never forget that.

Up at the house there were only two of them for dinner
that evening. Abigail and Dorothea had gone to a Hunt
Ball dressed, Margot thought, like a couple of
pantomime dames.

She was wearing her cinnamon-brown taffeta dress,
cut high at the neck to hide a faintly wrinkled cleavage.

'I saw the gardener's girl this afternoon,' she said,
when the parlour maid had gone back to the kitchen
after serving the lamb roast. 'I've taken her on to work
here in the afternoons.'

'Doing what, for God's sake?' Harry had already
drunk far too much. From now on he would laugh at
every word he uttered, finishing each sentence with a
loud guffaw. 'You can't turn round in this blasted
house without tripping over a wretched girl down on
her knees scrubbing the tiles in the hall or polishing the
blasted stair-rods.' He laughed till his eyes watered.
'You can't clear your throat these days without one of
the blighters jumping to attention. I put me boots down
t'other day and one of the interfering blaggards
whisked them away for a polishing they didn't need.
Chap with black shiny hair that reminded me of a
pontefract cake.'

This last witticism almost had him under the table.
His pleasant face was the colour of a boiled beetroot; he
beamed with the pleasure of his own conversation.

Margot looked upon him with a kind of love, an
affection that saw and accepted her husband for what he
was, a big blustering man who shouted and cursed his
way through each day, huffing and puffing, just for the
hell of it. She passed over a dish of sprouts. 'I've engaged
her as a seamstress. You won't set eyes on her unless you
go upstairs to the sewing-room.' She lowered her voice as
the parlour maid came and went with a dish of mint
sauce. 'Guess where she was living before Adam found
her wandering the roads?'

Harry leaned over and speared an extra roast potato.

'Surprise me,' he grinned, deciding to finish the whole dish.

'With Seth Armstrong,' Margot said. 'Not with him in that sense.'

'In *what* sense?' Harry wanted to know, trying to keep his face straight.

'Well, you know. Not as lovers.'

'Pity.' Harry pierced a piece of meat on his fork. 'If ever a man needed a woman's touch that man is Seth Armstrong. There's a sadness so deep in him it hurts to look at him at times.' He forgot to laugh.

'Harry!' Margot got up from her chair, walked round the table and planted a kiss on her husband's cheek. 'You're an old softie,' she whispered. 'Fancy you noticing a thing like that.'

Margot went back to her place. 'Adam's girl had made a dress for herself that wouldn't have looked out of place at a musical soirée. Where she's going to wear it, God only knows.'

12

Annie finished the dress in time. The bow at the back still didn't satisfy her, but she reassured herself that it was her front that mattered. At least there wasn't much wrong with the bodice with its tucks and covered buttons. She had pulled her hair up high on top of her head and the added height made her feel almost regal. She was glad the weather was fine. Rain would have frizzed her hair and muddied her boots, though Adam said it was much needed. The soil was dry and cracked for want of moisture, he grumbled.

He had been very quiet since Annie had showed him she wasn't going to stand for being bullied, but there was a quiet frenzy about him as though he could explode at any moment. He stared at her; his eyes followed her round the room; when she asked him to tell her more about the big house he sulked and said if she wanted to know its history she'd best ask her friend Mrs Gray, not him.

The winding drive seemed to go on for ever. Annie held her skirts well away from the dust. When she reached the house she saw two cock pheasants walking proudly across the lawns, and the sight brought tears of admiration to her eyes. Such splendour, such beauty – it was all too much to take in. Round the side of the house she saw tortoise-shell butterflies hovering over a bed of michaelmas daisies and actually clasped her hands together. Somebody ought to write a poem about it all, she decided, going right round to the back, as Adam had told her she must.

The girl who showed her up the back stairs to the sewing-room had a face on her that looked as if a smile would crack it. Annie beamed at her.

'What's your name? Mine's Annie Clancy.'

'Johnson.'

'No, I mean your *first* name.'

Nothing could wipe the smile off Annie's face. Certainly not this sulky girl with the slight cast in one eye. She wasn't to know that Annie could just as easily have been starting a thankless job, like picking coal over on the long belt at the mine, or standing at clacking looms in a noisy weaving shed, or washing other people's clothes. While here she was, wearing a dress that fitted, landing a job entailing nothing more than sitting on a chair and sewing.

Johnson's mouth curved into a sneer. 'Parlour maids are always called by their surnames. You don't know much, do you?'

'Nothing at all about working in a house like this.' Annie unfastened Clara's old cloak and took it off. 'How many rooms are there? Are they all furnished?'

Johnson's expression changed to one of stunned amazement. She backed away to the door, a hand held to her mouth. Annie heard her giggling with someone out on the landing.

'Pop your head in there and have a look at the gardener's girl. She's dressed up like a dog's dinner in a dress that shiny you can see your face in it. Wait till Kit sees her. He'll ask her for the last waltz!'

A tousled head appeared round the door, stared in disbelief, then disappeared, closing the door against the sound of hysterical laughter.

Annie looked down at the dress, the brightness fading from her face. Was it really as shiny as all that? And the colour? She frowned. To be honest, when she got it back to the cottage she had worried for a brief moment about the vivid shade of blue. She fingered the uneven bow at the back. Johnson hadn't seen that yet – she'd probably split her sides when she did.

Annie walked over to the window and stared down into the stable yard. Knowing too late that she should have worn one of Clara Page's drab cast-offs, in black or grey. Knowing she'd made a terrible mistake. A tear trickled slowly down her cheek, then another. She had wanted so much to look her best. This wasn't any old dress. She had dreamed of wearing one like this ever since she'd grown a bust and was old enough to care what she looked like. Her father had beaten her almost senseless for wanting to make a dress like this.

She dashed the tears away with the back of a hand. This dress was a symbol of the way things were going to be from now on. That's what it was, a symbol of how she felt inside, of how she knew she could be, given the chance. Annie perked up. Johnson wasn't going to spoil this day for her. Nothing could do that. Johnson was jealous. That was the truth. Not worth wasting good worrying time on.

Annie stood in the middle of the room looking round her. The carpet with its red and blue medallions must have cost a pretty penny, and there wasn't a worn patch in it. There were gilt-framed pictures on the walls and a long mirror fixed to the alcove at the side of the marble fireplace; there was a glowing fire in the basket-grate. The large work table was the only shabby piece of furniture in the room, and Annie bet she could have brought that up like new with a linseed rag.

In her shiny blue dress she matched the room. They were made for each other, she decided, nodding her head firmly up and down.

She wished someone would come in and tell her what to do. Sure in her mind that to sit down would be bad manners, she stood with clasped hands looking at the closed door. There were two chairs, both in basket weave, with chintz cushions, but knowing what was what, Annie wasn't to be tempted.

She had another look through the window and saw the two Gray girls being helped on to their horses by a stable lad with hair the colour of a butterpat. He stood back, touched a finger to his forehead and the girls rode off, sitting their horses like men. Annie could hardly believe it. Mrs Gray had been right. Those two wouldn't take kindly to being measured for elegant dresses with fish-tail skirts. Or to wearing long white gloves. Or flowers in their hair. She breathed on the window and rubbed it clean – and missed hearing the door open behind her.

'Annie Clancy?'

Annie whirled round, her heart sinking at the sight of a tall woman all in black holding a pile of snow-white linen out in front of her. She had a sharp nose, uptilted as if to avoid a bad smell, and a bunch of keys hanging from a wide stiffened belt. Another Johnson, if Annie was any judge, only older and nastier.

The blue dress was being stared at as if the very sight of it was enough to curdle milk. Annie's heart sank.

'Yes, I'm Annie Clancy,' she said.

After another long and telling silence, the tall black-clad woman seemed to have decided to make the best of a bad job. She walked with a strange gliding step over to the long table. 'I am Mrs Tunstall, the housekeeper. There are sheets, tablecloths, pillowcases and napkins. Hems and long seams to be done on the machine, everything else to be done by hand.' She stared at Annie's hands as if surprised to find them clean. 'Make a list of what you've done. I'll be wanting to check and I've not got the time to search everything.' She indicated a pad and pencil at the corner of the big table. 'You can write, I take it?'

'I was top of the class at school, ma'am,' Annie said. 'I used to get the sums right quicker than what the teacher could chalk them up on the blackboard.'

She was hoping for a bit of a smile, for a sign of warmth in the long angular face, but there was nothing, not even a slight quiver of the pointed chin.

'If you come down to the kitchen at going on a quarter to four there'll be tea. Cook likes the staff to get theirs over with before they have it upstairs.'

'That's a kind thought, Mrs Tunstall. I never expected to be having tea.'

214

The flourishing moustache on the housekeeper's upper lip moved slightly. 'I told the mistress you'd be better having it up here, but she thinks you ought to get to know us all.' The door was closed with a decisive click. 'God alone knows why,' her back said, loud and clear.

Annie decided that the housekeeper must have a secret sorrow eating away at her heart. She sat down at the long table and drew a pillowcase towards her, smoothing the fine material with her fingers. Linen. Fine bleached linen with that special sheen on it. Costing a fortune a yard. She ran an expert eye over the scallop-edges, hand-embroidered in cream silks. Two-ply, she guessed from the fineness of them. Holding the pillow-case to her cheek she breathed in its smooth coolness, imagined laying her head on it, night after night. What would she think, that hard-faced woman with a body like a stick insect, if she knew that up to leaving home the new seamstress had never known the touch of a sheet or a pillowcase unless she was washing and ironing them for someone else? That rough grey blankets had been her lot.

She had thought that the sheets on Mr Armstrong's spare-room bed had been the height of luxury, but what had they been but bleached twill? With a faintly superior smile she picked up a corner of a sheet and trailed it down her cheek again. Biddy had told her once that she'd read a story about a Countess who had slept between silken sheets. Black, according to Biddy, to match her nightgown. Annie had thought it was horrible then, and fingering the fine linen she thought it was even more horrible now. She began to thread a needle, licking the end of the cotton first and holding the needle up to the light.

She couldn't get over what she saw as the first sign that her luck was going to turn for the better. Here she was, sitting in a beautiful room with pictures on the walls, a carpet beneath her feet, a sewing machine decorated with gold scrolls, blue papers of pins to hand, a tray of coloured bobbins and a pair of scissors pretty enough to be hung round her neck on a chain. And she was getting paid for it!

With tiny perfect stitches Annie began to sew a loose border of hand-crocheted lace back on to a tray-cloth.

By the time the hands on the gilt clock on the mantelpiece moved round to half-past three she had worked her way through almost half a pile of linen, sitting by the long table with an unseasonable sun slanting through the windows and the fire flickering in the grate.

Once a small girl wearing a mobcap slipping down over one eye sidled into the room carrying a fresh scuttle of coal. When Annie spoke to her she jumped, but managed to whisper that her name was Gladys and that she was thirteen years old, before escaping. 'I'm Annie . . .' It was too late, the maid was gone, slipping through the door like a shadow, anxious to be off, but not before Annie had seen the disbelief flicker for a second in her eyes.

It was the quietness she couldn't get over. The peace and utter tranquillity of just sitting and sewing without having to get up every few minutes to see to something. She didn't even have to soil her hands by tending the fire. It was better than anything Biddy could have dreamed up.

At almost a quarter to four she crept down the back stairs into the large basement kitchen.

'Amen.'

A sombre-suited bald man at the head of a long table was just finishing grace. As Annie hesitated, every head lifted and turned in her direction. She saw eyes widen in astonishment, saw a nudge there, a snigger here. She knew it was the dress, and wanted to sink through the floor.

'In future you must take your place at the table at least two minutes before Grace is said.' The man in the black suit motioned her to a seat. 'And perhaps another day you could see fit to wear something more appropriate. The dress you have on would be more suitable for dancing round the maypole.'

The young girl with the slipping mob-cap who had tended the sewing-room fire gave a nervous snort of a giggle, but a buxom woman presiding over a large brown teapot smiled on Annie with kindness.

'I take it you have another frock, love?'

'Oh yes, ma'am,' Annie agreed at once. 'Mr Page – Adam – lets me wear all his wife's dresses. There's a dark-grey serge, a brown wool, and a black skirt and two blouses I've made over.' In an agony of embarrassment she patted her chest. 'Mrs Page was a lot less than me.' She floundered into unnecessary explanation. 'But then she was ill. The flesh just dropped off her.' Why didn't someone say something? Why did they all sit there staring at her with their mouths open? Annie gabbled on. 'I got carried away when I saw this material. It stood out from all the bolts of cotton and silks on the stall at the market . . .'

'I bet it did,' a voice from across the table said, and Annie saw that it was the parlour maid, Johnson.

The butler coughed and, as if at a signal, plates were passed, butter spread on scones, and a large glass jam dish handed round. Annie tried to eat but the food stuck in her throat. She tried to swallow and a crumb went down the wrong way.

'I think it's a beautiful dress. You suit it. With you having blue eyes.'

Annie raised her head, turning to the man sitting on her left. He was a black-haired man with a foreign look about him, and she wondered why she hadn't recognised him at first.

'You came to the cottage on the day Mrs Gray brought the box of preserves.'

'I did that.' The dark eyes teased so that Annie was reminded of another man, another place. But this man was even darker than Laurie, the face thinner, the

217

expression less kindly, more bold. He had a way of slowly nodding his head as he spoke. 'You were trying the dress on if I remember right.' Again he nodded, once, twice, three times. 'I bet old Adam thinks you look a fair treat in it.'

The words were whispered, but Annie had the feeling that everyone sitting round the table heard. She shuddered and moved quickly as she felt a leg pressed against hers. Could no one see what was going on? But everyone was eating as if there wasn't the chance of another square meal for months. The leg pressed even more closely, and to Annie's horror she felt it tremble.

Kit Dailey stared in open admiration. She was so close he could see a fine soft down on her cheeks. The lobes of her ears had a fragility about them that made him want to reach out a hand and touch. The neck of the peacock-blue dress was cut so low he could see the beginning of a sweet hollow between rounded breasts. The careful pin-tucks at her waist pushed up and exaggerated the full shape of her. Kit ran his tongue over his lips, and felt the heat rise in him.

'Would you like a piece of fruit-cake, love?'

Annie saw Cook smiling at her, knife poised over a rich brown cake risen to splendour, sultanas gleaming through its glazed surface. With relief she passed up her plate and took the opportunity to move to the far edge of the chair. She took a bite from the moist spicy cake.

'If you don't stop it I'll knock your chair over,' she whispered. 'I'm quite capable of it.'

Looking up she saw Johnson watching her with a look of boss-eyed hatred.

Suddenly Annie wished she had never taken the job, never left the cottage to walk up the long winding drive. Never made the dress. By this time her housework would be done and Adam's meal would be simmering in the black pan on the trivet or in the fire-oven. She turned her head to the right and met the blank gaze of the boy she had seen down in the stable yard. He was all wetness, eyes, nose and drooling mouth. Annie felt a stir of recognition.

'This is Toby Eccles,' Cook said, looking with fondness on the boy. 'There's nobody can groom a horse like our Toby.'

The butterpat head dropped to one side, as if the neck had suddenly snapped. Annie smiled on him. So this was the boy Barney Eccles had sent away, the 'idiot child', his mother had called him.

'You're wasting your time, Annie.'

Kit Dailey was talking directly to her, but she saw that his gaze was fixed on the furious face across the table. Johnson looked so angry Annie wouldn't have been surprised to see sparks coming out of the top of her head. Annie knew she was being used in some sort of game between them and decided to put an end to it.

'I'll be getting back to the sewing-room, if you'll excuse me.' She stood up and smiled round the table. 'Thank you for a lovely tea.'

'You will remain in your place until Grace has been said. Then you may go.' The butler's voice dripped scorn. 'You seem to be lacking in manners, Annie Clancy. We'll have to try and teach you some.'

'And finish your cake, love.'

Kit muttered the words from the side of his mouth, but he was heard all right. Annie frowned and looked down at her plate.

'For what we have received . . .'

The butler said the words with as much deliberation as if he intoned them from a high pulpit. As he rolled his eyes ceilingwards in an extra prayer of his own, Annie rushed from the kitchen and up the stairs, the blue dress with its elaborate skirt flowing out behind her like a bridal train.

She was breathless by the time she reached the sewing-room. Her hair had slipped from its restraining ribbon, and she'd caught her foot in the hem of her long skirt, tearing a flounce.

219

She was too angry to cry, too filled with humiliation to get the situation into any kind of perspective. Wearing the dress had been a tragedy, not a simple error of judgement. She *did* look ready to pick up a ribbon and prance round a maypole. The neckline *was* far too low. It was more than likely that the despicable greasy little man sitting next to her at the table had seen her front when she leaned forward in her chair.

Annie actually beat her brow. Accepting that she was a laughing stock, an object of scorn. Downstairs in the kitchen they would still be ridiculing her, pitying her, saying she knew no better.

'You're wanted downstairs in the drawing-room.'

The little maid of all work whispered her message, turned and ran. She wished she had dared to speak out at the tea table. She thought that the new girl looked like a fairy-tale princess in the blue dress, with her hair all wavy – without the nightly use of rags, she felt sure. Once when she had to see the school inspector her mother had put her hair in rags to make ringlets, but the nit nurse had said her hair was alive and had best be cut off.

Since then, hair had been the first thing she had noticed about people because from that terrible day when they'd shaved hers off it had never grown back quite the same. She tweaked her cap further down over her forehead, and got back to the kitchen as fast as she could. In case the unthinkable happened and they gave her the sack.

'Annie!'

Margot Gray tried not to show too much surprise as her new seamstress came into the room dressed to kill. She put a hand to her mouth to hide a smile. It was the dress, of course, the beautifully made, totally unsuitable dress Annie had been trying on when she called at the cottage. Whoever would have imagined she would wear it today? To work?

220

'I have . . .' she began, but Annie was determined to have her say, to get it over with and admit it was unforgiveable of her.

'I got carried away, ma'am,' she said on a rush. 'It's the first dress I've had that hasn't been made and worn by somebody else. I won't come in it tomorrow, and when I get the chance I'll make myself a dress as black as night with no trimmings, not even a lace collar.' She made a movement with her hands. 'It'll go straight up and down and bag over the chest. In the meantime I'll wear Mrs Page's dark-green serge.'

'Annie!' Margot put up a hand. 'You have a visitor, dear.'

From the tall winged chair with its back to Annie a man emerged, a fair-haired man with strangely light eyes. He was smiling at her.

'Mr Armstrong!' Annie didn't know what to say. He looked so different for one thing. Thinner in the face, shabbier, and surely Mrs Martindale would never have turned him out in a shirt with a frayed collar?

How different *she* looked. Seth thought she was thinner in the face, with cheekbones that showed, and what was she doing wearing a dress made for waltzing in? He came round the chair and held out his hand.

'I've come to take you back, Annie.'

'Why? Have you sent Biddy away?'

Margot sat up. That was quick. They were squaring up to each other as if they were old protagonists with a few more scores to settle. No polite preamble to their greetings. She leaned forward, in order not to miss a thing.

'No. Biddy's still there. I've come to take you home.'

'To *your* home?' The humiliation and the anger were still in her. What was he talking about, take her home? She stared directly at him. 'I saw you riding away from the Eccles's farm.'

'I didn't know you were there, Annie.'

'But you must have . . .'

He spread his hands wide. 'Suffice to say I didn't.'

221

Margot held her breath. She had known Seth Armstrong for a long time and he never used words like 'suffice'. There was a tiny nerve jumping near his jawline. He was clenching his hands into fists, too. She looked from one to the other. There was a 'situation' here, or she was much mistaken.

'Could you tell me where your gardener's working today?' Seth turned to her. 'I'll have a word with him and explain that I'm taking Annie back with me.'

'You mean *now*?' Annie looked at Mrs Gray. Had she heard that?

Margot was shaking her head. 'Sorry, Seth. You'll have to go down to the stables. Harry's bound to be there. He'll tell you.'

Nodding his thanks, Seth strode quickly to the door, shouting instructions at Annie over his shoulder. 'Be ready in half an hour . . .'

'Well!' Annie's face was a study. 'Did you hear all that, Mrs Gray?'

'Every single word.'

'An' do you think I should do as Mr Armstrong tells me and be ready for him in half an hour? As if I was his slave? As if I belonged to him?'

'I think he imagines that you do, Annie.'

There was a bleakness in the way Margot spoke, a certain hostility in the way she stared at the girl in the vividly blue dress. Once, a long time ago, she'd been able to reject men just for the satisfaction of seeing them tremble before her. Sure of herself, sure they would come back for more, she had played them off one against the other, till one day she'd realised they had all gone off and married younger girls, leaving her to accept the proposal of a middle-aged widower with two daughters who preferred horses to a new step-mama.

Suddenly she got up and swept from the room. 'You won't always be young, Annie,' she said. She spoke without kindness and with a certainty that seemed to give her a deal of satisfaction.

222

*

Since Annie had sent the animal doctor away with a flea in his ear – her own words – Adam felt a lot more settled. It was true he hated her working up at the house, but the cottage didn't seem to be neglected and he certainly wasn't. His meals were always ready, his clothes kept clean and mended, though Annie did always stand by his chair of a Friday evening holding out her hand for her wages.

He was careful not to touch her and quick to notice how she flinched away if he came too near. But when she brought the lamp from the dresser to the table of an evening and set light to the wick, he couldn't keep from staring. Staring didn't cost him anything.

After she'd lowered the globe over the flame it bathed the whole room in a soft yellow light. She looked so lovely sitting there with her sewing he had to clench his hands at times to stop himself from reaching out for her, though he knew better than that. Once he had come up behind her at the slopstone, so that as she turned round their faces were only inches apart. He had seen the way her eyes became wary, guarded, in the few seconds before she moved swiftly away, and he knew the time was not yet. She liked to chatter, and he would listen, watching her lips move, hardly heeding what she was saying.

Christmas came and went, as the seasons came and went, uneventfully, with a January so wet it was more like spring.

One night Annie sat at the table writing a letter and, fearsome less it was to the animal doctor, Adam asked her straight out who she was writing to.

'A lady who lived two doors down from us.' Annie put her pencil down. 'She looked after her mother as well as working in the mill. Her mother was bedfast, and I've had a feeling for a long time now that the old lady has died.' She began to write again. 'So the best way to find out is to ask.'

223

After she had gone up to bed Adam took the letter down from the dresser-shelf and examined the address. A slow reader himself, able to write only in capitals, he couldn't get over the neatness of Annie's joined-up script with small, perfectly-formed letters. He traced the name and address with his finger: Edith Morris. Miss Edith Morris. He put the letter back, took up his candlestick and climbed the stairs to his bed.

He didn't like the idea of Annie getting in touch with her past life. He drew the stone hot-water bottle up from the foot of the bed and cradled it to him. Still, writing to an old spinster about her mother was surely harmless enough.

When he woke up after an uneasy twitching sleep, the sky was beginning to redden, and the frost had at last arrived.

Edith showed Annie's letter to Mick the minute he arrived for his reading lesson.

'For practice you can read it aloud to me,' she said, handing him the single sheet of paper.

Mick took it from her with a sinking heart. He had begun to think that Miss Morris had stopped bothering about finding young Annie Clancy since that wasted visit to the Eccles's farm. Since then life had been so good to him, he could hardly believe his luck. For one thing he'd got himself a regular job bagging coal up to put on the carts. Forty on each cart, packed that tight you'd a job to separate them. He could have a bag on the weighing machine and up on the cart quicker than any man in the yard. It was the strength in him, he'd told Miss Morris, holding out an arm for her to feel his muscle.

He wasn't feeling strong now as he began to read, stumbling over each word, running a finger along the lines.

Dear Miss Morris,

I know you will be surprised to hear from me after such a long time, but I have stopped writing to my father. He said he would throw any letters I might write on to the back of the fire, and that is what he must be doing. But I would like to know how they are, especially the boys. Also I hope your mother is well. I hope you don't mind me writing to you. I am housekeeping in the mornings and working in a big house doing their sewing in the afternoons. I am well and happy. Hoping you are the same.

Annie Clancy

He handed the letter back, knowing he'd made a bad job of reading it, accepting as he stumbled over every single word that this life, this new shining life, would come to an end now that Miss Morris knew where to find Annie Clancy.

She looked as pleased as punch with herself. He'd noticed that the moment she had let him in. And there was a tantalising smell coming from the fire-oven. Oxtail, he guessed, slow cooked till the meat dropped off the jellied bones, with a sago pudding maybe afterwards, thick and creamy with a nutmeg crisp skin on top. All that would end now. It would be Annie Clancy getting her feet underneath the table, not him. He stared into the fire, sunk deep into a terrible despair.

Edith had gone quiet, too. She could read this big rough-spoken man like a book. She knew the effort it took him to present himself clean and tidy for his lessons since he worked as a coal bagger down at the yard. And she knew exactly how her finding Annie's address would have affected him.

'When are you fetching her back?' he said now. Then he made the supreme sacrifice. 'I'll come with you if you want.' He stared at Edith, a dull hopeless stare revealing all the terrible dread that had been growing in his heart day by day.

'I haven't thought yet,' Edith said. She couldn't bear to see the expression in Mick's eyes. It was as if his soul was revealed there for her to see. He was curling his big hands into fists, actually blinking to force back tears. He was suddenly disintegrating right there before her.

'I'd best not come any more,' he said in his low rumble of a voice. 'Best make it a clean break before Annie moves in.' He got up to go, snatching his jacket off the hook behind the door.

'Mick!' Edith felt rooted to her chair. His reaction to the letter hadn't surprised her, but she had never expected it to be so dramatic, so violent, so final.

'Mick!' She stepped outside on to the pavement, calling after him, but it was too late.

Within five minutes of leaving the cosy room, the fire built so that it roared up the chimney-back, Mick was down at the pub, pushing his way rudely through the men crowding round the bar. Shouting for a bloody drink at the top of his voice.

13

So Grandma Morris was dead. Annie folded Edith's letter and stored it away in the spare teapot on the dresser.

'Well? What does it say?'

Adam knew it wasn't any of his business, but he had to know. Ever since Annie had written to this Miss Morris he had lived in dread of her turning up at the cottage door, or worse still of Annie's father coming to claim her once he found out there was no illegitimate baby to bring them shame.

Annie didn't seem put out by his curiosity. 'She says the boys are all right, and that Billy is going down the pit when he leaves school at Easter. She says my father takes his wife out every Friday night, that they walk down the street to the Ram's Head arm in arm – would you believe it?'

'So that's all right then.' Adam was so relieved he could have shouted aloud. Instead, he went out of the back door, hiding his feelings by whistling under his breath. Annie wasn't going to leave him to go back to her old home. Things were going on all right there; this Miss Morris had said so.

'Are you going to write back?' he asked that evening, as they sat over the fire, Annie busy with sewing she'd brought with her from the big house.

'I don't think so.' Annie put down the length of crimson silk she was fringing and hemming by hand. 'She says I'll always be welcome, but from the tone of the letter it's obvious Miss Morris doesn't want to know any more than I've told her. I put myself beyond the pale when I got into trouble. It's just the sort of letter I imagined she would write – no feeling to it at all.'

Adam wished she wouldn't mention the trouble. It bothered him even to remember it. When Clara had first told him he hadn't liked it then. Annie was so lovely, so untouched, like a spring morning when the first cowslip appears dew-wet in the meadow grass.

'Aye, best let well alone,' he said.

Edith Morris thought she must be going mad. She was as lonely as ever now that Mick no longer came, and too proud to admit the reason for her despair. What was he, after all, but a rough-spoken Irish labourer who had warmed himself by her fire, eaten her food, pretended he wanted to learn how to read and write?

Why had she written in that cold way to young Annie? Why? When for so long she had dreamed of the day she would find her and bring her here to live. Now the thought of the red-haired girl sitting opposite to her in the chair where Mick had sat filled her with pain. Besides, Annie's letter hadn't been written by a lost and bewildered girl at the end of her tether. The baby was no more and Annie was well and happy. She had said so. She didn't need to be rescued. She was young and strong with all her life ahead of her.

Edith got up from her chair and walked slowly upstairs to her tiny bedroom at the front of the house. It was cold and damp. It had never known the warmth of a fire since the day the house was built, and in the tiny grate with its iron canopy Edith had pleated a fan of newspaper which she changed regularly once a month when she gave the room a thorough bottoming.

She paid no attention to the cold. It had seeped into her bones years ago and she accepted it as normal. Setting the candle down on her bedside table, she knelt by the wooden cross which stood on a lace-edged runner on top of a chest-of-drawers.

'Dear God, help me to cease this fevering of my blood. Thou knowest no man has ever touched me, so why should I be acting like a young and foolish girl? A foolish virgin, I should have said . . .' She felt the tears trickle through her fingers. 'Bring me to my senses, Lord, and show me the true way to Thy salvation. Amen.'

It was a terrible prayer to have said, a dreadful admission of weakness. But prayers were answered if the Lord saw fit to answer them. For the next few weeks she went as usual to the mill in the pitch-dark every morning, stood at her looms and concentrated on her work. She was a model weaver, sticking to the rules and abiding by them. She wore her hair high and close to her head to avoid the danger of it being drawn into the ever-moving belts; she paid no fines for faulty cloth, and she never needed to have her pay docked for arriving late in the mornings. She was, as usual, beyond reproach in every way.

But spring was on its way, even though the watery sun did no more than touch briefly the top half of the backyard wall. Edith walked home in the light, let herself in to her empty ordered house, and wept.

The wanting, the longing, the aching for the sight of a grizzled head and the sound of a deep rough voice in mid-curse was a pain deep down in her abdomen. 'Belly', Mick would undoubtedly have said. Every time a knock came to the door she expected to open it and see him standing there, holding his cap in his hand, shuffling his big feet, blurting out how bloody stupid he'd been for stopping away so long.

But he never came and during a sleepless night, when the March wind rattled the sash-window till she was sure it would collapse into the street below, Edith shouted aloud at the God who seemed to have turned His back on her.

Annie left the letter where it was, in the brown teapot, but she thought about it often as she sat with her sewing at the big house. What she had expected she didn't know, but every word was as cold and unfeeling as Edith Morris herself.

'She would run a mile if a man looked twice at her,' she told Adam, liking to make him smile.

'From how you've described her I don't think there's much danger of a man looking at her *once*,' Adam said, quick as a lick.

Annie could see he was getting over the shock of his wife's death nicely. She expected he was forgetting as well as regretting the proposal of marriage he'd made to her when still in deep grief. The arrangement of working afternoons up here in the comfortable sewing-room at the top of the big house was going well, now she had made Adam understand she wouldn't be bullied.

Annie folded her sewing and put it away for the next day. Dorothea was going to look splendid in the black velvet evening gown with the satin inlets in the puffed sleeves, in spite of the fact that she'd fidgeted and grumbled through every fitting. She was down there in the stable yard giving her horse its daily strapping, talking to a man who straightened up from his examination of the horse's foot, looked up at the window and gave Annie a curt nod of his head.

She turned away at once, but not before she was sure she'd seen a flash of mockery in the strangely light eyes.

Seth caught up with her as she walked back to the cottage down the long, winding drive.

'Everything all right, Annie?'

'Perfectly all right, thank you.'

'You're looking very tired.'

'That's because I'm busy.' She tried to walk on, but it was no use. He seemed determined to annoy her.

'You don't look all that happy to me.'

Annie was so angry she could have hit him. He had folded his arms, planted his feet wide apart, and was staring intently at her with his eyes narrowed.

'Having any more trouble with that ear?'

Annie's face flamed. 'I hear what I want to hear.'

'Your eyes are red. Maybe you should be wearing glasses for such close work.'

Was he serious? Did he really think he had the right to talk to her like this?

'I'm perfectly healthy,' she told him. 'I don't need glasses nor an ear trumpet. I suggest you keep your concern for those who appreciate and would benefit from it. Like Mr Gray's horses, or his pigs. And now, if you'll stand aside . . .'

She walked on, more than a little pleased with the way she'd dealt with that, but instead of going into the cottage she turned off the winding drive into a narrow field path, lifting her skirts clear of the mud-filled ruts where the shire horses had been exercised. She kicked a stone out of her way. She was tired and on edge, and her eyes ached from the strain of working on the black velvet.

Opening the gate and closing it carefully behind her, she walked along a barely visible path until she came to a small hump-backed bridge over what had once been a gravel pit. The long valley spread out before her, all in differing shades of green. The countryside, the real countryside with distant woods, so dense they were almost black, a meandering river lit to silver by the unusually strong light, all bisected by twisting ribbons of dry stone walls. The mines with their steep little streets of dark huddled houses and slag heaps seemed a million miles away.

Annie thought of her father, of Georgie and the four younger boys. All destined to work underground like moles, hardly seeing the light of day, never realising that all this beauty even existed.

How could Seth Armstrong suggest that she wasn't happy, when he had no idea of how it had been for her before he found her wandering the fells that dark winter's night?

She turned, and taking what she imagined was a short cut walked straight into a bramble thicket, with thorns that dragged at her dress. It would have been easier and

231

far more sensible to turn back and retrace her steps over the bridge, but Annie's mood was for fighting on, for finding her own way, for getting her bearings once she was free of the brambles. She was sure that if she skirted that wood, crossed that thread of a steam, picking her way over the two flat stepping-stones, she would be back at the cottage within minutes.

But when she climbed the long slope of a hill she looked down on a wide expanse of heathered wastes broken by isolated heaps of stone ruins. She looked up at the sky. She had no idea of how far she had walked, whether she had gone in circles or in a direct route away from the cottage. Town bred, she had none of the countryman's inborn instinct for survival, but surely it made sense to turn her back on that wild stretch of moorland and retrace her steps as far as possible?

She remembered a true story told to her by her mother years ago. A pitman, walking the hills one Sunday in summer, lost his way in a mist, fell down a gully and lay there for seven days and eight nights before being found by a search party. Still alive, but completely insane, his finger nails worn away in his frantic struggles to climb out.

Annie could see no sign of any creeping mist, but she was sure she could feel it in her bones. In March anything could happen – rain, snow, high winds, and days like today of pleasant warmth. There were signs of rabbits all around; purple violets flowered beneath a straggling hedge, but at any minute now she could be enveloped in a dank white curling mist, as lost as if she wandered alone on the far plains of the moon. Her next sliding, slipping steps brought her to a sudden totally unexpected clearing edged by the thick scrub and bramble bushes she remembered earlier. Sure now that the way back lay straight ahead of her she picked up her skirts and fought her way as carefully as her rising panic would allow her through the tangled undergrowth.

When she heard the soft murmur of voices she

stopped, a hand to her heart. For the past hour the only sound she had heard had been the bleat of a lone wandering sheep. It had seemed as if she would never hear a human voice again. She listened, not moving, standing quite still. Yes, there it was again, a muffled voice, followed by a scream of what sounded like a light-hearted protest. Moving cautiously, Annie edged forward.

The voices came, it seemed, from down the hill, carrying up to her, borne on the wind. Moving out into a sudden clearing, she looked down on a sight that brought a swift rush of colour to her face and started a trembling in her legs.

Lying on a dark brown blanket of bracken was Johnson, the parlour maid, with the handyman, Kit Dailey, straddled across her. His bare legs and buttocks shockingly white against the bracken. Deep in the throes of his passion his movements were rhythmic, fast and thrusting. Johnson was moaning, turning her head from side to side, her long, blue-black hair loosed from its neat bun.

Annie froze, stifled a cry by pressing fingers across her mouth, sank down on her knees on the hard stubbled grass. It was Laurie Yates all over again, groaning as he laboured in uncontrollable passion in the back room of her father's house. It was the realisation of what her father would have seen if he had come in through the door. It was the pain again, her sore back pressed down hard into the straw mattress; it was the feeling that she was being torn in two.

She got up, moved too quickly and dislodged a stone, a large stone which clattered and bounced its way down the slope.

'What the . . . ?'

Johnson's face was a mask of stunned disbelief. As the handyman scrabbled for his trousers, his voice was a bellowing shout of rage.

'Annie Clancy! Of all the dirty little tykes! Of all the

233

scum! *Watching* us, for God's sake! Up there snooping. Watching. Holy mother of God, I'll kill you for this!'

'I wasn't . . .' Annie knew this was no time for explanations; knew she wouldn't be believed anyway. Kit was hopping on one foot as he buttoned himself up, ready to come after her, while Johnson, hair flying, was already crossing the stream on her way up the hill.

But Annie was away, running as fast as she could across the uneven ground, mouth open, stumbling and falling, getting up and running on again. The inference that she had been watching horrified and sickened her. Those two had had it in for her since that first day. She had seen the look of undiluted hatred on the parlour maid's face. And Kit Dailey was just as bad. They made no secret of their dislike for her.

Annie was at the crest of a hill now. Over a ridge of trees she saw the familiar outline of chimneys. Sure that she was not being followed, she slowed down a little; as she saw the cottage in the distance, she began to run.

Adam was watching for her by the window. She could see him standing there, and the way he moved quickly away when he saw her coming. He had lit the lamp, tended the fire and the kettle was set to boil on the hob.

Gasping for breath, shaking with fear and disgust – how could they have thought she was up there on the hill watching them – Annie lifted the sneck on the cottage door and half fell inside.

Adam was there, kindly sturdy Adam, a father holding out loving arms to his child. In that moment he was the kind of father she had never had, one who would pat her troubles away and wipe the tears from her face.

Adam let her cry, knowing that whatever had distressed her so was best released in the bout of frenzied weeping. He stroked her hair, lifted it away from her neck. He tightened an arm about her, feeling her softness against him. Her hair was all mussed where he had touched it. She was damp and sweet-smelling and he could bear it no more.

'Annie . . . oh, Annie . . .'

He had meant to kiss her gently as he raised her face to his, but her eyes were tender with tears, she was looking at him with such feeling, the touch of her lips flamed his desire.

For Annie, it was as if the whole of her face was being swallowed up in a prickly thicket of hair, tobacco-smelling hair. His teeth were hard against her lips as he strained her to him, holding her with a strength that took the breath from her body. It came to her in that moment that no man had ever touched her gently, with tenderness, and without this greedy wanting.

She pushed him away from her so roughly, her strength matching his own, that he stumbled against a chair which gave against his weight and skitted across the floor. Somehow he kept his balance and would have reached for her again, but the expression in her eyes rooted him to the spot.

'Stay away from me!'

To his horror she picked up the lamp from the table and held it high above her head. He held out both hands, shaking his head from side to side.

'Annie! Annie, love, I don't want to hurt you. I would never hurt you.' He moved forward, only to step back as she swung the lamp high in an arc above her head.

'I mean it, Adam. Touch me again like that and I'll let fly. I will! I'm not pretending.'

Groping behind him for the armrests, Adam slowly lowered himself into his chair. 'Do I disgust you as much as all that, lass?' There were tears in his eyes. 'As much as all that?'

Annie lowered the lamp to the table. He wasn't to know that it was the humiliation, the terror of what might have happened if Kit Dailey had caught up with her that had wakened the violence in her. It was seeing them, it was them thinking that she . . . it was Adam comforting her . . . she shuddered. 'I think I'm going to be sick.'

Because she rushed over to the slopstone and had her back turned to him she saw nothing of the heartbreak creeping across the gardener's weather-beaten face.

'I won't bother you again, lass,' she heard him whisper.

When she turned round he was gone.

It took Harry Gray and his willing band of searchers four days to find him.

Adam, who knew the fells as well as his own back garden, had fallen down a long gully, broken both his legs and died there, face down on the dry and dusty bed.

They brought him back to the cottage, and two days later he was buried beside his wife in the old churchyard.

The weather had changed, and as the mourners walked back across the fields a sudden crack of thunder sent hailstones bouncing, while a gale from the west flattened the unseasonable daffodils in the flower beds that had been Adam's pride and joy.

14

'Well, then. It looks as if everything is settled, Annie.' Margot Gray nodded her head and smiled at her husband. 'That's right, isn't it, Harry? Annie can stay at the cottage till the new man and his wife work out their notice at their old place, then she moves in here on a permanent basis.'

Annie sat quietly, looking from one to the other, listening half-heartedly. Mrs Gray was being so kind, so generous, appearing not to notice that her husband was edging towards the door, eager to be outside with his dogs and his horses.

'You agree with that, dear.'

It was a statement, not a question, and it was Annie's turn to pretend not to be noticing when the big man in his checked jacket glanced over at her and closed an eye in a broad wink.

'Anything you say, my dear.' Harry felt behind him for the door handle. 'Now if you'll excuse me . . .' With a slam of the door he was gone. Annie heard the clump of his boots down the tiled hall and his bark of a voice calling out to someone to fetch his gun.

Margot smiled. She knew exactly what plans she had for this small flame-haired girl sitting on the edge of her chair, both hands clasped together in her lap. But as ever, she wanted Harry to think that the plans had been his idea. She had sensed a long time ago that the yelling, bullying manner hid an ego as fragile as an egg-shell. So, all the decisions were his – at least he believed so. The half of Margot that was French knew how to make a man happy, and still get her own way. Arguments, pouts, petulance, sulks were for other women, not her. She turned her full attention on Annie, one plump hand tapping on the arm of her chair as if to hurry her words along.

'Mr Gray's lawyer friend has everything in hand, Annie. With Adam's clear instructions in the letter he left behind, the money should come through in no time.'

'I don't want it, Mrs Gray.'

Margot ignored that. 'These things take time, and the most important thing was to take the money from its hiding-place and deposit it in the bank. You were right and very honest to tell me about it. Adam took a great risk in leaving it there. People talk, rumours grow and though he was a good and decent man, he did have a reputation as a miser.'

'I won't take it, Mrs Gray.'

'That's silly talk, Annie.'

'He ought never to have left it to me. He hadn't known me for long enough. I bet if you advertise in the paper for his relatives someone will come and claim it.'

'Undoubtedly.' Margot put up a hand. 'Did you ever hear him mention a relative? Or even a friend?'

Annie shook her head. 'He struck me as being a man who kept himself to himself. Like a hermit.'

'Exactly! Adam wanted *you* to have it, Annie. You made his life bearable after his wife died.'

'He asked me to marry him not long after.'

'He did?' Margot's eyes snapped their satisfaction. 'Well, there you are then. He looked upon you as his next of kin. For heaven's sake, child, don't disappoint me by going all pious and saying you refuse on principle to touch a single penny. Principles . . . pouff!' She snapped her fingers. 'It isn't exactly a fortune, when all's said and done, and don't go telling me that with your background it is because my grandmère once had to stay in the house for two years because her sabots were worn out and there was barely enough money for food.' She gave her trill of a laugh. 'You're a pretty girl and there's enough to buy clothes and a bonnet or two, then maybe bank the rest of your dowry. Money talks, Annie! This little legacy is

238

saying that you are now a woman of substance who will never have to go to her bridegroom empty-handed.'

'I can't take Adam's money, Mrs Gray.'

'Why not?' Margot's patience, always on a short rein, was beginning to give out. 'I know the world hasn't treated you fairly up to now, but this is the turning point. Can't you see that? One day you will marry and go over the hills and far away, then all this sadness and self-recrimination will be forgotten. Adam will be just a kindly memory of a man whose dearest wish was to make you happy. You brought joy into his life, Annie. Joy, where before there had been nothing but sadness and depression. Even cured of her illness his wife would still have faced each day expecting the worst – yes, and more often than not getting it. Because that was the way she was.'

Somewhere inside herself Annie was crying bitterly, sobbing tears of remorse. 'I sent Adam to his death,' she said suddenly, drooping her head into her hands.

Margot's heart contracted with pity. She sat quietly for a while, letting Annie have her cry out.

'You mean you quarrelled with him?' she ventured at last.

Annie raised tear-filled eyes. 'He . . . he kissed me in a certain way. I was unkind, no I was cruel to him, and he walked out. To his death,' she finished on a wail of despair.

'Nonsense! Absolute nonsense. Adam didn't commit suicide. He had tried many times to climb out of the place where he fell. The evidence was there for the search party to find. My husband told me about it. He was with them, remember? Adam certainly wasn't trying to die. He was struggling for hours to get out! They found proof that he had managed to lever himself up to the top using the powerful muscles of his arms before falling back on to his head.'

She stood up and began to walk about, swishing her long skirts. 'Adam Page wasn't the kind of man to kill himself, Annie. There wasn't the depth in him, the sensitivity. He got angry, he sulked. But you must know that.' Annie opened her mouth to speak, but Margot raised an imperious finger. 'So! You can stop wallowing in that silly trough of guilt, this minute. You brought Adam happiness; you put a smile on his face.'

'He kissed me and I vomited,' Annie said clearly.

The statement shot Margot's finely pencilled brows up almost to her hair-line. She walked across the room to the window, lifted a corner of the curtain and stared out across the lawns and down the tree-lined drive.

'But he didn't know that what had made me sick had really nothing to do with him.'

'What had it to do with?' Margot dropped the lace curtain back into place.

'Something that had upset me before.'

'Can you tell me?'

Annie shook her head and Margot, with uncharacteristic patience, went back to her chair and waited for Annie to compose herself. She knew exactly why this beautiful young girl interested her so much. Why her usually ordered thinking became diverted down strange pathways. Here in all her fresh loveliness was the daughter she would never have, the Lord in His wisdom having made her barren. And there, drowning in sorrow, was a girl who the same Lord should have seen fit to make happy. Somehow, somewhere the patterns had gone wrong. Birth, circumstances, fate had left the one with a searching need for affection, and the other, with the means and the will to give that affection, frustrated and unfulfilled.

'Of course you couldn't marry Adam,' she said at last, her voice brisk. 'But he would come back and haunt you if you refused the money.' She stood up to indicate the interview was at an end. She knew what had upset Annie before. Hadn't she seen Seth Armstrong ride away down the drive after her? Her hand went to the bell-rope by the side of the massive fireplace.

240

'I'm relying on you finishing the girls' dresses for the Mayday celebrations.' She gave the bell-rope a pull. 'Let's hope the weather keeps fine.' She smiled. 'One year we seemed to have overdone the liquid refreshments and Adam had to be carried back to the cottage on a plank. His wife never forgave him.'

With a bob of a knee and a 'Thank you, ma'am,' Annie left the room.

'That poor child . . .' Margot stood still, a hand to her heart. 'And poor, poor Adam Page.' Could a man who knew the fells like the back of his hand have fallen to his death like that? Had he really tried unsuccessfully to climb out, or had he lain there, heartbroken at Annie's cruel rejection, just waiting to die?

'Yes, ma'am?'

The maid Johnson stood, hands clasped together, in the doorway.

She had seen Annie Clancy going back upstairs to the sewing-room. Their glances had locked, but neither had spoken. Since that episode down by the stream she had completely ignored Annie, and told Kit to do the same. 'Look at her, but don't speak to her,' she'd advised. 'That way she won't know what to think.'

'But she'll think she's got away with it! The dirty little . . .'

Johnson had shushed him up. 'We know she hasn't got away with it, don't we? We know we're just biding our time. Don't we?'

That night Annie sat alone in the gardener's cottage putting the finishing touches to a blouse.

She was not afraid of being alone. Over and over again she impressed the truth of this on herself. What if the stairs creaked in the middle of the night, or a door swung open on rusty hinges? Adam had told her that the cottage was built just before the Great Plague down in London. It was said that a wealthy merchant had brought his wife and baby all the miles north, desperate

241

to save them from the terrible ravages of the disease, only to have them both die of the cholera not three months later. So if she thought she heard the thin wail of a sick baby before cockcrow, she was imagining it all. Adam had often teased her about letting her imagination run away with her.

Had Mrs Gray been right when she'd sworn that Adam had tried to climb up out of the gully? Was it all in her imagination that he had gone out and deliberately walked to his death? If he had, would he come back and haunt her with ghostly reproaches? Was that his whiskery face peering in at the window, that pale blurred wavering outline up against the glass?

Now, with the lamp lit and the fire glowing brightly, the little room was filled with peace. There was no need for her to keep on glancing over her shoulder as if she sensed a shadowy figure standing there. No need at all.

Bending her head over her sewing she put the finishing stitches in the button trim down the front of the white blouse, her stitches as fine as spiders' legs. The blouse was pretty with its lace-edged frill round the neck. Pretty, not smart like the blue gown she swore she would never wear again. She bit off a thread. Now it lay pushed down into the big chest in her bedroom where it could stay for ever.

A red-hot cinder fell into the hearth with a faint enough click, but Annie flinched and looked nervously behind her.

When she heard footsteps on the path outside the back door she held her breath. When she saw the latch slowly rise the sewing dropped from her fingers into her lap. She could actually feel the blood draining from her face and her scalp tightening of its own accord.

'Who is it?' She heard her voice, an alien voice, high and tinny, mechanical, like the squeak of a clockwork toy. 'Is anyone there?'

Her legs were trembling but if she was sharp enough about it there might be time to hurry across the room

242

and bolt the door. She started forward then backed away as the door was suddenly banged open to reveal Kit Dailey dressed for the road, a cap pulled low over his forehead, with Johnson in a long coat buttoned to her throat right behind him.

'You should have bolted the door, Annie Clancy.' Kit's voice was whisper-soft. 'We told you we'd get you one day – remember?' His dark eyes looked almost black. 'We haven't forgot you watching us, have we, Ruby?'

Johnson looked like a black crow in her floor-length coat, with her heavy boots showing beneath the folds. A black straw hat covered her hair and was tied beneath her chin with a trailing scarf. She looked as if she was ready for a long, long journey.

'We're not likely to forget a thing like that, are we, Annie?'

Her face was filled with hate; it smouldered in her narrowed eyes, and the twist of her thin lips. Annie forced herself to speak as calmly as she could.

'Just tell me what you want . . . then I can get on with my sewing.'

The white blouse had fallen to the floor as she stood up. It lay there, in a heap of white ruffles, delicate and pretty. Deliberately Johnson reached for it with a foot, dragged it towards her, picked it up and held it at arm's length, head on one side.

'I like this.' She nodded. 'I think I would suit a blouse like this.' She tossed it over to Kit. 'Do you think I would suit it?'

'Mebbe.' Before Annie could stretch out a hand to stop him, the blouse was on the back of the fire, smouldering briefly before bursting into flame. 'We'll never know now, will we?' His swarthy face darkened with an anger so fierce it almost stopped Annie's heart from beating.

'We've been given our marching orders, Annie Clancy! By her ladyship. The high and mighty Madame

Gray.' He spread both arms wide. 'And for what? For being found together in her room.' He jerked his chin at Johnson. 'Along with a few bottles of their precious wine.' He raised his fist. 'So who told on us, then? Who else but you, Clancy! You've been telling on us all the time. You told her about seeing us down by the pool, and she's been having us watched ever since. By *you*! Things were all right till the day you came up to the house toffed up like the bloody fairy queen. Kow-towing to your betters, sneaking your way into the drawing-room, making trouble for us.'

Annie stepped forward. 'I never told . . .' She whispered the truth. 'I never told a living soul. I wasn't following you. I was out walking, that was all. I walked too far and lost my bearings. Why should I want to get either of you into trouble? What would I have had to gain by that?'

'But we've got something to gain, Annie.' Kit thumped the flat of his hand down on the table, scattering a paper of pins in all directions. 'And you are going to give it to us.' He swiped two bobbins of cotton to the floor. 'The *money*, Clancy! The gold old Adam had stored away somewhere in this cottage. Mebbe even in this very room.' His eyes were everywhere as he shouted, flaying his arms about wildly, spinning round suddenly on his heels to point a finger. 'Oh, aye. He dropped hints often enough about being worth a bonny penny, an' don't tell us you don't know where he hid it, because we won't believe you!'

'Just biding your time, are you, till you can take the money and do a bunk?' Johnson shot out a hand to grasp Annie's wrist. 'Mebbe he *didn't* tell you where it was and that's why you're hanging on here on your own. Mebbe you hunt for it in the dead of night by the light of a candle. Searching, searching . . .'

'She knows where it is all right.' Kit suddenly took charge. 'Leave her be. She'll not tell us nowt. She's not that sort. Her sort will have their tongues ripped out before they'd tell. Here, give us that piece of stuff off the table. No, that's not long enough, the longer piece over there.'

Before Annie could guess what he was going to do her head was jerked back and the strip of white cotton material forced into her mouth. She choked on it, swung her head from side to side in painful protest, struggled in vain as her hands were bound together behind her back.

'Now, rope her to that chair!'

It was Johnson giving the orders and Kit Dailey carrying them out. The twine cut into Annie's wrists. The more she fought to free herself the worse the pain flared and burned.

'Are you going to tell us?' Johnson leaned so close Annie could see the way a tick jerked and flickered the soft flesh beneath the lower eyelid of her right eye. 'Well?'

Annie shook her head. Her eyes signalled defiance.

'Out of my way!' Kit elbowed Johnson aside, lifted a clenched fist and hit Annie full in the face, rocking the chair back on its spindles. 'Then we'll just have to look for it, won't we?'

With a nod at Johnson for her to follow suit, he began to pull the ornaments from the high mantelshelf, the matching pair of blue jugs, the ticking clock, sending them crashing into fragments on the stone hearth. Annie strained and jerked at the gag, sodden now and tighter than ever. Hardly able to believe what she was witnessing, Annie saw Johnson jerking open drawers, upturning their contents on to the floor. The brown teapot was hurled to the far side of the room, a copper jug dashed against a wall. Kit tossed the sticks for the morning's kindling out of the oven, scattering them everywhere.

'He'd keep it upstairs, Kit.' Johnson came out of the scullery with a sack of flour and a knife. 'The old skinflint wouldn't keep his money down here.' She slit the sack from top to bottom, tipping the flour on to the cut rug. 'Misers like to gloat, away from prying eyes. They like to

245

count it by the light of a candle.' The long full coat swung out behind her. Her normally pale cheeks were flushed, her small eyes shone with a strange light.

Kit Dailey's swarthy face was transfixed with an evil excitement. Annie watched him tear down the curtain at the bottom of the stairs, clawing at it until the worn material tore into hanging strips. In that moment she realised that they were enjoying themselves; that they were also half-crazed with drink.

She stopped struggling, closing her eyes to shut out the dreadful sight of a grown man and woman destroying for destruction's sake. But she couldn't shut out the sound of crashing crockery, of bentwood chairs that had lasted for two or more generations being dashed against a wall till they splintered into kindling sticks.

Soon their feet pounded on the bare wooden stairs as they climbed to the bedrooms. She heard them shouting and swearing; at one time she thought the ceiling would give, and wondered bleakly if she would ever come out of this alive. She wished she could pray, but found there were no words. The gag was choking her and the animal sounds coming from her throat were surely not being made by her? She felt sick and had a growing feeling of bowel discomfort. Her head slumped forward as she anticipated the moment when they came downstairs empty-handed.

Suddenly, Kit Dailey was standing in front of her, holding a section of wooden floorboard in his hand.

'Clancy!' He stabbed it into her chest. 'The money's gone! We found the hiding-place but the money isn't there!' He jerked the piece of wood up with such force that a rusty nail caught her cheekbone, tearing it down its full length. Beside himself with rage, he wrenched the gag from her mouth. 'So where is it? Them floorboards have been tampered with not all that long ago.' He raised the wood again, glanced round wildly, and sent the sewing-machine crashing from the table. His face was so contorted with fury that his features seemed to blur one into the other. 'Where is it, Clancy?'

246

'I don't know!' Shameful tears flooded Annie's breast, her throat; it was a pain swelling into more tears, but she blinked them back. 'I don't even know if there was any money. Why should Adam tell *me*?'

'Because you was his fancy woman!'

Johnson came from behind Kit Dailey, stepping suddenly into the pool of light from the lamp. 'She's telling the truth, Kit. Her sort's not capable of lying.' Her pale face now had a mottled look about it. The worst of her anger being spent, she looked ill and pinched, and very plain. She seemed to shrink where she stood, sinking down into the folds of the voluminous coat. 'The silly old fool most likely buried it. Out on the fells. So now it's gone for ever.'

Slowly Kit lowered the piece of wood, then tossed it on to the fire. 'So what do we do now? An' what do we do with her?'

Johnson's eyes were slits of venom. 'We can stop here till morning. Nobody up at the house knows where we've gone. An' she can stop here too.' She handed over the gag. 'Just make sure she spends a quiet night.'

'No!' Annie twisted her head from side to side. 'I can't breathe properly with that thing on me. Please . . . please!'

As he tied the sodden strip of stuff, knotting it three times, Kit got no satisfaction from Annie's stifled cry of pain. The euphoria of the past hour had drained from him; he felt weak, tired to the point of exhaustion. He saw the way the cloth was flecked with blood; he averted his eyes from the deep scratch down her cheek. Annie looked so ill, so beat, it came to him that of all the bad things he had done in his life, this was surely the worst.

'We can't leave her here like this. Not all night. She's gasping for breath now. Suppose she pegs out?'

Johnson could hardly bear to look at him. She'd suspected for a long time that he was all wind and shout and not much else. Picking up the lamp she gave him a push, almost sending him sprawling.

'Stop acting like a big soft lad. She'll still be here when we come down in the morning. Just make sure her legs are tied tight enough to the chair rungs, and stop taking your time about it. You've had a bit of a soft spot for her since that first day.' She walked to the foot of the stairs, holding the lamp high. 'You're only in on this with me because she wouldn't look at you!'

She led the way up the narrow stairway. What was she to do with Kit Dailey without the money to make up for his lack of spirit? He had sworn it was in the cottage, said that the gardener had dropped many a hint about having a tidy sum put by.

She banged her way angrily into the front bedroom, lay on top of the bed without removing her coat, and motioned for Kit to lie down beside her. The opportunity to make love was here, the privacy they had once thought they craved, but now the inclination, the lust she had once felt for him had gone.

'What are we to do without the money?' There were tears of anger in her voice, anger and frustration. 'There's no saying we'll get taken on, not without references.'

'Something'll turn up,' Kit said, without hope. He sat up, straining his eyes into the darkness. 'Suppose she dies? Suppose they come to look for her and find her dead? There's nobody going to come looking for us as it is, but if there's a corpse sitting in that chair they'll put two and two together and know it was us. Then there'll be nowhere for us to hide.' He swung his legs over the side of the bed. 'I'm going down to check I've not half throttled her.'

'So she can get free to run screaming for help?'

Kit felt his shoulder gripped as if in a vice, and when he tried to twist away she reached up for his hair with both hands, tugging and pulling till he thought his eyes would pop out with the agony of it.

'You go down those stairs and I'll kill you!' she hissed, her face not an inch away from his own. 'Then I'll kill her.' Her hands were on his throat now. He could feel the agonising pressure of her thumbs on his windpipe. His eyes strained and bulged from their sockets.

It was ludicrous, it was unbelievable. To be pinned down on a bed by a woman, even if she did have the strength of a man. He tried to prise her hands away from his throat only to feel the relentless pressure increase . . .

Annie heard them shouting and fighting up there in Adam's room. For a long time Johnson's voice was dominant.

Suddenly the house was quiet. The glow from the dying fire lingered on the upturned chairs, the spilled drawers, the shattered ornaments. The sewing-machine on its end, its bobbin of white cotton still in position.

The inside of her mouth felt raw where the gag cut into it. As she twisted her hands in a vain endeavour to free herself, the thick twine seared into her wrists sending waves of pain up her arms. She could see the blood from her grazed ankles staining her stockings. Soon the fire would go out, and in her thin working skirt and blouse she was already achingly cold. The afternoon sunshine had given way to rain; she could hear it splattering half-heartedly against the window. There was a sighing in the trees and when the last glimmer from the coals finally faded she would be in darkness, with a long night stretching ahead in blackness as thick and heavy as Laurie Yates had once told her it was down the pit.

Ember by flickering ember Annie watched the fire die, until all that was left was a tiny pinprick of a glow in the very heart of the grate. With the total darkness came the cold, seeping from cracks in the stone floor, whispering in from the gap at the bottom of the back door. It curled up round her numbed ankles; it turned her into stone.

Her eyes were wide, staring at nothing. The pressing dark was all around her. There could be anything out there in it, anyone, and she would never know until she felt their touch. She moved her head, then wished she hadn't as the gag tightened, thrusting her tongue back until she retched and heaved deep down in her throat. A sob burst from her, then another. The hard pain in her chest dissolved into tears. They ran down her cheeks, she tasted the sad saltiness of them as they trickled into her tortured mouth. She struggled yet again to free her hands, straining and twisting until she felt the warm stickiness of blood running down her fingers.

How much longer would they leave her like this? Was it God's way of punishing her for sending Adam to his death? Annie rocked her body to and fro, certain in her heart that the two upstairs had nothing in common with God. The devil then? She shivered. The maid Johnson was evil, she was sure of that. Johnson was capable of walking away when it came light and leaving her there.

How long would it be before they searched for her? Dear God, it could be days . . .

Seth woke up with a start, with the feeling he had heard some kind of noise from downstairs. Yet out on the landing he hesitated. If Biddy had got up from her bed, she would have taken a candle down with her and he'd be able to see the light shining beneath the kitchen door. He leaned over the banisters staring down into an inky blackness. Not a sliver of grey light seeped in from the tall landing window. It was all total darkness.

Feeling foolish he went back to bed, but not to sleep. He could hear the rain falling steadily and he knew that unless it stopped soon the stream would flood yet again. He could almost see the sloping stone floor of his surgery inches deep in water, the daffodils bent over, their heads trailing in a sea of mud. The picture in his mind was so vivid he could imagine the willow tree once again surrounded by a swirling torrent. He decided to go out at first light to make sure the new-born calves in Reynolds's farm were dry and safe and not up to their hocks in flood water.

An hour later he gave up trying to sleep and, pulling

on his long woollen dressing-gown, went downstairs and into his den where the banked-up fire needed only a touch of the poker to burst into flame.

He tried to read but found he lacked concentration. He reached for his pipe, but not even the comforting rigmarole of lighting it gave him ease. He cursed his restlessness, cursed the rain, wondered at the vague anxiety eating away at him. He went back to bed, to dream that he saw a woman's bloated body in the flood water, her full skirts caught by a hanging branch. Though her long hair was black-wet he knew that when it was dry it would be a glorious red-tinged gold.

The rain was keeping Edith Morris from her fought-for sleep. So she went downstairs and coaxed the fire into life with the pile of sticks drying in the side-oven.

The guttering along the roof was blocked again. She could hear the rain gushing down in a steady stream by the front window. It was almost two years since that same length of guttering had been cleared out, and even then the man next door had said it needed replacing. It would have to be done again, but not by the man next door. Now he spent his days crouched over the fire coughing was what left of his lungs away, a victim of the disease that came to so many miners.

Mick Malone would have the guttering cleared out in a jiffy. Edith warmed her hands round a mug of tea. Maybe he wouldn't charge her anything, as a gesture to their friendship, in token of their friendship. But she couldn't ask him, even though she'd have no trouble in finding him. It was said he was down there in the Ram's Head every single night till chucking-out time. It was said he was hardly ever sober.

Before she went back to bed she brought down and refilled her stone hot-water bottle, wrapping it carefully in one of her mother's old bed-jackets to protect her feet. When she slept at last she dreamed that Annie Clancy came back to the street. Dead in her coffin, strapped on to a cart. With her father and his terrible wife walking behind to the cemetery, arm in arm, swaying and laughing together, as they did every Friday night on their way to drink themselves sodden, with money that should be spent on food.

Hours later the weeping inside Annie stopped. Worn out, cold and cramped into a blessed state of semi-consciousness, her head fell forward, staying there for a short while until the agonizing pull of the gag jerked her cruelly awake for another few tortured minutes.

'We've got to untie her. She looks half dead to me.'

'What? And have her going straight to the house and setting them on after us! His lordship would hunt us down as if we were foxes.' Johnson snorted her disgust. 'Then we'd be up before the magistrates and clapped into prison for God knows how long. A fine start to a new life that would be!'

Kit Dailey's head throbbed like a tom-tom drum. By all that was holy she was a hard nut. He stared at her. In the cold morning light with her hair coming down, her face bloated with drink, he was beginning to wonder how he had ever desired her or ached in his bones to touch her.

Annie was a small slumped figure in the chair. The ashen pallor of her face was scaring him witless. When her eyes did open briefly they stared at him with a mute pleading. Reminding him suddenly of a puppy he'd had in County Down when he was a boy. Its paw had been caught in a snare. It had looked at him in just the same way.

'She won't be missed till this afternoon when she doesn't turn up for work at the house. She'll have been tied up for nigh on twenty-four hours.' He caught Johnson by the elbow as she moved to walk past him and swung her round to face him. 'Suppose she dies like I said? There'd be no place for us to hide then.'

With a careless shrug of her shoulders Johnson walked to the door and, as Kit fell reluctantly in step beside her, her mouth twisted into a sneer.

They walked for over a mile, keeping to the field paths. The overnight rain had left the ground bogged down with mud, but the floods had receded a little. The fences down by the river had been broken by the passing weight of logs and branches. The sun was already rising high in an almost cloudless sky and when they began to climb up the Nab's steep slope a lone sheep appeared from behind a stone wall, bleating anxiously.

Suddenly Kit dropped the sack he was carrying over his shoulder and whirled round to face back down the hill.

'Today's the Mayday feasting! Oh, dear God! Annie Clancy won't be working today. She won't be missed. Not today! They'll be run off their feet with us gone, too busy to miss her.' He yelled at the top of his voice. 'Are you listening to me, you hard-faced devil? She could sit in that chair for another day and another night! And beyond that mebbe. I'm going back!'

'Suit yourself.' Johnson made no move to follow him. Just stood there with her hands on her hips, laughing, the long black coat billowing out in a slight breeze. 'You're barmy! Pots for rags,' she called after him, cupping a hand to her mouth. 'I'm glad to be shut of you. You're not a man, you're a nowt! A weak, smarmy lump of nowt!'

When Kit stopped to catch his breath, turned back to look, shading his eyes from the sun, she was a mere speck in the distance, a bent black figure, for all the world like a Pendle witch. Kit shook his head. They'd burned the Pendle witches, but burning was too good for that one. She should be hung, drawn and quartered.

He stumbled on, leaping from one dry patch to another, as spry and nimble as a mountain goat. She was a bad lot, and he was well rid of her. He wouldn't try to meet up with her again, not him. Once he'd cut Annie

Clancy free then he'd be off. In the opposite direction. South, not north. It'd be easier to find a place without Ruby Johnson to hinder him. He'd done the right thing getting rid of her.

At the foot of the hill he risked leaving the field paths and set off along the narrow road. Muttering and cursing to himself, he missed hearing the sound of a horse's hooves and jumped clear only when the rider shouted aloud: 'Watch what you're doing, man!' Kit moved so swiftly he almost fell sprawled into the muddy ditch, regained his balance and looked up into the unsmiling face of the animal doctor.

'Mr Armstrong!' He touched his forehead in the gesture that owed nothing to respect. 'You're out this way early.'

Seth reined in his horse and nodded. There was something about this swarthy fellow that gave him the creeps. He looked like the type who would steal the pennies from his dead grandmother's eyes.

'What are you doing up here at this time, Dailey? I would have thought there would be plenty for you to do today. And wasn't that Johnson I saw back there? Running like a startled rabbit.' His eyes narrowed. 'Is something wrong? What's going on?'

'There's nowt going on, sir.'

Kit's mind was working feverishly as he summed up his chances of making a run for it up and over the stony ridge to the side of the bridle path. He took two shuffling steps sideways. By the time the animal doctor had dismounted he could be away, as far away as he could get. But first . . .

'I'd call in at the gardener's cottage, sir, that's if you're going to the May feasting.' He was backing away. 'I'd do that, sir. That I would. Indeed I would . . .'

'What did you say?' In one swift movement Seth slid from his horse, caught Kit by the collar of his jacket and swung him round. 'Why should I call at the gardener's cottage?' He lifted the handyman clear off the ground. 'I'm waiting, Dailey!'

Kit flinched away from the expression in the pale grey eyes. He had seen this man in a rage before now. He had seen him bring his whip down on the shoulders of a cringing stable lad for doing no more than beating an obstinate pony into submission.

'I'm doing mi best to help, sir,' he whined. 'It's a matter of life and death, sir. The gardener's girl. Young Annie Clancy. She's . . .' He was being shaken now like a rat held by a terrier's strong teeth. 'Go to her, sir,' he managed to gasp. 'There may not be much time . . .' The words were torn from him. He closed his eyes, waiting for the blow that never came.

Instead, with all his powerful strength Seth flung him to one side, leapt back into the saddle and rode away, as if all the winds of heaven and earth were behind him.

Leaving Kit rolling over and over on the steep and stony path, to lie dusty and bruised, but still alive, thanks be to God!

15

When Seth cut her free Annie moaned and opened her eyes.

Her hands were purple and swollen, the wrists inflamed where the twine had dug into them. One cheek was puffed and discoloured, and her torn blouse revealed scratches as deep and fiery as if a wild animal had clawed her. She was marble cold, her hair matted and sticky with sweat; she was wet and filthy, yet when he trickled water into her parched and bleeding mouth, she couldn't swallow.

Seth took off his cloak and wrapped it around her. He was filled with an anger so great he trembled with the force of it. Kicking aside the shattered debris of a stool, he carried her out into the bright morning, cradling her tenderly against his shoulder, shielding her face from the sun's glare.

When Margot Gray saw him coming towards the house, striding out, his face set like a stone mask, she ran towards him.

'Oh, *mon Dieu*! The poor child! Bring her into the house.' She called out to a boy with barley pale hair shambling aimlessly across the lower slope of lawn. 'Toby! Go and fetch the master. He's down at the stables. Go on boy! Run! Tell him it is necessary he comes at once!'

On the way up the wide oak staircase Seth explained what had happened. His words came out staccato sharp. He flung them at her over his shoulder. 'She's half choked and wandering in her mind. The cottage is in ruins. Wicked wanton destruction.'

On the landing Margot moved round him to open a door. 'In here.' She pulled back a silk counterpane, turned down the sheets. 'The first thing we've got to do is to warm her. Ring that bell.' She put a hand to her eyes. 'No, don't bother. They're all across in the meadow setting the trestle tables out . . .' Her voice spiralled after her. 'Dailey and Johnson have gone – taken half our wine cellar with them – today of all days, would you believe.'

Tenderly Seth laid Annie down, smoothed back her hair from her forehead. 'What have they done to you, love?' he whispered. 'How could anyone . . . ?'

The last time, that other time, he had known what to do. His hands had been gentle and sure as he touched her nakedness, feeling for broken bones. So why was he hesitating now? He buried his face in his hands. That had been the time when she was merely a stranger, a young girl he had found wandering in the darkness on the fells. He had tended her as he would a sick animal. Whereas now she was young Annie, a laughing girl he had talked to, argued with, watched blossom like a flower in the atmosphere of his home. He sighed. A girl he had frightened away.

When Harry came blundering into the room, red-faced, treading mud from his boots into the pastel-shaded carpet, Seth spoke to him through gritted teeth.

'She could have been tied to that chair all day. All night and the next day. She might have died.' He pulled back the top sheet. 'It wasn't a wild animal that did that. It was a man. He must have raked his nails so deep he's gouged the flesh away. He couldn't have done a better job if he'd taken a knife to her.'

Harry took blustering charge of the situation. 'The doctor'll be here in minutes, old chap. Young Toby Eccles went leaping and running to fetch him faster than if the hounds of hell were at his heels. Daft the lad might be, but he cottoned on to Annie here with a devotion that had to be seen to be believed.'

He went willingly from the room when his wife came in with towels and warm water. A sick room was no place for a man. He just prayed that when his turn came he would have the clout to curl up in a ditch, close his eyes and allow himself to stiffen. No funeral neither, with Margot and the girls done up like black crows. As far as he was concerned they could dig him into the soil, stamp it down and leave him be. If anyone wanted to remember him they could do that without crying over a headstone.

He decided to pour himself a whisky, though he never reckoned to start imbibing till midday. His teeth jittered against the rim of the glass as he raised it to his lips. Truth was, seeing that young lass in such a pitiful condition had shaken him to the mothballs.

Armstrong, too. He'd known the animal doctor for a long time. Margot had done a good job of supporting the stricken fella when his wife had died of self-inflicted starvation. They'd had her to dinner, and it had angered him no end to see the way the silly woman had pushed the food around on her plate, reckoning on to be eating it. Grief, they'd put it down to, a broken heart over the death of her baby. Harry refilled his glass and upended it. But the child had never lived, for God's sake! She hadn't had to watch it grow in grace and beauty, then have it taken from her. That he could understand – or could he?

It paid not to dwell, or even to think too much. Harry was glad he wasn't the introspective type. You could store a lot of bother up for yourself that way. Take Armstrong there. Finding the gardener's girl tied up like that, half dead into the bargain had almost pole-axed him. He'd had a look on his face that bit deep.

Harry shook his big head from side to side. Reached for the decanter again.

Margot noticed it too. The pain in Seth's eyes made her blink and look away from him for a moment.

'Dailey must be caught,' he was saying. 'I'd string him up myself if I laid hands on him.' Leaning over the bed he touched Annie's puffy cheek. 'It goes beyond me how anyone could . . . it really goes beyond comprehension.'

He turned to Margot. 'Her father used to beat her. Did you know that?'

Margot nodded. 'Life can be very cruel to some.'

'But the cruelty ends now.' Seth walked over to the window. 'I'm taking her home with me as soon as she's fit to travel. If it's within my power she'll never be hurt again. Never!'

Margot went to stand beside him, laying a hand on his arm. Didn't he realise, this lovely man with the build of a wrestler and the heart of a tender woman, that his feelings were plain to see? Feeling as he did, why in God's name had he ever let young Annie Clancy out of his sight? Annie had said she had left because he told her the truth.

For Margot, to think was to act. 'God knows how you came to let her go. Adam said he found her wandering the road like a tramp woman, escaping from the hill farm where young Toby Eccles used to live. You know that place, Seth. Come to think, it was because of what you told us of the conditions there that we had the lad brought here. How could you have let Annie go to a place like that?'

Seth stared down at the young-old face with its powdered wrinkles and misplaced rouge. He glanced behind him at the bed.

'Between us – Mrs Martindale and I – we frightened her away,' he said slowly. 'But I never knew she had gone to work for Barney Eccles.' He pounded a fist into the palm of his hand. 'Do you think I would have left her there, knowing? Barney Eccles expects to bed any servant girl foolish enough to stay. I called one day, not realising Annie was there.' His eyes darkened. 'She could have been only yards away, in the farmhouse, and I didn't know.'

'But she ran away. No harm came to her. Adam Page found her wandering the road and took her into his cottage. He was a kindly man. Over-thrifty, maybe, but kind.'

'Kinder than me.' Seth would not be comforted. When the doctor came into the room, Gladstone bag held out before him, Seth walked quickly out on to the landing and down the stairs, into the drawing-room where Harry sat slumped in his chair, third whisky to hand on the pedestal table by his side.

On the third day Annie swallowed a little of Cook's chicken broth in the morning, and in the afternoon managed a good two tablespoons of calves'-foot jelly. She was hazy in her mind about what had happened since the animal doctor had found her and brought her here.

Tincture of iodine had been painted on the deep scratches down her front. She remembered the sting of it going on, and she remembered a cold poultice being laid against her right eye, and the smell of linseed oil being gently massaged into her wrists and ankles.

There had been a man's voice; the sense of someone sitting by the bed, hour upon hour – day after day, for all she knew. She had called out and he had laid her back on the pillows, smoothed the hair from her forehead, trickled water into her mouth. She had been conscious of him being there, of feeling desolate when he went. Of waking in the night for what seemed like brief but terrible moments of fear when Johnson stood over her with the bread-knife in her hand, holding the tip of the blade against her throat, eyes blazing as she promised what she would do unless she was told the hiding-place of Adam's hoarded money.

Where was she now? Shuddering, Annie recalled the set face and the staring eyes, lived again the blind terror as Johnson's finger-nails had torn at her skin. Screamed again, but in her mind this time, at the memory of Kit Dailey's dark face as he forced the gag into her mouth.

On the seventh day Dorothea came into the bedroom and told Annie that Kit Dailey had been arrested by the police as he tried to sign on a ship leaving Liverpool Docks for Belfast.

'A small cargo ship,' she said, sitting down in the bedside chair with her knees apart, her skirts all rucked between them. 'He won't be sailing anywhere for a long time to come.' She gave an uncanny replica of her father's loud laugh. 'It's a pity they've stopped shipping criminals like him to Australia. Do him good to be clapped in irons below decks.'

She thought Annie looked a damn sight better than she had a few days ago, but the bruises on her face had faded to a sickly yellow, giving her a jaundiced look, and her mouth was still a bit lopsided where the gag had bit deep into the soft tissues of her mouth.

'You're looking splendid,' she lied, because there wasn't a mean bone in the whole of her big body. 'Doc says there'll be no lasting scars.'

She didn't add that the doctor had said it would be the mental scars that would take more time to heal, but she didn't really believe that sort of talk. You fell down, you developed a bruise. You cut yourself, it bled. Your head ached, you put a lavender-soaked handkerchief on your forehead, and you had a bad monthly pain and you cursed and wished for the umpteenth time that you'd been born a boy.

'The May feasting was a bit of a washout with all this excitement.' She laughed noisily, with her mouth open. 'You were lying up here on what looked like it could have been your deathbed, but we had to carry on with it or half the village maidens would have gone home in tears. Would you believe that some of them had been up at dawn to chase about the meadow kissing the dew?'

'Did you and Abigail do it?'

'What!' Dorothea leaned back in her chair, presenting the flat plains of her face to the ceiling. 'Take more than a splash or two of dew to make us even passable, but you should have seen the May Queen in her long white dress leaping round the Maypole. Pity she was in foal.'

Annie sat up and clutched her side. 'You shouldn't make me laugh. It hurts.'

A little colour had come into the pale cheeks and Dorothea was well pleased, though she didn't think that what she had said was as funny as all that.

'Abigail found a fox cub no more than a couple of weeks old. She's got it hidden in the barn in a cardboard box teaching it to drink milk from a saucer like a cat. If our father finds out he'll go raving mad. He's lost half his chickens to one of its relatives. I'll go now.' She stood up, her duty done. 'Seth's downstairs having tea. He'll be coming up to see how you are any time now.'

She missed the blush staining Annie's cheeks. The subtleties of blossoming relationships between men and women were lost on Dorothea. Naïve to the point of immaturity, she was happy to lollop her way through life skimming the surface of emotional involvements. She liked Annie for the simple reason that it would have been too much bother to dislike her.

'I'll see you tomorrow.'

She crashed the door to behind her and Annie heard her clomping down the stairs, making more noise than a herd of overweight elephants.

'You're better,' Seth said, coming in without knocking.

'As right as rain,' Annie agreed. 'I'm getting up this evening, then tomorrow I'm going downstairs.'

'In a few weeks' time you're coming back with me.'

'I'm going back to the cottage. It's been cleared up, they've told me.'

'You're never going back to the cottage. I'll see to that.'

'You?' Annie winced with pain as she twisted round too quickly. 'How can *you* say what I do, or what I don't do?'

'Because I'm responsible for you.'

She could hardly believe the things he was saying, standing there with his arms folded and his mouth set in a grim line. If it wouldn't hurt so much she would laugh.

262

He hadn't finished either. 'I made myself responsible for you when my horse knocked you down. I let Mrs Martindale make a fool of me. I should have known that you weren't such a little prude as to run away from me on account of one kiss.' He glared at her. 'A pretty chaste kiss into the bargain.'

He was making a total mess of what he had planned to say. Annie looked so awful sitting straight up in bed with her face a mottled yellow shading to purple beneath her eyes, and her mouth slipping to one side where the cuts had still to heal.

'Biddy misses you. She says the fun went out of the house when you left.' He nodded, well satisfied with his reasoning. 'She can act as chaperone between us, if that's what's bothering you.'

Annie's face was a study. 'Chaperone? So you think we'd need a chaperone?'

'Only till we're married.'

Annie's mouth dropped open, but it was so painful that she closed it again.

'Oh, my dear . . .' He came to sit on the edge of the bed. 'When I think of my chance meeting with Dailey up on the fells . . . when I think of what might have happened if I hadn't come across him . . .' He took her hand. 'There have been shadows in my life for a long time now, but when you were in my house they somehow went away.' Lifting her hand he gently kissed her swollen fingers. 'Come back with me and banish them again. Soon.'

'Marry you?' Her voice was tinged with disbelief. 'Did I hear you say that? I can't marry you, Mr Armstrong.'

He made a gesture of impatience. Couldn't she see that he hardly knew what he was saying? That never once, since his wife died her self-inflicted death, had he allowed his emotions to show. He frowned and turned his head away, so that all she saw was his profile.

'Yes, you must marry me,' he whispered. 'Oh, damn you! Do you have to look at me like that? Come back as a skivvy if that's what you want! Come back merely to wash and iron my blasted shirts. But just come back!'

If she hadn't looked so frail, so vulnerable, so touchingly fragile, he would have taken her in his arms and kissed the startled look from her face. Instead he stood up, well away from the bed, folded his arms and shouted at her.

'Can't you call me Seth? Is that too much to ask?'

'I'm not coming back with you . . .' she hesitated '. . . Seth.'

'Why? For God's sake, why?'

'Because I've planned the way things are going to be from now on.' She spoke with difficulty through her swollen lips. 'At first I wasn't going to accept Adam's money, but Mrs Gray made me see that if I refused it I would be insulting his memory because he wanted me to have it.' Her chin lifted. 'I have a gift for dressmaking, a real God-given gift. The girls actually wear the dresses I've made for them, when they see I'm not trying to make them look ridiculous in frills and flounces. With Adam's money I could have a shop with my name above it. *Annie Clancy. Modes!*' Her eyes shone. 'It's a fortune. With money like that you can do anything. So you don't need to bother about me any more. For the first time I'm going to be able to stand on my own feet.' Her voice dropped to a whisper. 'Without a man promising me, terrifying me, demanding of me what I haven't got to give, expecting things of me. Bothering me!'

'Into which of those flattering categories have you fitted me?'

Before she could answer he walked to the door, banged it behind him, making her wince as the sound set her head throbbing.

'A *fortune*? Eighty pounds?'

Seth stormed into the drawing-room where Margot sat dispensing tea from the silver spirit kettle, pouring it into egg-shell thin china cups rimmed with gold.

'How long would eighty pounds last if her little venture fails? As it surely will! I could tell her she'd be on a safer bet renting a corner shop selling meat and potato pies, oatmeal, paraffin and parched peas.' He waved the proffered cup of tea impatiently away. 'She must be out of her mind. For God's sake, Margot, who knows better than she that it's the pawnbroker's shop that's indispensable in the mill towns. Modes? From where did she coin an expression like that? From you?'

Margot stopped fluttering her be-ringed hands among the tea things. Once Seth had told her he could watch her doing just that indefinitely, but today she had to accept that she was wasting her time, and it badly irritated her.

'Not a shop as such. More a discreet establishment where ladies can go to choose their own material from swatches.'

'From what?'

'Swatches. Small samples of cloth.' Margot demonstrated with her hands, showing their approximate length and breadth. 'The clients can be measured and fitted and Annie will help them choose the kind of thing which suits them.' She smoothed down the skirt of her lilac silk afternoon gown. 'Lancashire women have good taste, given the money, of course. I don't expect many of them wear clogs and shawls from choice.' She sighed and took a dainty sip of tea. 'Annie was brought up in poverty, so she knows how to achieve the maximum effect with the minimum outlay. She'll be a tremendous success. I don't blame her for turning down whatever you had to offer.' If she hadn't known him better she could have sworn he was going to hit her. 'And don't go marching hell for leather out of here!' Her voice stayed him. 'I expect you proposed to her as if you were doing her a great big favour.' Her head went to one side. 'Well? Did you? Am I right?'

Seth stared at her for a moment, then actually beat his forehead with a clenched fist.

'It was when she was so ill . . . it was during the long hours I sat beside her bed. That was when I offered her my life, promised to cherish her for ever.'

'When she was unconscious?'

He lowered his head.

'And now, just now, upstairs, you talked as if it was a *fait accompli*?'

'I'll come back another day,' Seth muttered, striding from the room. 'Today I only make things worse.'

'Are we taking young Annie to France with us?' Harry came straight to the point. 'I've just bumped into Armstrong looking jealous as hell. Doesn't he want the lass to go?'

Margot picked up the heavy teapot. 'No. I don't think taking Annie with us would be a good idea at all,' she said firmly, thumping the pot back on its stand, making her mind up swiftly at that very moment, wondering why she'd ever considered it in the first place.

Harry wasn't surprised. He knew this dearly loved second wife of his very well. Knew that she had been thoroughly spoilt by fond and doting parents, so that in maturity she took up causes which interested and amused her, indulged herself with them for a little while, then dropped them when she became tired and bored. Annie Clancy had served her purpose. She had interested Margot at a time when she needed to be interested, and now could be discarded just as easily.

'So what do we do with her now we've finished with her?'

Margot had no idea she was being laughed at. She passed a fragile cup and saucer over to him, trying not to feel too annoyed at the way the tea was drunk at one gulp. 'She can stay here of course till we go away, and until she feels strong enough to . . .' the plump hands made vague circular motions in the air '. . . take up the threads of her life.'

'Do you think she'll marry Seth?'

A shrug of the plump shoulders. 'How should I know? After what has happened to her, she may never trust a man again. Never be able to surrender herself completely.' Margot yawned. 'I'm not too sure that a dress salon would be the right idea. Seth was quick to remind me that Lancashire mill towns are not in the least like Paris.'

She actually said 'Paree'. Harry downed a second cup of tea just as speedily. It was always the same. When she tired of anything she became more French than the Eiffel Tower; it was a way of detracting attention from what she was saying. It signified that in spirit she had removed herself from a tiresome situation.

'*Mon Dieu*!' she said now. 'Can that be ze time?'

Harry was troubled.

If Annie wasn't to marry Armstrong, then what to do with her? She was back in the sewing-room stitching what looked like acres of flimsy stuff into frocks for the girls to wear in the heat of Menton. Margot seemed to think that the lass would go back home, but from what he'd gathered there wasn't all that much of a home to go to.

'So you're not going into business, lass?' Standing by the window in the sewing-room, his massive bulk almost blocked out the light. 'Mrs Gray tells me the bank has advised you against.'

Annie put down the fine lawn neck-shawl she was hemming. 'If I had the premises and the goodwill, the money Adam left me would be ample to start me off with all I needed, but I haven't got either.'

'You could always go home.'

She shook her head. 'When I left my father's house I left it for good.'

Harry was flummoxed. Margot had told him that Annie's father had turned her out, and he hadn't been able to credit it. But now, looking at her sitting there with her hair tucked into a white cap, wearing a blue print frock with a white collar at the neck, she was a picture for sore eyes. How could any man banish a daughter like this from his door? My God, with a daughter like this a man should go down on his knees

267

every day and thank the Lord for heaping such a blessing on him. She wasn't afraid of hard work, either. Just look at her now, sewing away as if her life depended on it. Fourteen hours she put in some days, he'd been told, straining her eyes just so his wife and two daughters could go to France all dolled up in the latest fashion. Just so they could hold their own.

'Will the cottage be empty when you go to France, sir?'

Goddamn it, she'd read his thoughts. Harry cleared his throat. ''Fraid not. The couple move into it next week. The gardens have to be kept up while we're away.'

He stomped from the room before he found himself explaining to her about his problems with staffing, with the harvesting, with the animals while he was absent. He marched briskly across the tiled hall. No wonder Armstrong wanted to marry her. That lass had a wisdom, a strength, that went far beyond her years. It was the way she looked at you with those steady blue eyes, not a bold look, certainly not that, but a look of untutored intelligence that said she would understand if you confided in her.

He walked out on to the terrace. One of his favourite gun dogs had got out while in season. Producing her litter had almost finished her off. Now the sheer weight and volume of milk was making it impossible for her to walk. Something would have to be done.

Harry looked back at the tall window of the sewing-room. He reckoned a visit from the animal doctor was definitely on the agenda.

The men were at work with their rakes and pitch-forks when Annie left the house to walk along the meadow paths. The grasses bordering the brook had flowered; elder flowers bloomed in the place of whitethorn in the hedges; a skylark sang high above the bales of hay.

She no longer bore much resemblance to the girl in the greasy flat cap and the long woollen cloak who had trudged the roads looking for a place of work. The long night bound hand and foot to the chair in Adam's cottage had wiped the bright girlish expression from her face. Now she was fine-boned and achingly thin; her dark blue eyes had a wary look about them, and she kept her long red hair pulled tightly back from her face, tucked up into a serving-maid's white cap.

The men had gone home and the air was sticky and warm. Her dress clung to her back in damp patches. Over to the west a dark spiral of cloud curled across the sky threatening wind and rain. If it came the bales would have to be balanced against each other, to stop them from getting soaked through.

Annie raised her eyes to the changing sky and prayed that the rain would hold off. Lifting her skirts and bowing her head as if the rain had already begun, she ran back through the meadow, across the paddock and into the house by the back way, failing to look up and see Seth Armstrong framed in the window of the sewing-room. Waiting for her.

As she came through the doorway she snatched off her cap and shook her hair free, but when she saw him she immediately backed away.

'There's no need for you to do that.' She was so lovely he could scarcely bear to look at her. 'Harry tells me you won't be going with them to France.'

'No.'

'He also told me that you've dropped the idea of setting up in a dress shop.'

'That's right.' She sat down at the table and took up her sewing. 'Forgive me for carrying on working, but if everything is to be ready in time I can't let up.'

Turning a chair round, Seth sat down on it, resting his arms along its back. 'Annie . . .' He tried to speak calmly. 'Did you really believe that eighty pounds was enough to finance all you wanted to do? If you'd discussed it with me I could have explained, given you some idea . . .'

'Eighty pounds?' She raised her eyes and looked straight at him. 'Have you any idea just how much eighty pounds represents to someone like me? Eighty pounds would have kept my mother, father and their six children for nearly two years.' She raised her voice. 'Two years, Seth! Out of twenty-two shillings a week my father took two for his beer, or more when he felt like it. The rent was seven shillings, clothing club a shilling, boot and clog club another, burial insurance one and two-pence, soap and soda sixpence, lamp oil a penny, doctor's money sixpence . . . Do I need to tell you how much was left for food for all of us?' She stabbed the needle into the silky material on her lap. 'I could reckon things up to the last farthing; I could make a meal out of the dishcloth if needs must.' She bowed her head. 'An' you talk about eighty pounds as if it was nothing.'

'Why are you always so angry with me, love?' Seth spoke with a slow deliberation. 'What do I do that annoys you so much? You are punishing me for the things other men have done to you. Can't you see that?'

There was an aching need inside her to cry, so she became even more angry. 'Mrs Gray made me feel that my life was going to be so different from now on. But the truth is she can't wait to be rid of me.'

'She doesn't mean it, Annie. Mrs Gray is fickle, that's all.' He tried to keep his tone light. 'So why not come back with me? For the time being. Till you decide what to do next.'

There were tears glistening on her eyelashes. He saw the way she blinked them furiously away. 'No thank you, Mr Armstrong . . . Seth. I'm never going to be beholden to anyone again. Eighty pounds may be a mere pittance to you, but in my way of looking at things it's a fortune. And with a fortune behind them anyone can do any-thing. Because money talks!'

'What does it say, love?'

Her chin was up in a gesture of defiance. 'It says I never need to be beholden to anyone – to any *man* – again!'

270

16

On the day before Annie left the house Margot's conscience began to prick a little. Not too much, but enough to get in the way of her preparations for their long stay in France. The girls complained loudly that in their opinion Annie should be going with them.

'If we are to attend all the parties you've planned, who will dress our hair?'

'Or tell us what to wear with what?'

'I distinctly heard you tell Annie she would be going with us.'

Dorothea had tucked a torn flounce into the waistband of her skirt, and Abigail was wearing puce with bottle green. Margot could hardly bring herself to look at them, so she left the room and banged the door behind her.

Half-way up the stairs she stopped, a hand dramatically to her heart, not wanting to admit even to herself her real reason for withdrawing her affection from Annie Clancy. How could she explain, even to herself, her feelings about Seth Armstrong? Why did it hurt so much to see him falling more and more helplessly in love? Was it possible for a mature woman to covet, to desire a younger man, while loving her own husband as much as ever? All that flirting and teasing with the animal doctor, had it been half-way serious all the time, on her side at least?

On the stool in front of her tripled mirror she leaned forward to examine her face minutely. Were those fine wrinkles on her forehead the beginning of an ugly furrowed brow? By holding her chin up like this was she deluding herself into imagining that her double chin didn't exist? Was she turning into one of those pathetic

271

creatures who envied youth its bloom? Was she in fact sending Annie Clancy away for reasons beneath the contempt of the intelligent compassionate woman she imagined herself to be?

She got up and turned her back on the mirror. It was all too deep and complex a situation for her to fathom, particularly today when she was feeling far from well. Lately she'd taken to waking in the night drenched with perspiration, and sometimes her cheeks would flush up as though she had a fever. She was much too young for middle-aged nuisances like that to be happening to her, surely? When they did, if they did, she would ignore them so firmly they would have no choice but to go away.

She had no need to feel this niggling sense of disquiet and guilt. Annie had been treated more than fairly, and now she was ready to move on Margot had freely given her advice she would have had to pay for in some places.

'To look your best is to feel your best,' she had said. Who could quarrel with that? 'To look elegant always understate,' she had said. She had even bared her soul one day, telling Annie things she had never told before. 'On the day my husband came to bring me back from the hospital, I spent a whole hour getting ready. The specialist had told me I was never going to bear a child of my own, so I determined that when Mr Gray saw me he would see a smiling wife dressed in all her finery. You would have thought I was going to a Hunt Ball, or even to Buckingham Palace to one of the garden parties. I had my good pearls sent out to me, and I wore a hat with a feather curling all the way round the brim.'

'You have been very kind to me.' Annie had looked grave. 'What would I have done without you?'

'Survived,' Margot had said promptly. 'Like me.'

The next morning Margot came downstairs early wearing a pale green floating bedwrap. She smiled at Annie and held out both hands.

'Bartram is waiting outside with the trap.' She looked

Annie up and down with a critical eye. 'Yes. You'll do, but you still have to learn how to put up your hair properly. It looks in a state of collapse already.'

To stop herself from crying Annie smiled. 'The first time I saw you I wondered how you got your hair to stick up for itself like that, and I've been wondering ever since.'

'The next time we meet I'll show you,' Margot promised insincerely. 'Now you'd better go if Bartram's to come back tonight.'

When the clip-clop of the horse's hooves died away, Margot took off the pale green wrap and got back into bed.

'Well, no one can say we didn't do our best for her,' she whispered, then smiled as Harry grunted and turned over without waking up. Yes, there was no reason to feel like this. Kindness had been showered on the gardener's girl. Her own conscience was clear. She was blameless in every way.

So why couldn't she go back to sleep? Why, when the cock crowed three times, did she almost die of fright?

When Annie chose to sit up front with the driver he took a blanket and tucked it round her knees before laying another smaller one across her shoulders.

'You can throw them off when the sun gets through, but there's a nip in the air that's more like autumn, lass. It's more like back-end than summer; it's a case of three fine days then a thunderstorm. You can't rely on nowt. Still, they'll be well out of it abroad, though it beats me why the master goes year after year, but I expect his missus takes a lot of pleasing. The money's on her side, tha knows . . .'

According to the pit doctor Ed Bartram's lungs should have been finished long ago. He was as sparse and wiry as a hungry whippet. Since working for the Gray family – mostly outdoors – his already pock-marked skin had taken on the consistency and colour of seasoned leather, but his back was still stooped from his days of crouching underground. In many ways he reminded Annie of her father, but the eyes were different. Where her father's reflected only bitterness, Ed's brown eyes twinkled with contentment.

He chatted on, stopping only now and again to draw a necessary breath. 'You can tell a horse's age, up to about eight years old, by looking at its teeth,' he said, a couple of clip-clops further on. 'Then you look at their legs to see it hasn't got windgall.'

'What's that?' Annie's nerves felt so tightly drawn she was sure she would have twanged if anyone had touched her. She was grateful that Ed didn't seem to mind in the least that the conversation was totally one-sided, in fact she had more than a suspicion that he preferred it that way.

'Windgall? It's a spongy swelling on the side of the leg; it makes a horse lame if it's not watched, and if it gets a corn that's no good neither. You can't cure a horse with a corn. At least not many can. But I'd put me money on that animal chap who sees to the mester's horses any day. I've seen him cut a canker from a diseased horn wi' nowt to see by but a spluttering candle in a barn with a leaking roof. It were a pity his wife had to go that way. It's bad enough folks starving when there's nowt to eat in the house, but starving when there's a full table – that's another thing.'

'I used to work for Mr Armstrong,' Annie said in a small voice, but Ed wasn't listening to any other voice but his own.

'Aye, them hills over yon look as clean cut as if they'd been cut out with a pair of scissors. Mebbe it won't rain after all.' His burst of optimism seemed to depress him. 'Them mountains make up their own minds about the weather. Depends on their moods. Allus has and allus will.'

During the next hour Annie discarded the blanket round her shoulders, sitting up straight on the wooden

274

seat and holding on to the side as they turned into a rutted lane.

With every mile she was nearer to home. Home? She adjusted the brim of her hat to keep the sun from her face to ward off the freckles so frowned upon by Mrs Gray. It was hard to believe that so long had passed since she walked this very way, wearing boots too big, with her mother's cloak trailing in the mud, and a man's flat cap pulled low down over her forehead.

'Aye,' Ed said suddenly, as if he had been able to read her thoughts. 'Nowt stays the same. Like the seasons, everything changes. Take them hills, now, they'll still be here long after thee and me is dead and gone. Just listen to that quiet. There's nowt as deafening as quiet.'

At mid-morning they stopped at a horse trough and Ed showed Annie how his horse filtered the water through its teeth, shaking it about with its nose first to get rid of the dust.

'There's nowt as clean as a horse,' he said, fastening the nosebag into position.

Annie unwrapped the crusty bread and cheese packed for her by Cook that morning, but found she wasn't hungry. Ed disappeared through a gap in the hedge, and reappeared a few minutes later doing up his trousers, still talking.

A mile or so down the long winding road she interrupted him to point out the sight of a woman bent almost double, stumbling along by the hedges. Her head was sunk low on to her chest and when Ed stopped the trap and leaned out to her, the woman carried on, giving no sign that she had heard.

'Can we help you?' Annie climbed down and touched the woman on a shoulder. 'You're ill . . . look, we have food, and a skip of milk.' She bit her lips. 'I know what it's like to be on the road. Please – let us help you.'

The woman straightened up with obvious difficulty and stared Annie straight in the face.

'Johnson!' Annie stepped back a pace, but not quickly

275

enough to avoid the stream of saliva directed full into her face.

'*You* help *me*!' An expression of hatred slid across the well-remembered features, distorting them into an evil mask. 'Annie Clancy! By all that's holy! The gardener's little whore.'

Two claw-like hands came from inside the dusty rags, but before she could attack Ed came round the side of the trap and pulled Annie away. Lips curling, voice as hoarse as a raven's croak, Johnson yelled out her loathing to the clear blue sky.

'Just look at you! All dolled up for the next man who comes along. The gardener's whore spending the gardener's money!' A high cackle of a laugh burst from her throat. 'Got the money through lying on her back, an' now she's spending it on her back. You help *me*, Annie Clancy? I'd rather rot in me grave first.'

Turning her back on them, she stumbled into the hedge, righted herself and tottered on. Like a night woman far gone in drink.

Ed stared with concern at Annie's white face. Too shocked to move, he guessed; she was standing quite still, her eyes fixed on the staggering woman making her tortuous way down the road.

'Such hate . . .' Her voice was no more than a whisper. 'Oh, dear God, such hate. It was alive, wasn't it? Did you sense that? That hate was a living thing.'

When Ed took his handkerchief from his top pocket and gently wiped her face, she stood like a child submitting to the ministrations of a loving father. When he helped her back into the trap she sat hunched, her gloved hands joined tightly on her lap. It was an attitude of fear. Ed recognised it straight away. It was a tensing of the muscles against what had been, and what might be to come. He flicked the reins and urged the horse to a trotting pace, his lined face creased into anxiety. Fear . . . it could be a terrible thing. He'd known the smell and the taste of it many a time.

276

'All right, lass?'

She nodded, tried to smile, so he let her be.

That had been fear when he'd been buried with a wall of rock between him and his mates and it seemed he would slowly die. Fear when the doctor told him his lungs were shot – riddled with holes like the kitchen sieve. Had he made up his mind in that moment that he was going to survive? But the worst fear of all had been when his wife died, and he didn't know how to go on without her for a while. Folks had said that time would heal but unless they'd been down the same road they didn't know what they were talking about. The pain lessened, he'd grant them that, but he was never quite the same.

He coughed, glanced sideways, saw a hint of colour creeping back into the young lass's cheeks and nodded, well satisfied.

An hour later they drove over the crest of a hill and Ed pointed with his whip.

'Well, tha's home, lass. I'd forgotten how mucky it all is – all them rows of houses, and that black smoke. You'd never get me back there.'

Chunnering away he helped Annie down, then standing by the horse's head he watched her walk away from him. Her back was straight and her head held high, as if she was frightened of her hat slipping off. Silently Ed wished her well. He'd heard them talking about the gardener's girl in the kitchen at the house. Saying she was man-mad and that she would fleece Adam for every penny he possessed.

Ed climbed back into the trap. He'd always been good at summing folks up, and there was nowt much wrong with that little lass. He'd stake what was left of his life on it.

'Nay, it's never Annie Clancy?' The woman standing at her open door, arms crossed over the front of her flowered apron, stared with mouth agape. 'Nay, never!'

277

'Good afternoon, Mrs Isherwood.'

Looking neither left nor right, Annie acknowledged the greeting with a slight nod of her head, and kept on walking down the familiar street. Because it was a Friday the women would be busy indoors cleaning up for the coming weekend. Blackleading grates, whitening hearths with a scouring stone, scrubbing floors with hard yellow soap, polishing fire-irons with Brasso, and bringing up the shine on steel fenders with emery paper.

Grass sprouted from between the cobbles of the street, stunted blackened grass, hardly worthy of its name. The houses looked smaller somehow, the pavements narrower than she remembered. She stopped at the only unmopped step in the street, half raised her hand to the iron knocker set high in the shabby door scored and marked with the boys' clog irons. Changed her mind, lifted the sneck and walked straight in.

The shock and surprise slid over Florrie Clancy's fat face like butter slipping from a warm dish.

'Annie! May the saints preserve us!'

She wiped her hands on a rag looped over the front of the sacking apron tied round her thick waist, and sat down with a thump in the rocking-chair. Her small eyes bulged from their nests of puffy flesh, and when she found the breath to shout the noise she made caused Annie to widen her eyes in surprise.

'Jack! I know you're out there at the back. Come in here for a sken at what the wind's blown in!' She levered herself up from the chair and waddled across the room. 'Jack? Have you gone deaf all of a sudden?'

'What the 'ell?'

Strange that she had forgotten how small her father was, and yet since the last time she'd seen him he'd altered little. He was still whey-faced with the familiar cuts on his cheeks standing out like blue tacking stitches. His back had been so crippled by his years spent crouching in the mine that he seemed to be having difficulty holding his head up to stare in amazement at his daughter.

He'd been having one of his coughing fits in the privy out at the back. Annie could tell by the way his brown eyes watered, and by the way his voice seemed weaker than she had remembered. The mine was killing him. His destiny was written plain on his face. In that moment Annie saw it clearly. He looked, she thought, at least sixty years old.

Controlling her instinct to go to him and put her arms round him, she held out her hand. 'Hallo, our Dad. How are you?'

But the hand was dashed away with a swift swiping motion. There was no welcome in his eyes; no welcome and no love, either.

'Where is it, then?' he wanted to know in his croak of a voice.

'Where's what?'

'The little bastard! What have you done with it? Left it with your fancy man? Because dressed like that there's bound to be some man financing you.' He seemed to swell. 'Look at her, Florrie.' He stabbed a finger at Annie. 'Dressed up like the dog's bloody dinner! Thinking to impress.' His insulting glance swept upwards then downwards, taking in the blue-grey dress and matching hat trimmed with pink roses rescued from a hat thrown away by Margot Gray. 'I was right about you, madam. I knew what I was doing the day I gave you a leathering for wanting – nay, demanding – a new dress. I had your measure right from the start.' He nodded at his wife. 'I've kept telling you the sort she was an' now here's the living proof, because never in a million years could she have found a job of work that paid enough to put clothes like those on her back.' He moved a step closer. 'An' there's no ring on her finger under them fancy gloves. I'd stake me life on that.' His voice was giving out, but his tone was so menacing it was as if he shouted the words aloud. 'There's no husband you could find who would have the brass to dress you up like that. I wasn't born yesterday.'

279

'Give her a chance to speak, Jack. She *might* be married.' Florrie was all for giving young Annie the benefit of the doubt.

'No, I'm not married.' Annie turned to her gratefully. 'And it's true a man gave me the money to buy the material to make this dress. But I didn't earn it the way you think I did.'

Her father's snort of derision started him off coughing again.

'I landed a good job as a seamstress,' Annie said, when the spasm was over. 'In a house where the pantry is bigger than this room.'

'A seamstress?' Jack clutched his chest. 'I don't remember you being apprenticed to a dressmaker. I don't remember you being good for bloody owt but possing the muck out of other folk's clothes.'

Annie began to feel sick. It was as though she had never been away. If anything, it was worse with the hate her father felt for her festering away inside him. He was never going to be proud of her, never feel glad for her sake. He would never talk about her with that tinge of pride in his voice that most men have for their daughters. He didn't even like her, never mind love her. Why hadn't she known that and kept away instead of coming back looking for something that had never been hers and never would be.

'It was my own mother who taught me to sew, our Dad. You know that. She was gifted at dressmaking, really gifted – you know that, too. She set me to hem pieces of fent as soon as I could hold a needle. It was from her I got the flair. Why won't you let me tell you how it's been? Why won't you even let me talk to you?'

He was making for the stairs, but Annie called after him. 'Why must you always put me in the wrong?'

'You put yourself in the wrong, madam.'

'But I'm different now.' Annie put her hand on the narrow stair-rail, looked up after him. 'That could never happen to me now. I wasn't properly grown, our Dad.'

280

She followed him as far as the third stair. 'I lost the baby . . . I nearly died losing it. Let me tell you. Please.'

But he was gone, turning into the front room to the left of the little square landing, closing the door so quietly it was like a slap in her face.

'Mrs Greenhalgh – sorry – Florrie?' Annie didn't know what to call her. 'Why? Why does he hate me so much? He looks at me as if I was less than the dust under his feet.'

'He'll not stand for you stopping here.' The loose jowls of Florrie's big face quivered as she jerked her head at a chair. 'Sit you down, and don't moither about your dad. He'll come down again when he's had his bit of a sulk.'

'I know I'm not stopping here.' Annie sat down, her face still turned in the direction of the stairway. 'I may stay with Edith Morris for a night or two. I wrote to her as soon . . . as soon as I knew I'd be moving on, telling her I was coming.'

'An' you've not heard back?' Florrie's boot-button eyes lit up.

Annie shook her head. 'It doesn't matter. I won't be there long.'

When Florrie laughed, every spreading inch of her flesh laughed with her. Her tiny eyes disappeared completely into the loose pockets of flesh, and the chair set itself rocking as she shook uncontrollably.

'No, you won't be there long, I can grant you that.'

'Is Miss Morris all right?'

'All right?' Florrie had laughed herself into almost a state of collapse. 'Oh, aye. She's all right, chuck. Like a dog with two tails, you might say.' She winked so hard that her left eye disappeared completely. 'Best not leave it too long or you might find she's gone to bed.'

'At seven o'clock?'

'Five o'clock sometimes.'

'Is she ill?'

Suddenly Florrie tired of the conversation she seemed to find so comical. Leaning forward, she steadied the chair by planting both wide feet together.

281

'Now then, chuck. You tell me what you've been up to, because I'd like to hear even if him upstairs couldn't give a toss. I might as well tell you I've thought about you many a time since that morning you walked up the street carrying that little cloth bundle.' She scratched underneath an armpit. 'I didn't really hold with your dad throwing you out, and if I hadn't been full of my own troubles I would have stuck up for you more. But I was too bothered about me own problems. It's a bad job when your own son shows you the door. We've never spoken since, not a word. I cross the street if I see me son's wife coming towards me and stick me nose in the air. She's had a baby since you went, but she won't give me house-room even though I'm its grandma.'

'The boys?' Annie took her chance as Florrie paused for breath. 'Are they all out playing?'

'Except Georgie. He's on the second shift.' Florrie looked proud. 'Timmy's been put up at school an' he's holding his own with lads a full year older than him. Miss Shrubsall came round last week. She says with extra tuition and stopping on at school a bit longer he could go as a pupil teacher one day in Salford, or somewhere where they can't get teachers. He'd only get his keep for about two years then he might be able to take a course, or he could even study and work at the same time. But he'd be a teacher at the end of it, Miss Shrubsall was sure of it.'

'That's wonderful!' Annie was so pleased she felt tears fill her eyes. Now she knew what part of Adam's money could be used for. Money was the key to everything, she'd seen enough evidence of that.

'There's no question of it of course,' Florrie was saying. 'Miss Shrubsall said he'd be expected to pay back every penny his training had cost him, so what chance is there?'

'But there has to be a chance.' Annie could hardly contain herself. 'I can help in that direction.'

Florrie almost fell off her chair, and when she spoke

her gruff voice was sharp and high with greed. 'With a bit of the ready?' She rubbed finger and thumb together.

Annie nodded and bit her lips. She tried not to blush but felt the warmth spreading up from her throat. 'A friend died and left his savings to me. A man I was housekeeper to.'

'Oh, aye?' Florrie winked again. 'Left you right for life, did he, chuck?'

'Enough to see Timmy through his teaching course, and put a stop to him going down the pit.'

'Jack told Miss Shrubsall that there'd be no difference made with Timmy. "One son down the pit, all my sons down the pit," he said. He won't treat one any different from the others.'

'But Timmy *is* different,' Annie cried.

Miss Shrubsall had said exactly the same, banging her fist down on the table till the pots rattled. She had rounded on Jack, pointing at him with a finger. 'Your daughter was different too, and you knew it. It was pure sacrilege when that clever child had to leave school. All right, I know you hadn't much choice when her mother died – but you have that choice now, Mr Clancy. Tim has imagination as well as brains, and that's an unbeatable combination, believe me. Timothy can do it. With my help and a lot of hard work on his part, he can make something of himself. He can be kept out of the mine!'

'I couldn't repeat what your father said to Miss Shrubsall.' Florrie jerked her head up to nod at the ceiling. 'She was away and up the street faster than if he'd set a match to her drawers.'

At the sound of her laughter Jack Clancy stopped his pacing of the narrow gap between the double bed and the window. She was a loud mouth all right, but she looked after him – him and the kids. She could feed the lot of them on ten shillings a week; though she was no cook she could slice bread and slap jam on it, and serve a

283

tasty haddock poached in milk on a Saturday, as well as a bit of meat now and again on a Sunday.

He leaned his forehead against the grimy window pane. In a strange way he was happier than he'd been for a long, long time. Even though Florrie had insisted on going with him to the pub, threatening to follow him and show him up if he didn't take her. An' she would too. He wouldn't put it past her elbowing her way up to the bar counter, getting him by the scruff of his neck and frog-marching him up the street. She certainly had the build. You had to laugh at her – his expression softened a little – as long as you never tried to best her. Big Florrie had to be the boss. Or at least think she was.

Because she always left the lads alone, not bothering them to keep clean, to wipe their noses when they ran, or mend their torn britches, they too seemed happier than they used to be when Annie was always on at them to do better, to try harder, to reach for the moon when he could have told her they didn't particularly want it.

Annie . . . His expression hardened again. She had looked so much like her dead mother when he came in from the back and saw her standing there, he had thought he would have a stroke. Like her, apart from the hair. He closed his eyes, and held a fist to his mouth. That glossy wavy red hair, the colour of flame.

Just like before, he had wanted to hit out at her, thump her till her eyes swam. Hurt her, because that was the only way he could get even with her. Jack bowed his head. Even in drink, even in the worst of his rages, Jack Clancy had known that beating the living daylights out of Annie was the only way he could stomach her living with him, underneath the same roof.

How in the name of God could he admit the truth, when the truth would have made him appear to be less than a man? He sat down heavily on the side of the unmade bed, holding his head in his hands. Oh, aye, the truth would have given his mates a good belly laugh; it would have turned him into an object of pity. Pity? He groaned. There was nobody ever going to pity Jack Clancy. Nobody!

Mary, his first wife, had been pregnant when he married her, but they'd had their bit of fun and he was willing to pay for it by marrying her. He got up again and began his pacing. He'd never forget the relief on her parents' faces when, hand in hand, they'd said they were getting married. In the street of tall brick houses up by the Corporation Park in Blackburn a little bastard would have put paid to all her father's big ideas. Superintendent at the nearby Methodist Sunday School, spouting from the pulpit as a lay-preacher, kow-towing to the Town Clerk in his position of clerk in the accounts department, oh aye, Mary's father set a lot of store on his good name. Even though his daughter marrying a miner was a bitter pill to swallow, he'd stuck by her till the ring was safely on her finger.

Then the severance took over. Jack curled his lip. Not even when Annie was born did they visit, even though it was a safe bet that Mary's apology for a father was telling about the compassion of his Lord from the bare pulpit in chapel. 'Suffer the little children to come unto me.' Jack wouldn't put it past him using that as his text.

'It takes a man to make a girl,' his mates had teased him six months after the wedding when Annie was born. Jack could still remember the pride in him as he'd looked down at the tiny puckered face and held out his finger for her to take in a light and clinging grasp. 'A proper father's girl,' folks would say, as she held his hand to walk up the street, a right little princess in the dresses her mother could make out of remnants from the material stall on the market.

Then one morning, when the sky outside was dark and the rain swept down spattering against the window, they had overslept, lying in each other's arms in the billowing feather bed. It was in the days before they had sunk the second shaft, when jobs were hard to find, and the day after the pit deputy had warned Jack about the amount of stone in his tub.

285

'One more like this. One more late morning. One more stepping out of line, and you're *out*! Think on!'

Jack could remember as if it was yesterday, staring at the clean-shaven face with the tell-tale markings on it. He had actually looked at the ground and apologised, swearing it would never happen again. Knowing he would have licked the deputy's boots if that would keep him his job. The stern and unyielding man was long since gone, but Jack could still remember him with a deep unforgiving loathing. Even as he was obeyed he had been despised, but what was the bloody alternative with a wife and child and another on the way? Jack lifted his head and saw his distorted reflection in the large brass knob on the bed-end.

How had what should have been no more than a normal row ended so disastrously? Jack covered his grotesque image with a hand. He was shouting at her because he was going to be late again, and she was yelling back at him because she felt sick and the fire wouldn't light. She was hugging her neck-shawl round her; she was shivering in the early dawn. The street outside was quiet, with the early shift already on their way down the mine, standing motionless in the cage, bull-necked, their shoulders sloping forward as if they were already at the face. Jack could even remember the way his thoughts had run that morning.

How in God's name had his angry words goaded Mary into bursting out with the truth? What had he said to inflame her till she lost all control? Was it the seeping cold in the fireless room? The pitch-dark sky outside? The coming here to live after living in a house with a square of carpet on the floor, and cups and plates that matched. Was it her saucerless existence that had finally cracked her?

To the end of his days Jack would never know, but one thing was sure. He had known from that minute that never again would he be able to look upon Annie with love. Even now, after all those years, he could still hear his young wife's voice; he could still smell the acrid smell of the ashes she had been raking out from the grate till she stood up with the shovel in her hand. Is this all there was? she wanted to know. Was this the way her life was set from now on? Was this existing from day to day a marriage?

'You want to think you're lucky to have a ring on your finger.' Why had he said that? Why had she answered him straight off telling him something he would have given his right arm not to hear.

'I never meant to tell you,' she had sobbed. 'But there was another man, a married man, and I went with him just once.'

'And he is Annie's father.' Jack spoke what he instinctively knew to be the truth. In the time it took him to say it, his love for Annie died.

After two dreadful days of weeping, with him threatening to leave, with Mary saying she would kill herself, they had come to some sort of compromise. It must never be mentioned again. In the eyes of his mates it would make him appear as less than a man. He'd be a laughing stock, and that he could never stomach.

Now, seeing Annie dressed up, hearing her speak, the agony was there again, the deep festering anguish that came on him every time he looked on his first-born child. He began to tremble. Mary had sworn that Annie could – might possibly – be his daughter, but there was not one feature, gesture or mannerism to suggest that the beautiful girl downstairs could be flesh of his flesh. She was her mother's daughter all right. She'd proved that, hadn't she?

He winced as a sudden burst of raucous laughter spiralled upstairs. His second wife was a blab-mouth and a slut, and yet . . . and yet . . .

He turned his head from side to side as he remembered Annie's mother sitting quietly by the fire, her sewing on her lap. Small, subdued, a little brown mouse of a woman, with a spirit that had been seared out of her the day she had told the truth and known from that moment that he would never forgive her, never forget.

Wrenching open the top drawer of the chest by the wall, Jack rummaged among the untidy jumble of old socks and unironed shirts, and took out a folded letter.

'Here!' he said, clattering his way back down the stairs. 'Read that!' The gloating expression on his face sent a prickle of fear down Annie's spine, but she took the folded sheet of paper and began to read. 'Out loud! So Florrie here can hear it.' He gripped Annie's wrist, forcing her up against the table. 'Let's be knowing what happens to women who will lay with anybody.'

'Leave go of me!'

This was not the terrified girl who had once cowered at his touch, shrank from him with pleading in her eyes. There was a strength in her that surprised him as she twisted away from him, as she put the width of the table between them.

'I'll read it. To myself,' she said quietly.

The letter was written in pencil, faded now, but the message was clear. Laurie Yates had written to say that he was never coming back again; that he had seen the Light and gone back to his wife and two children, to try to make amends to them for his wandering years. He was never going back to sea again, he swore, or down another mine. He was sorry for making a promise he couldn't keep but he would always have pleasing memories of a girl he had once known by the name of Annie Clancy.

When she raised her head the gloating, sly, satisfied expression on her father's face was an obscenity. For a long moment there was silence, even the rocking-chair was still.

'If I had received this letter when it first came, it would have broken my heart.' She paused, her dark blue eyes steady. 'But now it doesn't matter. You kept it too long, don't you see. Nothing in it can hurt me now.'

Moving round the table, she stared quite calmly into the fire, down at the letter, then directly at him. Jack was struck again by the quiet dignity in her, a way of standing, of holding her head, that had always set her apart from the yelling, fighting, Clancy family. Her mother had been just the same, a cut above, dignified even when her life was anything but, and he had worshipped the difference. He felt a choking sensation in his thick bull-neck.

Annie held the letter over the fire for a moment before letting it drop into the flames.

'That's that,' she said softly. 'He'll always be a travelling man, it's in his blood, but I'll tell you something – it would take a lot more than a length of blue ribbon to make me that trusting again.' She looked straight at Jack. 'It's not the mistakes we make, it's what we do afterwards that counts.'

There was a droop about her that belied the flippancy of her words. Jack was gazing at her, seeing her as the little girl who had once walked up the street with her hand in his. He swallowed hard, might have stretched out a hand towards her, but on that instant Florrie set the chair rocking with an irritating rhythm that wiped the passing gleam of understanding from his face.

Annie could have been echoing her own mother's words. She was even standing in the same spot, by the fire, a mute pleading in her eyes. Over and over again her mother had cried out that wasn't everyone allowed to behave like a fool, make a mistake, all right then, *sin*, just once in their lives?

'Is there to be no future for us because I made one mistake?' she had sobbed. 'Just one bad mistake?'

'Don't most folks make a fool of themselves just once in their lives?' Annie asked then.

Jack's anger flared as bright and fierce as the flames dancing up the chimney-back. In that instant the murder was in his heart again. When he raised his hand it was stayed by a grip of steel. As he gawped in astonishment, his features out of flunter by the force of his emotions, Florrie's voice was the outraged bellow of a charging bull. Cheeks wobbling, pig eyes starting from her head, she confronted him.

'Nay you don't, Jack Clancy! You're not belting her while I'm here to stop it. Your Annie brings out the very devil in you. Always has done, from what I've heard.'

'Do you want to know why, woman?'

Florrie had him by the lapels of his pit jacket. She was hissing into his face, jowls working convulsively.

'Do you think I'm daft, you silly bugger? Do you think me and a lot more have never wondered where that red hair come from? One copper-knob among a family of black-haired little lads?' When he hit her she fell back against the table, clutching her face. 'Go on! Tell Annie she's not yours! Set her free! Stop her trying to make you like her. Or give her your blessing and let me put the kettle on and brew us all a nice cup of tea.'

She was amazing, she was unbelievable. When Jack began to sob and shake she pushed him down into his chair to stand over him, hands on the wooden arms.

'Well? Can she stay? Or can't you spare the lass a sup of tea?'

17

Seth had never driven his horse as hard before. There was a certainty in him that he had to get to Annie before she saw her father.

It was the memory of her face as she'd talked about Jack Clancy; it was the memory of the weals on her back, the distinctive mark of a large belt buckle, and it was the knowledge that the heavy blows had perforated an eardrum. All this spurred him on through the early evening of a day that had been more like April, with its slanting sunshine and sharp heavy showers.

He had thought to meet Bartram making his way back, but instead took a short cut, leaving the main road and branching off into a lane fringed by grassy borders, only just wide enough for trap and horse.

The superficial friendship between him and Margot Gray was vanished for ever. She had smiled first at his concern for Annie, then laughed, trying to tease him out of his anxiety.

'Let Annie Clancy go, Seth! It's time she went home.' She had led the way into the drawing-room. 'Those kind of people always go back to where they were born in the end. She was a girl of the streets. She belongs there. She'll marry some young collier or some millhand. He'll beat her every Friday after he's drunk most of his wages away. She'll have a baby a year, and grow fat, and the money Adam left her will be squandered in the first few months. Those people don't know how to budget; it's a hand-to-mouth existence. It's what she was used to, Seth. Let her alone. She's even got the money with her, sewed into her clothes. Can you believe the stupidity of that?'

He had walked away from her to look out of the

window, hardly able to control his voice. 'Have you stopped to think what's happened to Annie since she left home?' He whirled round, jerking his chin up out of the soft collar of his leather over-jacket. 'Any kindness she's been shown has evaporated just as she was getting used to it. Time after time. She's started to trust, then been let down. By me, you, Adam . . .'

'Don't forget the sailor, the travelling man.' Margot was totally unmoved. 'Why is Annie always the victim, I wonder? Does she cast herself in that role on purpose, knowing that men fall soft for her wide-eyed appeal?'

Seth rounded on her. 'Don't you see that life turns some of us into victims? Fate, luck, environment? Circumstances, Margot. The very accident of our birth?'

'Come now, Seth.' She had gone to him, raised her over made-up face to his.

He turned away from her scented breath. 'Devoid of all this . . .' he swept an arm to encompass the over-stuffed opulence of the pink and grey drawing-room '. . . do you think *you* would have lived through what Annie has had to live through, coming out of it in the end with your spirit unbroken, your courage intact?'

'Mon ami, mon ami . . .' The look in her eyes had been unmistakable, the swivel of her wide hips a clear invitation. 'You are bewitched, just as all the others were bewitched. Wake up, my dear . . . my very dear one . . .' She pressed herself against him.

Seth took her firmly by the arms and put her away, seeing clearly for the first time the grotesquely piled hair, the flesh – wrinkled like the skin on a glass of hot milk – flowing from the top of her low-cut muslin dress. Her eyes, misted with emotion, were fixed on him with a naked longing that revolted him.

Margot Gray was no fool. In that moment she saw the calculating expression in the silver-light eyes and, worst of all, the disgust on his face. She stepped back as smartly as if he had slapped her, mistress of her emotions in an instant.

'We go to France tomorrow,' she said, speaking through clenched teeth. 'We will be away for almost three months. You know our address, but you will not be writing to Harry about the animals, his livestock, because they are no longer your responsibility. I shall tell him that you made advances to me.'

Seth gave a short laugh. 'He won't believe a word of it!'

'I shall tell him you embarrassed me so much that I never wish to see you again. I shall remind him of the times you flirted with me, and how in innocence I flirted back. I shall tell him that I had no choice but to terminate the arrangement he has with you about the medical care of the animals.'

'You wouldn't do that. You're not serious, surely?'

'Perfectly serious. Harry will believe me for the simple reason that I can make him believe anything.'

'What is to stop me telling him the truth?'

'Your perfect English manners, which will tell you that no gentleman would dream of compromising a lady, even if his loyalty costs him a friendship.' Her lip curled. 'I though you were more of . . . how do you say? . . . a sophisticate, Seth. I know you have a paramour in Manchester. I also know that you don't live alone. I thought you were a man who knew exactly what he was doing, but I was mistaken. By the time we come back from France you will have left my mind completely. As easily as that!'

She snapped her fingers in his face, turned her back on him and swept from the room, flounced skirts billowing, small heels clicking across the tiled floor of the hall.

Seth's horse was visibly tiring so reluctantly he dismounted and led it over to a trough set outside a low-thatched inn, kept clean and replenished by a kindly landlord.

His anger with Margot Gray had cooled a little, but the fear for Annie was still in him. It was a sickening

293

dread of what might be happening to her, a helpless feeling deep inside him that harm was coming to her.

As he climbed back into the trap he saw the bent figure of a woman shuffling along in the shadow of a hedge bright with elder flowers. An old tramp woman, from the look of her. Seth caught only a fleeting glimpse, but she seemed to be cursing him, shaking her fist, a witch-like creature obviously riddled with madness. And yet there had been something familiar about her.

Seth shook his head and drove on, forgetting her in the same instant.

'Your Annie's come into money,' Florrie said, when Jack had calmed down a little. 'An' she's giving it to us for Timmy's schooling. So he can be a teacher one day.'

'Where is it?' Jack's beetle-brows drew together. 'Where's the money?'

Instinctively Annie clutched her draw-string purse to her, too late to prevent her father leaping from the chair in one bound and snatching it away from her.

Tearing at the string, thrusting his hand deep inside, not finding what he was after straight away, he upended the purse over the table, scrabbled among the contents and found what he was looking for. Five, six, seven, eight, nine, ten . . . ten gold sovereigns rolled in all directions, to lie among the unwashed pots, the greasy plates, the jam jar with its scraping of red plum jam in the bottom.

Jack stared at it in disbelief, rubbing one hand over the dark stubble on his chin. 'Ten bloody pounds!' He gathered the coins up and thrust them deep into his trouser pocket. 'Now then. Where's the rest?'

'There's no more.' Annie backed towards the door, but again he was too fast for her. 'Hold her, Florrie!'

Annie screamed. Just once, but the sound of it brought her father's rough hand up to the side of her head, striking a hard blow that dislodged her hat so that it hung loosely, tethered to her head by the long hat pin.

294

'Where's the rest?' Jack was beside himself with pent-up rage. 'You dare to come back, flaunting yourself at us in your finery!' He hit her again, so that her head rocked back, sending a sharp shaft of pain through her ear. 'You've been nothing but trouble since the day you were born!' His hand came out again. 'Now where's the rest? D'you hear me?' This time the pain brought her teeth down onto her tongue, so that she tasted blood, then suddenly he stopped hitting her to twist her arm high behind her back. With his other hand he tugged at the hat, tearing it from her head, bringing a bright tuft of hair with it.

'Feel round her skirts, Florrie. The hem of her skirts.' His face was no more than an inch away. 'That's where she used to hide her money from me. Feel round her skirts, woman! Not like that! Down on your knees, so you can see what you're doing.'

It was a long, long time since Florrie had been down on her knees and the hard discomfort of it made her draw in her breath sharply. As much as she disliked seeing Jack hit out at Annie like that, money was money and never to be sneezed at. Moving awkwardly, wincing at the sound of Annie's moans of pain, she fumbled round the machine-stitched padded hem of the blue-grey dress.

'There's nowt here, Jack.' She sat back, puffed.

'Not in her dress, woman! Her petticoat!' With his free hand Jack gathered a fold of Annie's skirt in his hand and yanked it up above her waist. 'There'll be a pocket somewhere. There! I knew it! Old habits die hard, especially for whores.'

The sound of the petticoat being ripped from her released Annie from the numbed horror of what was happening to her. In Adam's cottage, tied to a chair, she had been helpless, but now . . . The anger at what her father had done to her all her life, was trying to do now, broke from her in a piercing scream.

'Give that to me!' Like a wild cat she flew at Jack, wrenching the torn white petticoat from him before he

295

could react. 'I'll give you the money of my own accord, of my own free will!' She pulled the thread from the pocket. 'Here!' Before their astonished gazes she tossed a chamois leather bag on to the table. 'Take it! Take it as payment for bringing me up, as payment for all the times you reminded me how much it cost you to feed me.' She lifted her chin. 'Take it so I can walk free from this house and never ever feel the need to come back again. And remember I gave it to you, not the other way round. It belonged to a man who was prepared to see his wife die rather than use it to buy medicine for her and care for her, so it's tainted already. May you both have joy of it, because it's brought none to me!'

Tears flooded her heart, but she would not let them fall. The carefully arranged hair was slipping its bun, her hat lay in a corner where her father had tossed it away. She looked desperately ill with her white face marked by red patches, showing clearly the imprints of Jack Clancy's stubby fingers.

'I tried to love you, but I failed,' she shouted. 'I'm not going to try any more, because I don't care! You're my family, our Dad, and I had need of you, but not any more.' She gestured towards the money on the table. 'I know you'll drink all that away and there'll be none to spare for Timmy.' She rubbed her eyes with a fist. 'There's nothing I can do about that, neither.' She went to pick up her hat. 'As soon as I can I'll be gone from this town and you'll never see me again.' She turned at the door. 'Do you know what you do to someone when you withhold love from them, our Dad? You kill them inside so that they no longer trust, because always, every minute, they're expecting to be let down. You make them more ready to see the worst in folks than the best!'

It was a long speech for someone who had never been taught to express herself, but Annie knew she felt all the better for the saying of it. The two she'd left inside, gawping at her with blank faces, would be quarrelling about the money even now. Florrie, who wasn't all bad, would be wanting to put some aside, but her husband would have different ideas.

Annie leant against the wall and with trembling hands pinned her hat back on her untidy hair. The men were coming up from the early shift, clogs and heavy boots clattering on the cobblestones, bait-tins slung round stooped shoulders, jacket pockets bulging with their water bottles. One or two of them stared curiously at Annie, the whites of their eyes gleaming from dust-grimed faces, but they were tired to the point of exhaustion, with pinched-hard apathetic expressions. They were going home to a tub of hot water, to a bowl of stew with a dabbing of shin beef in it if they were lucky, and to sleep till it was time to get up and begin all over again.

Annie could smell the thick meaty stew the minute she got inside the house two doors down. It was like stepping back into her childhood, with Edith Morris, neat as ever in long black skirt and high-necked blouse, bending over the soot-blackened pan to stir what looked like a full-bodied lentil soup. The only thing missing was the bed in the window, the commode by its side, and Grandma Morris sitting up and listening, bird-small head on one side, eyes as shrewd as if she guessed exactly what you were going to say long before you said it.

She would have known at once that Annie's father had been laying about her again, but her daughter seemed not to notice that her visitor was swaying on her feet, with her hair coming down, almost on the point of collapse.

The usually self-possessed prim woman was so agitated that she let the spoon drop into the hearth, picked it up and stuck it back into the pan without washing it first. How was she going to explain to this smartly dressed young woman who bore not the slightest resemblance to the Annie Clancy she remembered that it wasn't convenient for her to stop here, not even for the odd night? Not just inconvenient but impossible, to judge by the way Mick had carried on when the letter came.

'She's looking for a place,' he'd thundered, letting Edith read the letter aloud to him because it was quicker that way. 'If she comes through the front door then it's me out of the back!'

For the first time in her life Edith was being bossed, cherished and dominated, and it thrilled her to the marrow of her big bones. The act of love had astonished her at first, then pleased her so much she was ready for Mick any time he wanted her. Which was every single day. Sometimes he would come in from the woodyard and lower her down onto the cut-rug by the fire and pleasure her even before he sat down to his tea, and by the hours of sleep she'd lost it was a wonder she could keep awake at her looms in the weaving shed.

He was so tender, so gentle, so brutal. He worshipped her. Every inch of her body, he'd said, kissing her in places she'd been brought up to think were downright rude. The red rough hands that could wield an axe or lift sacks of coal up on to his shoulders had such liquid passion in their touch that Edith's whole being would melt with longing when he trailed his fingers down her cheeks, her throat, fumbled with the buttons of her blouse, and feather-touched her breasts, rolling her nipples round between finger and thumb till they stood out hard.

'I know you wanted Annie here at one time,' he'd said, and then gone on to explain that their sweet freedom would be all gone with a third person in the house. 'We'd be like other folks then,' he'd said. 'Making love only in bed, in the dark, trying to be quiet. I couldn't come home and do this,' he'd whispered, his hands at the fastening of her blouse, even as he stood by the door in muffler and cap, ready for work.

Edith blushed like a young girl, turned round and looked properly at Annie for the first time since she'd opened the door to her.

'What's he done to you, love?' She wiped her hands on her apron, pushed Annie down into a chair. 'He's a wicked man. My mother, who wouldn't have hurt a fly, always said he was a wicked man.'

Her sudden change of mood from apparent indifference to warmth was too much for Annie. Her head went down so that all Edith could see was the carefully trimmed hat with its wreath of artificial daisies and dog-roses.

'I'm never going into that house again.' Her voice came ragged with tears. 'I've bought my freedom from him, Miss Morris, and when I've had a chance to get myself together I'll start afresh. I've still got a bit sewed away where he couldn't feel it for the padding, so it won't be like the last time I was on my own. Nothing could be as bad as that.'

Edith went to sit in the chair opposite, watching Annie's face when she raised her head. Even blotched red and wet with tears there was beauty in the high cheek-bones, the curve of the generous mouth.

'Take your hat off,' Edith said, too loudly, wondering at the flood of resentment and jealousy rising up inside her. 'I tried to find you,' she said, feeling her conscience dictate that she make amends. 'But you'd run away.' She stared significantly at Annie's dress with its lace frill and pearl-buttoned bodice. 'You must have found yourself a good job?'

'I was a seamstress in a big house.'

'Was?' The significance of that wasn't lost on Edith. She began to feel hot and bothered again.

'I lost the job.' Annie suddenly realised that Miss Morris was frightened of something, that she was continually glancing towards the door, twisting a corner of her apron round and round as if it was wet and she was trying to wring it out. 'The family I worked for are going to France.'

'Oh . . .'

Annie knew she'd been mistaken in thinking that Miss

299

Morris had altered. She was just the same, with her thin mouth buttoned up prissy and her eyes looking at you and finding you wanting.

'So you're out of work?' Edith looked positively distraught. 'And looking round for a place to stay?'

'Only for a while. Till I find a living-in job.' Annie hated to say it but felt she had no choice. 'Your mother said that there would always . . .'

But the chance to remind Edith exactly what her mother had said was lost when the front door banged open as violently as if someone outside had come at it with a battering ram. Annie turned round to see a huge man with hair only a mite less red than her own, with tangled eyebrows meeting over a bulbous nose. Bagging and delivering seventy bags of coal that day had brought the sweat up on him. His face was streaked with coal dust, but the fastidious Miss Morris went straight to him and kissed him.

'Mick! Look who's here! It's Annie Clancy!' Annie watched in amazement as she simpered, widening her eyes, laughing at nothing. 'You remember Annie?' Tripping over to the oven she opened the door, then stood back, wafting the heat from her face. 'She came to see her father, and now she's popped in here to see me and have a bite to eat before getting on her way.'

'So that's the way of it?' Mick was swaying on his feet, very much on his mettle, certainly not drunk. Annie had seen too much of insobriety to know when a man was stone-cold sober.

For a second – a tiny fraction of time – she hesitated, fighting to get a hold on herself, to make sense of what was going on. To steady herself she took a deep breath. Edith Morris, Miss Morris, with the hatchet face and prissy ways, was married to Mick Malone, the town's drunk, an Irishman with a tongue on him like the floor of a pigeon loft! It was incredible, but it was true. There was a wide gold ring on Edith's finger, and for the first time Annie noticed that the table was set for two. The last time she had seen Mick he had been clomping in loose pit clogs across Barney Eccles's filthy yard. She had seen him blow his nose through his fingers on to the greasy cobblestones. She remembered turning away in disgust.

'Go through and have your wash, sweetheart,' Miss Morris was saying, laying a hand on her husband's arm. 'It's lentil soup, then tatie-pie, and pineapple chunks if you can still find a corner to fill.'

'Then I'll say goodbye, Annie, seeing as you'll be gone when I come back like a nice clean boy.' Mick was talking to Annie, but his eyes never left his wife's face. 'I expect you'll be wanting to be away before dark sets in, won't you, lass?'

With a squeeze of Edith's shoulder he left the room, king of his castle, monarch of all he surveyed. Annie could hardly bear to look at the tall woman cringing in embarrassment in front of her.

'It's all right,' she said quickly, getting up from her chair. 'He's right. It's best I go now.'

Edith was actually wringing her hands. 'He doesn't like company.' She lowered her voice. 'Having visitors in the house threatens him.' Her eyes were pleading with Annie to understand. 'This is the first home he's ever had, the longest he's ever kept a job . . .'

She was so bitterly ashamed she hardly knew what she was saying or doing. Her mother had kept open house for anybody who happened to drop in. Another potato would be popped into the pot, another chair set at the table. No fuss, no bother at all. For Annie Clancy there had always been a special welcome. 'That child is treated something shocking at home. If ever a man deserved to go to hell when he dies, that man is Jack Clancy. I could watch him dangle from a rope without batting an eyelid.' Edith could hear her mother saying it now.

It was terrible having to walk by on the other side, terrible knowing that Annie Clancy had nowhere to go. Showing her to the door just the same.

Florrie saw Annie pass the window on her way up the street. She had a hand over her mouth as if she was crying. Florrie went to the door for a proper look.

She tut-tutted into her chins. The poor little beggar had her bag with her, so she hadn't managed to get her feet under next door but one's table after all. Fat chance of that happening now. Edith Morris might have been lagging behind when it came to the wicked ways of men, but she was catching up with a vengeance. With Mick Malone, too. There was no accounting for tastes! Personally, Florrie wouldn't have touched her distant cousin with a barge-pole.

All the time she was chunnering to herself Florrie was down on her knees in front of the cupboard under the slopstone, rummaging behind the pans set on a rickety shelf. The parcel was there where she'd hidden it when it first came, knowing it was the one spot in the house safe from prying eyes. Cursing and groaning at the discomfort in her swollen knees, she turfed out two grease-encrusted meat tins, a broken pie funnel, a rusted vegetable slicer, a heavy pair of iron weigh scales with cushions of dirt growing on them like black moss, a bent toasting-fork and a goffering iron. They made an almighty clatter on the floor but Florrie was in a hurry. If Jack came in from the backyard and caught her he'd kill her as likely as not. An' he'd take his time about it as well if he knew what she was about to do.

Florrie got to her feet with even more of a struggle than it had taken her to get down. She opened the door, closed it quietly behind her, and set off up the street.

'Annie?' If she hadn't been frightened to death that Jack might hear her she could have let rip. With the wind in the right direction she could have been heard four streets away, but she daren't risk discovery. 'Annie?' Her slippers were that thin she could feel every nick in the flags through them. Her heart was thumping fit to bust, and there was a woman across the street mopping

302

her window bottom for the second time that day, the silly beggar, staring with her gob open as if she was catching flies.

'Annie!' Florrie stopped to catch her breath. Why wouldn't she turn round? And why was she swaying from side to side like that? That last blow with the flat of Jack's hand had nearly knocked the lass's block off. He didn't know his own strength, never had. It was to be hoped this was the end of it, because Annie Clancy was like a red rag to a bull to Jack.

Huffing and panting, Florrie set off again. It was wicked the way hate could fester inside a man without healing or even scabbing over. Florrie had always been the bottom of her class at school, but you didn't need brains to know that when Jack landed out like that it was Annie's real father he was punishing. The unknown red-haired man his first wife had dared to love before she met him. 'With Jack it's all or nowt.' Everybody who knew Jack said that about him, and they were right. By God, they weren't wrong.

Her big face was blood red; she held a hand over a raging stitch in her side; she was unkempt and far from clean, but as she caught up with Annie at last and pushed the parcel at her, the small button eyes brimmed over with compassion.

'It's yours, chuck. I hid it from him,' was all she managed to gasp before setting off back down the long street, enormous behind wagging, tomato-red heels slipping from the shabby shoes.

It was a brown paper parcel, tied badly with dirty string. It had been at the back of the grimy shelf for so long it was covered in grease marks. Annie opened her bag and pushed it down as far as she could, too dispirited to open it or even care what it could be.

When she reached the top road leading to the open countryside she turned round to look down on the straggled rows of little houses, the tall mill chimneys, the

303

grey slag heaps, touched to a kind of splendour by the rays of the setting sun.

Common-sense told her that the best thing would be to find lodgings for the night. All she needed was to produce one of the seven sovereigns hidden in the padded hem of her dress and she'd be welcomed with open arms. She knew of a particular row of houses where the theatricals lodged. She could stay in one of them while she looked round for a job, a living-in job at one of the big detached houses on the far side of the town. If she went back now there was the possibility of at least temporary security; if she turned her back on the town there was little ahead but moorland, beck and fell for miles.

Annie looked far out to the distant hills, purple now but green, she knew, when you got nearer to them. The leaves on the trees were already beginning to be tipped with yellow, and across a far field she could see a farmer and his men still working.

The pain in her ear, in the whole of the left side of her head, was agonising. When she moved her head too quickly the ground swayed and dipped, making her feel sick. She took off her hat to let the evening breeze lift her damp hair away from her forehead. She wished she could decide what to do next – what to do for the best. The only way she could contain the knife-point stabbing pain was by holding a hand over her ear, so she let her hat drop to the ground and walked on without it.

She turned into a field path and stumbled along the deeply rutted ground. The pains were red-hot now; they were bringing a mist to her eyes; they were taking her reasoning away. Suddenly the agony slicing through her head, the weight of her bag, the chill wind that cut through to her skin, were all too much. She tripped and fell, to lie there whimpering into the damp earth, all control gone.

She began to cry, and once started couldn't stop. She cried not only with pain but because she was tired of fighting, tired of being rejected, weary of having to make her own way in the world, terrified that she would still be going on fighting when she was an old, old woman.

'Oh, God,' she sobbed, 'help me now. Help me, please.'

All the time she cried she could hear a little voice deep inside her telling her that once the relief of letting go was over she would get up and walk on, in one direction or another. Lying in a field feeling sorry for herself wasn't going to help. Nor was it dignified. She would manage, she would soldier on – she always had and she always would.

But oh, dear God, it was a relief to let go, to stop being brave and proud and quietly dignified. She could scream as loud as she wanted to, or tear at her hair, knowing no one could hear, knowing no one could see.

Ten minutes later she was walking back towards the town, making for the top road again. When she came to where her hat lay she picked it up and plonked it on her head. Defiantly.

There was nothing Seth could do when Jake Tomlinson, a farmer he knew well, stood in his path waving both arms in the air. The awful dread was still in him, but Jake's best cow was in the middle of calving and Seth soon saw that something was badly wrong. She bellowed her anguish, straining so hard she was in imminent danger of toppling over.

The front legs and nose of her calf were sticking out, but as fast as Seth tried to get a length of baler twine round them they slipped back, making the cow sway dangerously and her heart to palpitate visibly. Seth passed a piece of wood through the loops of twine to make hauling easier, but again and again the calf's legs and the tip of its nose appeared briefly only to be sucked back immediately. Seth took off his jacket, shouted for a bucket of water and rolled up his shirt sleeves.

'She's tekkin her time, Mr Armstrong.' Old Jake

looked almost as distressed as his animal. 'She wasn't like this the last time. D'you reckon it's a big 'un?'

There was milk spurting from the cow's udders and her eyes were rolling. Seth decided to ease her agony with his hands.

'You're right about it being a big one,' he panted, trying to slide his hands into the best position. 'Move that clean straw over here. I think . . . I think . . .'

With a gigantic push that almost toppled the cow over, the calf slithered out on to the straw, blinked and tried to sit up.

Jake was a bit put out when Mr Armstrong wouldn't go into the farmhouse for a sup of tay. His cow was lowing with pleasure, busily licking the wet slime from her calf. Jake shuddered to think what might have happened if the animal doctor hadn't chanced along the road. It was a miracle, that's what it was, an' you didn't come across them all that often. Seth Armstrong had the gift of healing in his hands; Jake's missus thought the world of him. Yet here he was rubbing himself dry on a bit of sacking and putting his jacket and shirt back on, positive he hadn't time to stop, not even for a brew.

'It's my belief there was summat sorely bothering him,' Jake told his wife.

'Nowt a sup o' tay wouldn't have put right,' she said, aggrieved.

Seth was so glad to see Annie trudging along the top road he leaned from the trap and shouted at her, all control gone.

'For God's sake, where d'you think you're going? Give me that bag and let's have you up here.' In one bound he was out of the trap and by her side, wincing at the sight of her bruised cheek. Almost without volition he stretched out a hand to touch it, then drew back as she jerked her head away. 'Your father?' Surely he had the right to ask that?

Annie nodded. 'But it's for the last time. He tried to

take Adam's money from me, but I said he was welcome to it. As a sort of payment. I felt I needed to make it clear. Can you understand?'

Seth did understand. He knew exactly what she meant. He admired her more than he'd admired any woman in his life before, but he knew he must subdue the longing in him to put his arms around her and hold her close. There was mud down the front of her dress, her hair was coming down, and he wanted to hold her tenderly as he would an injured bird, calming her, soothing her until her heartbeats slowed and her eyes lost their aching sadness.

'So where are you going now?'

She nodded towards the town with its slag heaps and tall mill chimneys. 'I'm going to find a place to stay till I can get a living-in situation. I've got enough money to see me right for a while.' She tilted her chin. 'I won't starve.'

'I can offer you a living-in situation.' He was very business-like, trying desperately not to show his eagerness. 'Biddy is finding the house too much for her to manage on her own, and besides, people are beginning to talk.'

Her glance was sharp. 'Is there reason for them to talk?'

Solemnly he shook his head. 'There has been no physical contact between us at all.'

He was laughing at her again. Annie searched his face, but he was gazing ahead, apparently perfectly serious, the brim of the slouch hat hiding his expression.

'You don't care what people say,' she accused. 'You never did.'

'I admit I am broad in the mind,' he said, still in that pompous voice, making her lips curve up in the merest semblance of a smile which, if he noticed, he was careful not to comment on.

Annie put a hand over her mouth in the familiar gesture of self-comfort. She was forcing the tears back, experiencing again the moment when she had turned to see the black horse galloping towards her, the trap being driven as if it was part of a chariot race. For a brief second it had seemed to be surrounded by a shimmering white light.

'You may wear a uniform if you wish,' he was saying, 'but the cost will of course be deducted from your wages.'

Her bag was already in the trap, she had only to say the word and she could be turning her back on the town. She could be feeling safe and protected. She could. This man watching her so carefully knew the score now and accepted it. It would be master and maid, just as he had promised.

'You have to start trusting sometime,' he said softly, almost as if to himself.

Annie made up her mind. 'I accept the position, thank you,' she said, then wondered if the surge of emotion inside her stemmed from laughter or tears.

A bit of both, she suspected.

Biddy had known all along that this would happen. She would look through the window one day and see Mr Armstrong bringing Annie Clancy back. Even though it wasn't the romantic scene she'd imagined with Annie leaning against him, her face upturned for his kiss. Instead, they just walked in together as if there was nothing extraordinary in it at all.

Biddy thought that Annie looked as if she'd gone three rounds with a fairground boxer. She was covered in mud and her face was the colour of unrisen dough.

'Rustle up some supper quickly, and bring mine through when I've stabled the horse. Annie's joining us again,' Mr Armstrong said over a disappearing shoulder.

'Oh, I'm glad! Really glad!' Biddy clasped her hands together. 'He's not best pleased,' she told Annie. 'He's been in a rare old state since the day you left.' She unhooked a ladle from the fireplace alcove. 'Like a man

308

possessed he's been. Pacing the carpet in his den, backwards and forwards, forwards and backwards, like a caged lion.'

Annie had forgotton that Biddy talked just like an 'a penny book. She sat down suddenly as if her legs had given way and stared round at the familiar kitchen. Biddy brought a crusty cob of bread to the table and began to slice it into thick chunks.

'In the morning you can tell me all you've been doing, but for now just get some of that broth down you. Do you feel as ill as you look?'

'Worse,' Annie said, but she was smiling properly for the first time that day. The warmth of her welcome, the kindness in Biddy's eyes, the fact that she was prepared to wait till the next day to hear Annie's story, was almost too much to bear.

When Biddy came back from taking Seth's supper through to the den, Annie was fast asleep where she sat, her head down in her arms, the bowl of broth pushed to one side.

Biddy felt extremely frustrated, if the truth were told. She could have wept. It was like reading a story with the last page missing.Annie had gone up to her bed in her old room without opening her eyes properly, without even hearing Biddy tell her how she'd kept the bed made up and aired for this very moment.

When she'd cleared away and banked the fire up for the night, she went to bed herself. There was a light showing underneath Mr Armstrong's door, so it looked as if this could be one of the nights he spent sleeping in his chair by the dying embers of the fire.

Biddy felt personally let down. Things weren't working out at all in the way she'd dreamed they would. There was Annie upstairs and Mr Armstrong down, with hardly a word exchanged between them since they came into the house.

She set her candlestick down on the high table by her

bed, took off her cap and pulled the pins from her hair. At least they were under the same roof again, and this time there was no Mrs Martindale to put a damper on things. The best romances were the ones that took their time – the blossoming of true love couldn't be hurried. Mr Armstrong had given a meaningful look up at the ceiling when she'd told him that Annie had gone to her bed worn out.

Biddy took off her stays and had a good scratch.

She was sure, positive, that when he raised his eyes like that his expression had been one of utter yearning.

'Utter yearning,' she said aloud, liking the sound of the words on her tongue.

The pain in Annie's ear woke her up around three o'clock in the morning. At once her hand went to her head and she sat up, rocking herself, whimpering till the dagger-sharp agony faded a little.

Gradually, as her eyes became used to the darkness, she made out the shape of the wardrobe, and the tallboy set beneath the window. The blind had been pulled down but she could see the pale yellow outline of the window. There was no fire in the grate, but that last time the flames had touched the walls to a soft rose, and whenever she opened her eyes the animal doctor had been there, waiting and watching, his presence solid and reassuring.

After Kit Dailey and the maid Johnson had almost killed her, Seth had sat in the bedroom at the Grays' house, watching and waiting in just the same way.

'I'll always be there if you want me to be.' Had he said that, or had she dreamed it?

'I'll never forget you,' Laurie Yates had said. 'You are so lovely,' he had whispered as he kissed her.

'You're so lovely,' Seth had said, and his mouth had been hard and demanding on her own.

Annie swung her legs over the side of the bed, lit the candle, held it up – and saw the parcel on the dresser. In the half-light it was a dirty tattered bundle.

'I hid it from him, chuck. It's yours. It came in the post. From foreign parts.'

Florrie's big face was running with sweat as she'd handed the parcel over. Annie could see her now, slopping her untidy way back down the street.

The paper came away easily as she tore at it. It was damp to the touch and smelled of rancid mutton fat. Annie pulled one layer away, then another, and yet a third – then caught her breath in astonishment.

The white lace tablecloth was so fine, so delicate that at first she thought it was a bridal veil. But when she stood up and shook it out she saw the round shape of it, knew that the delicate lace would hang down in perfect folds when it was draped over a rounded table.

'So Laurie remembered my dream,' she told Biddy the next morning, holding the lace cloth up for her to admire. 'It was just a silly daydream really, but he remembered.'

Biddy had no intention of listening to anything good about the travelling man. Mr Armstrong had taken one look at the cloth and gone straight out, calling for his dog in a voice that had it running as fast as if he'd fired a starting pistol.

Biddy told Annie that she bet at least four poor foreign women had gone stone-blind making the lace cloth, and that Laurie Yates would have paid no more than a shilling for it, if that.

'It's his conscience talking,' she said scathingly. 'He thinks that a handful or two of hand-made lace can make up for all the anguish he's caused you. If it was mine I would toss it on the fire to show my contempt.'

'That would show I was still foolish enough to care for him,' Annie told her, examining the cloth with a critical eye. 'I think it would come up beautifully if I starched it lightly and pressed it on the wrong side with a hot iron. It would look different again.'

'Oh, Annie . . .'

311

The next minute they were holding on to each other, laughing so much they failed to see Seth watching them from the doorway.

'You've chased the haunting sadness from his face already,' Biddy told Annie, after he'd gone out.

She thought how beautiful the phrase had sounded when she'd first read it in a story about a scullery maid who had brought joy and love back into the life of an embittered lord of the realm, who owned half of Cumberland, four houses in London and a chain of shops, but who was spiritually as poor as a cripple with a begging bowl.

They worked together through the days, settling back into their old rhythm of Annie doing the bulk of the work and Biddy skiving off to read whenever she got the chance.

Seth came and went from the house, eating alone in his den and twice in that first week not going to bed at all. Annie worried about him, and one dark evening took the swinging lantern down from its nail and walked to the verge of the long garden to see if there was any sign of him coming back down the hill. There was a heavy drizzle in the air, the wetting kind. She couldn't think why he hadn't set off for home much earlier as he must have seen the cows lying down in the fields. She had seen them – she had known that rain was on the way.

'Does he never take any account of the time?' she asked Biddy.

'Never.' Biddy looked up from her book, keeping her finger on her place. 'Sometimes he doesn't come home at all.' She said this for the benefit of seeing Annie's face change, her expression grow bleak.

'You mean when he goes to Manchester?'

Biddy excelled herself. 'Oh, when he goes there he's often away for as long as a week, coming back mighty pleased with himself.'

'He has his own life to lead.'

'And of course he's a man,' Biddy said. She glanced down at her book. 'A virile, handsome giant of a man,' she read. 'With passion throbbing in his veins.'

Annie, she noted with immense satisfaction, had gone as red as a new scald.

Seth had found Jake Tomlinson's cow down with milk fever, though the calf was doing well.

'The loss of a deep milker like her'll cripple me financially, Mr Armstrong.' Jake shook his head mournfully. 'I can see by the look on th' face tha doesn't hold out much hope.'

Seth tried to look more optimistic than he felt. If the animal had been conscious he could have given it a sedative. As it was, he would have to give choral by the rectum. He would also, if necessary, spend the whole day stimulating the cow's spine with embrocation. It was too late to tell Jake that if his precious cow had been kept on oat-straw and hay for the six weeks prior to calving, this might never have happened. Jake had his own methods and wouldn't be moved from them, and at the moment his distress was so great that Seth could hardly bear to look at him.

'D'you reckon she'll pull through, Mr Armstrong?'

Seth continued his massaging, using long deep strokes in a soothing rhythm. 'We're not beaten yet, Jake. Not by a long chalk. You go and do what you'd normally be doing. I can manage on my own.'

He was lying so uncomfortably on the dirt floor that his whole body ached. A draught from the ill-fitting door was the only breath of air in the badly-ventilated cowshed. Jake's pastures were poorly drained, almost bare of trees, so that his animals found little respite from summer fleas. Yet they thrived, with an inborn capacity for adapting themselves to circumstances, as if knowing how dearly they were cherished. Dearly-loved wouldn't be too strong a word, Seth supposed.

Twice during that long day Jake's missus came out

with food and drink, and twice Seth refused the food but drank the hot sweet tea laced with sugar. By the late afternoon he was able to tell Jake with truth that the cow was responding. When the shadows lengthened and the drizzle of the day had turned to a good honest rain, he knew the animal would live.

He was so stiff and weary, he stumbled as he walked away from the small farmholding, still hearing Jake's overwhelming gratitude in his ears. Rain dripped from the overhanging trees which lined his path as he trudged through the mud. He marvelled, not for the first time, at the patience of the farmers and their almost passive acceptance of whatever the weather could chuck at them. With no more needed than a few days of sunshine the corn would be ripe, but only the other day a large flock of swallows had flown over the fields making for the south, at least a month earlier than usual – a bad sign, even to an optimist.

Seth crossed the lane in order to skirt the dark wood, walked on down the familiar road until he turned a corner and saw the lights of his own home, shining out from every single window. Smiling because he knew that Annie was there.

Lying sleepless in her bed that night Annie wished she hadn't sounded so much like Mrs Martindale, fussing over him, giving him a towel to dry his hair, telling him that she would fill the hipbath, put a handful of mustard in it and leave him to soak away what she was sure could easily be the onset of pneumonia.

'He's as strong as an ox,' Biddy had reassured her. 'I've seen him come in, shake the drops from him, then stand by the fire till his clothes steam-dried. He hated you mothering him. Anger was flashing from his eyes like living sparks, and a pulse was throbbing in his strong jaw.'

'Stop talking like that!' Annie had heard herself shouting, then she had yelled at a cat for doing no more than raking its claws along the already tattered chair cushions.

Now at last the house was quiet. Biddy had gone to bed telling Annie that she understood, that however Annie behaved she would always understand. Annie gave a deep sigh.

What was it making Biddy so annoyingly understanding? Why had she scuttled off to bed with that silly expression on her face? That simpering look, as if she was a bit doo-lally.

There was an ache in Annie's head that had nothing to do with the beating her father had given her. She was trembly without being cold; her heart was beating rapidly though she lay perfectly still. She was bewildered, unhappy, so nervous that when Seth had slammed the door of his room behind him, obviously irritated by her fussing, she had wanted to run after him to say she was sorry.

Sorry for what? Only one way to settle that.

Annie was half-way downstairs, her long nightgown trailing behind her, and still she didn't know what she was going to say.

'I've come to say I'm sorry,' she told him, standing in the doorway still shivering from a cold she couldn't feel.

He was reading as usual, with his empty pipe on the small table beside him. He was wearing his dressing-gown; his fair hair was sleeked back – still damp, she guessed.

'For what?' The light grey eyes were steady. 'For what?'

'For fussing you when you came in. For moithering till you took your wet things off. For behaving as if I was your mother.'

'Do you feel like my mother, Annie Clancy?'

She hung her head. 'No, I don't.'

He got up from his chair, came round her and closed the door. 'Then what *do* you feel like?' He was standing very close to her. 'Is that what you've come downstairs in the dead of night to tell me?'

'I don't know . . .' The admission came from her on a long drawn-out sigh.

'Look at me, Annie.'

Slowly she raised her head, looked straight into his eyes. She had always thought they were the kindest eyes she had ever seen in a man, but now, in the darkened room, they were filled with a tenderness that couldn't be mistaken for anything else but the deepest love.

'Seth?'

She had never of her own volition touched a man like this before. Her fingers traced the line of his eyebrows, the curve of his cheek, lingered at his mouth. She swayed towards him, tracing the shape of his lips, parting her own in anticipation of a kiss, closing her eyes. Failing to see the hesitation in his expression before he took her in his arms.

But this time there was no terrified rejection, no shrinking from his caresses. This time it was how he had known it could be – all sweet surrender and an awakened passion that drove away every vestige of his carefully guarded control.

The pity of it was that Biddy, who had imagined this very moment, lived it for them, adding more than a few embellishments of her own, was fast asleep upstairs, totally oblivious of the fact that what was happening downstairs was more romantic than anything she'd ever read. Or was ever likely to.